RIGHT CONNECTIONS

SEAN HARDIE

MICHAEL JOSEPH
LONDON

MICHAEL JOSEPH LTD

Published by the Penguin Group
27 Wrights Lane, London. W8 5TZ, England
Viking Penguing Inc., 375 Hudson Street, New York, New York 10014, USA
Penguin Books Australia Ltd, Ringwood, Victoria, Australia
Penguin Books Canada Ltd, 2801 John Street, Markham, Ontario, Canada L3R 1B4
Penguin Books (NZ) Ltd, 182–190 Wairau Road, Auckland 10, New Zealand

Penguin Books Ltd, Registered Offices: Harmondsworth, Middlesex, England

First published in Great Britain 1991

Typeset, printed and bound in England by
Clays Ltd, St Ives plc
Filmset in 11½/13½ pt Sabon

A CIP catalogue record for this book is available from the British Library

ISBN 0 7181 3291 2

RIGHT CONNECTIONS

Also by Sean Hardie
THE LAST SUPPER

. . . For Kerry and Willie

I

HARRY WAS LATE. The cab circled round Hammersmith Broadway and turned right into Beadon Road and dropped him in the forecourt of the Metropolitan Line station opposite an Indian restaurant called the Bombay Duck. Outside it was darkness at noon, brake lights and headlights and indicators flashed through the lashing rain, a wet day in a wet November.

The Duck had two General Election posters in the window, one Tory, one Labour. Two weeks to polling, and the catering trade was hedging its bets. From behind the net curtains Pete and Shirley Pattichis watched Harry get out of the cab, head down against the gale.

'Is that him?' asked Shirley.

'Could be,' said Pete. He lit another cigarette, gripped it in his teeth, pulled a comb out of his jacket pocket, and started combing what was left of his hair. 'I don't know what he looks like.'

Pete was short and stocky, maybe five seven, beginning to go bald, dressed in built up shoes and a flared brown suit with wide lapels and trousers a little short at the ankle, a beige shirt with long, pointed collar tabs and a wide brown and orange tie. His wife Shirley sat beside him, gift-wrapped in a white blouse and black leather trousers with a gold belt, bulging to contain the overweight contours of her body. There was something liquid about Shirley, like a brimming jug of perfumed treacle, threatening to spill over you. She was the same height as Pete, but maybe twice as wide. They'd been married nine years.

'Taki the Sikh says he looked fit, like he goes to the gym a lot.'

'Taki's met him?'

'He's seen him on TV.'

'They never look the same on TV,' said Shirley. 'The TV companies hire people to make them look healthy, buy them the right clothes, get rid of their wrinkles for them.' She blew a long column of smoke at the roof and worried at her ear lobe. 'Do you think the gold's too much?'

'You look fine,' said Pete, not looking.

'If it's his own show how come it's not called after him?' Shirley demanded. She twisted her arm behind her back and pinched at her bra buckle. 'Wogan has a show, it's called Wogan. Aspel's the same. David Frost talks to someone, they call it *The Frost Interview*. What's his name?'

'Kapowski,' said Pete. 'Kapow. Like in the comics, when someone hits someone, KAPOW. Harry Kapowski. He's good.'

'Says who?'

'The Sikh, for one. And Stavros, and Tony Dimas. Tony says he's the best.'

Shirley had moved from her bra to her shoulder pads, smoothing them into place so they didn't show through her blouse.

'So how much are you going to tell him?'

'What do you mean how much am I going to tell him?'

'I mean about Terry. You going to tell him about all the other stuff?'

Pete didn't know, he was sort of leaving it to see how things went.

Harry pushed through the door. He was in his mid

thirties, tall and thin, like a heron, with straight blond hair and a long, lantern face, not exactly handsome but striking, a presence you'd remember. He wore a tweed jacket with the collar turned up against the storm, a navy sweater, well cut corduroy trousers, brogues. The Sikh was right, he looked fit, fit and well groomed.

'Mr Kapowski?' said Pete, stubbing out his cigarette in the glass ashtray before getting up from the draylon-covered wrought-iron bench.

'Harry,' said Harry. 'I'm sorry I'm late.'

'No problem,' said Pete. 'We have plenty of time.'

Harry bet they did. He'd met a lot of Petes and Shirleys, had sat for hours in railway buffets and bars and the front rooms of cheaply furnished council houses listening to them stuttering their way through confused and improbable explanations of how their loved ones had been stitched up by the police. Most of them had difficulty selling their cases to themselves let alone to an impartial outsider.

The Pattichis were Cypriots, out of Larnaca, via New Cross and latterly Finsbury Park. Poor bastards, Cypriots weren't even an interesting minority. Pete was thirty-two, drove a minicab. At weekends he stuck a sign on the roof of the '83 Escort and became a School of Motoring. Shirley was a couple of years younger, and told Harry she was an interior designer, chose wallpaper and furnishings for people. Friends mostly, they told her she had a natural eye for style, so she helped them with their houses and business premises.

'Like a cushion consultant?' asked Harry.

'Yeah, that sort of thing.'

They moved through into the restaurant and sat uncomfortably close together at a table between the kitchen door and the pay phone. Pete and Harry ordered curries, Shirley a mixed grill. The Pattichis were nervous.

'Tell me about Terry,' said Harry.

'He didn't do it, Mr Kapowski, I swear to God,' Pete said quietly. 'It looks like he did it, but he didn't.'

'Can you prove it?'

Pete knew he couldn't, not as such. Eight years ago he might have, but he was only a kid when his brother got sent down, didn't speak much English, didn't understand what to do. In Cyprus he could have talked to people, called in favours, used his family influence. But not in New Cross.

'Maybe, I don't know.'

The waiter brought drinks, lagers for the men, vodka and tonic for Shirley who sat listening, one arm clamped across her stomach supporting her bosom, the other holding a cigarette with a pillar of grey ash.

'To get a case reopened,' Harry explained, 'you either need to prove the original trial was defective, or you need new evidence. Alibis, forensic, witnesses, something that wasn't known to the jury at the time of the trial.'

Pete Pattichis' letter had arrived ten days before. Harry'd talked to the Home Office to check Terry was where he was for the reasons Pete said, thought about it for a couple of days, then phoned Pete and arranged to meet. It was as well for a reporter to look busy at election time, unless you were the sort of reporter who liked elections. Harry liked elections about as much as he liked pot noodles, maybe even less.

He'd re-read Pete's letter in the taxi, six sides of cheap lined paper, light on grammar and spelling and littered with underlinings and unprovoked capital letters. Pete had spent the last eight years in Broadmoor at Her Majesty's Pleasure. Always supposing Her Majesty had much pleasure to spare, which Harry often doubted.

Harry had built his reputation as a TV reporter on miscarriage of justice cases. The trick with miscarriage of justice cases isn't knowing which cases to take up, it's knowing which ones not to touch with a barge pole.

4

Terry Pattichis was unpromising material. Even if he had a case, eight years had passed, no one liked to go back that far. Witnesses die, people forget things.

Pete knew he'd screwed up. To start with he'd dressed wrong. What felt right in Finsbury Park felt embarrassing in Hammersmith. Not that Hammersmith was fancy, but it was English. Finsbury Park was all sorts of things but not English – even the English in Finsbury Park had given up being English. Second, he shouldn't have brought Shirley. He'd thought it might look better if they arrived as a couple, more respectable, a family thing. Instead the pair of them looked like a freak show. Also, the Indian was a bad idea, he didn't even like Indian food, he only suggested it on the phone because Harry had asked where he'd like to have lunch, and Indian had seemed sort of classless, neutral territory. Everyone goes to Indian restaurants. Except the Chinese, you never saw a Chinaman in an Indian restaurant.

Kapowski wasn't going to believe him. The man had the easy life written all over him, comfortable clothes, comfortable smile, comfortably concerned eyebrows. He'd listen politely and nod and make notes, and go home, and that would be that.

'I don't know about all the legal stuff,' said Pete. 'That stuff is why I need help. You mind if I smoke?'

'Not all all,' said Harry.

Pete pushed away his chicken tikka and tried to figure where to go next.

'Tell me about Jo O'Brien,' Harry suggested.

'He was, like, Terry's boss.'

'Lover,' Shirley corrected him. 'He was his boss, but he was his lover too.'

Pete put down his lager.

'You leave this to me, OK?'

'They went to clubs,' Shirley continued. She put a cigarette to her mouth, held her lighter in both hands, bent forward to reach the flame. 'The kind of clubs they don't let women in.' She blew out a mouthful of smoke. 'As if women would want to go in places like that.'

'You don't know that,' Pete objected. He was getting agitated, starting to gesticulate, knew he shouldn't, couldn't help himself. 'It's just talk. Anyhow, if they don't allow women how do you know you wouldn't want to go in?'

'That's why I wouldn't want to go in. You go in those places they think you're a man in a dress, it's like in Singapore, I read about it in a magazine one time.' She wiped her lips on her napkin. 'This Terry is a bum-boy, Mr Kapowski.'

Pete had given up. He wanted to go home.

'A bum-boy,' Shirley repeated. 'Why lie about it? Rich men took him home to live with them in their apartments for a week or two, they went out to work, he had to stay in and wait for them to come back, get bathed and dressed up for them, have a drink ready when they come in the door. Like a housewife. And he stole things.'

'He didn't steal, they were presents from admirers,' Pete interrupted.

'What did he steal?' asked Harry.

'Money,' Shirley continued. 'Cheques. Credit cards. Anything he could flog. He thought no one would go to the police. But he was wrong, wasn't he.'

'Did he do time?' asked Harry.

'He did three times,' she continued. 'After the times he didn't do time, on top of probation and that.'

The waiter brought more lagers.

'OK,' said Harry. 'And Jo O'Brien?'

'Another bum-boy,' said Shirley. 'Only a lot older, maybe forty. I don't know what you call them when they get old. Invited people to parties, waited until they started doing things they might be ashamed of later, took photos of them, all that kind of business.'

6

'Shirley,' Pete stubbed out his cigarette. 'This is my brother, are you going to let me tell the story?'

'You tell Mr Kapowski the story, but don't give him crap. He's a TV man, he knows his job, you tell him crap and he'll find out it's crap and he won't believe the rest of the story. Isn't that so, Mr Kapowski?'

Harry nodded, and stole a glance at his watch. It was already two o'clock: he was due to play squash at three.

Pete went over the story in numbing detail. Terry had worked – in what capacity wasn't clear – for a South African called Jo O'Brien. Jo ran a GLC-funded charity called the Latchkey Trust with offices in Shepherd's Bush. There'd been a fire one night at the Latchkey offices. The building survived but the office was a wreck. When the police got there Jo was dead, the back of his head stoved in with a chair. They found Terry wandering around Shepherd's Bush Green, took him down to the cells in Uxbridge Road, started asking him questions. Around three in the morning he signed a confession. The next day, when they got to work on the charred shell of the Latchkey offices, the story began to come clear. Money was missing, records had been systematically removed from the files to feed the blaze. Terry was charged, convicted on his own confession and sent to Wormwood Scrubs. Three months later he went off his trolley, and was transferred to Broadmoor, where he'd been ever since.

All this happened on the same day the IRA put a bomb outside Harrods, killing six and injuring another ninety, which meant the Latchkey affair missed the front pages: it wasn't until the trial six months later that Fleet Street really got its fangs into it. Harry half-remembered the case, the capital the Tories had made out of it. A GLC enquiry into Latchkey revealed that over £200,000 worth of public money had been siphoned off into O'Brien's personal accounts. Jo and Terry had been living like kings, jetting round the world, entertaining sportsmen, politicians and pop stars, furnishing Jo's Maida Vale flat with the best that money could buy.

'And what makes you think Terry didn't do it?' asked Harry.

'I know,' said Pete. 'I just know.'

Harry put down his pen.

'We'd need more than that, I'm afraid.'

Pete had been dreading this moment.

'The confession,' he said. 'It doesn't feel right. And some other things.'

He reached down, extracted a sheaf of dog-eared letters and newspaper cuttings from his bag, and passed them one by one across the table. Harry scanned the headlines. He'd stopped taking notes.

'Not now,' said Shirley. 'Let him take them away to read.'

He takes them away, I'll never see them again, Pete wanted to say. He'll put them in his briefcase, and then he'll leave them on his desk, and the cleaning lady will tidy up the office, put them in a corner, jumble them up with other stuff. And that'll be the end of that.

Harry saw the panic in his face.

'Do you have copies?'

'No. I can get some made.'

He should have thought of that before, had them in a binder. A lot of things he should have done. But mostly he should have left Shirley at home.

'Do that,' said Harry, 'and put them in the post to me.'

He handed Pete his card. A nice card, embossed red BBC logo, and underneath in a small typeface: harry kapowski, bbc tv, wood lane london w12, no capital letters, very stylish. Pete put the card in his pocket. The waiters were hovering.

'Tell me something,' asked Harry. 'All this happened eight years ago. Why now?'

8

'It's because of his mother,' Shirley explained. 'His mother just died, in hospital she made him promise to do something for Terry. I don't know what, maybe go and see him more, take him cigarettes and stuff.'

Pete ignored her.

'I read about your programme last week,' he said. 'It was the same as Terry, they had a confession, only it couldn't have been a confession, he said things he couldn't have known about. Terry wouldn't have said the things they said he said, not normally.'

'Why not?'

'Drugs,' said Shirley. 'He took a lot of drugs.'

Pete's eyes flew to heaven.

The West Indian had been watching the restaurant ever since Harry and the Pattichises went in, the pillion of the Honda nifty fifty, head in his helmet. Every few minutes he looked up and down the street and then at his watch, acting as though he was waiting for someone who was late; sometimes he wandered across the pavement and looked in the window of the Victoria Wine off-licence, watching the reflection of the Bombay Duck in the well-washed glass between the Beaujolais Nouveau posters.

Shirley came out first, then Harry, then Pete. Harry was shaking hands, making goodbye small talk. Pete turned to leave, then he noticed the ProntaPrint shop across the road.

The nifty fifty moved off from the kerb.

'Hey, you wait here a moment,' Pete told Harry as he started past him. He saw the Honda coming, but there was plenty of time to reach the centre of the road, plenty of space for the bike to pass behind him.

Only the West Indian didn't want to pass behind him; instead he pulled out to try and get between Pete and the shop. Harry shouted a warning, Pete looked round, saw the Honda, started to run towards the far pavement.

9

The garbage truck must have been doing thirty miles an hour when it hit him.

Harry was luckier: all he got was the Honda. He started across the road to help Pete, stopped for a moment and looked right to make sure there was nothing coming. Only the bike wasn't coming from the right this time, it had gone on up the street, turned, and driven straight back at him on the wrong side of the road.

It was another ten seconds before Shirley started to scream.

2

HARRY NEED TWENTY STITCHES where the Honda's mudguard cut into his calf and had a bruise the size of a pancake across his chest, otherwise no damage. He was sitting up in hospital trying not to talk to his neighbours when Roger Carlisle arrived.

Roger was a tribal northener, a skinny, angular undertaker's son from Bolton, with the Lancastrian's rain-washed skin and soot-black hair and a weakness for hillwalking, Marks and Spencers and W. B. Yeats. His real gurus, though, were Paul Simon and John Hampden, which is what happens if you send a northern nonconformist to university in the 1960s. Roger was Harry's boss.

He sat down on the edge of the bed, trench-coat still on, hands deep in his pockets.

'Ow,' said Harry, shifting his weight on the pillows. His breath was still raw and toxic from the lunch-time curry.

'How was lunch?' asked Roger.

'A gay Cypriot junky with three previous convictions who killed his lover and torched the building. Eight years ago. His mum thinks he's innocent, but she's dead.'

'You're meant to seek out the best in people, Harry.'

'I've looked,' said Harry. 'There's nothing there. But

he has a very entertaining sister-in-law with a dodgy marriage.'

'Widow-in-law.'

'Pete's dead?'

'Died an hour ago.'

The first thing Harry felt was guilt: guilt that he hadn't asked about Pete and Shirley first, a deeper guilt that he'd felt no curiosity about what had happened to them. The accusation that TV journalists treat their fellow citizens as inanimate objects, inert building blocks in the construction of programmes, was a raw spot in his self-image.

'The garbage truck went right over him,' Roger continued. 'The police are downstairs, they want to know if you got a look at the guy on the bike.'

'Sure. Black and orange helmet with a black Perspex visor, one-piece body suit. He probably had boots on, they usually do. And a small mole on his left buttock. Could have been a woman or a monkey inside for all I know. What happened to him?'

'He junked the bike and ran off into the Broadway underpasses.'

'Did anyone see him with his hat off?'

'No. But he's coloured.'

'Says who?'

'The bike was nicked in Clapham this morning. A bike goes missing in Clapham, they look for a black man. Or so I'm told. He'd been waiting outside the restaurant, a girl in the off-licence saw him. The three of you came through the door, he mounted up, headed off towards you. The Greek sees him coming, starts to run across the road, the moped gives chase until he sees what's about to happen with the Greek and the truck.'

'He chased him on purpose?'

'It sounds like it, but you don't know. It could have been an accident.'

'A garbage truck – wouldn't you know it? Poor bloody Pete.'

'That might have been an accident,' Roger went on, 'but you were no accident, Harry.'

'What do you mean?'

'It took real skill to turn and get back in time to hit you. Classy riding, by all accounts. Grand prix stuff.'

Harry looked straight in front of him, thinking, trying to remember the moment before the Honda hit him: the noise of the traffic. Pete with his back to the truck, looking round towards Harry. Roger was right, the bike had been way out from the curb, maybe twenty feet away. It hadn't swerved to avoid Pete, it had swerved to hit Harry. Jesus.

Journalism, despite what its practitioners would have you believe, is not a dangerous profession. The number of British reporters who've been injured in the line of duty is tiny. Harry had worked in Belfast, Beirut, Rhodesia; ridden on the back of Israeli tanks into Southern Lebanon, rendezvoused with ETA gunmen in Spanish cellars, interviewed hooded spokesmen for the Red Army Faction in the backs of cars in Berlin. In fifteen years he'd hardly taken so much as a scratch. Occasionally, in spontaneous street riots or in bars when too much drink had been taken, he'd been jostled or punched in the heat of the moment. But most men of violence are sophisticated enough to know it's in their interest to treat the Press gently. Even in war zones, let alone Hammersmith Broadway.

Statistically the most likely person to attack you is a member of your own family. Wife, husband, child, parent. Harry was a bachelor, as far as he knew he didn't have children, his parents were dead. He had a fat sister called Barbara living somewhere in Herefordshire with a Neanderthal hippy and six children whose names he could never remember. They got on fine, sent each other birthday cards. Not Barbara, had to be someone else.

If it's not family then it's likely to be someone you
know already, someone you've annoyed.

'Be frank with me, Roger. Do a lot of people hate
me?'

'I was wondering that.'

Roger opened his document case and took out a
single sheet of paper. He was the only journalist Harry
had ever met who carried a document case. Every time
he opened it Harry thought he was about to be sold
something, probably life insurance. Instead he got a list,
all the programmes with which Harry had been involved
in the past five years.

Harry ran his eyes down the paper, but he wasn't
reading, he was still coming to terms with the idea that
someone – anyone – was out to get him. Kill him even,
though a Honda 50 isn't much of a killing weapon; if
someone wanted you dead they'd use a car. Then he
thought about Pete Pattichis, worried little Pete and his
photocopies, stretched out on the slab. He dropped the
list on the bed.

'What happened to Shirley?'

'She's downstairs. Physically she's fine, her trousers
got ripped. She seems very upset about her trousers.'

Harry remembered the trousers. Black leather,
pleated at the waist, loose at the bum, tight at the ankle,
must have cost two hundred quid.

'She wants to see you sometime.'

'Sure,' said Harry. 'Any time.'

He picked up the list again.

'You're certain the guy on the bike was black?'

'I'm not certain of anything. The police seem pretty
sure.'

Harry waved over a passing nurse.

'Excuse me, is there a pay phone round here?'

The nurse looked at him. She was young, eighteen at
the oldest. At first he thought she smelled of soap, but
then he decided she smelled of nothing, she was just

very clean, as if she'd been steamed. Her name was Kate. If you were into women in uniform Kate would be a Grade A sex object, but Harry was never too fussed by uniforms.

'You're on TV, aren't you,' said Kate.

'Sometimes,' said Harry modestly.

'I've never seen you, but one of the other nurses said she recognized you. How often is sometimes?'

'Once a month.'

'That must be nice for you. What was it you wanted?'

'A phone.'

'It's in the corridor,' said Kate. 'Do you need a wheelchair?'

Roger pushed him down the ward and out into the passage. Harry still had the list, and was probing his shoulder bag for his contact book.

'You got any change?' he asked Roger.

Roger took a 50 p out of his pocket. Harry pushed it into the pay phone.

'Walker,' he told Roger. 'Pigfoot Walker.'

He dialled. The phone rang three times, and then a woman answered.

'Hi.'

'Is that Yvonne?' said Harry. Only his voice didn't sound like Harry now, it sounded like anyone and no one.

'Who's calling?' asked Yvonne.

There was loud music in the background.

'Lazarus,' said Harry. 'Is Pigfoot there?'

Roger had begun to distance himself from Harry, studying the health and safety regulations on the staff notice board, still listening but not wanting to seem involved.

'I dunno,' said Yvonne.

Harry was examining his finger tips.

'Yvonne, there are five rooms in that flat. The phone's in the hall. To get from one room to another you have to go through the hall. From where you're standing now you can see into the kitchen, the living room and the dining room. The bathroom has a frost-glass panel in the door so you'd know if there was someone in there too. Which leaves the bedroom. No one's in the bedroom because no one could sleep through that shit. How come you don't know who's there?'

There was a pause.

'Who shall I say's calling?'

'I'll tell him when he gets here.'

Harry listened to the rasta music. Now there was an argument and a TV going on in the background as well. Then Pigfoot picked up the receiver. Harry spoke first.

'You hit the wrong guy, Pigfoot.'

'What the hell you talking about? Who is this, man?'

'A real fuck-up. You killed a Cypriot minicab driver called Pete Pattichis.'

Pigfoot wasn't saying anything.

'He left a widow. You still dealing, Walker? How much cash you got in the house at the moment?'

Another pause. Harry heard Pigfoot pull on his cigarette.

'Kapowski,' he decided.

Harry thumbed through his contact book.

'The widow's called Shirley,' he told Pigfoot. 'You got a pen there?'

'Hold on.'

Harry heard him shouting to Yvonne to get him something to write with, gave him time to get ready, then read out Pete's address.

'First thing you do, you take all the cash you can lay your hands on, put it in an envelope, and post it to Shirley Pattichis. First Class. When I find out how much is in it I'll decide what happens next.'

'You kidding?' said Pigfoot.

'Not for a moment,' said Harry.

'Hey man, hold on. What's all this about?'

'Some soul brother on a nifty fifty followed me from home this morning, hung around while I ate lunch, then took a run at me outside an Indian restaurant called the Bombay Duck, opposite Hammersmith underground. Only the poor fucking Cypriot got in the way. You hearing this, Pigfoot.'

Pigfoot wasn't saying.

'And who would want to harm an inoffensive guy like Harry Kapowski?' Harry continued.

'That's a list, man. Long list.'

'You on that list, Pigfoot?'

'Me? Why no, Kapowski, why would I want any harm to come to you? You do your job, I do mine, that's fine by me.' Pigfoot sounded like he was thinking again. 'You serious about the money?'

'Absolutely.'

'What happens if I pay?'

'You mean what's it going to cost you?'

'I mean, I put some notes in an envelope, send them off to the Cypriot, that's the end of it?'

'Maybe,' said Harry. 'And maybe not.'

'I need to think,' said Pigfoot.

'You do? That's all I need to know.'

'Shit, man – I only meant to scare you.'

'You did, Brother, you did.'

Harry rang off.

Roger wheeled him back to bed.

'Are you going to tell me what all that was about?'

'Eventually,' said Harry. 'Not now.'

Roger smiled.

'I'll wait. Meantime they want you to work on the election. As of yesterday.'

Harry moaned.

'Dead or alive?'

'Dead or alive.'

'Tell them it'll have to be dead.'

Harry had covered four general elections, and four

was enough. He got into bed and settled back on his pillows.

'You don't need reporters to cover elections any more, Roger. The parties do it themselves: dictate the agendas, fix the photo opportunties, decide what questions they want to be asked, and who by. Anyway, I'm not that sort of reporter any more. What happens to *Not Proven*? They're taking us off the air?'

'They're thinking about it. We'd only lose one show.'

'Tell them I'll do polling day, they can shunt me off to Middlesbrough or somewhere for the count.'

'I've tried that,' said Roger. 'They want you as soon as you can walk.'

'You're going to let them?'

'Why not?'

'I'm a committed member of the Socialist Workers Party.'

'Since when?'

Harry scratched at his dressing.

'Fuck it, Roger. The building's crawling with ambitious little shits all itching to get their feet on the campaign trail. They must be oversubscribed by a factor of nine. Tell them I'll be free on the day.'

'I did. They're thinking about it.'

After Roger came Chief Inspector Norman Calloway, a bovine man with gobstopper eyes who wore his suit and tie with about as much grace as a fifteen-year-old wears a school uniform. A working cop, top side of forty. Probably divorced, Harry guessed, they usually are by that age. Not a lot of friends outside the force. Spends his evenings off drinking with the same men and women he's been working with all week. Six foot one, long-jawed, a dusting of dandruff on the shoulders of his black raincoat.

Harry was impressed: not a lot of CIs bothered turning out to interview road accident witnesses in hospital these days, not unless there was a photographer present. He realized this was precisely why Calloway was there: Harry mightn't be a tabloid TV star, but he might have friends on the *Standard* or somesuch.

'How are you feeling, Mr Kapowski?'

Harry was feeling fine, apart from the hole in his leg and the bruise on his chest that hit him like a sledgehammer if he moved his rib cage too far to either side. Calloway asked him what he remembered of the accident. Harry told him all he could remember, but it didn't amount to much. He didn't tell him about Pigfoot. He was so full of painkillers and tranqs that he didn't trust himself to go making allegations to the police. And anyway he couldn't prove anything.

Shirley came next.

'Hi,' said Harry, wondering what the hell else you're meant to say in a situation like this. Neither his concentration nor his social emotions were at their best.

'Hello,' said Shirley.

There was a long silence.

He could see she'd been crying. Two raw scars of exhaustion were etched beneath her eyes. He wondered if she was crying for Pete, or something else.

'It's not your fault, Mr Kapowski,' she said before Harry had time to say he was sorry.

'Harry,' said Harry, heaving himself further up on to his pillows. His leg was coming round from the anaesthetic, a deep, sharp pain. 'I don't think this was to do with Pete, I think it was me they were after. You probably know that.'

Shirley pulled up a chair.

'Pete never had much luck, Kapowski. A man gets hit by a falling tree, you can't go blaming it on the tree. You're just the tree hit Pete.'

Harry still couldn't think what to say. He looked at her, wondered what she'd do, marry again, or slip into professional widowhood.

'Do you have kids?' he asked.

'Two,' said Shirley. 'They're young, they don't realize what's happened yet.'

'Did Pete have other family?'

'Brothers and sisters? No, just Terry, his parents are dead. He had uncles and aunts, there are cousins and stuff.'

Another silence. A bus passed in the street outside.

'You got any idea why he done it?' asked Shirley.

'I made a programme a while ago about protection rackets and drug dealers in South London. They play by their own rules down there; someone messes with your business, you get rid of them. Has a certain logic in Brixton, and those guys never leave their manor, they don't know we do things differently north of the river. There's a man called Pigfoot Walker who got four years in the Scrubs, two suspended, a year off for good behaviour, got out last month.'

Harry pictured the big West Indian, the flat with the multicoloured brickwork and the deep-pile purple carpets and goat-hair rugs, the smell of dope, the coffin-sized hi-fi speakers, the triple brass locks and tempered-steel plates on the door; Yvonne with her sexy little arse vacuum-packed in stretch denim, big breasts wobbling as she walked, fetching beers from the fridge; another couple of guys flaked out across the big sofa smoking joints and fiddling with the TV remote control. Ten o'clock in the morning, watching kids' cartoons and housewives' chat shows and a bit of racing. Ask them what they're watching, they say they don't know, still staring at the screen.

Pigfoot had been under the impression Harry and his crew were making a documentary about successful black businessmen, which in a sense they were. He co-operated to start off with, let them film him driving down Clapham Road in the big white Chevie convertible, hood down, cameraman in the passenger seat focusing on the big close-up, Pigfoot in a clean red shirt and dark glasses, music up loud, noisy rap with an excitable DJ on the radio. Eight hundred pounds, that car radio cost whoever bought it before Pigfoot liberated it.

In the edit Harry's director had replaced the rap with Alan Price singing 'Ain't Nobody Gonna Know' from the Lindsay Anderson movie. And there were other times when Pigfoot didn't know they were filming him, the crew crouched in the back of a Ford Transit looking out of the one-way mirror in the back door, night-sight on and a radio mike hidden on a BBC researcher outside a club off Brixton Road.

Harry hadn't been after Pigfoot, he'd been after the police. They had a deal going with the West Indian, who among other things wholesaled dope and tranquilzers. The deal was that Pigfoot gave the cops the names of some of his smalltime buyers, in return for which they left him alone to get on with the big stuff. They got a regular supply of convictions to keep their figures looking good, and Pigfoot went about his business unmolested.

The night the programme went out Pigfoot phoned Harry at home and said he loved all that shit, they didn't have to go hiding in vans and planting microphones, he'd have been happy to let them do it in the open, tripod on the pavement. People had been calling up all evening to say how great he looked on TV. The next morning after some MP came on the *Today* programme demanding action, the police called and arrested him. Harry had to give evidence, and Pigfoot gave him a look from the dock. Nothing personal, just a new definition of their relationship.

Shirley had a lot of make-up on. Not to look good, but to hide what was going on underneath. Harry wondered what she'd do if the money arrived through her letterbox the next morning.

'If he's after you, Kapowski, how come he chases Pete under a truck first?'

'The man takes a lot of drugs,' Harry explained. 'Same problem as Terry, he gets a little confused sometimes. When's the funeral?'

'Thursday. You gonna be there?'

'Sure,' said Harry.

'No flowers,' said Shirley. 'Peter never had much time for flowers.'

3

THEY KEPT HARRY IN hospital overnight and then sent him home, told him to take it easy for a while, make sure his wife looked after him. He told them he didn't have a wife, he was part of the new Underclass that didn't have anyone to care for it when the post-Thatcher Health Service turfed them out on to the street with the blood still wet in their wounds.

His chest was tender and his leg hurt, but otherwise he was not in bad shape. Monday morning found him on his way into work again, singing high harmonies against the car cassette, straining his throat to reach above the Righteous Brothers, then spooling the tape back for a second attempt at the middle eight as he slowed down for the traffic lights at the junction of the Shepherd's Bush Green and Wood Lane. In the grey and yellow November sky a hundred thousand starlings rose as a cloud above the Westway, banked in front of the tombstone silhouettes of the Westbourne Park high-rises, and turned north towards Harlesden.

He wound down the car window and offered his ID card to the BBC commissionaire at the gates to TV Centre. A small knot of pubescent girls sheltering against the perimeter wall glanced across to make sure he wasn't George Michael, turned back to their fanzines.

'Morning, Les,' said Harry cheerfully.

'Morning, Harry,' said Les. 'You reckoning on parking that thing in there?'

'Just dropping some stuff off,' Harry lied. 'Five minutes.'

'I'll give you an hour.' Les raised the barrier. 'After that we tow.'

Harry abandoned the Golf in the News car park, two wheels on the pavement, and walked up the curving ramp towards the tiled concrete doughnut that forms the heart of TV Centre. A coven of BBC executives in black suits, attentive as undertakers, were pouring a delegation from Conservative Central Office into black chauffeur-driven limousines. Harry stood aside to let them past. Tony Mangan, Deputy Director of News and Current Affairs, gaunt, silver-haired, with the slight stoop of a man used to bowing, held back from the group.

'Fixed up the knighthood, Tony?' Harry asked him.

Mangan smiled. He was in his mid fifties, one of that breed of television executives who rise smoothly through the organization without ever making a memorable programme – not making programmes being the best way of keeping your nose politically clean. At Cambridge there must have been a minuscule spark of something in him that persuaded him to join the BBC rather than the Foreign Office or Barclays Bank, but whatever it was had long since died. People like Harry unsettled Mangan because they possessed the confidence and social manners of his class without sharing his assumptions.

'Don't joke, Harry, this is serious stuff. You on board for the campaign?'

'I'd love to, Tony, but I have to wash my hair.'

Mangan smiled again, then asked Harry about his leg. Harry told him the story.

'Is it giving you much pain?' Mangan asked when he'd finished.

'Not too bad, in the circumstances. You don't seriously want me on the election, do you?'

Two stage hands passed them pushing a trolley of discarded scenery labelled 'Oliver Twist, Dead.'

'Afraid so,' said Mangan.

In the lift to the third floor Harry started worrying about the election again. With luck he'd be spared the campaign, but there was no avoiding the count. Everyone worked on polling day: he'd be shipped off to the shires with some teenage natural history producer to cover the declaration in Plymouth North-East or Kircudbright Central. Maybe get on air once or twice, maybe not at all. As a programme idea, election night was insane: the country would be better off going to bed and switching their sets on again at breakfast when there was real news to report. But *Election Special* wasn't really a programme, more a religious ceremony. In fact it sometimes occurred to Harry that the whole BBC was a bit like a church: preaching, explaining, celebrating, confessing sins. Mangan was a bishop, sleek and well fed; Roger Carlisle a turbulent priest; Harry himself a keen chaplain with good prospects, provided he held the faith.

The *Not Proven* production office was open plan, grey-carpeted, a low false ceiling with textured tiles in an aluminium grid and recessed strip-lights; half a dozen desks with VDUs, bendy-backed office chairs, scarlet filing cabinets, pot plants; a soft acoustic broken only by the muffled rattle of computer keyboards. There was a long conference table scattered with half-read newspapers in one corner. Roger Carlisle had a room of his own off the far end, a small glass booth with venetian blinds, a desk, a sofa, a good carpet and a framed Gerald Scarfe etching on the wall: the Queen on horseback, horse and Queen being eaten from the inside out by Harold Wilson maggots. 'To Roger with love

Gerald,' written in felt tip at the bottom, 'In memory of the 1972 Labour party Conference.'

There were a dozen people in the office, the men in shirtsleeves, ties at half mast, women in careful casuals, typing scripts, making phone calls, chatting among themselves. Harry got a lot of sympathy for his leg, particularly from Joan. Joan was forty-five, shaped like a pear, with eyebrows that met in the middle: she looked after the programme paperwork, booked crews and studios, and had a new-fangled BBC title Harry could never remember – Programme Co-ordinator, Production Liaison Manager or somesuch. Ray, the Assistant Producer, somewhere between career collapse and early retirement, put on a show of motherly concern.

Harry helped himself to coffee from the machine and dumped his briefcase on his desk. There was a parcel waiting for him: a dustbin liner wound round with string, his name and address scrawled on a sheet of lined blue writing paper stuck on with Sellotape. Crude, careful writing, like someone sitting a school exam. From Shirley, he guessed. Pete's papers.

Roger's office door was open, Roger standing at the window, watching a skinny freckled girl with ginger hair cross the central courtyard.

'God but she's lovely,' said Roger wistfully.

Roger who daily committed a thousand mental infidelities, but lived a life of faultless domestic virtue.

'Her name's Miranda. Twenty-five years old, and not a care in the world. Single but selective, or so I'm told.'

'You're a married man, Roger. She's young enough to be your daughter.'

'She's got better legs than my daughter. She might have better taste in music, too. I got the brat a ticket for the Dylan gig at Wembley last week, she looked at me sadly and asked what I'd have said to my father if he'd breezed in one day and offered to take me to see Perry Como.'

'Have you hired her?'

'Mmmm. But not for her looks, her looks are coincidental. Joined at the beginning of the week, I sent her straight off to Ulster, baptism of fire – she's never worked in television before. She got back last night.'

People were drifting over to the conference table for the programme meeting. Roger was still looking down into the courtyard.

'You don't have much luck with women, do you, Harry,' said Roger. 'People think you do, but you don't. I mean I don't doubt you get laid, but – how old are you?'

'Thirty-six,' said Harry.

'How many women have you known well? I don't mean one night stands, I mean serious relationships?'

'Serious relationships – that's what I should be aiming for, is it? You're envious, that's your trouble, Roger. You have a wonderfully serious relationship but no sex.'

He picked up a newspaper, limped out into the main office and sat down at the table next to Robert Kettle. Not Bob or Rob or Robbie: Robert, like The Bruce. Robert was a documentary director, age twenty-eight, carried a director's shoulder bag, wore aftershave and open-necked denim shirts and a diver's watch that told him the right time to phone Tokyo, if he ever needed to. A handsome but deeply dull human being, possessed of that odd quality of not knowing when he was being insulted, something which Harry looked on as a crusading challenge. Robert was reading the *Star*, 'The Best of Twenty Things You Always Wanted To Know'.

'Julius Caesar, Lawrence of Arabia and Admiral Nelson all suffered from travel sickness. Fifty thousand American children disappear every year. Israel has over three hundred ex-colonels and generals registered as unemployed. Fancy that.'

'What a wonderful world,' said Harry.

'You want more?'

'Frankly, no. That stuff sticks to your brain, takes up valuable cell-space.'

Robert appeared not to have heard him.

'Animal biologists,' he read, 'have found that four per cent of male elephant seals are responsible for eighty-eight per cent of observed seal copulation.'

'Observed being the operative word,' said Roger, joining them. 'Some of us prefer not to be observed.'

The door opened and in came Miranda, freckled and elfin but with something wild in her eyes that reminded Harry of Sissy Spacek in *Badlands*, only seven or eight years older. She wore a faded green short-sleeved floral blouse and bleached-out jeans held up by an old canvas snake-buckled belt: one of those women who didn't care what they wore, but the less they cared the better they looked.

Roger did the introductions. Harry took his papers off the chair beside him. Miranda gave him a quick look and sat down next to Robert.

'How did you get on?' Roger asked her.

She ran her fingers over her scalp.

'It's all true, the police fixed the whole thing.'

'What's the story?' asked Harry.

'A kid called Sean Walsh,' said Miranda.

She looked straight at him as she talked; Harry couldn't work out if she was being aggressive or simply direct. She had restless green eyes, very clear and sharp, full of curiosity and intelligence.

'He's doing fifteen years in Long Kesh for blowing up the railway station in Derry city. Only he couldn't have, he was breaking into an off-licence in Strabane at the time. He has an impressive record, joined the Provisionals when he was still at school, ran errands, kept lookout. No one I spoke to seems to have liked him — he sounds like a boastful bully. A young RUC superintendent was put on the railway station case. New in the job, wanted a quick conviction. The Provisionals wanted

Walsh out of the way, he'd become an embarrassment to them. They did a deal: the Provos got rid of Walsh, the RUC super got a conviction, case closed. The kid didn't have a hope. As far as I can see the only person who minded was his dad.'

'What makes you so sure it's true?' asked Roger.

'There's a witness, someone who saw the off-licence break-in happen.'

Roger was taking notes.

'Did you talk to him?'

Miranda waited for a moment before answering. Harry watched her carefully, wondering what was going on in her head. She looked down, teasing out her hair with the tips of her fingers.

'Yes. He's called Liam O'Kelly. He's married with a pregnant wife, two children under three. Lives in Strabane, at the head of the town on a housing executive estate with seventy per cent male unemployment. He's part of the seventy per cent. He didn't want to talk. I told him he could trust me. It took rather a long time, but in the end he agreed to be interviewed.'

'Under what conditions?' asked Harry, trying to figure the sub-text.

'With his back to camera, voice distorted.'

'So when can we tape him?' asked Roger.

Miranda kept fiddling with her hair.

'We can't.'

They all looked at her, and for a moment the office was quiet, just the sound of someone tapping a keyboard, a phone ringing somewhere down the corridor.

'Why the hell not?' Roger asked softly.

'I persuaded him not to. I'd told him he could trust me. I said that my job as a researcher was to persuade him to talk, that's what I was paid for. And I'd done my job, earned my money. I said that speaking as a BBC researcher I thought he should do it, but speaking as a human being I thought he'd be mad to. I'd done a sixteen-hour day for the BBC, and come midnight I was on my own time. I told him disguises wouldn't work, it's a small community, wouldn't take long for people to figure who he was.'

Robert's eyes were on stalks. Miranda took a mouthful of coffee, swallowed, put down her cup. She wasn't finding this easy.

'I figured that for me it was just a job, next month I'd have moved on, I'd be doing something else. I had a return ticket, he didn't. He's stuck there in that damp cramped little council house, there's nowhere else for him to go. He could leave, I suppose, jump the country. But for what? So that we could polish up our haloes, pick up another award from the Royal Television Society, purr over the reviews in the Sunday papers. I'm sorry, I know I screwed it.' She corrected herself. 'What I mean is – I'm not sorry I did it, I'm sorry I wasted your time.' She gathered up her papers, ready to leave. 'Thanks for the job. It's just not my kind of work. I don't mean that critically, I know it's important, I know someone has to do it. But not me.'

Harry was in love.

'Hold on,' said Roger. 'Where are you going?'

Miranda hesitated. Harry could see that she just wanted out. He wanted to go with her.

'The Job Centre.'

Roger gestured with his hand.

'For God's sake sit down.'

Harry was thinking about what she'd done, going all that way, trudging round Derry in the wet, knocking on doors, drinking all that tea, eating all those thick-cut ham sandwiches and slabs of fruit loaf – Ulster hospitality would kill you years before the IRA did – playing on the guilt and the goodness in people, being nice to their children, admiring their houses, seducing them with TV talk until they abandoned their better judgment. And then undoing it all. Madness.

Miranda sat down again, but tentatively.

'Did you believe Liam?' asked Roger.

'Absolutely.'

'So the story still holds up?'

She shrugged her shoulders.

'I suppose so, yes.'

'Then let's think of another way of getting at it.'

Bloody Carlisle, thought Harry. There were times when working for Roger was like having a north-country Martin Luther for your programme editor, stubborn, uncompromising, refusing ever to cut his losses and move on. Roger's scruples and moral convictions were a nuisance to everyone. As editor of *Newsnight* he'd been in trouble with the authorities over Ulster, and the Official Secrets Act, and Hong Kong refugees, and insider trading in the City, until finally the Board of Governors insisted on his removal from mainstream current affairs, gave him a BBC-speak title (Head of Special Projects, Television News and Current Affairs) and effectively shunted him sideways to run a monthly programme on the law. *Not Proven* – the only Special Project on air – was meant to explain to the punters how the legal system worked. Roger interpreted the brief as an excuse to demonstrate that it didn't. Harry asked to be transferred across from *Newsnight* with him because life with Carlisle was difficult but never dull.

'The story stands up,' Roger continued, 'but you don't want to put Liam on camera, am I right?'

Miranda wasn't saying anything. Roger was on his feet, hands in his pockets, pacing the carpet like a ship's captain.

'Listen, it doesn't matter what else bloody Walsh has done, doesn't matter if he is or isn't or was or wasn't in the Provisionals: if he didn't blow up the tax office he shouldn't be in prison for it. If the UK government breaks the rules it can't expect the rest of its citizens to be law abiding either.'

'What are you suggesting?' asked Robert.

Roger didn't know. But he didn't see why the fact that Liam O'Kelly had been persuaded not to put his neck on the line changed the story.

'There must be other people who know what happened. So far we've talked to one.'

'But the same veto would apply to anyone else involved,' Robert objected.

'Then find another way to tell the story.' Roger took his hand out of his pocket and punched the table. 'God, if every miscarriage of justice case depended on people agreeing to go on television we might as well give up, scrap the whole bloody legal system. Do it as a drama. If the case is as shot through with holes as you think it is, reconstruct the court case, use the transcripts. Or get someone to write a comic monologue, mock them into submission. But don't just give up.'

Harry watched Miranda, who had the puzzled look of someone who has picked a fight only to find the opposition agree with her. She caught his stare. He blushed.

'Who else did you talk to?' asked Roger.

'She got out her notes and thumbed through the pages. She'd been to see the BBC newsroom in Belfast, then Radio Foyle, then Walsh's father, and his solicitor, and the PP, and the local paper, all the obvious calls. Harry was watching her, but he was hardly listening, just wishing he was twenty-five again. He remembered that burning enthusiasm, that appetite for an argument, the unquestioning assumption that you were right, even if you couldn't always explain why. At twenty-five it doesn't even matter much if you discover you've got it wrong, because at that age mistakes don't count – if something doesn't work out in your career or your relationships you can simply move on, start again.

But then again he wasn't sure he could face being twenty-five again. Just looking at Miranda made him feel tired. Harry was thirty-six, well-respected, decently paid, on top of the job. But thirty-six was an awkward age for a TV reporter, no longer young and eager, not yet old enough to have real gravitas. The next few years could go either way.

Roger was talking again, briefing Miranda, telling her to write the case up chronologically, in as much detail as she could, giving sources, identifying which were on the record and which off.

'And then?' she asked.

'And then we'll work out what to do next. One day at a time, sweet Jesus.'

After lunch Harry opened up Shirley's parcel and read through the cuttings on Terry Pattichis. Pete's research was utterly undiscriminating: every newspaper cutting, every letter, every photograph.

There was a photo of Jo O'Brien, taken at a function of some kind, sitting at a restaurant table. A big man in his early forties with prematurely white hair, long at the collar, jacket off and raising a glass of wine to the camera. He was smiling, but his eyes had that panic about age you sometimes see in middle-aged gays. Terry was beside him, neat and pretty but with a hard mouth, a cigarette in his hand, gold bracelet on his wrist. Jo was drinking wine, Terry had a short on the table in front of him. It must have been the only photo of them together, because it kept cropping up time and time again.

Harry rather liked the sound of Jo, who appeared to have been an accomplished, articulate con-man, utterly without scruple, but curiously without malice. He'd jumped South Africa on a fraud rap in the late sixties, moved to London, and announced he was a political refugee, which is how he picked up his political connections. He earned his living as a fund raiser, promoting charity events, organizing sponsorship. *Private Eye* and the *Sunday Times* Insight people had been after him a couple of times, but nothing was ever proved, and the Left screamed persecution.

No one had much to say about Terry, except that he was Jo's lover, Greek Cypriot, eighteen, with a string of minor convictions.

On 17 December 1983, Jo and Terry were working late at the office. Around eight, according to Terry's confession, he and Jo had gone round the corner to the Balzac bistro for a bottle of Beaujolais and something to eat; later they'd moved next door to the Beaumont Arms for more drink. Harry knew the Balzac and the Beaumont well, both were popular BBC watering holes, which was probably why Latchkey had it's offices in Shepherd's Bush in the first place. Jo and Terry got back to the office at eleven. They had an argument. Terry knocked Jo unconscious with a chair, put his body in a stationery cupboard, helped himself to the petty cash and then set the place on fire. All this he admitted to Detective Superintendent Brian Natkeil at Shepherd's Bush police station. Signed and witnessed, all very proper. No evidence of physical abuse or threatening behaviour by the police. At the trial Terry claimed he'd been tricked into signing but neither the judge nor the jury believed him, and nor did the Court of Appeal. The papers ran both the murder and the trial, but it was a busy summer – the Falklands War, the birth of Prince Harry, the Pope's visit.

Harry didn't know if Terry Pattichis did or didn't kill Jo O'Brien, but the way Terry was heading, at the age of eighteen, he was either going to wind up in a cell or dead. The kid was a male prostitute, drug-abuser, thief, alcoholic, mental patient, compulsive liar, knife-man. The best you could say for Terry was he had a nice brother and an entertaining sister-in-law: and that getting into Broadmoor probably saved his life.

He'd go to Pete's funeral, be nice to Shirley, and that would be that. Afterwards he'd help Miranda sort out Sean Walsh. At least the Walsh case was about something.

Grace arrived with the tea trolley, two urns and a bottom shelf of biscuits and buns; cheerful Grace from Trinidad who knew everyone's names and never stopped laughing. Everyone liked Grace, though no one knew her surname, or where she lived, what made up her life away from the corridors of Television Centre.

'Hey Harry, what's up with the leg?'

'Did you ever come across a compatriot of yours called Pigfoot Walker?' asked Harry, eyeing up the macaroons.

'Pigfoot? Never heard of him. He done that to you?'

Harry took a slice of clingwrapped fruit cake.

'One of his employees.'

'And what you gonna do about that?' asked Grace, big grin, laughing so her whole body wobbled.

'I'm not sure yet,' said Harry. 'But I'm working on it.'

4

THERE WERE MAYBE THIRTY mourners at Pete Pattichis' funeral, standing around outside the crematorium
in small groups of four or five, sombre as crows,
stamping their feet and punching their hands, checking
their watches. Relatives and neighbours, by the look of
them, with a few of Pete's colleagues from the minicab
trade, uncomfortable in their suits and ties and over-
coats and scarfs, leaves clinging to their shoes. The
women wore head scarfs, handbags hanging from
crooked elbows. The day had begun with cloud bursts
and a bitter gusting gale from the north, but by noon
the rain had cleared and a thin sun silvered the tarmac,
chill and dishonest, like a hot bath-tap running cold.

Harry parked the Golf and limped across to where
Shirley was sheltering by the double oak doors of the
chapel, one arm battening her hem to her calves, the
other clamping a black felt hat to the crown of her
head, receiving condolences. She had her two young
sons beside her.

She smiled sadly at Harry.

'I didn't think you'd come.'

'I did.'

'Thanks, I appreciate it, Mr Kapowski.'

'Harry,' said Harry.

'I'd rather call you Kapowski, I only just learned how
to pronounce it. Like in comics, Pete said – KAPOW!'

Without thinking she leaned forward and lifted a hair off the shoulder of Harry's jacket. 'You know something? An oak veneer coffin costs the undertaker thirty-two pounds ninety-five p. It costs you or me a hundred and thirty quid. Solid oak costs them a hundred and sixty-one quid, we pay five hundred and seventy. We're waiting for Terry,' she explained.

'They let him out?' asked Harry.

'If you can call it that.'

Harry looked around at the laurel and ivy, the scavenging starlings and well-swept Tarmacadam paths. Beyond, on the verges, the undertakers hovered, their dress mirror-perfect, looking at their watches and fingering their breast-pocket handkerchiefs, just in case. There was a sense of everything rented, in-out, time's up, like paid-for sex.

Terry arrived in an unmarked black limousine: two plain clothes prison officers in the front, two more in the back sandwiching a small figure in a dark suit. The limo parked under a dripping beech, and out got Pete Pattichis, walking down the asphalt path towards the white concrete prow of the chapel, dwarfed by his minders.

No one had told Harry the Pattichis brothers were twins.

Close up you could tell the difference, but only just. Terry looked fitter than his brother, had pumped iron and looked after his body while Pete was slouched over the wheel of his minicab, had eaten meagre institutional food while Shirley fattened Pete up on mutton and honey cakes. He wore glasses, and dressed better than Pete, a sharp suit, white shirt, black silk tie. Broadmoor was technically a hospital not a prison, and the inmates had a lot of freedom about that sort of thing.

Terry and his minders sat at the back in a pew of their own. Harry found a seat across the aisle, watching out the corner of his eye.

The verger coughed into his cuff and led Shirley and the two boys off up the aisle. The coffin followed on a chrome trolley, like a room-service lunch. Overhead an asthmatic organist elbowed her way distastefully through 'You'll Never Walk Alone', picking the unfamiliar notes off the staves like head-lice. Then the priest said a few words.

They reached the oven door, and slid the casket into the void. Harry watched Terry's face, utterly impassive, a soldier on parade. At one point he raised his hand-cuffed wrist to scratch his cheek, and the guard had to raise his too, wait with his hand suspended in mid-air until Terry had finished, then the two of them lowered their arms together, like schoolboys in a three-legged race.

Harry watched, but his mind was on other things, on the general election, on Pigfoot Walker, and Miranda, and whether to go away to Wales for the weekend.

The music stopped, the congregation sat down. A clergyman said a few words, then Shirley walked back down the aisle and took up her position for the Shaking of Hands, and the congregation filed out past her muttering regrets. Outside it was raining again. There were a few brief attempts at conversation, heads tortoised into collars, shouting at each other above the gale. Terry disappeared back into the Ford. As far as Harry knew, he'd spoken to no one.

'You do something for me, Mr Kapowski?' Shirley asked Harry as he was about to make his excuses. 'Don't go yet. It means something to these people having you here. Come and eat lunch.'

'Sure,' said Harry, not wanting to, unable to think of a reason not to.

They drove in convoy to an early fifties mock-Tudor roadhouse hotel set in the middle of an enormous car park bordering a dual carriageway, and followed the Private Function signs upstairs to a low-ceilinged room

38

with a lurid carpet that smelled of spilled beer and stale tobacco. The waitresses looked as though they'd had a bad week, nothing personal but don't make any jokes. Harry got a cup of tea and a plate of ham and limp salad and stood on his own by the window, wondering what to do, who to talk to. For ten minutes he stood there, nodding and smiling at other guests as they passed. They'd nod and smile back, no one taking the initiative.

It was Taki the Sikh who broke the ice. Taki watched a lot of TV, read the feature articles about TV celebrities in the papers and magazines, knew things about TV that people who worked in TV didn't know themselves. Like: how many TV channels does New Zealand have? Or: which well-known weather forecaster used to be a professional ballroom dancer?

Taki didn't want to ask Harry about himself, he wanted to tell him, describe in detail programmes Harry had made, things he'd said in interviews in *You* magazine or on *Start the Week*.

'You were on Sue Lawley with Annie Burgh and Victoria Wood and' – closing his eyes, biting his lips – 'Bryan Robson?'

'Jackie Charlton.'

'Right,' said Taki.

Harry asked Taki about Pete and Terry. Taki didn't know a lot about Terry, but he knew a bit about Pete. Tony Dimas knew other bits of the story.

The Pattichis brothers were born in Cyprus and sent to England as teenagers to join their Uncle Micky and Aunt Tina. Micky and Tina lived in an Edwardian brick terrace in New Cross, just off Loampit Hill. Micky ran a panel-beating business under the railway arches, Tina cooked lunches for a council geriatric home in Deptford and worked in a chipper in Lewisham in the evenings. They had five children of their own. The twins were sixteen, spoke bad English, and disliked their relatives.

Terry more than Pete: Pete was the quiet one, with a conscientious streak and low expectations. He didn't much like London, but he got fed and paid, watched a lot of television and stuck pictures of girls on the wall above his bed. Terry wasn't interested in girls, and he didn't want to spend his life fixing Ford Cortinas.

'They were good-looking boys,' Tony Dimas explained. 'Some skin problems, but good looking enough when they took the trouble to fix their hair and dress up right. Terry had a taste for clothes. On Saturday night he'd put on tight black trousers and a white shirt and some jewellery, medallions and that, shave very close and splash himself with cologne, and take the bus up to Waterloo. Often he didn't come home until Monday morning, after a few months he didn't come back at all.'

Harry asked them if they thought he'd killed Jo O'Brien. Taki looked at Tony, Tony looked at Taki, then both looked over their shoulders to see who was listening.

'Who knows?' asked Tony eventually.

'Sometimes he went a little funny,' Taki added.

'Funny like what?' asked Harry.

'Funny like he was dreaming,' said Tony. 'Like he'd pinch himself to see if he felt anything.'

Harry stayed for a hour before making his excuses, explaining to Shirley that he'd do what he could about Terry but he doubted much would come of it. He signed an autograph for Tony Dimas, and went down to find his car.

It was gone. He walked round the hotel, out on to the main road, hoping he'd had a brainstorm and left it somewhere else. He hadn't: he'd parked nose on to the hotel, remembered the rasp as he'd scraped the front numberplate on the kerb.

'Navy blue Golf?' asked the pump attendant at the

filling station across the road. 'Yeah, went about twenty minutes ago.'

Harry asked who went with it.

'Guy on his own,' said the attendant. 'He had keys, I assumed it was his.'

'Black or white.'

'Brown.'

At least Harry wasn't suffering from racial discrimination this week.

Shirley gave him a lift back into London in Pete's Escort with the School of Motoring sign on the roof. Her children had gone ahead with relatives. She drove with a cigarette in her mouth, one eye on the rear view mirror. When she wasn't smoking she ate toffees out of a bag in the glove compartment. Harry tried to decide if she was fat and ugly, or just fat.

At the junction with the North Circular a truck had shed its load and they sat for twenty minutes not moving, waiting for the traffic to clear.

'Thanks for the money,' said Shirley. 'At least I suppose that was you?'

'Not entirely,' said Harry. 'How much did he send?'

'A lot, fifty-pound notes in one of those padded envelopes, I haven't touched it. I didn't know what to do.'

'In Saudi Arabia,' Harry explained, 'if they catch a murderer, the relatives of the deceased decide what they want the authorities to do with him. Or her. Often they'll spare the killer's life in return for compensation. The widow has the final word.'

'They do a lot of things in Saudi Arabia. As far as I'm concerned the police can have whoever did it.'

'That's what I reckoned, too,' said Harry. 'So what do you want to do about the money?'

'He'll want it back, won't he?'

'If he does he's going to have to explain why he sent it to you in the first place.'

'You told him to.'

'His word against mine. He's an ex-con, I'm a nice middle-class boy with a clean record.'

'Bloody hell!' said Shirley. 'Whose side are you on?'

'I wonder about that sometimes,' said Harry.

Shirley bit her cuticles. The traffic was starting to move again.

'OK, I'll think about it. But believe it or not, Mr Kapowski, I don't give a shit about the money. I mean, I appreciate the thought, but it's not what matters.'

She put on a cassette, Cat Stephens, 'Morning Has Broken', music for people who don't like music. Harry winced.

'Were you fond of him?' he asked.

'I don't know.' Shirley laughed quietly. 'He was just Pete, I never thought about it really. Like the weather, you got used to him.'

'I meant Terry,' said Harry.

'Terry? Yes, I like Terry, I suppose. I couldn't begin to explain why. I've never heard him say sorry for anything, not once. He's got religion now, did you know that? Jesus has entered his life; he has a picture of Cliff Richard by his bed and letters from all kinds of people promising to pray for him – Archbishops, Cardinals, all that stuff. But you never hear any regrets for the old days.'

'Is he serious about religion?'

'He was for a while. Terry never does anything by halves, he becomes what he decides to become and that's that. Like an actor, he should have been an actor. He was in something on TV once, they wanted a lot of people sitting in a pub, in the background while someone got shot. He enjoyed that.'

Harry hadn't noticed where they were going: now he realized Shirley was heading north-east, way off course for him.

'You can drop me at a tube,' he suggested.

'Don't you want to pick up your car?' asked Shirley.

Harry looked at her.

'What the hell do you mean?'

'Taki took it.'

Harry was speechless. Shirley was smiling, a sad little smile.

'Why?' he asked finally.

'I wanted to talk to you is why. About Pete and Terry.'

Harry still didn't believe her.

'Are you serious about this?'

'Of course. Tony kept you talking, Taki took the keys.'

'Fuck me!' said Harry, and gave an indignant snort.

He looked out the side window, wondering what to do, get angry or go along with it.

'I guessed you had no real intention of doing anything about Terry,' said Shirley. She lit another cigarette. 'I wouldn't have. I'll be honest with you, Mr Kapowski, I don't know if Terry did it or didn't do it. More honestly, I think maybe he did. Not certainly, maybe. But maybe is not meant to be enough, am I right? Has to be sure. Some lawyer told me that once. It can't be likely, or probably, or it looks as if – it has to be beyond doubt.'

'Reasonable doubt,' said Harry. 'So why now?'

'I told you, Pete promised his mother he'd do something.'

But Pete's dead, Harry didn't say.

'Pete would do that out of respect for his mother,' Shirley went on. 'Not because he thought anything would come of it, but out of respect.'

'And you feel the same way about Pete?'

'More or less.'

Harry shook his head.

'It's hopeless, but you probably know that, don't you?'

'Of course it's hopeless. I figured it like this. To let someone out you have to have a reason why it's

43

necessary for them to be out. Not because they're innocent, but because it suits people better to let them go than hang on to them. Am I right?'

'More or less.'

'I mean, just having innocent people in prison doesn't worry the government. What worries the government is people making trouble, signing petitions, painting slogans on buildings. If politicians reckon keeping a particular person in prison might cost them votes, then maybe they let that person go. Tell me if I'm wrong, Kapowski, this is just what I figure.'

'No, you're still making sense. You didn't have to steal my car to tell me, but you're making sense.'

She was fat and ugly, he decided. Her eyes were too small, set too far apart, and she had sharp little teeth, like a fish. But for a cushion consultant, she'd make a hell of a lawyer.

'So who would want Terry Pattichis out of jail?' she asked him. 'No one. Even if he's innocent who cares? A Cypriot bum-boy who never did anyone a favour in his life, suddenly looking for favours back from the world. Plus he's nuts; who knows when he'll do it again?'

'Is he really nuts?'

Shirley wasn't sure.

'He went funny after the trial. Pete reckoned it was just coming off chemicals, being without the drugs and that he couldn't blur the edges any more. Me, I don't think he's nuts. You read Pete's papers?'

'Mostly. There doesn't seem much to go on.'

'There isn't. Except for the money.'

Harry looked at her.

'What money?'

'His mother's money. Came every month in the post, ever since Terry went down. A money order, one hundred pounds it was to start with. Then it got a bit more, for inflation and that I suppose. Buys a lot in Cyprus, that does.'

Harry asked her who sent it.

'You're the detective. It was just a money order. She died and it stopped. Pete didn't want to mention it, he assumed maybe Terry sent it, like he had some money tucked away from before, he wanted to make sure his mother was all right. Pete figured that if anyone started sniffing around where it came from they might make more trouble for Terry, that's why he didn't tell you.'

'Did he ask Terry about it?'

'He asked but he didn't get much of an answer.'

She turned off Seven Sisters Road at Finsbury Park, on up Stroud Green Road. Harry saw the Golf parked by the kerb, Taki standing beside it, big grin on his face.

'The other thing I don't understand,' said Shirley, 'isn't why they won't let him out. It's why they keep him in. He's done eight years, behaved himself. They normally let them out after less than that, don't they?'

'Usually,' said Harry.

He was halfway out of the car, collecting up his coat and bag. Taki tossed him the keys to the Golf.

'So what are you going to do about it?'

'Nothing,' said Harry.

'You sure about that?'

'Certain.' He put on his best sincere, I'm-talking-to-you-as-a-friend voice. 'Listen, Shirley . . .'

'Mrs Pattichis. You're Kapowski, I'm Mrs Pattichis, let's get that straight at least.'

'All I can suggest is that you try going through your MP, see if you can get him interested.'

'That's all?'

'That's all.'

'Even if I tell you who wants him kept inside?'

Harry smiled, shrugged his shoulders.

'You know?'

'Ben Webb.'

'Are you serious?'

Shirley nodded.

'The Ben Webb who's deputy leader of the Labour party?' asked Harry.

She nodded again.

'The Ben Webb who in two weeks' time may be Chancellor of the Exchequer?'

'I told you, you're the detective, Kapowski. I don't know much about all that stuff. All I know is that there were three people working for the Latchkey Trust – Terry, Jo O'Brien, and a boy called Ben Webb.'

'Shit,' said Harry.

'You say that a lot, Kapowski. Anyone says anything surprising you say "shit". You should get yourself a new word.'

'Tell me about Ben.'

'The thing to tell about Ben Webb is that there isn't anything to tell because everyone shut up about him. He was there the night it happened, earlier on. He worked there, he must have known a heap of things about what they were up to. Come the trial he's not there, no one calls him as a witness, no one puts his name in the paper. Like those photos the Russians used to have, someone falls from power and the next time they print the photo he's not there, like he never existed. Only he exists all right now, everyone's heard of Ben Webb now, they just don't talk about the time he shared an office with Terry Pattichis and Jo O'Brien.' She sucked at her cigarette. 'You know him?'

'Sort of. I know Angela – his wife. Or I used to.'

'Then ask her to ask her husband what the hell Terry is doing in Broadmoor. And how come he sent a hundred pounds a month to an old lady in Cyprus for eight years.'

'How do you know he did?'

'I don't, that's for you to find out. You're very clever, Kapowski. But you don't seem to feel very much.'

Harry's leg gave him a twinge.

5

THAT NIGHT HARRY'S STITCHES tore. Not badly, but enough to keep him hanging around doctors and hospital outpatients for most of the following day. He tried ringing Angela Webb, but she was away, off campaigning with Ben. He left a message on her answering machine, took a taxi round to the police station and signed a statement for Chief Inspector Calloway. He mentioned Pigfoot this time, didn't accuse him, just suggested he might have a motive, then went home to bed. It was Friday by the time he got back to the office.

Miranda was sitting at her desk, writing up notes, absorbed in her work. Harry dumped his bag on his desk, grabbed a coffee and wandered across to the conference table to join Robert. Robert wore a white linen shirt and tight black trousers today, and a black leather jacket, collar up, sleeves turned back at the wrist. Harry thought he could smell a whiff of Kouros.

'You know your problem, Bob?' Harry sniffed the air like a Bistro kid. 'You smell great, you're hugely talented, creative, witty, intelligent, have impeccable taste in food, wine, art, underwear and hairdressers, and a natural gift for conversation. But you're ugly.'

'Huh,' Robert grinned. He knew he was handsome. Talented, too.

Roger joined them.

'Good funeral?'

47

'Miserable,' said Harry. 'You know what I hate about funerals? The way the Church uses them to put the fear of death into the rest of us. Join up before it's your turn for the urn.'

Roger asked him what he was going to do about Terry Pattichis.

'I suggested to Shirley that she get in touch with her MP. I might make a couple more phone calls. It's rather an odd case, but the law doesn't seem to have done much wrong.'

'Odd because . . .?'

'Because Pattichis is still inside after all this time. It's not like the Krays, he wasn't into organized crime or anything. We'd need to talk to the doctors, find out if there are medical grounds for keeping him in. It's worth a couple of letters.'

Roger nodded.

'Oh,' Harry added, 'there's one other thing. According to Terry's widow, Latchkey had another staffer at the time. Ben Webb.'

Roger blinked.

'You're joking.'

'Not at all.'

Roger lifted *Who's Who* down from the shelf behind his desk and read out Ben's entry.

'Webb, Benjamin Franklyn Giles, MP – God, the names parents give their children – born twelfth of May nineteen fifty-three, only son of the late etc. etc., educated Marlborough, Oxford etc., Fulbright Scholar, University of Chicago etc. etc., elected to Parliament nineteen eighty-four, blah blah blah, married Angela wotsit, two kids . . . publications, address . . . No, not a word about Latchkey.'

'Maybe it's a different Ben Webb,' said Robert.

'Quite possibly,' said Harry. 'Doesn't affect the rights and wrongs of the case. I'll check it out anyway.'

Roger closed the book.

'Why not. Listen, Harry, Tony Mangan was on again this morning about the election, they want – '

'Phone for you, Harry,' Joan called from across the office.

Harry took the call at his desk.

'Kapowski?'

'Pigfoot?' said Harry. 'How are you doing?'

He gestured to Joan to record the call.

'I'm doing shit, man. Twelve pigs just busted down my front door. Nobody knocks, they just took out the frame with sledges, busted right in. We had a deal, Kapowski. I send the package round to the Greek woman, you leave me alone.'

'Cypriot,' Harry corrected him. 'Pete was a Cypriot. Different thing entirely.'

'What the fuck,' said Pigfoot. 'We still made a deal.'

Harry glanced across the room. Roger and Robert were arguing. Miranda was making phone calls.

'No we didn't. I said send the money, and we'll see.'

'A deal, Kapowski, you fucked up on a deal, you shouldn't do that. And you know what else those pigs did? Stole my leather jacket, I saw it with my own eyes. Just as they're hauling me out what's left of my front door one of them nips back in, lifts it off the pegs. What they want to do that for?'

'Maybe they thought it was stolen in the first place,' Harry suggested. 'Maybe they wanted it as evidence.'

'Of course it was stolen, man. But not by me, I got it off a friend. Nothing to stop you getting presents from your friends, is there?'

'What did you give him in exchange? Angel Dust? Ice? Ecstasy?'

Pigfoot didn't answer.

'Where are you, by the way?' asked Harry.

'Brixton police station. I get one phone call, arsehole, to my solicitor or whoever. You're my whoever,

Kapowski, I'm making it to you instead. Maybe when I'm done you call me a lawyer, you do that?'

'Tell them you got a wrong number first time.' Harry lit a cigarette. 'Was there something particular you wanted to talk to me about, Pigfoot?'

'You dead, Kapowski. That's all. Whatever happens to me, you dead.'

He hung up.

Harry waited a moment before putting down the phone, wondering what to do. You blabbermouth with these guys and it feels like a joke, a game of dare. And then it isn't a game any more, Pete Pattichis is dead. He was fairly sure Pigfoot hadn't meant to kill anyone, just scare him. The rest was an accident. Didn't make any difference, Pattichis is dead, Pigfoot's inside and screaming revenge, probably has enough money stashed away to get someone to do the job for him.

He picked the phone up again, rang Chief Inspector Calloway and told him about Pigfoot's call. Calloway asked if he wanted protection.

Not yet, Harry told him, not yet. Not because he meant it, but because it sounded good.

'Did you order these, Harry?' asked Joan, offering a News Information file on Ben Webb.

It was a fat file, the cuttings folded into neat little stacks piled two inches deep along its length. Some were little more than snippets, others full-page features and magazine articles. The first reference to Ben's name would be underlined in red biro, and Harry wondered sometimes if the poor bastards who spent their days cutting and filing the papers ever read any further than that. 'Labour MP Ben Webb,' started one, 'was among three thousand demonstrators protesting outside the Chinese Embassy in London . . .' Then three full columns about the demonstration, without another mention of Ben.

There were goodies, though: an anonymous *Observer* profile, a long and anecdotal piece from *GQ* magazine, four or five extended interviews in which Ben talked about his background and his career. Most of it Harry knew already, but he re-read it all, looking for clues and omissions.

Ben was an only child, adopted and brought up by a Home Counties solicitor and his church-going wife. It had been a happy childhood, spent playing on his own among the beech woods of the Chilterns, with regular trips up to London to visit museums and Madame Tussauds. His real mother, he later discovered, was unmarried and Irish, sent to relatives in England when she was found to be pregnant. Ben had traced her later, shortly before her death, to a housing estate in Waterford, where she'd married and raised five more children.

He went to a local prep school in Aylesbury, and then on to Marlborough, where he played cricket and rugby and joined the drama society – there was a photograph of him as a nymph in Offenbach's *Orpheus in the Underworld*, dragged up in pink chiffon with a wand in his hand. Academically he was the star of his year, and won an open scholarship to Oxford to read politics, philosophy and economics. He was a handsome, intelligent undergraduate, but by no means a political ideologue. He'd joined the Union, and by his third year been elected president. Another photograph showed him standing on the steps of the Union with Norman Tebbit and Eric Heffer before a debate. Angela was there too, her hair long, wearing a padded Chinese cotton jacket and a CND button, Ben's hand on her shoulder.

Ben went straight from Oxford to Chicago on a Fulbright Scholarship to study twentieth-century American socialism. He was lonely, and found the contemporary American Left in-bred and demoralized, still fighting the battles of the twenties and thirties. But mainstream American politics fascinated him. He got a campaign job during the mid-term Congressional elections, learned about computers, and political advertising, and how plain-speaking and enthusiasm could snowball into a national crusade.

Back in England, he set about establishing his own political career, making contacts, involving himself in the activities of his local Labour party. There was no mention of Latchkey in the cuttings, just a passing reference to a period spent working for the homeless. In 1984, the year of Terry's trial, he'd got himself selected as a candidate for a by-election in a South London constituency, and held the seat. Within two years, following a succession of brilliant performances at party conferences, he was on the National Executive, and the ball was well and truly rolling. 'Mr Unstoppable', one of the papers had dubbed him.

Harry closed the file and wandered across to Roger's office. Roger was still on about the election.

'Mangan's prepared to lay off for a couple of days. But they want you on board from Tuesday.'

'Full time?'

'Full time,' said Roger. 'Robert too. Don't look so bloody miserable, it's sizing up into rather an interesting campaign.'

'Fascinating,' Harry agreed. 'And what about you?'

'Me? I'm on obituary stand-by,' said Roger. 'In case someone gets shot.'

Robert and Harry took Miranda to lunch in the waitress-service canteen, a sort of ersatz BBC bistro patronized by the more leisured class of producer and the odd minor celebrity. Robert was in his element, shirt cuff folded back to show off his tanned forearms, greeting prestigious acquaintances, Hi Esther, Hallo Barry, How-you-doing Michael? He'd brought his mobile phone with him too, balancing it on the table-cloth beside the miniature porcelain vase with the single

52

carnation in it. Robert loved phones. Harry hated them.

'I've got this thing,' he explained, 'that the waves are passing through our heads, what's being said is absorbed into our subconscious. The air's full of garbage we can't see, radio signals, TV signals, satellite footprints, God knows what. They're building high-powered portable computers now that talk to each other via radio waves, some guy in Brighton is offloading spreadsheets to his mate in Birmingham, the whole lot passes through my head on the way. It's a wonder we can think at all.'

Robert shook his head sadly. Harry kept going.

'Just think of what's out there – hundreds of TV and radio channels, personal pagers, taxi drivers, police and ambulance, air traffic, remote controllers – are you telling me all that stuff ignores the human body, Bob?'

'It doesn't work like that, Harry.'

Harry wondered whether to go on, whether to gamble on Robert knowing how that stuff did work. If he didn't it would be fun, if he did they'd be there all afternoon.

The waitress arrived to take their drink orders. Harry ordered a carafe of wine.

'So what were you doing before this?' Robert asked Miranda.

Girls in Robert's life-experience always liked to talk about themselves, all you had to do was listen, nod, show how seriously you took them as human beings. You want to sleep with a woman, pretend to take her seriously.

'I was in Honduras,' said Miranda, just like that.

Robert couldn't believe his luck.

'Honduras? I was there in eighty-nine. Lovely beaches, if you can find them. I spent three weeks on the Bay Islands, down on the Caribbean coast. Marvellous place. A bit like the Seychelles, but without the crowds.'

'Marvellous for what?' Miranda asked innocently.

Harry didn't know her well, but well enough to guess what was coming.

'Swimming, sunbathing, scuba, photography. Very cheap, too.'

'It's the same everywhere you go now, isn't it,' Miranda smiled sweetly, and drained her wine glass. She was a thirsty woman, but she semed well able to take it. 'Gucci boutiques and picturesque poor people. Buy a Nikon on the duty free, take pictures of the poor people. The trouble is there are some places where the poor people aren't even picturesque. No one takes pictures of London's beggars.'

Robert was lost for words, mouth frozen in one of those smiles opera singers put on between verses.

'How long were you out there?' asked Harry.

'In Honduras? I left last summer when the Foreign and Commonwealth Office cut our budget in half.'

'What were you doing?'

'Primary health care. At the time I left we were sorting out the mess left by the Americans. They have teams of women travelling round Central America in minibuses inserting contraceptive coils. They drive into town one day, show a video explaining the benefits, fit the IUDs and move on. Coils need to be checked after three months, of course, but by then the people who fitted them have left the country. It was worse in this case because the coils were part of a job lot rejected by the Federal Health and Safety people. There were a lot of complications.'

'How very interesting,' said Robert.

'Not really.' She still wasn't being aggressive, just matter-of-fact. 'It's part of daily life in most of the Third World. The IUD merchants were nothing compared to the born-again missionaries.'

'So why did you join the Beeb?' asked Harry.

Miranda smiled.

'I need the money.'

'No better reason,' said a voice behind Harry's shoulder: Freddy Piperidge, Presentation Duty Editor, braggart and bore, a loathsome creature but a man to be humoured by anyone wanting their programmes trailed and promoted on air.

'Hallo Harry – who's the lovely lady?'

Harry didn't bother looking round.

'Miranda Cunningham, Freddy Piperidge,' he said wearily.

Freddy dropped his safari jacket over the back of a chair and sat down. Striped shirt, slacks, packet of Dunhill in his breast pocket.

'You're a wise one, Miranda. Money – why else would anyone choose to spend their lives poking around the nation's sewers looking for misunderstood delinquents? All this there-but-for-fortune, *tout-comprendre-c'est-tout-pardonner* shit Roger and Harry hawk around the airwaves – bloody madness. Some guy trashes your flat, rapes your wife, and Harry here thinks: If I were in his shoes I'd do the same, we all would. The only hope for us all is if we wouldn't. There was a man on *Breakfast Time* the other week who seriously believed bank robbers were social revolutionaries. Can you believe it? As though the first thing criminals did with their loot was hand it out to the poor and needy. Do they hell. They buy big houses in Surrey with swimming pools and stables, or clear off to some mock-Roman palace in Spain, buy in some blondes and draught champagne, get themselves photographed by the *News of the World*. One thing I know about successful hoods is they all vote Tory. They don't want to help the poor, they want to get away from them, same as the rest of us. How many of the people you've got out of jail are what you'd call useful citizens, Kapowski?'

'Are you?' asked Harry.

'Hugely,' said Freddy. 'What puzzles me is that I don't imagine you lot have much fun doing it, either. I mean, you could be on the *Holiday Programme*, or the *History of Wine*, out and about in pleasant places. It's OK for Harry, he gets his physog on the box. You love all that, don't you Harry?'

Harry wasn't saying.

'Tell me honestly, Miranda,' Freddy asked. 'Which Harry do you like best? Deeply sympathetic and understanding, or morally outraged and aggressive? Criminals get the one, police and politicians the other. You can guess which gets which.'

'I'm afraid I don't watch much television,' said Miranda.

She looked at Harry, wondering why he didn't fight back. She couldn't figure him at all: half the time he knocked the system, the other half he seemed completely at ease with it.

'You mean you've never seen the great Kapowski at work?'

She shook her head. She'd stopped toying with her salad and was taking out her contact lenses, pulling her eyelids open with one hand, pinching the lens out with the other, putting them one by one in their neat little container.

'Lucky woman,' said Freddy. 'So what have you on the stocks for us, chaps? Anything you'd like plugged?'

How about your arsehole? Harry refrained from saying.

'Nothing definite, Freddy,' Robert said instead. 'We'll let you know as soon as we can.'

'Do that,' said Freddy. 'Nice meeting you, Miranda.' And he was off.

'Jesus,' Miranda laughed. 'Is he real?'

'Entirely,' said Harry.

'He's wonderful.'

He couldn't figure Miranda either. One minute she

seemed self-assured, the next nervous, almost frightened. First vulnerable, then dangerous. Not because she was likely to have a go at you, but because she didn't seem to mind what happened. He couldn't keep his eyes off her, had to force himself to keep looking away.

She slipped her contact lens case back into the pocket of her jeans.

'Can I ask you something, Harry? What chance do you think there is of getting Sean Walsh off?'

Harry reached for the wine bottle and re-filled his glass.

'About twenty to one against.'

'Are those good odds?'

'The Home Office gets over four thousand allegations of miscarriage of justice a year. You can imagine how much paperwork each one involves. And you can guess what priority the Home Office gives miscarriage of justice cases in the first place. Even to sift them, make up a short list of which ones to investigate further – it's a huge job. There are a few cases which are so self-evident they have to do something. Most of the rest never get out of the in-tray. You have to manoeuvre yours to the top of the pile, which can take years. Once it's got to the top of the pile, you have to win it. Preferably on an appeal of some kind, very occasionally the Director of Public Prosecutions intervenes and drops the case. Not good odds.'

'And if the case is in Ulster?'

'Much worse. When are you going back?'

'This afternoon,' said Miranda. 'Robert's giving me a lift to the airport.'

'Am I?' Robert enthused.

'No,' said Miranda. 'I'm not going until Monday.'

6

THE PHONE WAS RINGING when Harry got home. It was Angela Webb.

'Harry?'

'Hallo Angela. Where are you?'

'I'm not sure. Scotland, I think. Monday we were in Wales, Tuesday was Lincoln and Ipswich, yesterday was Newcastle, today Millom. I think. You know where Millom is?'

'Not Scotland. Cumbria. I know because it's next door to Haverigg prison.'

'Wherever it is it's sweet. There's a youth training scheme, Ben had to be photographed at a lathe wearing a hard-hat. In Barrow-in-Furness he went swimming with the disabled.' She laughed. 'I wish you knew what it felt like to be in this kind of circus, Harry. It's as if you're in a movie. You wake up at six every morning, put on your make-up and start acting. Most days we don't finish until after midnight. Everywhere you look there's a camera crew waiting for you to say something dumb or do something undignified.'

'Admit it, you love it,' said Harry.

'You're right. I love it. I think I'm probably quite good at it too – Best Supporting Actress In A Socialist Soap.'

Harry and Angela had known each other since University. At Oxford they'd been friends; but it was only later, in London, that they'd become lovers. Angela was already involved with Ben, but he was off in America doing a year's scholarship, so Harry and Angela's was an illicit liaison, and they both looked on it as a temporary thing, driven more by lust than emotion. Ben was two years older, a different generation, altogether more adult and mature. It never occurred to Harry that Angela might look on him as a permanent replacement. Ben and Angela were an acknowledged match, everyone among their friends and family looked on them as a well-suited couple. Shortly before Ben got back from the States Harry was posted to the BBC in Glasgow for a year. Angela moved in with Ben. They got married early in 1984, shortly after Jo was killed.

'I'm serious, I'm a star,' she went on. 'In Wales I went on Radio Cardiff and talked about motherhood and in Southampton BBC South interviewed me about the famine in Eritrea. They don't seem to have a radio station in Millom. How are you, Harry? Long time no see.'

'Someone drove a motor bike into me earlier this week,' said Harry, tucking the receiver under his chin while he lit a cigarette.

'On purpose?'

'I think so.'

'Who?'

'No one you know – a West Indian called Pigfoot Walker, it's his idea of a protest. He thinks there isn't enough violence on TV so he beats people up in the hope that TV will copy him. Maybe he's right. He killed the man I was having lunch with by mistake, and he's threatening another go at me. Otherwise I'm fine.'

The night before her wedding, Angela turned up on Harry's doorstep at three in the morning, unannounced, just like old times. He was still working in Glasgow, but he'd kept on his flat off Primrose Hill, often came down on business or for weekends.

'One for the road,' she'd explained as she unbuttoned her blouse and slid into his bachelor bed.

She had a good body, Angela, kept herself in good shape, knew a lot of tricks. She could be a bit emotionally uninvolved in the sack, but she knew a lot of tricks. And she was fun to be with, in bed and out of it.

'Why?' Harry'd asked.

'I think I'm just curious,' she told him. 'I want to remember what it was like with us, but pleasure's like pain, you can remember having felt it but you can't remember what it felt like.'

'Which were we – pain or pleasure?'

'That's what I'm trying to remember.'

She'd left at dawn, while Harry was still asleep. Evidently the memory was pain: he hadn't seen much of her since, saw her picture in the paper with Ben sometimes, and there'd been a couple of dinner parties. But he'd kept his distance, aware that the bond that had existed between them might re-form if he wasn't careful. From what he'd seen she'd weathered the years well, taken care of her looks and her figure. The Webbs had money, and she'd always had good taste in clothes, nothing too flamboyant but enough to get noticed. Magazines wrote articles about her sometimes, silly Woman-Behind-The-Man features where she revealed the secrets of her complexion and posed in the kitchen preparing meals, the Philippino maid and the au pair firmly out of shot.

She and Ben had two children at a fashionable London State primary school. They got written about in magazines too. Meanwhile Ben had worked his way up through the Labour party, authored political pamphlets, got himself elected to Parliament, and then the National Executive Committee. He was still under forty, good looking, charming – people were already calling him the new J.F.K. Angela was his Jackie. If the Labour party won the election Ben would be Chancellor; if they lost the party leader would resign, and it was a racing certainty that Ben would succeed him.

'I was wondering if I could buy you a drink,' said Harry.

Angela hesitated.

'Why?'

'I'll tell you why if you'll say yes first.'

'It'll have to be after the election. You want Ben there too?'

'It'll have to be sooner than that, I'm afraid.'

She let out a short laugh, like an actress, clean and clipped. The teeth would be clean, too, the gums fresh and healthy, the breath sweet. Angela was careful about things like that – not fussy, but careful.

'Have you any idea what my diary's like? I have to store it on the computer.'

'Dangerous things,' said Harry, who'd recently succumbed and bought one for himself. 'Just a drink, an hour would do.'

'In London.'

'Anywhere.'

'Is this important, Harry?'

'Definitely.'

'But you're not telling me why?'

'Have you said yes?'

'I suppose so. I can always cancel if I don't like the reason.'

Harry took a long drag on his cigarette.

'Does the name Terry Pattichis mean anything to you?'

She waited a moment before replying, which Harry guessed answered his question.

'Is he a boxer?'

'No, he's a murderer. He used to work with Ben.'

'You'll have to give me a clue, Harry.'

'Jo O'Brien. The Latchkey Trust. Terry killed Jo, set

fire to the place. Or not, depending on who you talk to. Ben was the only other person on the Latchkey payroll at the time.'

Angela remembered.

'It seems such a long time ago.'

'Early eighties,' Harry confirmed.

'And that's why you want to take me out – to talk about the Latchkey Trust? Very romantic. You don't call me for eight years, and when you do it's because you want to pick my brain on some story you're working on. What happened to the art of romantic foreplay?'

'Life got too short. How's the diary looking?'

'Like an air traffic control log. Friday I'm in Glasgow. I have to be in London on Saturday afternoon, it's Mark's seventh birthday. Ben can't, he has to do a TV show in Aberdeen. I fly up and meet him again in Leeds on Sunday morning.'

'Why the hell do you need to fly to Leeds? Isn't the train quicker?'

'Image,' Angela explained. 'Trains are for losers. The plane makes us look busy and successful.'

'Is that what impresses the Labour voters these days?'

'Don't ask me, I'm only doing what I'm told. Where do you want to meet? It'll have to be somewhere discreet, the Press are very intrigued by my private life.'

'You still have some?'

'Not a lot, frankly.'

'My place,' Harry suggested. 'Or would you like to check with your image people and call me back?'

Angela laughed again, a real laugh this time.

'It's nice hearing you again, Harry. What's your address?'

'Nine Elms Lane.'

He gave her the number.

'No one lives in Nine Elms Lane,' she objected. 'It's

not that kind of road. It's got concrete cold stores and truck parks and stuff in it, hasn't it?'

'Other side of the road. Mine's a new block, looks out on the Thames. You can stay awake all night listening to disco parties on the river boats.'

'This is just a drink, Harry.' He heard her sucking on her cigarette. 'Penthouse by the Thames, eh? You and Jeffrey Archer.'

'No such luck, I'm on the first floor. The greenhouse effect means I'll be underwater by about 2050. If Pigfoot doesn't get to me first.'

'Are you living alone these days, by the way?'

'Just me and my memories. I'll see you Sunday.'

He hung up, took off his jacket and poured himself a drink. It was half past six, an empty evening in front of him. It surprised him to find how pleased he was to hear Angela's voice again after so many years. Some people you see or hear after a long gap and they've changed, or you have, and it's a struggle to remember why it was you liked them before. With others the years vanish and you pick up the same jokes and conversations again as though you'd never been interrupted. He remembered her body, too, the cunningness of her affection.

Most of the flat was occupied by an open-plan living room, twenty feet by fifteen, with a breakfast counter and a miniature kitchen. Two big picture windows looked down on the mud-flats and across the Thames to Pimlico. The furniture was modern, bought in a day the same week he bought the flat, a sofa and chairs from Heals, fitted carpets from John Lewis, a TV and stereo, a desk from Habitat with an Apple Macintosh and a row of red box files and jars of pens and magic markers. There were framed prints and posters on the walls, and an oil painting of two naked old men in the style of Lucien Freud, an impulse buy from an exhibition at the Serpentine Gallery, and an upright piano behind the door. Harry didn't play the piano, but he meant to one day. His accountant had phoned him up and told him to go out and spend a thousand pounds in a hurry, and the only thing he could think of was a piano.

Apart from the living room there was a bedroom, a bathroom hung with TV awards and memorabilia, and a small hall with a TV monitor that showed you who was ringing your bell down in Nine Elms Lane. The monitor never worked. It occurred to Harry that with Pigfoot in his present frame of mind he might finally get it fixed.

He carried his Bushmills out on to the little balcony, hardly wide enough to take a chair, and stood looking down on the river. The Thames always made him think of dead bodies, face down in the water, police launches, men with boat-hooks, old black and white films where the Flying Squad wore trilbies and drove Riley saloons. Some days the river was brown, today it was grey, slow and strong as a python. A barge struggled doggedly upstream against the current, and to the East under Vauxhall Bridge two cormorants were diving into the murky waters. Why would a cormorant choose to live in London? Same reason as the rest of us, he supposed.

The phone rang: it was Angela again.

'I'm not sure your flat's a great idea when I come to think of it, Harry. You know Dolphin Square?'

'I'm looking at it now.'

He glanced across the river. Dolphin Square, like New Delhi, was a late Imperial afterthought, a vast and tidy flat-roofed red-brick edifice the size of a small town, a strange hybrid of hotel and sprawling apartment block, discreet and private, home to the better class of MP, Foreign Office people home on leave, company directors with houses in Hampshire or Suffolk who need a London *pied-à-terre*. It had a health centre with a swimming pool and a squash court, a wing of short-let rooms and apartments, and a bar and restaurant. The courtyard gardens alone covered over three acres, guarded from the intrusions of the late twentieth century by a small army of smartly uniformed commissionaires and porters.

'I go there to swim,' said Angela. 'We could run into each other in the bar afterwards. What could be more natural?'

There were a number of answers to that, none of which Harry thought it prudent to suggest. He arranged to meet her there at eight.

His leg was giving him trouble again, a numb pain that turned acute if he put weight on it. He rang off and checked his answering machine. Two dinner invitations for next week, Dillons to say a book he'd ordered was out of print, and an unidentified West Indian woman, possibly Pigfoot's friend Yvonne, calling to say Pigfoot was thinking about him, sleep well whitey. Harry liked Yvonne, and hoped it wasn't her.

He sat down on the sofa and turned on the TV. On BBC 1 Peter Sissons and a clutch of party spokespersons were talking to what Peter claimed was a studio audience of Ordinary Voters, though they didn't look much like ordinary voters to Harry, not a lot of ordinary voters ask each other questions about GATT negotiations or public sector borrowing requirements or the mathematics of arms limitation talks. Over on Channel 4 a man with a beard was discussing tactical voting mechanisms.

Harry turned off the TV, and went to inspect the contents of the fridge. It was almost empty: a stale Camembert, a jar of olives, two slices of curled-up bacon, three eggs, butter, a carton of milk the same age as the Camembert. Enough for an omelette of sorts. Harry could cook, but living alone he hardly ever did: mostly he ate out or went to dinner parties. When he did cook it was usually to entertain.

65

He wondered how Shirley Pattichis was spending the evening, tried to picture her in Finsbury Park, getting supper together for the kids, coming to grips with life without Pete. He doubted there was much money there, Pete didn't strike him as the sort of man who'd carry much life insurance. In TV you were always passing through other people's fucked up lives, feeling something at the time, forgetting about them two weeks later.

He suspected he hadn't seen the last of Shirley, though. The Terry business would give her something to distract herself with. Didn't matter if she believed Terry was innocent or not, he was a Cause, and in circumstances like hers a Cause is what matters, whatever the outcome. He got Pete's folder out of his briefcase, poured himself another whisky, switched on his computer and started typing notes.

The tabloids had milked the Latchkey trial for everything they could, but there was little of substance: it was all MP Demands Action, Gay Reds in Corruption Probe stuff. The broadsheets went into a bit more detail, particularly during the trial, conducted by Mr Justice Wasson, Sir Patrick Brabazon for the prosecution, Antony Tree for the defence; not a bad brief considering Terry was on Legal Aid. His solicitors were McKenzie and Clark, young and keen but a bit nervous if Harry remembered them right.

Most of it was about Jo — even the serious papers couldn't resist him. If the *News of the World* set out to invent a rogue they'd have trouble coming up with anyone as richly mischievous. He was flamboyantly gay, a self-styled friend of the famous, ostensibly left-wing, utterly dishonest. His lifestyle was shameless, an unending procession of sex and drug parties and dubious liaisons, organized from a lavish six-room flat — mirrored ceilings throughout, including the kitchen — in

66

Maida Vale. On their frequent trips abroad he and Terry stayed in five-star hotels and drank champagne like water. All paid for out of public funds and private donations intended to save London's waifs and strays. The Press hadn't enjoyed themselves so much since Jeremy Thorpe.

He went over to the computer and typed up a few notes, then drafted a letter to the Home Office, one more sheet to add to the daily midden arriving in the in-tray in Queen Anne's Gate.

Miranda lived in Marylebone, in a low-rent flat in an Edwardian block owned by the Church Commissioners: a bedroom, a bathroom with naked pipes and a gas geyser, a small living room with paint-encrusted steel-framed windows and a view on to a tiny patch of municipal park; a kitchen with lino on the floor, a twin-tub washing machine and a scotch airer hanging from the ceiling. The flat was cheap, warm, central and cheerfully furnished.

She dropped her bag in the hall, got a glass of orange juice from the fridge, carried it through to the bathroom, turned on the geyser and began to undress. She was down to her underwear when the phone went.

'I just wanted to say I admire what you did in Ulster,' said Harry. 'I don't know why, but I admire it.'

Miranda carried the phone through into the bathroom, finished undressing, turned off the tap and got in.

'I thought I made a fair prat of myself. But thanks anyway.'

There was a pause.

'And I wondered if you were doing anything this evening,' said Harry.

'Why?'

'Why what?'

'Why did you wonder what I was doing?'

'I thought . . .' Harry was getting nervous. 'I wondered if you felt like dinner.'

'I'm going to the cinema,' said Miranda, grabbing a copy of *Time Out* off the cistern.

'Oh,' said Harry. 'Fine.'

'Is it?'

'I don't know. What's on?'

'*Television as Popular Art in Latin America,*' she read at random. 'Two hours of Cuban soap opera. At the National Film Theatre. It's in Spanish.'

'Would I like it?'

'You'd probably hate it. You could try.'

Cuban soap opera wasn't what Harry had in mind at all, but what the hell, it was that or Peter Snow on the state of the Liberal Democrats.

'OK,' he said cautiously. 'Is that an invitation?'

'Of a sort, I suppose. But don't be surprised if you have a miserable evening. It starts,' Miranda checked the listing, 'at eight.' Then she paused. 'Are you safe to be around?'

'In what sense?'

'In the sense that people are likely to drive motor bikes at you.'

'That's a risk you'll have to take,' said Harry.

'Do you know who it was?'

'I think I must have offended someone.'

Miranda reached out for her orange juice, took a mouthful, swallowed, put the empty glass back on the ledge among the shampoo bottles.

'Maybe they just wanted to wipe the smile off your face, Kapowski.'

7

THE KID DIDN'T LOOK like Elvis, or sound like Elvis, but you knew in his head he was Elvis, that the iron catwalk connecting the South Bank arts complex with the Hungerford railway bridge was Vegas, or someplace in Tennessee in the early days, and that somewhere among the commuters was Colonel Tom Parker. Parker was a fraud, of course, a crooked, mean, spirited Dutch circus operator and illegal immigrant, who wouldn't let Elvis tour outside the US because where Elvis went Tom went too, and Tom was afraid if he went with him he'd never get back into the States again. He was also too mean to pay songwriters their full whack, so the best paid singer in the country had trouble finding halfway decent material. But he was good enough for Elvis, and what was good enough for Elvis was good enough for the boy croaking 'Heartbreak Hotel' to the damp November drizzle.

Harry wanted to tell the kid he should wear incontinence pads if he wanted to get the real Elvis look, but hadn't the heart. He tossed a fifty pence coin into his guitar case and walked on past the line of teenage dossers, 'Homeless' scribbled in felt tip on torn squares of cardboard beside their damp sleeping bags, down the riverside walkway towards the Festival Hall and the National Film Theatre. It was quarter to eight.

He should have guessed about Miranda. Gone are the

days of the quiet dinner and the bottle of Blue Nun in a candle-lit restaurant: you want to spend the evening with people like her these days, you have to do something serious. Go to a lecture on shamanism, or a Welsh language video workshop open day, or a vegetarian reception to meet the backstage crew from the Bratislava Modern Dance Ensemble, grab what time you can along the way.

In the overcrowded concrete bunker of the NFT bar the affluent unwashed stood like long-stranded passengers in a fog-bound airport, drinking lukewarm lager and smoking acrid roll-ups, here for the all-night Boris Karloff retrospective. The ugliness wasn't accidental – these people had gone to trouble to look drab – thought and even misled vanity had gone into it: they ripped artistic holes in the knees of their best jeans, boiled their shirts and blouses a grim shade of laundromat grey, used gel to keep their hair angry and dishevelled. The hair wants a quiet life, wants to lie limp on the scalp. No chance.

Miranda was standing beside a poster display outside the bar, reading a dog-eared paperback of Genet's *Funeral Rites*.

'Nice place you have here,' said Harry. 'Very intimate.'

' "The desire for solitude is pride",' she read aloud, without looking up.

'What the hell does that mean?' asked Harry.

She laughed, closed the book and put it in her bag.

'I haven't a clue. I thought you might know.'

She wore a white T-shirt and black cotton trousers under a belted raincoat, neutral enough to blend with the one-size-fits-none fashions around her without becoming a party member. Harry's sports jacket and Levi's made him feel like a bank manager.

'You come here often?' he asked.

Miranda grinned.

'Hardly ever. I've been on foreign ground at the BBC

all week, I thought I'd ring the changes and take you somewhere you'd feel uncomfortable.'

'Thanks,' said Harry.

He rather enjoyed the soaps. They came in twenty-five minute episodes, and between each an intelligent, wry little Cuban explained the style and context, apologized for various minor defects in the prints, and answered questions from the floor, most of them designed to show off the questioners' detailed knowledge of Latin American cinema through a plethora of subsidiary clauses and semantic clarifications. It was half past ten by the time they emerged into the darkness of the South Bank. The Thames gleamed black and silver in the darkness, and to the North the high-rise behemoths of the City twinkled above the skyline.

'If they're going to build that kind of shit,' said Harry, 'the least they could do is turn the lights off so we don't have to see them at night. Not that we should worry, I suppose. A hundred years from now the banks will have gone the way of the docks, all those places will be abandoned. Smart young people will be buying up the NatWest tower and the Shell building on the cheap and converting them into chic lofts for trendy young professionals.'

'And what will the trendy professions be?' asked Miranda.

'Lawyers,' said Harry. 'It doesn't matter how poor a country is, they still need lawyers.'

He wondered where they were going, if he was meant to suggest somewhere or if she'd already decided.

'Are you hungry?' he asked.

'Are you?'

He still couldn't figure what was going on.

'I could be.'

'OK,' she smiled. 'Why not. Are you beginning to feel uncomfortable yet?'

'Absolutely.'

71

'Good. What nationality do you fancy?'

'Austrian,' said Harry, for no reason at all except that he thought it sounded interesting.

Neither of them knew any Austrian restaurants, but the cab driver did. He drove them North of the river to Swiss Cottage and dropped them outside The Eidelweiss, a drab cellar staffed by elderly Austrian-refugee waiters with cigarette-ash skin and terrible surgical problems in their intestines, the kind who look at you pityingly knowing that what happened to their lives will happen to yours sooner or later, only you're too English to know it. The menu offered Central European stews and veal in heavy sauces. Harry badly needed a drink, and ordered a bottle of wine.

Ask her about herself, ask her about her family, his training told him.

'You really want to know?' said Miranda, pouring herself a glass of water. 'I'm twenty-five, born in Hong Kong. Daddy was in the British Council. We moved back to England when I was three. I went to a girls boarding school in Worcestershire, then Bristol University. I have a brother who's a social worker in Sussex and a sister married to a schoolteacher in Lancashire. My hobbies are reading and playing the piano.' She picked up the menu and hunted for a salad among the schnitzels and oxtail pies. 'My favourite author is Joseph Conrad and my favourite composers are Bach and/or Jerry Leiber and Mike Stoller. I don't have a favourite colour. Will that do?'

'To be going on with.'

'And you?'

Harry lit a cigarette.

'Much the same, really. Father's a Polish refugee, that's where the name came from. Stayed on after the war and opened a small factory making shoes for the disabled. He's retired now. Mother gardens and sits on charity committees. I was educated in Scotland, then

72

three years at Oxford, then journalism. I have a sister living in Herefordshire. My favourite composers are Felice and Boudleaux Bryant. That's about it.'

'How long have you been divorced?' she guessed.

'Widowed. My wife died in childbirth on her eighteenth birthday. I've never really got over it.'

'You're joking.'

'I'm joking. No wife, no divorce.'

'Well that's got the dinner-date crap out the way,' said Miranda, folding up the menu. They didn't seem to eat much salad in Vienna. 'Let's talk about something serious. Why did you ask me out tonight?'

'To be honest, I can't remember,' said Harry. 'Why did you accept?'

'Curiosity, I'm always curious about people. There's nothing personal about it. Fifteen thirty, your serve.'

She was beginning to slow down a little. Not a lot, but then Harry doubted if she ever relaxed completely. Maybe if she did yoga, or TM. Across the room a fat, dignified little man ordered a second glass of wine from the waiter. The man was really quite small, so that his trousers waisted at the breast of his business shirt, lifting them too far up his ankles, clear of his polished black shoes. He wore a shirt and tie, no jacket. Facing him was a fat little woman in a loose lawn cotton print dress, belted at the waist. Both were quite young, in their late twenties or early thirties. He ate very slowly, lowering his face to meet each fork full, lifting it as though it weighed a ton, then chewed each mouthful maybe thirty times while he poked over his plate with his fork, looking for the next mouthful, like a woman sorting jumble in a church sale. Neither of them were saying anything, but as they chewed they smiled sweetly at each other across the table. Newly-weds? Lovers?

'Something bugs you about me, doesn't it,' said Harry.

'Not particularly. I've never been out with anyone

famous before, I suppose if I'm honest that came into it. I want to find out what it is about yourself that you're so pleased with. And I've had a strange week, I thought I might as well keep it going a bit longer.'

'How am I doing?'

'I'm not sure yet.'

'You must give me the name of your aggression coach sometime.'

She laughed – not at him but at herself.

'I'm afraid I can't help it, Harry, it comes as part of the package. If you think I'm bad now you should have known me as a teenager. I'm a victim of autocratic parents. My father would never let us change the TV channels – even when he was asleep in his chair, if one of us tried to sneak over to the set and switch over from the rugger he'd always wake up. We weren't allowed any control over our lives. The main theme of my childhood was an absolute determination that as soon as I grew up I'd never do what I was told again. Ever.'

'Even if it was something you did want to do?'

'Precisely. That's the problem.'

'You're grown up now?'

'Getting there.'

'Are you going to let your own kids change the TV channels?'

She laughed again, elbow on the table, hand supporting her chin, biting her little finger.

'Of course not.'

'What sort of people do you normally go out to dinner with?' asked Harry.

'Oh God, I thought we'd finished all that stuff. Depends how hungry I am. Let me think. In Honduras I generally ate with the nuns. Overseas nuns are a very different breed from the domestic variety, not at all inhibited. But you have to go Dutch with nuns, they don't have expense accounts. Since I got back I've been out with my father twice, he comes up to town once in a while to check if I'm married yet and to give me career advice. And then there was – ' she stopped. 'If you want to know if I'm spoken for the answer is no, but it's not something that worries me.'

Harry looked across the table at her and thought: twenty-five. Normally when you take a twenty-five-year-old out to dinner you go through all the shit of pretending to be interested in their minds, their ideas, their worries and ambitions, when all you really want to do is get them into bed. Miranda wasn't like that at all. He wasn't even sure if he wanted to risk trying to get her to bed for fear of what might happen if he tried and failed.

'How about you, Harry Kapowski? I bet you take a lot of younger women out, don't you?'

'I used to,' said Harry.

'How come you're still single? Most successful men have a first wife they dump when their situation changes.'

Harry didn't know the answer to that either. A lot of his friends were divorced, remarried to younger women. He often wondered what would have happened if he'd married in his twenties, whether it would have worked out.

'I think I decided I'd be a lousy husband.'

'Why?'

'I suppose because I'm selfish – I like things my own way, but I don't like passive women. Catch twenty-two.'

Miranda had eaten her way through a bowl of goulash soup and a large plate of schnitzel and potatoes and moved on to the mixed vegetables. Across the aisle the lovers had finished their entrées and were wiping their mouths on their napkins and studying the sweet trolley.

'Me too,' said Miranda. 'It's a bitch, isn't it. I suppose you get used to it after a while. Was Freddy right about you and television? The fame, I mean.'

75

'No.'

'Then why do you do it?'

'I do the job because I think it's worth doing. Not always, but sometimes. I think someone needs to ask awkward questions of the Establishment. TV let you do it in public.'

'But you're part of the Establishment too, aren't you?'

Harry shrugged.

'Maybe. Maybe it's no bad thing. It worries people more if they know the person grilling them comes from the same class – you understand them better.'

Miranda laughed.

'You reckon?'

'I reckon,' said Harry. 'Now tell me what you're doing in the BBC. And don't tell me it's the money, there are plenty of people who pay better than the Beeb.'

She helped herself to one of his cigarettes.

'You're right, I don't give a toss about money. I happen to think the justice system in this country sucks. It seems to me that if you feel that way you can either join lefty pressure groups and write letters to *Time Out*, or you can get a job somewhere and see if you can do something about it. I'm not optimistic, but I thought I'd give it a try. Did you really get the West Indian to pay blood money to Shirley Pattichis, by the way?'

Harry looked at her.

'Who told you that?'

'Joan recorded the call, I listened to the tape later. I also listened to your call to the police. You're a wanted man, Kapowski. I'm risking my life taking dinner off you.'

Said with a grin. Harry blinked.

'Do you always listen in on other people's phone calls?'

'Only when they're important enough to tape. I

shouldn't be smoking this thing, I'm meant to have given up.' She stubbed out the cigarette. 'Do you mind being bugged?'

'Of course I bloody well mind. I could go to prison for something like that.'

'Why did you do it?'

'You want an honest answer? Because I was scared. When I'm cornered my first impulse is to do something, anything, take the initiative. I wanted to hear Pigfoot Walker admit he was involved, because I need to know who's after me. If it's Pigfoot then the danger is definable – I doubt if he'll do anything again. He's like that: he has an idea, goes out and does it, then if it doesn't work he shrugs his shoulders and finds something else to do. It may sound odd, but we're fond of each other in a bizarre sort of way. But if I'd accused him outright, he'd have denied it. So I told him I knew he was involved, but offered him a way out of the problem. At least that was my reasoning at the time. He's not a very subtle man, Pigfoot.'

'And what about Pete Pattichis?'

Harry scratched the back of his head.

'That's up to Shirley. I mean it: Pigfoot didn't intend to kill him, it was an accident. Locking him up for ten years won't bring Pete back.'

Miranda wasn't buying it.

'That's crap. You did it to show off.'

'To who?'

'To Pigfoot, to Shirley Pattichis, to me, anyone who might be listening. That's how you put legends together, isn't it?'

'So what were you doing with Sean Walsh and Liam O'Kelly? You made yourself famous too. That's who you are in the BBC now – the woman who persuaded Liam O'Kelly to talk and then told him not to.'

'I thought you admired me for it. Or was that part of the chat-up?'

'Get to fuck,' said Harry.

'Up yours too,' said Miranda.

And then they both laughed.

By midnight they were the only people left in the restaurant. They'd disposed of a litre of white wine and moved on to brandies. The Austrian was sitting by the till, tidying up his paperwork.

Harry paid the bill. As they walked to the taxi he put his arm round her waist, feeling the warmth of her skinny body through the loose cotton, wondering what would happen. She didn't flinch, but she didn't co-operate either. Normally you get a clue, a reaction. Nothing. Harry tried to figure what to do next.

'Decision time,' she said quietly, almost to herself. 'I'm not very good at this bit, I'm afraid Harry. I think you're meant to make a pass at me, isn't that how it works?' She looked straight in front, away from him. 'I suppose we could give it a try,' she said finally. 'But I warn you, it's not going to be easy.' Then she turned and reached across and kissed him gently, broke off in giggles, then kissed him again. 'And no bloody smiling. Is that understood?'

8

Angela Webb stood at the back of the studio control room watching Ben being interviewed. She hadn't had a worthwhile conversation with him in a fortnight. They'd said things to each other in the backs of cars, backstage at rallies, in hotel rooms in the few brief moments between checking in and collapsing into sleep – practical things, about schedules and laundry and alarm calls. But they hadn't talked like husband and wife, about the children, or the hospital tests she was having on her uterus, or the discreet affair Ben was conducting with the pretty young psephologist from Nuffield College who was writing a book about the campaign. Angela didn't mind too much about the psephologist, almost took her for granted: Ben had always strayed a lot, even in the early years of their marriage. But the tests worried her, and she'd have liked to share her worry. Polyps on your uterus aren't something you can discuss with room-service waiters or constituency agents.

'Look at what we've done to the language,' Ben was telling Alastair from Radio Scotland.

It was half past nine on Saturday morning, and this was Glasgow, which a Labour council had transformed from a by-word for industrial and urban decay into the Dream City of the nineties. Not the Tory Government, or Michael Heseltine, or the Enterprise Culture: the Labour party.

79

'What used to be called Usury,' Ben went on, 'is now called Financial Services. The only Financial Service most people want is a decent wage.'

He was a handsome man, tall and fit, with a fine head of flaxen hair and a smiling, intelligent face with plenty of laugh lines. He wore a sports jacket in a rich Donegal tweed, cord trousers, a loose denim shirt, designer socialist, very healthy looking, and the only man in the studio or the control room not wearing a suit. Angela chose his clothes, always had. Left to himself Ben would have worn Daks and a shirt and tie under a V-neck Pringle sweater with a lion embroidered on the chest. The Labour party weren't the first ones to get to work on his image.

'You get mail order fashion catalogues called things like "Essentials". "Essentials",' he repeated with a chuckle. Alastair chuckled too.

'That's the Thatcher legacy for you – all of a sudden fifty-quid Lycra swimsuits and hand-printed silk Italian shorts are Essentials. Consume, consume, consume. Ask the people who live in high-rises out in Easterhouse what conspicuous consumption is and they'll tell you it's the disease their grandparents died of. Incidentally I was reading a batch of social work reports the other evening that describe people in Easterhouse as having had "Inappropriate Childhoods". Are you hearing this, Easterhouse?'

Next to Angela a Labour party aide man smiled, pleased Ben had used his consumption line. A gram-spinner was lining up 'Batchelor Boy' on the turntable. 'Batchelor Boy' was Ben's favourite record.

Alastair was still chuckling, ha ha ha.

'I'm sure they are. Inappropriate Childhoods, eh? How do you spell that? And if you're listening out there in Easterhouse, which of course you all are, and you can find a phone that's working, maybe you'd like to give us a ring. Meantime let's have a record.'

He flicked his wrist towards the gram-spinner. A few bars of the Norrie Paramor Strings, then Cliff and the Shadows came in with the melody.

An open-topped bus was waiting outside ready to take Ben and Angela across town to a rally in George's Square. Lunch in City Hall, and then a limousine would whisk her out to the airport in time to catch the three o'clock BA shuttle to London. Another car would take her straight from the tarmac at Heathrow to the Wandsworth townhouse where the housekeeper and the caterers were setting up for Mark Webb's seventh birthday party. No one had asked Mark if he minded Press photographers and TV cameras at his party, or explained to him why the three photogenic black kids and the pretty girl in the wheelchair had been added to his list of schoolfriends and neighbours. But at least he'd see his mother for a couple of hours, and get to open the large box from his father which had arrived by taxi from Hamleys earlier in the week.

Cliff was coming to an end.

'Batchelor Boy', Alastair reminded the listeners. 'And I'm talking to the Deputy Leader of the Labour party, Ben Webb, live in studio. You have a wife of course, Ben. How's Angela coping with the campaign?'

Angela tried not to listen.

Outside hanging curtains of grey rain were lashing in from the Campsie hills, which put paid to the open bus. Ben's managers substituted a Range Rover, but Ben was having none of it.

'Where's the nearest underground?' he asked, raising his voice a little to make sure the Press could hear.

Mayhem followed. Ben grabbed his raincoat and trotted up the ramp from Broadcasting House out into Queen Margaret Drive. Someone gave Angela an umbrella, and they set off across Great Western Road towards Hillhead. The punters loved it, cheering them through the traffic. Opposite the Grosvenor Hotel Ben stopped to sign his autograph for a traffic warden; outside the Bejam Centre a street seller presented him with a bunch of roses, which he chivalrously handed to Angela. The photographers made him do it again, and this time he kissed her on the mouth. Angela kissed him back then laughed, brushing the hair back off her face. The picture looked wonderful, handsome Ben Webb and his carefree sexy wife in the short red dress and high heels, embracing over a bunch of roses in the middle of a Scots monsoon. They made the front page of every national Sunday the following morning.

'Give my love to Mark,' said Ben when they found themselves briefly alone in an anteroom in the City Chambers.

'I will,' said Angela. 'Thousands wouldn't, but I will.' She lit a cigarette. 'I'm having a drink with Harry Kapowski tonight, by the way.'

'Harry? God, there's a name from the past,' said Ben, thumbing through the notes for his speech. 'Old Mr Self-Righteous himself.'

'I thought you liked him.'

'Maybe I did once. It's so long since I saw him. Which is he these days, a was-kid or a hasn't been?'

'He wants to talk about Terry Pattichis.'

'Terry Pattichis?' Ben put down his speech. 'Oh dear.'

Miranda didn't think much of the flat. She liked the view of the Thames, and the oil painting, but that was about it.

'It's like living in a hotel,' she complained. 'As though you eat and sleep here, but you don't live here. Everything's so bloody tidy. Do you have a chambermaid?'

She was standing at the breakfast counter, naked but for one of Harry's shirts, making herself scrambled eggs. Harry was stretched out on the sofa, a towel round his waist, reading the *Guardian*. He nodded.

'Mrs Perrymede. A terrifying woman. She comes twice a week, Mondays and Thursdays.'

The first egg Miranda cracked open was bad.

'Jesus. When did you last go shopping?'

'I thought we weren't going to try and change each other's idiosyncrasies,' Harry objected.

'This isn't an idiosyncrasy, Kapowski, this is a health hazard. Do they do Room Service in this block?'

'Probably. I never tried. The nice thing about living here is that you never see anyone. The only time I ever met the neighbours was when I let the bath overflow, a Swiss woman came upstairs and let fly at me in German. She had a dog with her, one of those horrible little things that look like rats on stilts, yap a lot.'

Miranda gave up on the fridge and made herself toast and a cup of instant coffee. Harry looked around for his, but there wasn't any.

'How long have you lived here?' she asked.

'Three years.'

'On your own?'

'Yup. I've had overnight guests. Not a lot.'

She sat down at the far end of the sofa, legs tucked under her, holding the coffee cup in both hands.

'This is a terrible mistake, Harry. You know that, don't you.'

'Why?'

'Because I'm a very difficult woman and you're a very opinionated man.'

'Am I?'

'Of course you are. Not about whether the Americans should invade Libya or what the government should do about public transport, I'm sure you're open minded to a fault about all that shit, that's all theory. But I bet you mind like hell about the little things.'

'Like what?'

'People talking to you while you're reading the paper, for example. Or girl-friends who put your books back

83

in the wrong place on the shelves. This morning's OK, you're on best behaviour. But on a week-day evening, just back from the office, feeling pissed off with the world, I bet you can be really cantankerous.'

She was right, Harry knew it. He turned to the sports pages, still reading.

'I bet you get jealous, too,' she added. Right again.

'So tell me why you're difficult,' said Harry, putting down the paper.

'Me? Same reasons as you. I like living on my own, I'm used to taking my own decisions, not having to explain why I do things.'

'Is that why you went to Honduras?'

She took a sip of coffee.

'Yup.'

'And where were you before that?'

'Bristol.'

'Doing what?'

'Modern European History. Dull stuff. If there's anything you need to know about postwar Yugoslavian history, don't be too shy to ask.'

'If it was that dull why did you do it?'

'Oh, Bristol wasn't dull, far from it. And I travelled quite a bit. You can get quite addicted to academic life once you discover how long the vacations are.'

'Did you travel alone?'

She laughed out loud.

'You're obsessed, Harry Kapowski. What do you want, a full list of lovers?'

'Just a précis would do.'

'There weren't that many, in fact. I don't mind men, but they can be terribly clinging if you give them the chance. I also quite enjoy my own company. The only serious affair I had was with a guy called Danny, and I'm not sure "serious" is the right word to describe our relationship; we sort of drifted in and out of each other's lives as it suited. Forty-eight going on twenty,

84

handsome, energetic, very ambitious. He's fun to be with and he's good in bed.'

'Who left who?' he asked her.

'It wasn't like that,' said Miranda. 'It ended quite amicably. I'd finished at Bristol, and he wasn't about to leave it for my sake. He's not a chauvinist, he really likes women, but he believes in planned obsolescence as far as relationships are concerned. I do too. I went to Honduras. He didn't.'

Half what you want in a lover, Harry reflected, is security, the other half is danger. The trick is finding the balance. Miranda was strong on danger, but there didn't seem much security in sight. He wandered across to the book shelf and picked over a stack of music cassettes, looking for a box that had something inside it.

'Where do I come into all this?' he asked her.

'Oh, that's simple, you're my father. Sad, isn't it. Women spend twenty years loathing their fathers, then fall in love with someone who precisely mirrors all their faults. The only evidence I can see for the existence of a God is that random chance couldn't have created such cruelly ironic little jokes.'

Harry got up, walked over to the kitchen and made himself a cup of coffee. This was evidently going to be a self-catering relationship.

'Why am I like your father?' he asked.

'You're a successful middle-class Anglo-Saxon male, for starters. And I suspect deep down you're also a company man. A thin veneer of anti-establishment gloss hiding a granite faith in the system.'

Harry sat down beside her again.

'Is this analysis based on your life experience,' he asked, 'or is it something you read in a book?'

She lifted her legs on to his lap and sat back against the cushions.

'I'm making it up as I go along. Is it any good?'

'The first part's crap.'

'I thought it probably was.'

'Sixth-form feminism,' Harry continued, 'circa 1974. The second half I don't know, there may be something in it.'

She was right, of course. Harry was a careful man, careful with his career, and his emotions, and his possessions. Not shy, or passive, but careful. He knew what he was and wasn't good at, and avoided putting himself in situations where his weaknesses were exposed.

'And that's as far as I've got at the moment,' said Miranda.

'Thanks,' said Harry. 'What's the treatment?'

'You have to work that out for yourself.' She got up. 'I'm glad you've found the session useful. That will be thirty guineas, you can pay the receptionist on the way out.'

'Will you take a cheque?'

'I take everything I can get, Kapowski.'

They showered, and got dressed and lunched in a pub on the river, queuing among the ersatz timber beams and flickering fruit machines for plates of cottage pie and lasagne.

'Did your friend Danny put up with this character assassination for three whole years?' Harry asked as they settled into a corner nook.

'Not at all, it would have been wasted on Danny, he was beyond changing.'

'And I'm not?'

'You tell me.'

Harry wasn't sure.

'The older you get the harder it is to change into who your lover wants you to be. Not just your lover, it applies to your own plans for your life. By the time you reach your mid-thirties you lose the chameleon ambition of youth – it's getting a bit late to turn yourself into a rock star, or an international footballer, or a future prime minister.'

'That's what you want to be, is it? Rock star, foot-baller, prime minister?'

'What had you in mind for me?'

'Just an ordinary, kind, decent human being.'

'You'd hate me. Goodness is dull when you're twenty-five.'

She laughed.

'I suppose it is. Who do you want me to be, by the way?'

Harry shrugged his shoulders. He didn't know how long he could keep up with her as she was, but didn't want her to change either.

'This is getting ridiculous,' he decided. 'I ask you out to dinner, and less than a day later you talk about me as if I was an old farmhouse you've just bought, in need of some refurbishment. Knock down the interior walls, box in the beams, rip out the fireplaces and chimneys. What's the hurry?'

'I'm an impulse buyer. You love me, don't you?' said Miranda, looking him straight in the eye.

He looked back, a memorable frozen moment, very strong. She was right, it had been love at first fuck, the moment their bodies touched. Twenty past one on the morning of Saturday November the twenty-eighth, an anniversary to remember. He knew nothing about her, but she felt terribly familiar.

'Did I say that?' he asked cautiously.

'No. At least I don't think so. You just acted that way.'

'And how about you?' he asked.

Her eyes hadn't moved.

'I like you, Harry. I don't approve of you, but I like you.'

They walked back along the river to Nine Elms.

'Visitor for you, Harry,' said Walter the porter as they crossed the lobby.

'Where?' asked Harry, looking around.

'In the car park.'

87

9

SHIRLEY PATTICHIS WAS SITTING in the front of the Ford Escort smoking a cigarette, sucking on it in short violent gasps, as though it was a life support machine. She glanced at Harry, then at Miranda; looked her up and down, then up again, as though she were a dress in a shop window, then stubbed out her cigarette.

'You better get in, Kapowski. We don't have much time.'

'For what?' asked Harry, not moving.

'I tell you on the way. She coming too?'

'Ask her. Miranda, this is Mrs Pattichis.'

The two women nodded at each other.

'Pleased to meet you, Miranda,' said Shirley. 'You coming?'

Miranda raised an eyebrow at Harry, who gave her what he hoped was a discreet nod.

'He does that he means yes,' said Shirley, twisting round to unlock the rear passenger door. 'She's welcome to come for the ride, but she stays outside when we get there. We're late, have to be there by four.'

'Fine,' said Miranda.

Harry got in the front, Miranda behind. Shirley was using the stub of her old cigarette to light another with one hand, turning the steering wheel with the other, engine revving painfully as she backed up the Escort, turned round and squealed out into Nine Elms Lane.

'Where are we late for?' Harry asked innocently.

'Broadmoor.' She took the Queenstown Road traffic lights on amber, heading for Battersea Bridge and the Hammersmith flyover. 'I got the visiting docket in the post, says two persons, me and Pete. So I phone them up, say Pete's not going to make it, I bring a friend instead. They say that's fine, doesn't worry them who comes so long as they got a docket. The docket says Mr Pattichis, no initial, so you're Pete's Uncle Micky. You find his driving licence in the dash in case they want some ID.'

Harry took out the licence and looked at the details.

'I know what you're thinking,' said Shirley. 'They're gonna check the age, see how old you look, see how old Micky is. They have the age written at the top, like by a computer, only they change the figures round so it doesn't look like someone's age, just a number.' She reached across and pointed at the licence. 'P-A-T-T-I, for Pattichis, they just do the first letters. Then the number. Says you should be forty. I figure you not too far off forty.'

Harry could feel Miranda's smile on the back of his neck.

'You do this a lot, turn up on people's doorsteps and take them off to prison?' he asked.

'It isn't a prison, it's a hospital. And I'm doing you a favour, you try and get a visit on your own it takes weeks. Plus they ask Terry if he wants to see you, and maybe he says no.'

'He doesn't know I'm coming?'

Shirley shook her head.

For fifteen minutes no one spoke, each looking out their separate windows as they drove west across the city, Shirley concentrating on her traffic manoeuvres.

'So what you do, Miranda?' she asked once they were safe on the motorway.

Miranda said she was a researcher, same business as Harry.

89

'You know about Terry then?'

'Only what Harry's told me.'

Shirley said she'd love to know what that was.

'Crazy Cypriots is what he told you, am I right? Fat Mrs Pattichis who steals cars and her brother-in-law who kills people and then sets them on fire. What's he told you about himself?' Her left arm poked the dashboard in front of Harry. 'I've been doing some research on you, Kapowski, I been reading Taki's magazines. You're a scorpio. Your favourite dish is gravelax, did I get that right? Something they do with fish in Norway or some place. You don't have a lot of hobbies, reading, I think it said, and travelling. How come you don't have a fancy hobby, collect old pictures or fly airplanes or something? The only reason most people don't have fancy hobbies is they can't afford them, they have to stay home and watch TV instead.'

'I'm not rich,' Harry explained. 'And I work hard, I don't have a lot of spare time.'

'I reckon you've got money.' Shirley took a bag of toffees out of the parcel shelf, selected one and passed the bag back to Miranda. 'I bet you don't even look at the price of most things when you buy them. How much you pay for a loaf of bread?'

Harry didn't know.

'Then you got money. Not enough for an airplane maybe, but enough to enjoy yourself when you need to.'

It was a grey November day, the sky full of rooks and magpies. They were out of London now, driving through the Tory woodlands of the Thames Valley, out into the dry-cleaned countryside of Berkshire, immitation Tudor pubs with log tables in their orchards, pony jumps in the paddocks, low ridges lined with beech and elm, Intercity 125s thundering through the cuttings. In England you liked the North or the South but rarely both. Harry was a moorland man, unfond of this placid, comfortable countryside.

'Tell me about the money,' he asked Shirley.

She sucked at her toffee.

'I told you. A hundred pounds, every month. More later, he adjusted it.'

'How did it arrive?'

'A draft, like a postal order, she cashed it in the Bank of Cyprus in Larnaca.'

'It came by post?'

'Yeah. Brown envelope. Typed, only he didn't type it every time, it was photocopied.'

She reached inside her jacket, took out an envelope and passed it to Harry. A very ordinary cheap brown A6 envelope, the kind people use for invoices or charity circulars. A white panel glued to the front with an address on it, an Air Mail sticker in the top left hand corner.

'Can I keep this?' he asked her.

'No. You can show it to your friend, but you can't keep it. Pete was right, people like you lose things.'

Harry passed it back to Miranda.

'What makes you think it was Ben Webb?' he asked Shirley.

'It's a guess. Just a guess.'

Broadmoor was commissioned in 1856 by the Lunacy Commissioners from Sir Joshua Jebb, who also designed Holloway and Pentonville prisons. Its three-storeyed buildings – Railway Terminus with a distant nod to Venice in the miniature romanesque windows – are brick, red for the main walls, with decorative capitals and architraves in a sort of mustard yellow. Long before you enter it the soul starts to smell boiled cabbage, disinfectant and linoleum. Close up the impression is less daunting: there's a graze of ivy and Virginia creeper against some of the walls, the gardens and lawns are well if rather militarily tended, and there are intermittent signs of low-cost modernization. But there's no mistaking where you are, inside the walls of a booby-hatch for the criminally insane.

Harry and Shirley left Miranda in the car and passed through electric sliding steel doors into the hospital. No clanking here, no rattle of keys – if you heard something rattling in Broadmoor it was probably the medicine trolley. Once through the doors there was no sound at all, just an eerie silence. They sat for five minutes in a drab reception room while their credentials were checked.

The security search was brief: they'd left their bags in the car. No one queried their papers, but they knew who Harry was.

'You're that prick from TV, aren't you?' their nurse/minder said pleasantly as he conducted them through to the visitors' lounge. 'Here to get another psychopath back on the streets, I presume.'

'Only doing my job,' said Harry, grinning back.

The visitors' room was like a works canteen, brightly lit, with half a dozen tables and upright plastic chairs. Terry was waiting for them in a corner, immaculately dressed in a dark suit, white silk shirt, polished shoes, gold watch and a black arm-band in memory of Pete on his left sleeve. As they approached he pulled down his shirt cuffs and fingered his tie like a nightclub manager greeting important guests. Nightclubs being where Terry learned most of his style.

'Hello Terry. This is Uncle Micky,' said Shirley with a wink.

'Harry Kapowski,' said Harry, and extended his hand.

Terry shook it politely and gestured to a table.

'Pleased to meet you, Mr Kapowski.' He spoke slowly and formally, like a man who'd learned his manners from a phrase book. 'How are you, Shirley?'

'Awful, since you ask, Terry. Bloody awful.'

She sat down, lit a cigarette and put the match in the

foil ashtray. Terry clicked his fingers at a youth in a white jacket.

'Tea and biscuits?' he asked his guests. 'Or perhaps you'd prefer a hot meat pie?'

The youth took their order then disappeared through a swing door.

'Who's that?' asked Shirley. 'He's new, isn't he?'

'That's Napoleon. Sad case, he thinks he's Arthur Scargill.' Terry smiled sadly at his little joke. 'No, his name's Benny Marks, he killed his mum and dad with an electric hedge-trimmer, you probably read about the case.'

There were perhaps a dozen visitor-groups scattered round the room, patients and their relatives. Harry ran his eye over the pale, polite, grey-faced men talking quietly to their mothers and wives, mad axe-men and serial rapists and child molesters who in their prime graced the front pages of the *Star* and the *News of the World*, now looking after their budgerigars and writing doggerel poems and studying for their GCSEs.

'Is this your first visit, Mr Kapowski?' Terry asked him.

'No, I was here once before, years ago. Making a film for the BBC.'

Cost him a good leather jacket, that trip. They'd come down the day before on a recce, been taken round the whole building, selected where they wanted to film. The first location of the day was the canteen. Harry and his director walked into the room and felt something strange, something different. They leaned back against the wall, asking each other what had changed. What had changed was the paint, still wet, sticking to the backs of their jackets. Every room they'd selected had been redecorated overnight.

'I saw you at the funeral,' said Terry. 'It was good of you to come.'

'I made him,' said Shirley.

Harry had decided that the best way to cope with Shirley in this kind of mood was to ignore her, the way he used to ignore his grandmother at mealtimes. Not rudely, just pretend you haven't heard.

'I hadn't realized you were twins,' he told Terry.

'Us and the Krays both. Yeah, we used to look alike. Not mentally, though: mentally we were different.'

'In what way?'

Terry fiddled with his watch strap.

'I think he was a better person. He didn't have a lot of fun, but he was a better person.'

Napoleon brought the teas and a plate of custard creams, and Terry took a dispenser out of his pocket and dropped a Sweetex into his cup. Harry asked him what medication he was on.

'Stemetol capsules four times a day. They're meant to quieten the nerves, which they do, but they make your limbs shake so they give me Disipal to cope with the side-effects. I get an injection of Modicate once a fortnight for bad dreams and depression. That's about it.'

Putting a drug-user like Terry Pattichis in a mental hospital, it occurred to Harry, was like locking an alcoholic up in a brewery, or a paedophile in a dormitory full of boy scouts. Not that Terry slept in a dormitory, he had his own room, with a shelf of books and a washbasin and a radio and a view out across the fields to the woods.

Terry liked Broadmoor.

'It's a very good neighbourhood – Windsor, Ascot, Sandhurst. Berkshire's not what it used to be, of course,' he smiled. 'The motorway's brought in a lot of commuters.'

'Do you ever get out?' asked Harry.

'No need, really.'

He laughed, showing off his teeth, crisp and white and even. Harry tried to imagine him ten years ago, during the good times, camping it up with Jo and his

94

friends. I bet he was a lot of fun in those days, he decided. In small doses.

'The food got to me a bit until I went vegetarian,' Terry went on. 'The vegetables are good, we grow them ourselves. Otherwise there's not a lot to complain about. Monmouth House is a bit rough, that's what used to be called Block Six, where they put the howling wolves, the real nutters.'

'You're not a real nutter?'

'I can be, Harry, I can be.' He looked him straight in the eye. 'When the occasion calls for it.'

'Is that what happened with Jo O'Brien?'

'Maybe.' Terry's eyes shot to Shirley, then back to Harry again. 'You want to talk about that?'

'That's why he's here,' Shirley confirmed.

Harry picked up a spoon and stirred his tea. Normally when you go to see someone inside it's because they want to get out. Terry seemed entirely happy where he was. A roof over his head, three meals a day, all the chemicals he could eat.

'What did Pete tell you?' asked Terry.

'He'd seen a programme I'd done about a phoney confession. He thought your confession was phoney too.'

Terry looked up at the ceiling for a full thirty seconds, as though he was doing some kind of mental exercise.

'Can I ask you a question, Harry?' he said eventually. 'Do you believe in Jesus?'

'Up to a point,' said Harry.

'No such thing,' said Terry. 'Either you do or you don't. I do. You have to understand that. Eight years ago I found Jesus, and my life became full of meaning.'

Harry was used to the religious ones. Mostly they faked it for reasons of convenience, like Terry and his vegetables. Sometimes it was real. When it was real they went overboard on it, morning noon and night, as though their brains had been taken out of their heads and steam-cleaned.

'God moves in a mysterious way,' Terry continued. 'Things happen to all of us that we don't understand. I don't know what happened with Jo, but God does, he had a reason.'

'That's it, is it?' said Harry. 'All part of the Divine plan.'

'I reckon,' said Terry, very dead pan. 'At least that's the Authorized Version.'

'And what's the rumour?'

Religious cons were easy to sort out: the real ones didn't mind how rude you were to them, they just smiled and prayed for your soul. The phoneys were liable to get jumpy. Terry didn't get jumpy, he just grinned.

'All sorts of rumours, Harry.'

'What I heard,' Harry continued, 'is this. You and your friend Jo are working late at the office, have a few jars and maybe the odd powder or two, retire to the pub and start discussing your relationship.'

'Football,' Terry corrected him. 'It started as an argument about football. Spurs were playing QPR in the Cup Final. He had a thing about QPR, Jo, couldn't stand them. So it started about football – we only got on to the relationship later.'

'Whatever. By the time you got back to the office it had got serious. You'd been seeing other men, and Jo threatened to throw you out. You said fine, throw me out and I'll blow the whistle on the Latchkey scam. Jo said hold on, got out the vodka bottle, you both dropped more chemicals, talked it over a bit more. At which point you had a visitor. Or maybe the visitor was waiting for you when you got back, having a look through the files. By this stage neither you nor Jo are making much sense, the sky's gone green and the furniture is beginning to melt and move around the room. Maybe you passed out altogether.'

'You make this stuff up yourself,' asked Terry, 'or you have script writers working for you?'

'I get visions,' said Harry.

'Maybe you should see a doctor about it. But keep going.'

'Next thing you know it's two in the morning, you're crawling around Shepherd's Bush Green on your hands and knees talking to the dog turds. The cops pick you up, take you down the station, start asking you questions. They're quite nice about it, give you cups of tea, aspirins for your head. In return for which you sign a confession. They already know all about Latchkey, the Special Branch have a file a yard deep on Jo O'Brien tucked away in a corner for a rainy day.'

'If they knew about Jo,' Shirley objected, 'how come they hadn't done anything before?'

'Odds are he was working for them in the first place. Even if he wasn't they wouldn't touch him until the time was right. The cops love the Loony Left, nothing like the old Enemy Within to scare the politicos back in line. So you sign on the dotted line. You're fucked anyway, you had the motive, the opportunity: no one's going to believe you didn't do it. Either you sign right away, or the heavy boys get to work on you. How am I doing?'

'Brilliant,' said Terry. 'But there's still something I don't understand, Inspector. Who killed Jo?'

'Maybe you did. Maybe there wasn't a visitor. I don't know; and I suspect you don't either. At this point it doesn't matter. What matters is that you signed a confession you didn't make. The police stitched you up.'

Terry helped himself to a custard cream.

'Why would they do that?'

'Maybe they were convinced you'd done it anyway and took a few shortcuts to save themselves the unnecessary trouble of looking around for extra evidence. Or maybe they were trying to protect someone with powerful connections.'

'Like who?'

'Like Ben Webb.'

Terry stirred his tea, eyes down on the table. Harry waited for him to pick up on Ben's name, but he didn't.

'You're right, I don't remember a thing. The honest truth is that I have no idea if I did or didn't kill him. I may have done. And if I didn't, who the hell did?'

'Jo blackmailed people, didn't he?'

'When he needed money. He was never very serious about it. He looked on it as his savings account, something to dip into when he was short of cash.'

'Did you?'

'Sure. In my business it was the nearest you could get to a contributory pension scheme. But only when they could afford it, I wouldn't want anyone to suffer too much.'

There was a disturbance across the room: a bone-thin, stubble-skulled man of perhaps thirty stood up, overturning his chair, and began waving a long fleshless arm at the woman he'd been talking to.

'Whore!'

'I tell you, Peter, I don't fancy him,' she whispered indignantly.

He pursed his lips and spat at her. Two male nurses moved quickly through the tables, took him gently but firmly by the arms and led him away.

'Cabaret time,' said Terry. 'What were we talking about?'

'Money,' Harry reminded him.

'What, the Latchkey money? We ate it. Ate it, drank it, sniffed it, smoked it, partied on it, sunbathed on it. Not a penny wasted.'

Harry didn't mean the Latchkey money, but he wanted to know about that too.

'You ate a quarter of a million quid?'

'Is that what they're saying? Bollocks, we never ate that well. It's always the same, some guy sticks up a bank, helps himself to a hundred grand, picks up the paper the next day and bank's saying they've lost a hundred and fifty thousand. The manager splits the spare fifty with the police. We did well, though, I mustn't complain. Stayed in some lovely hotels.'

'And what about the cheques to your mother?'

Terry shot another glance at his sister-in-law.

Shirley shrugged her shoulders.

'We're washing the family laundry, Terry. I figured we might as well throw the whole lot in while we're at it.'

'Some things you send to the laundry, some you wash at home.' He'd stopped smiling. 'That was private business, nothing to do with this. It was my own money.' He smiled again. 'I stole it myself.'

Time was up. A bell rang, the attendants lined up by the doors, the visitors began getting to their feet. Harry put away his notebook.

'Are you going to make a programme about this?' asked Terry.

'I might.'

'Waste of everyone's time.'

'Not if it gets you out.'

Terry laughed, a quick spontaneous laugh, like a child at a pantomime.

'What on earth makes you think I want out? Listen, Harry. I've been inside eight years. Last week, on the way to Pete's funeral, I saw what's happened outside. It's all changed – the shops, the people, the clothes, the buildings, what I think of as modern is old now. What's waiting for me outside? No job, no money, a reputation. Every time I walked into a bar people would start whispering. I told you, I like it here. I've got friends here. I don't know anyone out there any more.'

They were at the door now.

'Thanks for coming,' Terry told him. 'I know you mean well, but you're wasting your time. Stick to Irish bombers, they've got homes to go to.'

Shirley and Harry walked down the corridor in silence, back out into Berkshire. It was dusk: the floodlights were on, pools of yellow light dissolving in the drizzle. Miranda was still sitting in the back of the Escort, reading the AA handbook.

'He's a funny boy,' Shirley said finally as she got into the car. 'But I'm fond of him.'

Miranda asked how they'd got on.

'Brilliant,' said Harry. 'I have a whole new career ahead of me campaigning to keep innocent men in prison.'

Shirley shrugged her shoulders, started the engine and turned on the radio.

'Maybe some music would be nice.'

It was seven o'clock by the time she dropped them back at Nine Elms Lane. Upstairs, Harry flung his bag on the sofa. Miranda lifted the whisky bottle down from the shelf.

'Aren't you going to ask me how I got on?' she asked.

Harry stopped kicking the furniture and looked up. Miranda had a glass of whisky in one hand, Shirley's brown envelope in the other. She was grinning.

'You just nicked it?'

'Just like that.'

Harry took the envelope, turned it over in his hand.

'Thanks. If nothing else I can frame it, a souvenir of a wasted afternoon.'

'It was that bad?'

'He probably didn't do it, but he doesn't care. We make a programme proving he's innocent and at the end of it he'll be there in the dock at the Appeal Court begging the judge not to let him go.'

He told her what had happened at the interview. She sat on the arm of the sofa, sipping her drink and teasing the tips of her ginger hair between her fingers, watching, listening.

'So that's that, is it?' she asked when he'd finished.

'I don't know,' said Harry, draining his glass. 'He's happy where he is. If something ain't broken, as they say in Detroit, don't fix it.'

Miranda got up from the sofa.

'What if he's lying?'

'It doesn't matter, it's still his choice. If he wants to stay in Broadmoor, so be it.'

'If he wants to stay inside it doesn't have to be Broadmoor. If he's innocent he could get transferred to an ordinary mental hospital. That's point one.'

'You've got more?'

'Lots. You only have his word for it that he sent the money to his mum. That's point two. Three is about money as well. Who pays for his suits? Point four: he was paying the HP on Pete's car.'

Harry looked at her.

'How the hell do you know that?'

'I got bored,' Miranda explained. 'You were a long time inside, there wasn't a lot to read. I read the atlas first, cover to cover, then the car handbook, then an old copy of the *Daily Mirror* that had got lost under one of the seats. After that I did twenty minutes' transcendental meditation, re-read the atlas, listened to the radio. Then I thought why not? I did your bag first, just out of curiosity. Then I did Shirley's. First thing I found was her diary. She's a very methodical woman, all her accounts are there. Tenth of each month, eighty-five quid to Lombard Finance, then Terry in brackets. The eighty-five quid doesn't appear in her overall budget.'

'Shit,' said Harry. 'What else was in there?'

'Lots of things.'

'Tell me.'

She collected her notebook from her jacket pocket and sat down beside him.

'The widow Pattichis is still sexually active, carries her cap with her. She takes something called Tazodone HCL, pretty little blue and green capsules.'

'Anti-depressant,' said Harry.

Miranda looked up from her pad.

'I didn't know you were a pharmacist too.'

'I'm not. I just happen to meet a lot of people in stressful conditions. What else was in there?'

'Toffees. Cosmetics. A bus pass.'

'That's it?'

'That's it. How did I do?'

'Ten out of ten for technique, seven out of ten for analysis, three out of ten for results.'

'You still on the case?'

'Maybe.'

Harry wasn't sure. The ostensible reason for keeping going had disappeared – Terry Pattichis didn't give a fuck. But there was still Ben Webb.

And then he remembered Angela.

'I'm afraid I have a problem this evening,' he said as nonchalantly as he could manage. 'I have to see Angela Webb.'

Miranda looked surprised.

'Why's that a problem? I was about to go anyway.'

'Fine,' said Harry. 'I just wondered if we could meet up later?'

She shrugged her shoulders.

'Do what you want, Harry.'

There was no guile or sarcasm in her voice, she just wanted to get home and get on with her life.

10

HARRY WALKED ALONG Nine Elms Lane, and crossed
Vauxhall Bridge. It was raining hard now, the east wind
blowing gusts of airborne litter across the road. North
of the river he turned left into Pimlico, the land of the
waxproof jacket and the four-wheel drive, a museum of
1950s Home Counties society, men in pinstripe or
British Warms, women in cashmere and gabardine,
walking their dogs up and down tree-lined private parks
and portico'd Victorian terraces, conversing unselfcons-
ciously with one another at a volume that could be
heard three streets away.

He was due to meet Angela at eight. By five to he was
in the bar at Dolphin Square, a whisky in his hand,
settling back into one of the beech-framed tapestry
chairs. The decor was thirties-plush, very Noël Coward,
as though you'd wandered into the saloon of a pre-war
transatlantic liner: art deco lights, soft pastel murals on
the walls, a lot of chrome and glass and bamboo. A
long way from the worlds of Pete Pattichis and Liam
Walsh and Pigfoot Walker. A long way from Miranda
too. He had her address in his pocket – Marylebone,
two blocks south of the Euston Road – and was trying
to decide if he had the bottle to go there after he'd
finished with Angela. She'd given it to him without any
indication as to when she next expected to see him.

Through a glass wall he could see down into the

swimming pool, where half a dozen residents were putting in their daily lengths, middle-aged ladies in rubber hats and overweight gents in boxer trunks, wallowing slowly through the water like so many clockwork whales. No sign of Angela. He hid himself behind a newspaper and settled in for a long wait. Angela's attitude to other people's time had always been casual.

He wasn't entirely sure why he was there, what he wanted to ask her about: the Cypriot rent boy who'd worked with Ben twelve years before, or what she meant when she talked about pain and pleasure the night before she got married. Either, both. Nor was he sure why she'd agreed to meet him at such short notice – she must have a thousand other social and domestic tasks to attend to at a time like this.

At the bar a youth in his early twenties was sipping a gin and tonic and chewing cashew nuts. Neat fair hair, mathematically parted, a blazer, a shirt with broad stripes and a tie with insignia, brass buttons on the blazer, the face of an eager child: an army officer if ever he'd seen one, waiting for mummy or daddy. What simple lives some people lived: public school, Sandhurst, plenty of squash and rowing, Queen and Country, marry a Colonel's daughter, retire at forty and get a job with the Forestry Commission or the National Trust.

At least that's how it looked for a moment to Harry, preoccupied with Angela and mad Terry and Miranda and Pigfoot Walker. Some week. Of course the kid was probably due to fly out to South Armagh in the morning, shit scared he'd come home in a body-bag. What the hell, at least he had something he believed in.

Angela kept Harry waiting three quarters of an hour. He smelled her before he saw her, a soft breeze of Rive Gauche wafting in over the top of his paper. She looked stunning, a scarlet dress as tight as a tourniquet, cut short above the knee to show her legs, long and sexy if not quite as long as her fuck-me high heels made them look. Lipstick, a short page-boy cut to her blonde hair, no bra; a subtle blend of pre-feminist female artifice and nineties working woman. She didn't look as though she'd been swimming, she looked as though she'd spent the last two hours getting ready for a date. Harry couldn't help but feel flattered.

She made a reasonable stab at looking surprised.

'Harry Kapowski! What are you doing here?'

Harry was too absorbed in the red dress to remember what his alibi was meant to be.

'Angela!' he stuttered. 'Good heavens.'

They kept up the pretence for a while, Angela protesting she was on her way to meet friends, Harry persuading her at least to sit down so they catch up on each other's news. The soldier's parents arrived and carried him off to the restaurant. Angela reached into her bag for a tissue, looked round, and then slid a room key under Harry's newspaper.

'Hood House,' she said quietly. Each of Dolphin Square's wings was named after a British admiral. 'Third floor. Give me five minutes' start.'

When she'd left Harry went through the motions of worrying about the late arrival of his fictional assignation, then got up and asked the barman where he could find a phone. The barman directed him to the main reception. He took the lift to the third floor and followed the signs down the carpeted corridors looking for the right number. There was a smell of brasso and varnish in the air. Distant sounds of television and muffled laughter came from behind the closed doors of apartments, hinting at the world of cut-glass sherry decanters and chintz sofas inside.

Angela's flat was one of six which had been refurbished for the short-term rental market. The decor in the living room was modern, clean and tasteful, decorated in shades of mushroom and claret, with Audebon prints in thin gold frames on the wall. At one end a white dining table with four white ladder-back chairs, school of Charles Renée Macintosh; at the other a brown leather sofa and two easy chairs arranged around a glass coffee table with fresh roses in a porcelain vase.

Angela was sitting on the sofa with her shoes off, legs tucked under her, a vodka and tonic in one hand, a cigarette in the other. She waved her glass towards the sideboard.

'Help yourself to a drink.'

Harry poured himself a large Bushmills and looked around the room.

'What the hell is this place?'

'My safe house. It's less hassle than having a permanent flat. And they're very discreet here, the place is so full of Foreign Office spooks that they hardly notice if the rest of us come and go at odd times.'

'What's wrong with the hotels?'

'I'm getting a bit old for hotels, Harry.'

He sat down on the arm of one of the chairs, maybe eight feet away from her.

'Bullshit. In your early twenties you go to each other's flats, in your late twenties you're married and raising kids, in your mid thirties you start meeting people in hotels, it's all built into the biological clock. Does Ben know you have a love-nest?'

'I expect so. If he did he wouldn't complain. It's not what you'd call a monogamous marriage. You know Ben, he'll fuck anything if it stands still long enough, just for something to do.' She reached forward and put her glass on the coffee table. 'So how have you been, Harry?'

'Do you want the long answer or the short one?'

'Short for now, you can save the long one for later.'

'I can't complain. And you?'

'Ditto. I have two healthy and intelligent kids, enough money, a successful husband, plenty of male admirers.'

'Are you happy?'

She laughed.

'Compared to what?'

'Compared to what you expected, I suppose.'

'I'm not sure what I expected, but not this. No, that's wrong – I suppose I've got exactly what I did want. It's the old cliché – be careful what you wish for, it might come true. Ben's good to me in his way, we're just neither of us very good at marriage.'

She got up to pour herself another drink. As she passed Harry she brushed her hand lightly against his shoulder.

Concentrate, he reminded himself. Remember Miranda.

'Do you really want to talk about Terry wotsisname?'

'Yes.'

'Why?'

He told her the story, about Shirley and Pete and Pete's mother's deathbed request. He didn't tell her what had happened that afternoon in the tea-room at Broadmoor. She listened carefully, running her fingertip round the rim of her glass, licking her lips, eyes very open, watching him watch her. It had always been part of Angela's technique to leave men with the impression that there might be circumstances in which she would sleep with them, without ever making clear what the circumstances were. Tonight the circumstances looked clear and immediate.

She sat down again.

'Fancy Harry Kapowski going soft over Terry Pattichis. So what do you want to know?'

'Tell it from the beginning,' said Harry.

'Do I really have to?'

'Please.'

She untucked her legs and lit another cigarette.

'Did you ever go to somewhere called the Leduce Club in Wardour Street? Very popular with transvestites in those days, Ben took me there once for a giggle; everyone thought I was a man in drag.'

Harry hadn't been to the Leduce, but he got the picture.

'That's the world Terry came from. I rather liked him, in a bizarre sort of way. This was pre-AIDs, of course, gays were still allowed to have fun then. He was completely amoral, I don't think I ever met anyone with less scruples. Which was fine once you knew the rules, or rather the lack of them. There was very little malice to him – I don't think he understood the concept. He'd steal, but he was never offended if anything of his was taken. He drank a lot, and he took anything chemical that came to hand. Uppers and downers, barbiturates, amphetamines, the works. He couldn't resist a medicine cabinet, none of that crowd could.'

'What did he do at Latchkey?'

Angela smiled at the memory.

'Messed around, played practical jokes. He used to pretend to be a woman when he answered the phones. He sent letters to people on Latchkey stationery telling them he was conducting a survey of sleeping habits, asking them questions about their sex lives. He could be very mischievous.'

Harry took out his pocket book, started taking notes.

'That was on the better days,' Angela went on. 'On bad days he could be frightening, out of his head. Often he didn't come in at all, or the police would phone to say he'd been found in Hyde Park spreading butter on tree trunks.' She sucked at her cigarette. 'It's funny, I'd forgotten all about Terry. Is he still in prison?'

'Broadmoor.'

'Poor bastard.'

'And how about Jo?' asked Harry.

'Mad. Clever, but mad. You know those people who seem entirely plausible on the outside, but inside there's something missing? Professionally he was a great operator. He'd ring up one of the ex-Beatles, tell him one of the Stones wanted to do a benefit gig with him. And vice versa. Often it worked – he had half London eating out of his hand at one time. But it was bound to fall apart sooner or later. Someone was going to look at the books.'

'Did any money go to the waifs?'

She laughed.

'I doubt it – I suspect the nearest any homeless kids got to Latchkey was posing for the photographs. You must have seen the posters, all those grainy black and white photos of urchins sleeping in doorways. White kids, black kids, Indian kids – ethnic minorities were all the rage then.'

'Didn't that worry Ben?'

'I think it did a bit. But he was still very naïve in a lot of ways then. And everyone was having a good time, I think he was reluctant to ask too many questions.'

Harry stole a glance at his watch. It was twenty past nine.

'How did he get involved with Latchkey?'

'He wanted a job that would get him started in politics. He wrote to all sorts of people in the Labour party asking for advice. I think it was Willie Walpole put him in touch with Jo. You could check with Ben.'

First Ben Webb, now Willie Walpole. The erstwhile Labour MP and minister, once famous for his gourmet tastes and flamboyant dress, was a Tory peer now ('For Service to the Wine Trade', someone had unkindly remarked). Harry had done a film on him once, around the time he resigned the Labour whip, must have been around 1985. Walpole was one of the Old Brigade, elected in the landslide in 1945, a bright and flamboyant grammar school boy, just out of the army. Like Randolph Churchill he had a great future behind him: twice a PPS under Atlee, a minor front-bench portfolio in the fifties, a succession of unspectacular ministerial posts under Wilson, until he finally lost out in a cabinet reshuffle in 1969. Wilson made him a life peer in his resignation honours seven years later.

Judged by his political career, Willie Walpole would have been no more than a minor footnote in other people's memoirs, a Fred Peart or a Bob Mellish or an Edmund Dell. What guaranteed his place in the head-lines was the company he kept. Musical hall comedians, crooners, fag-hag actresses, boxers, East End villains – dear old Willie, such a character, too fond of sounding off in newspaper columns to be taken seriously, too fond of the fleshpots to get as far as his brain deserved. He made the news almost as often as George Best – libel cases and drink-driving charges, tired and emotional behaviour on TV chat shows, scandalous scenes in West End nightclubs. Despite it all he was still popular and not without influence on both sides of the House, a regular guest at dinner tables and in private boxes at the races during his increasingly rare visits to England. He spent most of the year in Spain.

'Willie knew Jo?'

'You could say that,' said Angela with a sly grin.

'In the biblical sense?'

'Among others.'

Walpole had never made much effort to conceal his homosexuality.

'What was his role in Latchkey.'

'Patron, I think. Jo had a lot of famous names on his notepaper. Some of them he even checked with first. But Willie was around a lot, yes.'

'This was when – nineteen eight-two?'

Angela paused.

'Eight-two, eighty-three, sometime around then. Before we got married. You will have been in Glasgow. I thought of you there this morning, Ben did an inter-view for Radio Scotland.'

Harry'd been happy in Glasgow. He'd been twenty-five, the same age as Miranda, living in a first-floor flat in a tree-lined crescent with a view across the Kelvin to the Botanic Gardens. Two minutes from work, one and a half from the BBC Club. There'd been a girl called Sara, small and pert, with a neat little bum that stuck out like a parcel shelf, a ready laugh and a passionate nature. All those girls you used to go out with, thought you knew well, now realize you never knew at all, nor they you. What a waste.

He asked Angela what she knew about the night of the killing.

'Terry and Jo were working late in the office. Jo was working on a list of sportsmen and TV personalities to deliver a petition to Ten Downing Street the following weekend. He was trying to get in touch with Seb Coe but he was out of the country, no one seemed to know where he was. Ben had stayed to help. He left around seven, he was meeting some friends round the corner at the Vanderbilt Raquets Club in Sterner Street. We didn't find out that Jo was dead until the following morning.'

'Do you think Terry killed him?' Harry asked her.

'It seemed pretty clear at the trial. He more or less admitted it.'

Harry checked his watch again. It was ten o'clock. He got up, poured himself another whisky, went over to the window and opened the drapes a little. The gardens were empty, narrow floodlit paths meandering through the darkness of the shrubbery.

'Does Ben think so?'

'Ask him, Harry.'

'I will.'

Angela had her hand on her shoulder, stroking herself.

'Do you think Terry did it?' she asked, not looking up.

Harry hadn't a clue.

'The confession is dodgy, far too articulate. And someone paid blood money to Terry's mother until she died. Not a lot, a hundred quid a month.'

He watched her carefully, but there was no reaction.

'How do you know it was blood money?'

'I don't.'

Angela was playing with the hem of her dress.

'He wasn't involved, I promise you.'

'That's what puzzles me,' said Harry. 'He may not have been directly involved, but he must have known something about it. How come he wasn't called as a witness? How come he kept his name out of the papers?'

'I think Willie Walpole may have had something to do with that. Willie's had a lot of experience at handling scandal. Ben was quite happy to go into the box, but Willie persuaded him not to. He couldn't have told the court anything they didn't already know. The whole business could have been very damaging to Ben's political career – he was looking for a Labour seat at the time. The selection committee met two weeks before the trial.'

That's Ben, thought Harry – the sins are all sins of omission. Why get involved when it's not going to make any difference? Six months later he was a parliamentary candidate, within a year there was a sudden by-election and he was an MP. First things first.

'Try not to be too hard on him, Harry,' Angela continued. 'It would be rough on him if Latchkey came back to haunt him now. He was only a bystander.'

'I'll do what I can,' said Harry.

She got up and came over to the window and stood behind him, almost touching.

'What are you thinking about?' she asked.

'I was thinking what an irony it is that the only time anyone ever believed anything Terry said was when he confessed to a murder. It must have suited them all to believe him.'

'Is that all you're thinking?'

Harry turned round.

'Of course not. I was also wondering how many men you've slept with here.'

'Not that many. Do you want names?'

'Not particularly.'

She put her arm round his waist, more like an old friend than a lover.

'No one very important. To me, that is. Once in a while I get fed up, feel like a bit of excitement for a change. It's not much fun being an MP's wife – not as bad as some of them make out, but the hours do get to you. I mean it when I say Ben's good to me in his way. And you were right when you said I enjoyed the celebrity bit – I do, quite. It's a nuisance sometimes, that's all. I don't mind him being unfaithful. If you've slept around a lot, then sex doesn't seem such a hugely significant thing. Infidelity's a sin, but a small one. I can always tell when he's found a new lover – burned letters in the grate, all those "And-I-You" phone calls, then the guilt, all this unprovoked affection suddenly descends on me like a warm wet cow-pat.' She released her arm. 'Talking of which, you have to go, don't you?'

'Bad timing,' said Harry.

'It always was with us. We should have stayed together after Oxford. I was mad about you then. You didn't seem terribly interested.'

Harry sighed.

'I never knew.'

'Are you serious?'

'I saw myself as a gauche, rather unpleasant twenty-year-old. I thought you were the most beautiful woman in the world. It never occurred to me to do anything about it.'

He wanted her now too, despite Miranda. Or even because of Miranda: the time you're most likely to betray a lover is when sex is at its best, the appetite nicely wetted. They were facing each other, all he had to do was put his hand on her hips, hold her against him.

'Fear of failing?' she asked.

'A bit. Fear of losing a friend too, I suppose. By the time we were together, Ben was around. You were very clear about that.'

She shook her head.

'You're a fool, Kapowski. What's her name, by the way?'

'Miranda.'

'Have you been together long?'

'No.'

'You going to marry her?'

'She hasn't asked me yet.'

'Don't ask her to love you for yourself, Harry. No one's going to love you for yourself. Money, power, wit, sexual prowess – but not yourself. I'm joking, of course.' She kissed him gently on the mouth, then pulled away. 'It's OK, I know you have to go. It's been nice seeing you again.'

'For me too,' said Harry, picking up his raincoat off the back of the chair.

'Another time, maybe.'

'Another time,' said Harry.

Suddenly she looked very tired.

I I

HARRY MADE IT TO Marylebone a little after eleven. Miranda was sprawled on the sofa in the little living room, lights off, watching an alternative chat-show on Channel 4, some cor-blimey cockney host who probably had a PhD in linguistics or Serbo-Croatian literature pretending he'd never read a book in his life, coming on all cheeky and down-to-earth and loveable with a Liverpool boxer who was launching a new career as a fashion model. Alternative entertainers, in Harry's experience, knocked things for one of two reasons: because they want to knock them over or because they want to be let in. Cor-blimey badly wanted in: give him another couple of years he'd be driving a Bentley and getting himself photographed handing over Variety Club cheques to Dr Barnardo's.

'I thought you never watched TV,' said Harry.

'I thought I'd better learn.'

'Did you miss me?'

'Not a lot.'

He dumped his bag on the floor. Miranda flicked the remote control to change channels.

'Did Angela offer to sleep with you?' she asked.

'Of course.'

'Were you tempted?'

'No.'

She grabbed his trench coat, unbalancing him backwards on to the sofa. She was slightly built, but she knew how to fight.

'I bet you were. It's so easy with old lovers, you don't need to go through all the preliminaries. "Fancy a fuck, Harry?" "Not particularly." "Come on, why not . . ." "OK, if you're having one yourself. But I mustn't be long, I promised Miranda . . ."'

Her bedroom was tiny, just large enough for a double bed and a pine wardrobe with a built-in mirror in which they watched each other make love, Harry taking care of his wounded leg until he forgot about it altogether. Miranda had some grass and rolled joints, and sometime in the small hours they moved the TV through and balanced it on a chair at the bottom of the bed and watched *Where Eagles Dare* dubbed into Italian on one of the satellite stations; then made love again, then Miranda watched Major League Philippino Baseball while Harry cooked toast and scrambled eggs. Afterwards, lying smoking dope and watching TV, she asked him about Angela again.

'Did she really ask you to sleep with her?'

'Not in so many words.'

'You don't need many words for that sort of invitation.'

He sucked at the joint and passed it down to her.

'I think she's genuinely lonely. I think she's boxed so clever for so many years that she's wound up with no one she can talk to. Sleeping with someone is a way of getting close to another human being without having to say anything. It's easiest with someone you've known a long time.'

Miranda inhaled and blew a column of smoke towards the ceiling. Outside they could hear the first sounds of the new day, the early morning traffic moving along Marylebone High Street.

'Why did you go to see her?'

'Habit. If a famous name comes up in this business, you check it out. If only out of curiosity.'

'That wasn't what I meant. Why Angela, why not Ben?'

Harry'd been asking himself that, too.

'You wouldn't get within a million miles of Ben at the moment. He knows me, but he doesn't owe me any favours.'

'Unlike Angela,' said Miranda.

'For fuck's sake,' said Harry.

It was late morning by the time they woke. Harry went out and bought milk and Sunday papers from the Indian supermarket round the corner, and they idled the day away, walked across Regent's Park to Primrose Hill, poked at the stalls in the market on Camden Lock, drank pints in an Irish pub in Kentish Town, Harry waiting for the moment when she'd wise up to him or get bored or decide she really had made a mistake. She didn't, but she argued a lot. It was hard to get away with anything with Miranda: she despised the least hint of sentimentality, jumped on what had always seemed to Harry to be harmless conversational platitudes, mocked his political speeches. There was no clear pattern to her own politics: she had no respect for male posturing, but let him pay for everything; when he attacked politicians she sprang to their defence, when he defended them she was quick to question his assumptions.

They were both exhausted by the time they got back to the flat. Harry washed up the breakfast while she made more scrambled eggs.

'What do you want to do about us and work?' she asked him.

'Do you have a preference?'

He was learning that the only way to begin to cope with Miranda was to throw her questions back at her.

'Cool,' she'd suggested, with uncharacteristic caution.

Cool was fine by Harry too, at least in theory. In practice he felt anything but.

They arrived at work separately on Monday morning, and by the time Harry got in Miranda was in conference with Roger Carlisle, gesticulating, laughing, making notes. She was due to fly to Belfast at lunchtime and drive on to Derry: not to try and make Liam O'Kelly change his mind, but to talk to Sean Walsh's father about the possibility of turning the story into a drama. Harry sat at his desk pretending to read the morning papers, watching her through the glass window of Roger's office. He felt jealous. He had nothing to feel jealous of, but he felt jealous, out of control. It was a long time since he'd felt this way about a woman.

He glanced down at *The Independent*. The newspaperwas running inconclusive opinion polls and clever pictures of photo-opportunities, in the background a publicity-minded politician picking up dog-shit in a pooper scooper, in the foreground an aide hovering with a tray of spare turds, just in case. The IRA had put a bomb in the British Forces Broadcasting studios in Paddington, injuring a West Indian typist. The travel industry was going through its annual spate of bankruptcies. In Norfolk a man had reached the age of a hundred and eleven. 'I'm really not at all interesting,' he'd told the Press Association. 'I've never done anything interesting, I've never said anything interesting or been anywhere interesting. I'm just old.' There was a picture of him with a large birthday card and a bottle of champagne on his bedside locker. He was watching children's television.

Miranda was still in Roger's office. Harry wanted to touch her, remind himself she was real. One of the troubles with an office affair was that it made you behave so ridiculously in public. Last week he would simply have gone across and talked to her casually, made a joke. Now he assumed everyone was watching them, which they were, because forty-eight hours ago they seemed to get on fine and now they were treating each other like complete strangers, the surest way of broadcasting to the world that the two of you are having an affair.

Roger was laughing a lot now, thumbing through his contact book, leaning across the desk to let her copy out useful numbers. Harry clammed his jaw tight shut, looked around for something to do to distract himself. If he touches her I'll kill him, he decided. He looked at his watch. It was quarter to eleven. Miranda's flight was at one. She was still talking to Roger, but not about Ulster.

The phone on his desk rang. It was his daily, Mrs Perrymede.

'I think you'd better come over,' she told him.

The flat was a wreck. Overturned furniture, torn-down curtains, walls smeared with food and cosmetics, books and papers and clothing scattered, drawers, emptied, pictures smashed, food and wine and garbage tossed at random across the floor – as if a family of elephants had been suddenly struck by food poisoning, Walter the porter suggested helpfully.

Mrs Perrymede was in something approaching shock, bending to pick something up or right a chair, then stopping herself, as though afraid of catching some contagious disease.

The glass door to the balcony was open. Harry went out and stood looking down into the damp strip of garden that separated the building from the river. The drop from the parapet to the ground was maybe ten feet. Getting from the garden into the riverside walkway didn't present much of a problem either, a white clap-board fence that had seen better days.

'In through the front door,' Mrs Perrymede supposed.

'And out through the window. They must have had a key.'

That was what Walter reckoned too. What he couldn't work out was how they got it.

'Have a look in the bedroom,' he suggested to Harry.

Harry got as far as the door and froze.

His duvet had been pulled back, the mattress soaked in red wine. A carving knife was sticking out of the pillow. On the knife was impaled a pig's trotter.

He felt what he'd seen on the faces of men in police custody and in the dock, the realization of impotence, when the systems that have protected you in the past are suddenly no longer available. From here on in what's done is done to you, not by you. Someone wants to kill you, someone who knows where you live, where you have lunch, how to get into your bedroom in the middle of the night and stick knives in your headboard.

And then the door bell rang.

'Looks like you had a good party,' said Chief Inspector Calloway. 'Any idea when this happened?'

Harry had no idea. He hadn't been back to the flat since he left to see Angela on Saturday evening: the break-in could have taken place any time in the previous thirty-six hours.

Then Walter remembered the fire. Saturday evening, about eight o'clock, someone had put a match to the rubbish skip by the garage doors.

'Kids,' he guessed. 'I smelled the smoke, ran round to see what was happening.'

By the time he reached the fire whoever'd started it had vanished. The fire was a feeble affair, smouldering refuse, nothing to get upset about, he'd put it out with a hose.

'How long were you gone?' asked the sergeant.

Five minutes, Walter reckoned.

Long enough for someone to slip into his office and help themselves to the keys?

He supposed so. By the time he got back they'd be safely upstairs. It looked as though they'd left by the balcony, dropped down into the garden and out into the riverside path.

Mrs Perrymede had made tea and was handing it round.

'You reckon this is friend Walker again, do you?' asked Calloway looking around for biscuits. Harry didn't keep biscuits.

'Could be, I suppose,' the copper continued. 'He's out on bail at the moment.'

'You're joking.'

The Chief Inspector ladled three spoons of sugar into his tea.

'Not at all.'

'But he's on a murder charge, you can't let a man out when he's in the middle of trying to kill someone.'

'Not murder: manslaughter.' He had his notebook out, checking his facts. 'Or driving without due care and attention, the CPS can't decide which to go for. A thousand pounds on his own surety, another thousand for a Miss Knight.'

'Yvonne,' said Harry. 'She's called Yvonne, she lives with him. I don't think she has what you'd call independent means. If she put up bail for him, it's his money not hers.'

'She signed the papers, that's all the court needs.'

'This man tried to kill me,' Harry repeated. 'He not only tried, he admitted it. He killed Pete Pattichis instead. It's either murder or attempted murder.'

'*Actus non facit reum nisi mens sit rea*, I'm afraid Mr Kapowski. As I'm sure you know from your own work.'

Oh God, Harry realized, he's one of those.

'An act does not itself constitute guilt unless the mind is guilty, Fowler versus Padget, 1798. No one as far as I know is claiming that Mr Walker intended to kill Mr Pattichis. Or you, for that matter, perhaps he just wanted to scare you a little. We don't even know for sure he was riding the bike.' He was enjoying himself now, lecturing the great Harry Kapowski on the basics of the criminal law. Something inside Harry snapped.

'This is because he's black, isn't it? You've been told to lay off him because he's black, because he knows how to make a noise and claim police harassment, judicial bias, all that stuff.'

Calloway just smiled, letting Harry listen to the echo of his own words.

'Come come,' he said finally. 'I thought we were meant to be the racist pigs around here.'

As soon as the police had left Harry phoned Miranda and asked if he could move in with her for a few days.

'Is this a proposal, Kapowski?'

'Just a cry for help.'

'Most psychiatrists agree attention seeking is best ignored.'

In the background he could hear Roger Carlisle and Robert Kettle arguing. Harry told her what had happened.

'The excuses men dream up,' she said drily.

'I'm afraid this isn't a joke any more,' said Harry.

'I know, Harry. You have to remember I'm only twenty-five, I don't have the vocabulary to verbalize real emotion yet. I feel things, but it's not part of my self-image to show them, so I hide behind a sense of humour. I have to be at Heathrow in an hour, I'll leave a key on your desk. This is just while I'm away, remember, in case you're getting any ideas.'

'That's fine,' said Harry. 'Thanks.'

'Not at all. I like crises. Give me any kind of disaster – birds with broken wings, punctures, abscesses of the inner ear, central heating breakdowns, unexpected guests, drug overdoses, bodies in car boots, I promise I won't even blink. It's normal life I can't handle.'

'Where are you staying in Derry?'

'The Everglades.'

She realized people in the office were watching her, Ray looking over the top of his newspaper, Joan pretending to water a pot-plant, eyes diverted, ears flapping.

'I'm late, I'd better go, Harry.'

'I'll call you tonight.'

'If you want,' said Miranda.

The thing about Miranda, Harry was beginning to realize, was that when she said something like that she meant it, exactly and literally. There weren't any undertones or overtones: the woman was entirely and unnervingly straightforward.

Mrs Perrymede had begun the big clear-up, swabbing the walls, moving the furniture back in place, constructing piles of papers and clothing and crockery in the middle of the room for Harry to sort through. The blitz had been worse, she told him, during the blitz people lost everything.

'And not just because of the Germans. People used to go out thieving during the blackouts, a villain's paradise. And afterwards, there was always a lot of looting after a raid. The poor stealing from the poor. Shocking.'

Harry wasn't in the mood for conversation. He picked up his teacup and went and stood by the window and looked out at the Thames, wondering if he should go and see Pigfoot. Normally he had a simple rule when he was threatened: find out who it is and go to see them, talk about it. In Ulster, in New York, in Central America it usually worked.

In Brixton he wasn't too sure, they played by funny rules down there. Not just Brixton – whole areas of South London seemed to be turning into an urban Afghanistan. Illegality had become the norm: everyone stole their electricity, their furniture, their cars and TV sets, aborted on their HP, dealt drugs, fiddled their social security. Harry knew an estate in Wandsworth where the ten-year-olds ran their own home-shopping scam: you cut a picture of a particular brand of camera or video recorder out of a magazine, gave it to the kids, and they went out and stole one for you. Pigfoot had told Harry that in Brixton people buy so much stolen stuff that they often pay more for it than they would in the shops, you can go out and buy a video in Dixons and take it round the corner to a pub, say it fell off the back of a lorry and get fifty quid more than it cost you.

'They don't talk about the war like that now, mind you,' Mrs Perrymede continued, tearing a dustbin liner off the roll. 'All you hear about now is Flannagan and Allan and singsongs on the Underground. They make the blitz like a Max Bygraves concert. Wasn't like that at all.' She picked a waterlogged Walkman out of the sink. 'What do you want me to do with this?'

'Chuck it,' said Harry.

He decided to take the risk. He had to be back at Television Centre by three for a General Election conference. Which left him two hours to drive down to Brixton, see Pigfoot, and then get back across town to Shepherd's Bush. He picked up the phone.

'He's not here,' Yvonne began, shouting above the shit music.

'I don't give a fuck if he is or isn't, Yvonne,' said Harry. 'Just tell him to be in the Mason's Arms in thirty-five minutes. You own a watch?'

Of course Yvonne owned a watch. Yvonne would have something Swiss and showy on her wrist, a fake Cartier on a gold chain round her neck, and probably something else on a thong round her ankle. Failing that there was a gold and smoke-glass wall clock in the hall, a hideous thing about the size of a cabin trunk which played Three Blind Mice on tin chimes every twenty-six minutes.

'What time do you make it now?' asked Harry.

Yvonne made it different times by different clocks.

'The one on your wrist,' Harry suggested.

'Half past twelve.'

'OK. Then tell him I'll be in the Mason's Arms at five past one. Not five past two or five to five, five past one. You got that?'

He rang off without waiting for her reply and switched on the answering machine.

12

THE MASON'S ARMS WAS a mixed pub, three parts black to one part Irish, with a leavening of downwardly mobile white middle-class urban misfits. There was a long mahogany bar backed by mirrors, a glass display cabinet containing a half-empty tray of shepherd's pie, two cellophane-wrapped sausage rolls and a twig of plastic parsley, marble-topped tables and vinyl-covered stools with wrought-iron legs, a pool table and a line of noisy game machines. A dozen lunchtime drinkers sat reading the *Sun* and the *Sporting Life* and watching Newmarket on the wall-mounted TV, the colour turned up high so the sky looked orange and the grass purple. At the far end, beside the jukebox, four fat girls were smoking roll-ups, bovva-gear punks in Doc Martens and tight cotton trousers, shirt tails hanging out under their black leather jackets. The air smelled of disinfectant and tobacco and stale beer.

There was no sign of Pigfoot. Harry checked the Gents, then bought a pint of Guinness, sat down at a corner table and pretended to watch TV while he tried to work out what to say to him. It was the violence of what was happening that was worrying him – not just the danger of it, but how unlike the man it was. He never looked on Pigfoot as that kind of villain. The man liked money and style and his reputation; he stole, dealt, fenced, pimped, bribed, bounced cheques, borrowed people's cars and wrecked them, slept with their wives and daughters. But he didn't seem the killing kind, not unless he got drunk and hit someone, or if someone made what he took to be a pass at Yvonne.

The bar was noisy but not with conversation, just the thudding bass of the jukebox, the electronic bleeps of the game machines and the excitable commentary from the TV.

'He's not coming.'

Harry looked up. Yvonne was behind him, all five eleven of her, high heels and braided hair, a wide toothpaste grin on her face, her body wrapped in a skin-tight purple wrap that stopped three inches below her crotch. She had a hell of a body, Yvonne, long legs and a thin waist and big cheerful breasts. She was alone.

'If you were in less of a hurry to hang up I'd have told you. He's in Luton, gone to see his aunt.'

'He has?' said Harry with mock innocence. 'When did he go?'

'Saturday morning.' She sat down on a stool, legs apart, and leaned forward to help herself to one of his cigarettes. 'You buying drinks, honky, or do I have to brew my own?'

He bought her a vodka and coke from the bar.

'Is this a real aunt?'

'You want blood tests?'

'The police may. He's going to need a hell of an alibi.'

'For what?'

'Someone trashed my flat on Saturday evening, went to a lot of trouble over it. They didn't steal anything, they just dismantled the place. Before they left they stuck a pig's trotter on my bed.'

'Like in *The Godfather*?' Yvonne giggled. 'Wait till I tell him. *The Godfather*'s his favourite movie, that and *Conan the Barbarian*; he must have watched it fifty times. But it can't have been him put it there. He phoned me from Luton Saturday evening, been there all day.'

'Maybe he got someone else to do it for him.'

Yvonne bit at the varnish on her fingernail, studied it, bit again.

'Could be. But I don't reckon. He thought up a stunt like that, he'd want to do it himself. Someone else did it, they might screw up – you know how he is.'

'When's he getting back?' asked Harry.

Yvonne shrugged her shoulders.

'Soon as he's finished his business.'

'Get him to call me, will you?'

He knocked back the dregs of his Guinness.

'You still living at the same place?' she asked, eyes down, picking at her nail varnish.

'If I'm not there he can leave a message on the answering machine. Or he can get me at the BBC.'

'Doesn't answer my question,' said Yvonne. 'Sounds to me as if you might be moving out. You got yourself a woman yet, Kapowski? Someone don't mind you sharing their bed for a few days?'

'For fuck's sake,' said Harry. He put his notebook in his pocket.

Yvonne picked a lump of ice out of her glass and crunched it between her back teeth.

'Listen,' said Harry. 'I don't know what Pigfoot's trying to prove, but whatever it is tell him I'm happy to talk to him about it.'

'Sure. I'll tell him to call you. You want my opinion, he's sore but he's not that sore.'

Harry looked at her, wondering if he should believe her. Yvonne stared straight back, eyeball to eyeball. No clues.

Harry loathed Shepherd's Bush. Neither city centre nor suburb, a dreary square mile of brick terraces and junk yards and worn-out corner pubs that had stubbornly withstood the gentrification of its neighbours. Grimy For Sale signs shared the tiny gardens with dirty laurel bushes and anaemic hydrangeas. The nearest Shepherd's Bush ever came to a sheep was the revolving spit of hot gristle that dribbled fat into tin trays behind the counters of the Greek cafés on the Uxbridge Road. Eventually the place would vanish like Acre under the midden of its own litter, and in years to come archaeologists would pore over their troves of crisp packets and burger cartons and used condoms, trying to deduce who it was lived here. And why.

Harry looked in his mirror. The green Vauxhall van that had been behind him since he left Brixton was still there, hanging three cars back in the traffic. The concrete and glass barrel of TV Centre loomed to his left. In the thirty odd years since it was built, the BBC building had grown like a malignant tumour, throwing up wings and spurs, portacabins and multi-storey car parks, marching inexorably north towards the Westway and the mirror-glass monstrosity of the new Corporate Headquarters. Harry slowed at the entrance, then changed his mind and drove on up Wood Lane to the motorway flyover and turned right up the slipway heading back into central London. He checked his mirror again. The Vauxhall had gone. He doubled back at the first roundabout and retraced his route to TV Centre.

Over two hundred people were standing around in studio TC7 waiting to be briefed on the final run-in to the election. Producers, directors, researchers, reporters, technical managers, secretaries and PAs and graphic designers, a whole army preparing itself for battle. Some were already working on the campaign, others due to join in the coming days. Harry picked up a Fact-Pack folder from a table by the entrance and walked over to where Roger Carlisle was sitting at the end of a line of plastic chairs.

'I hear you got broken into,' said Roger.

Harry sat down. His leg was playing up again.

'Who told you that?'

'Miranda.'

'Did she tell you about the pig's foot?'

Roger let out a nervous laugh.

'What pig's foot?'

'Impaled on my headboard.'

Roger relished emergencies. He didn't wallow in them, he didn't indulge in mock bravado, he worked out what could be done and did it, fast and with a minimum of fuss. Harry told him about his conversations with Calloway and his meeting with Yvonne.

'OK,' Roger began. 'Assume it's Walker. We can try for an injunction against him but I doubt it would work. I'll talk to the lawyers. I'll also talk to Calloway, put his head on the line. Did he offer you protection?'

Harry said he had but he didn't want it. Partly a gut reaction, partly because he didn't fancy being followed round town by gumshoes from the Met for the next couple of months. Though remembering the green Vauxhall it also occurred to him that he might be getting it whether he wanted it or not.

'Anyway, you know what coppers are like – hate students, hate blacks, hate politicians, hate journalists – if someone like me gets worked over by a big black man they kill two birds with one stone, the black goes down and the journalist ends up in hospital. The Met would be out celebrating for a week.'

Roger didn't argue with him.

'It's up to you, Harry. Meanwhile you need somewhere to live. I'll give Margaret a call, you can have the spare room for the time being.'

'Thanks,' said Harry cautiously. He was going to have to tell him about Miranda eventually, but not yet. 'I'll think about it.'

He didn't need to. Roger might be all heart, but his wife was all bowel, a mountainous earth-mother who ran their Greenwich household like a transvestite major-domo, looked after six children and their innumerable pets, baked, knitted, ironed Roger's shirts, dug the garden, ran the Community Association and the Girl Guides and the PTA, published a Greenpeace newsletter, and somehow found time in between to write a succession of obscure books on medieval herbal medicine. He might as well move in to London zoo.

The meeting was about to come to order, senior executives and programme editors taking their seats on an improvised rostrum, a sound-man checking mikes.

'Are you up there or down here?' Harry asked Roger.

'With the politbureau, I'm afraid.' He gathered up his papers. 'I'll talk to you afterwards.'

Harry opened his Fact-Pack. On top was an introductory essay by Tony Mangan on the Representation of the People Act and the BBC's Standing Instructions on the Interviewing of Politicians, then page after page of who-does-what and who-answers-to-whom, phone numbers, outside broadcast locations, the dos and donts of presenting opinion polls, an idiot's guide to the computerized results and graphic operations.

There was a class of producer for whom general elections were the peak of their careers. Ex-studio directors, mostly, technology junkies who judged the success of a programme by the number of satellite lines and microwave feeds they'd managed to get into the mixer desk. These men (all men) called telephones two-way audio links and blackboards manual systems indicators; they wore short-sleeved cotton shirts with pens and Hi-lighters in their top pockets, just like the guys at NASA, and said 'affirmative' instead of 'yes' and 'check' when they meant 'OK'. There were three of them on the top table, each with a wad of computer printouts in case someone wanted to know further details of the multiplexers at the Manchester switching centre.

None of the audience gave a fig about microwave

links or multiplexers. This was church again, sermons and lessons, time to sit back and think about life or finish the Quick Crossword in the *Evening Standard*. What Harry wanted to know was where he'd been posted, and when. He thumbed through his papers, checking names. Robert Kettle was off to Cardiff. He'd like that, a nice room in the Post House, his own desk in the newsroom, a welcoming drink from Controller Wales. Wales didn't need him, of course, they were well able to handle these things on their own, but London didn't trust the regions, they wanted familiar voices at the far end of talkback.

Tony Mangan was at the microphone now, explaining the etiquette for granting airtime to minor parties. Harry ploughed on through his papers until he found a page headed Reporters, and ran his finger down the list of names. Isherwood R., Jenkinson C., Jessell D., Johnson I., Kapowski H.

General Pool, as of 22 November. Not Brentwood and Ongar or Staffordshire South East or Oldham Central: General Pool.

November 22 was Wednesday, two days away.

General Pool meant whatever they wanted it to mean. Stand-in for sick colleagues, fire-man on a big story, daily reports on the road with party leaders.

'Do you need the bed?' Roger asked him afterwards. The meeting was breaking up, the congregation melting away.

'Thanks but no thanks.' Harry rubbed at his leg, trying to ease the cramps. 'Or not yet.'

Tony Mangan came over to join them.

'What's so special about Wednesday?' Harry demanded.

'Don't ask me,' said Tony, 'ask the computer. Did you have something else planned?'

'I'm washing my hair.'

'The safest place you could be at this moment,' said

Roger, 'is out on the road with the politicians. It's crawling with policemen out there.'

Harry looked at Mangan, the grey suit, the sober spectacles, white shirt and tie, a slight bulge in his jacket pocket – he must be the only man in the building who still carried a handkerchief, ironed by his wife. She probably ironed his hair while she was at it, scrubbed his neck, dusted his ears, washed his arse with Harpic.

'So which part of the General Pool are you dropping me in?'

Mangan took out the handkerchief and wiped the lenses of his glasses.

'Do you have any preferences?'

'Webb,' said Harry. 'I'd like to do a film about Ben Webb.'

Mangan thought for a moment.

'OK. Why not?'

13

HARRY PHONED THE Labour party headquarters in Walworth Road to get a copy of Ben's campaign itinerary, and asked Phyllis to run a check with the film and tape libraries to see what they had in the way of archive footage and interviews. He rather liked the idea of making an old-fashioned political film again. No lawyers, no court transcripts, no more shopping bags of dog-eared letters and photographs and disintegrating newspaper cuttings, no more Pigfoot Walkers and Sean Walshes and Terry Pattichises. Not for at least two weeks.

Except Terry, he wasn't ready to let go of Terry yet.

He spent twenty minutes talking to Roger Carlisle about the case. Roger wanted him to drop it. He had thirty other stories in his in-tray; Terry didn't want to be saved; so far Harry had come up with nothing concrete, the most he could offer was a feeling that things had tied up too cleanly, as though it suited everyone.

'As far as Ben Webb's concerned this is a General Election campaign, not the Old Bailey or the gossip pages of *Private Eye*,' Roger instructed him. 'For the next week you're not working for me, you're working for Tony Mangan.'

Harry had all the time in the world for Roger but the man could be a pompous bore at times. Harry looked at the books on the shelf behind his desk. Harold

Wilson's *The Final Term*, Peter Rowland's *Lloyd George*, Robert Rhodes James on J. C. C. Davidson, Gerald Kaufman on Israel. Every programme editor had a shelf like that in his office, lined with free copies of political tracts and memoirs. Publishers sent them out by the container, month after month. No one ever read them, no one ever mentioned them in a broadcast, people just scattered them around their offices to add a bit of gravitas, or sold them on to bookshops. Except Roger, Roger would have read them.

'Yes. Sir,' said Harry.

And that was that. Tuesday to get his thoughts together, organize some laundry, clear his desk; on Wednesday he'd be on the road. Eight days later the nation would decide.

He wondered who they'd give him as a director. Some twenty-three-year-old squeaky-clean kid from *Newsnight* in a bankers' suit, with glasses and short hair and an MA in political science from Edinburgh or Bristol or the Manchester Business School. They turned those guys out like battery hens these days, efficient little automatons, computer-literate, Q-tips in their washbags, passionate as breeze-blocks. They switched to mineral water after their second glass of wine, went to bed early, put off having their first orgasms until their careers were well established. There's nothing quite as loathsome as the generation after your own.

Ben Webb's schedule had arrived over the office fax. His itinerary said a lot about Labour's strategy. Walworth Road knew they couldn't hope to gain seats in the grazing lands of the Tory fat-stock – the South West, or East Anglia, or the Home Counties. Nor did it matter – if things went well elsewhere they could do without them. Scotland and the North-East were fairly safe. The crucial battlegrounds were London, the Midlands and the North-West, a belt of marginal constituencies running diagonally across the country from

Merseyside to the Thames. And that was where Ben was spending most of the next week. Rochdale, Bolton, Ellesmere Port, Wolverhampton, Derby, Birmingham, Coventry, Luton, Slough – his itinerary read like a check-list of places no one goes to for pleasure. Harry could see them all in his mind's eye, acres of grimy pedestrian precincts, mile upon mile of Hallmark stationers and Sainsbury's and Building Societies. Whatever happened to variety?

Miranda's key was in an envelope on his desk with Personal written across the top left hand corner and a note inside telling him how to work the gas geyser and where to find clean towels, very straightforward and practical. He put the note in his pocket and rang his answering machine at Nine Elms Lane to see if there were any messages. There weren't. He spent the next hour reading up on Ben Webb and the election. The opinion polls in that morning's papers were showing a close race, only two points between Labour and the Tories, with over twenty per cent of the electorate undecided. Anyone's race, with a strong chance of a hung Parliament. By six o'clock the office was almost empty. Harry packed up his papers and headed for the BBC Club. He wasn't ready for Marylebone yet.

The Club was on the fourth floor and divided into two bars. The first was a large split-level lounge giving on to a rooftop patio, big enough to accommodate the bulk of casual lunchtime and early evening drinkers. Harry walked through into a smaller room, known affectionately as the Home of Lost Causes, where the serious customers gathered, career-stunted know-alls and under-employed poseurs who felt their talents ignored by their masters. *Not Proven* had its own representative in residence in the person of Robert Kettle. The director was perched on a plush-topped high stool against the end wall, one hand in the back pocket of his jeans, the other clasping a glass of lager, telling a middle-aged production manager from Light Entertainment why John Cleese was an overrated comic, but nowhere near as overrated as Tony Hancock. The production manager was nodding but not listening, getting an anecdote organized in his head for when Robert stopped talking.

Harry fancied a chat with Robert, the way he sometimes felt like settling down to watch junk TV: tank yourself up on alcohol, find a comfortable seat, put the brain in neutral and float away on a warm tide of second-hand ideas and third-hand emotions. After a couple of hours the most banal aspects of reality seemed fresh and exciting.

As Harry approached, a once-pretty make-up supervisor, bleary with drink, grabbed the production manager by the arm and pulled him off to a corner table to join someone's leaving party. Harry took his empty stool.

'Cardiff, eh, Bobby? How come you manage to get all the best trips?'

Robert took the compliment calmly.

'Friends in the right places. What about you?'

'Cap D'Antibes. They want a European perspective on things.'

'You're serious?'

'No. Six days following Ben Webb around by the bootstraps. What are you drinking?'

Harry never bought the drink. Halfway across the room on his way to the bar he heard Archie Bain's voice coming from the television in the corner, and looked up at the screen. Archie was a gamekeeper turned poacher, a TV reporter who had gone into politics, now a Labour MP, talking to Jeremy Paxman about the party's prospects in Scotland. Harry'd known Archie since his time in Glasgow, ten years ago, when they'd worked together on the local news.

The interview ended. Harry grabbed an internal

phone, rang the studio gallery and asked if it had been live. It had. He ran out of the bar and took the lift to reception. Archie was getting into his taxi. Harry got in beside him.

'Kapowski! Get the fuck out of here, will you?'

A big Glasgow grin. Harry settled back in the seat. The cab drove down the ramp and out into Wood Lane.

'Where are we going, big fella?'

Archie got a pack of Embassy out of his raincoat pocket. He wasn't just big, he was enormous, eighteen stone, all of it alive with energy.

'Heathrow, sunshine. The delights of the British Airways eight o'clock Shuttle. You coming for the ride?'

'Why not,' said Harry, and took a cigarette.

'Fucking ridiculous – there's a perfectly good studio in Glasgow, Paxman's people are perfectly happy for me to talk to him down the line, but Walworth Road won't have it, has to be face to face. Some PR fart in a BMW tells them down-the-line interviews have an alienating effect on the viewer. Six hours' travelling for four minutes on air blabbing on about devolution. How's yourself, Kapowski? You in on this circus too?'

'On the fringes, Archie.'

'Lucky bastard.'

The polls suggested that Labour candidates would sweep the carpet north of the border. Archie already had a majority of over fifteen thousand in his own constituency, and hoped to add another five next week. Harry asked him how the campaign was going.

'In Scotland? Unreal, pal. Scots Tories are an endangered species, they're thinking of putting a preservation order on them. It's between us and the bloody Nats, and even that's not much of a contest.'

'They going to give you a job after next Thursday?'

Archie coughed on his cigarette at the idea.

'Me? In government? You must be fucking joking "Dear Archibald,"' he mimicked. ' "I am instructed by the Minister to offer you the post of parliamentary private secretary to the parliamentary under-secretary of state for defence procurement. Although the job is not salaried as such, it provides a useful opportunity for a back-bench MP to gain experience . . ." – they actually write letters like that, Harry, can you believe it? And the buggers fall for it, sign on as bag-carriers to some junior bloody minister because they think that's the way to get on. And then they find out the why. The why is that the moment you become a PPS you have to shut up and toe the party line. Which is not my style, Harry boy, as you well know. All of which supposes we win, by the way, which the way England looks is by no means a bygone conclusion. You found yourself a wife yet?'

'Still interviewing the candidates,' said Harry.

'Anyone you fancy?'

'Mmm.'

'She fancy you?'

'The interview's still in progress.'

They were in the Goldhawk Road now, heading West for Hogarth roundabout and the M4.

Archie butted his Embassy and lit up another.

'You really coming all the way to Heathrow with me?'

'They told me to make sure you were out the country by midnight, I'm not to let you out of my sight until you're on the plane.'

'Are you telling me this isn't simply a social call?'

'It is and it isn't.'

'What's the isn't?'

'I'm making a film about Ben Webb.'

'And?'

'I wanted to ask you some questions about him.'

'You mean you want dirt on him?' Archie laughed. 'There isn't any. At least not until after the vote.'

They were on the motorway now, the cab rattling up to sixty in the outside lane.

'Not dirt,' said Harry. 'Politics. I want to know how he's got so far so fast.'

'Talent,' said Archie sarcastically. 'Talent, charisma, a good brain and a cute eye. End quote.'

'And friends?'

'That too. Christ, Harry, we all need a few pals in his business, there's nothing sinister about it. If you're asking me if Ben's been groomed, of course he bloody has. Old men who never quite made it to the top, passing on a few tips of the trade – it happens in any party. Happens in the BBC too, for that matter.' He studied the end of his cigarette. 'Is this about something specific?'

'It could be.'

'Are you going to tell me what?'

Harry hesitated. Archie wasn't a journalist any more. He still wrote for the papers, did the chat shows when they wanted a bit of political iconoclasm, wrote the occasional book. But he was a Labour party man, in the middle of a finely balanced election campaign, a campaign that could easily be derailed by a political scandal.

'I'm thinking about it, Archie. Do you like Ben?'

'Of course not. I told you, he's talented.'

So was Archie, but he had too many appetites and too little ambition, didn't take himself seriously enough to be a successful politician.

'That aside.'

'There are worse.'

'Do you think he's straight?'

'Relatively. Which isn't necessarily a compliment – you could say the same of Major. Am I to assume that you don't?'

Which was when Harry decided to tell him the story.

'So where's the dirt on Ben in all that?' asked Archie when he'd finished. There was disappointment in his voice. 'Willie Walpole may have pulled a few strings to make sure an innocent bystander didn't get his face dragged through the courts. Good on him. I thought you had some real gossip for me.'

'I know,' said Harry. 'It's just an odd coincidence that two ghosts from my past should land in simultaneously. First Pigfoot, then Ben and Angela.'

'And that's the best you can come up with, eh?' Archie sighed. 'God, conspiracy theories aren't what they used to be. You might at least throw in a Libyan connection.'

'It's early days,' said Harry.

The cab had reached Heathrow. Archie heaved himself out on to the pavement, pushed through the doors into the Terminal, glanced up at the departures board and cursed. Glasgow was delayed by an air-traffic controllers' work-to-rule. He grabbed Harry by the lapels.

'You fixed this, didn't you, you fucker.'

'I have friends too, Archie. What are you drinking?'

They waited upstairs in the bar with a hundred tired and grey-faced Scots businessmen, shoulder to shoulder under the low ceiling, briefcases at their feet, eyeing the monitor in the corner, waiting for news.

'Have you no home to go to, Kapowski?' asked Archie as Harry handed him a double whisky and a chaser. 'What about this wife-to-be? Does she have a name?'

'Miranda.'

Archie choked on his whisky.

'Miranda? Jesus!'

He couldn't stop laughing. Harry looked at him helplessly, said nothing.

'It's that bad?'

'Afraid so,' said Harry shyly.

'Miranda,' Archie repeated. 'You poor bastard. Sounds like a Japanese car – the Honda Miranda. How long's this been going on?'

'Three days.'

Archie dried his tie on the back of his hand.

'Three whole days? Get to fuck, will you?'

The bar was solid now: orders had to be shouted, glasses passed back over the heads of the other drinkers. Archie bought another round, four pints and four doublers this time to cut down on the queuing. British Airways announced a further delay. They carried their drinks out into the main concourse and sat down on the stairs.

'So what are you going to say about Ben in this film?' asked Archie.

'There's not a lot you can say – the image seems pretty watertight. You got any ideas?'

Archie took a sip of whisky and rinsed it round his gums.

'Politically? He's a cute whore, that one. His trick is to appear to take everyone seriously, never dismisses you out of hand. He makes sure you know he's listened to what you have to say, nods to show he's thinking about it, so that when he does venture an opinion you're left with the impression he's been through all the arguments carefully and dispassionately. Unlike most of us who just sound off our prejudices at the nearest vertical object.'

'Still doesn't explain how he managed it so fast.'

'More conspiracy theory, eh?' said Archie.

'No, just a question.'

'William Pitt was seventeen when he was made Chancellor of the Exchequer. Or thereabouts.'

'He didn't have to get elected to the National Executive along the way.'

'Ach, that's no problem. That's just a question of being in the right place at the right time. You know why I think Ben's done so well? Looks. Name me three Labour front benchers who are attractive to women.'

Harry thought about it, and couldn't.

'Always been our bloody trouble. We're an over-weight, potato-faced, bag-eyed, balding lot who sleep in our suits.'

By nine o'clock both of them were well oiled.

'Tell me something, Archie,' said Harry a little uncertainly. 'How would Willie Walpole have gone about keeping Ben out of the limelight?'

'You still on about that, pal? Easy. You or I would do the obvious, wouldn't we, take a look in our address book and see if we could find a few strings to pull. But then we're new on the block. But someone like Willie wouldn't need to bother with that crap, begging favours off police commissioners and newspaper editors. Willie and his ilk aren't friends with the system, they're part of it.'

Harry emptied his glass. He was drunk, he realized, out of training for this kind of session. The tannoy was calling the Glasgow flight.

'Conspiracy theories again?'

Archie got to his feet.

'Of course, pal. If the facts don't make sense, make up a conspiracy theory. Preferably one that can't be proved or disproved. But if you're planning to put it on air before the election, do me a favour and make sure it's a Tory conspiracy. I'm not sure we could cope with one on our side this week.'

The taxi dropped him at the corner of Paddington Street and Marylebone High Street. He swayed slightly as he cut down the narrow entry beside the park, running his hand along the iron railings, the light from the street lamps flickering through the trees; he stopped to search his case and pockets for Miranda's keys, found them and swung open the little gate that led into the dank courtyard of number forty-five.

The flat was on the third floor, and there was no lift, just a stone-flagged staircase. He was two hundred yards

143

from the grand terraces of Harley Street, but this was artisan territory, a warren of nondescript Edwardian barracks tucked out of sight of the main roads. The climb left him breathless, and he paused for a moment before unlocking the door, checking through the letter-box to see if there was a light on. The place was in darkness.

He went into the kitchen first, drank two glasses of cold water and turned on the electric kettle. It took him some time to find a mug and a jar of instant coffee. There were baked beans in the cupboard, frozen burgers and peas in the fridge, a half loaf of white bread in the bin. Women weren't meant to eat this way nowadays, they were meant to live off bean-curd and seaweed and cottage cheese. He made himself a jam sandwich and started thumbing through the pile of circulars and utility bills stacked behind the pot-plants. There was a bank statement: Miranda had a balance of £178 with the National Westminster Bank in Cavendish Square, most of which would be swallowed by standing orders by the end of the month. A Visa statement showed two pur-chases: £12 at Boots the Chemist, £16.50 for petrol at a filling station in Baker Street. Dull stuff.

Next he went to work on the rest of the flat, looking for nothing in particular, simply curious. The sitting room yielded a letter from Miranda's mother ('The Wilkinsons are in Teneriffe for two weeks, your father is thinking of changing the Renault . . .'), and a bottle of duty free Grand Marnier. He took it into the kitchen, looked for glasses and couldn't find any, poured himself an inch in the bottom of a jam-jar, and topped up the bottle with tap water. Putting the bottle back on the bookcase he knocked over his coffee, and spent ten minutes blearily scrubbing the stain off the beige carpet. The kitchen clock said half past eleven: it was time for bed.

It was only when he turned out the sitting room light

that he noticed the red Message Received light on the answering machine and remembered that he hadn't phoned Miranda. Blame it on the hotel, he decided: I phoned but they said you were out.

Not that Miranda would bother with that shit: in his position she'd simply say she'd got drunk, and forgotten.

14

THE SOUND OF TRAFFIC woke him. He opened his eyes slowly, feeling head-sore and foul breathed, wanting to go back to sleep, knowing he wouldn't; trying to engage his brain, work out where he was and why. The faded patched-up hand-me-down curtains were closed, billowing gently in the breeze, a line of grey light seeping through the join and round the edges.

He hadn't closed the curtains last night. There had been no draft to billow them, either: the window had been shut. He'd gone to sleep with the radio on: it was silent now, the glowing green numerals of its clock showing ten to nine. He hadn't folded his clothes, or put them in a neat pile on the chair.

As he turned and raised himself on his elbow, his body met soft warm flesh. Miranda was sleeping silently beside him, hunched in a foetal curl, one hand holding the duvet over her face.

He eased himself gently off the bed, gathered up his clothes and slipped out. He dressed in the kitchen, collected his wallet and keys from the kitchen table, tiptoed across the hall and let himself out.

In Marylebone High Street the day had already begun. Some shops were open, others pushing up their shutters, the fishmonger in Paddington Street sluicing down his slabs, the greengrocer stacking up boxes of apples and satsumas on the pavement. A steady stream of pedestrians flowed south towards Oxford Street. The weather had cleared, bringing blue skies and a cold wind from the north, the London air almost fresh after it's nightly detox.

He bought croissants at the French patisserie, fresh orange juice, Greek yoghurt, bacon, sausages, a melon and a bunch of freesias from the over-priced Lebanese delicatessen next door, and an armful of morning papers from the newsagents.

Miranda was still asleep when he got back. He put the croissants in the oven to warm, laid breakfast, made himself a cup of coffee and set to work on the papers. The Tories were accusing Labour of trimming their education policies to placate the Muslim vote. Harry could believe it. The SNP were claiming widespread defections from the Liberal Democrats in Scotland: he believed that too. A man with one leg had drowned while trying to swim the English Channel to raise money for charity.

Poor Miranda. He wondered what had gone wrong in Ulster this time. Scruples, he guessed – once more and she'll get herself eliminated for three refusals. The fiasco couldn't have taken long: she'd have landed in Belfast early afternoon, picked up a car and driven seventy miles across the Sperrins to Derry, turned straight round in time to get the last flight of the day home to Heathrow.

'What's all the guilt-geld about?'

She was standing in the kitchen door in a cotton nightdress, rubbing her eyes and nodding towards the freesias.

'Love,' said Harry.

'Bullshit. You've been misbehaving, haven't you.' She gave him a sleepy kiss on the forehead, sat down and poured herself an orange juice. 'Who with, Angela Webb?'

'A piss-head called Archie Bain. I was worried about

you. I tried phoning the hotel all evening. You weren't there.'

'More bullshit, I suspect. You can't have been that worried – if you were really worried you'd have stayed awake a little longer. I was home by half past twelve. The perfect end to a perfect day – you have my keys. Fortunately you'd also forgotten to close the front door. I thought you wanted to stay here because it was safe. You're lucky Pigfoot didn't call by.'

'I'm sorry,' said Harry.

'Not at all. Women love clearing up after drunks, it satisfies our need to care and nurture.'

Harry put on the kettle and got the croissants out of the oven. Miranda picked up the *Guardian*.

'What happened?' he asked her.

'Didn't you hear?' She kept turning the pages, scanning headlines, looking for something. 'It must be in here somewhere.'

'What must be?'

'If this happened in England they'd put it on the front page. Walsh did a deal. Names, people, times and places. In return for which he gets to go and live in New Zealand or Mexico or somewhere. His own father's disowned him.' She put down the paper. 'No one told me what the dropout rate was in this business, it's worse than bloody evening classes. So what's been happening in the big city while I've been away?'

Harry told her about his conversations with Yvonne and the police.

'When do they think it happened?' she asked.

'Saturday evening. Just after we left.'

She brushed the croissant crumbs off her lips and poured herself more orange juice.

'And you reckon it was Pigfoot?'

'You tell me. Who the hell else is it likely to be?'

'Angela, of course. She knew you'd be out. I'm joking, by the way. How long are you intending to stay?'

148

Harry hadn't a clue, he hadn't thought that far ahead.

'You're not meant to do things this way, you know,' she reproached him. 'You're meant to keep taking me out for a few weeks, buy me dinners, then maybe suggest a weekend in the country, and if that works out OK we go on holiday together. Then you ask me to marry you, and I say no, let's try living together for a while, see how it works out. Then I move in with you, not the other way round.'

'Will you marry me?' asked Harry.

'Of course not, don't be ridiculous. You can have three days, on approval. Separate toothbrushes, and if I want you to move on to the sofa at any stage you do so. Why aren't you at work, by the way?'

'Condemned man's last breakfast. I start on the election campaign tomorrow.'

'No more Terry Pattichis?'

'I'm doing a film on Ben Webb.'

Miranda laughed.

'You cunning bugger. Can I come too?'

'As what?'

She grinned.

'Director.'

Up to that moment the thought hadn't crossed Harry's mind.

'You've never directed a film in your life,' he objected.

'I could learn.'

They moved through to the bedroom, and Miranda started to get dressed. Harry wondered what she would be like to work with. Murder, he decided. You had to believe in the system to some extent to get things done. You could rebel, argue, cheat, bluff, bully, lie: but deep down you had to keep to the faith. Harry took risks all the time, but they were calculated risks, and he never took them without knowing what he'd do if things went wrong. If he talked to the IRA, or put a hidden microphone on someone, or pretended not to be a television reporter, he cleared it first. He might be vague in his intentions and justify what he did afterwards on the grounds of operational necessity, but he made sure he was covered. Miranda only answered to herself.

'Have you told Roger about Walsh yet?'

She was sitting on the edge of the bed now, putting on her plimsoles.

'No. I suppose I should.'

She rang the office from the phone in the sitting room. Harry was surprised at her nervousness, the way she doodled on an old envelope while she made the call. He could hear Roger Carlisle's voice at the far end, very straightforward and matter of fact. After they'd talked for a couple of minutes she suddenly covered the mouthpiece with her hand.

'He wants to talk to you, Harry.'

Roger wasn't supposed to know Harry was there. Harry hadn't told him, nor had Miranda. He took the phone.

'How the hell did you know where I was?' he demanded.

'Years of training,' said Roger. 'Tony Mangan's office have been looking for you. They've got a director for the Webb film.'

'Who?'

'Robert Kettle.'

Harry's eyes flew to heaven.

'Shit. I thought he was going to Cardiff.'

'Me too. Cardiff decided they didn't need him.'

'Shit,' he repeated. 'Where is he?'

'Here, he got in about ten minutes ago. What's the matter? You guys have worked together enough times before.'

'That's exactly the point.'

Harry had worked with Robert a dozen times. It wasn't Robert's work that upset him, it was the prospect

150

of a week on the road with him, the smell of after-shave, the self-serving anecdotes, the man's chronic inability to differentiate between content and style. Robert's talent, such as it was, lay in pointing cameras, or rather telling people where to point them. That, and strutting the TV Director act around Groucho's and the Edinburgh Festival, anywhere where talking about programmes was rated higher than making them. You could trust him with the visuals, but that was as far as it went. He relied on researchers to do the groundwork, Harry to write the script, and then Robert would package it all together.

'Do you want to talk to him?' asked Roger.

'Not now,' said Harry. 'I'll be in after lunch.'

'What happened to this morning?'

'Annual leave, I'm owed seven weeks, you can dock it any time you want.'

Miranda and Harry walked together down to Oxford Circus to catch the Central Line. Harry had left his car at Television Centre the night before, and Miranda didn't approve of taking taxis. No reason, she just didn't. If Harry didn't want to do something he'd think of a reason, even if there wasn't one. Not Miranda.

Halfway down Upper Regent Street she slipped her arm into his.

'I thought you said you weren't coming in to the office this morning?'

'I wasn't. I changed my mind.'

They steered their way through the mid-morning crowds, the harikrishnas and language school pamphleteers and bag-laden West End shoppers. The clothing shops were full of Country Classics – used to be the other way round, people from the country used to try and look like Londoners, now all the townies want to look like Princess Anne.

'What's the worst mistake you've ever made,'

Miranda asked as they walked down the broken escalator to the Central Line platform. 'Professionally, I mean.'

Harry thought for a moment.

'I don't know. Most of them were stupid. I got caught out once by two people with the same name. We were chasing a guy called Bernie Wiggins who was pyramid-selling dry-cleaning franchises. We checked on him in the files and at Company House, he had a record a mile long. He wouldn't talk to us so we ran the story anyway, bales of evidence. Only it was a different Bernie Wiggins. Same name, same age, same business, both Rhodesian exiles. That cost the BBC a lot of money. And I flew all the way to Brazil one time to try and find a man who'd been dead for three years, not an easy call back to the office. But I suspect the really bad mistakes are the ones you don't know you've made, people who had a defence they couldn't use. Like they were in bed with someone else's wife at the time – the Long Black Veil syndrome.'

They decided to get off the tube a stop early to take a look at what had once been Latchkey's offices. Shepherd's Bush Green is a large triangle of flat and muddy grass, dotted with sycamore and limes and crossed by narrow asphalt paths. It's not really a park, though people sometimes take their mastiffs and Rottweilers there to crap; its main function is to act as a four-acre roundabout for the traffic which grinds three lanes deep along its perimeter. On the south side there's a rain-washed concrete shopping mall, a filling station and two blocks of high-rise council flats, on the west a pair of what used to be cinemas, one converted into a TV theatre for BBC Light Entertainment, the other a bingo and social club. The north side is made up of a succession of mucky brick Edwardian terraces, shops and fast-food outlets on the ground floor, flats and offices above.

They walked past the Spud-U-Like and the bookie's and the Job Centre, checking the numbers. Ten years before the shop below Latchkey had sold hardware and novelties, but the business had long since passed on, and its windows were block-boarded up and papered with pop posters and left-wing flyers. If you looked carefully at the brickwork on the second and third floors you could still make out the smoke-marks from the fire, but there was modern double-glazing in the frames now, and a new roof above. The sign by the bell said Greene and Willis, Insurance Brokers. Harry didn't ring, he was just curious.

The back entry was round the corner in Bulwer Street, a flaking wooden door in a brick wall topped with broken glass. The door was bolted. Harry pulled over a dustbin and climbed on top, balancing his weight against a lamppost until he could see over. A narrow alley strewn with rubbish led between two more walls to an iron fire escape. He wondered which way they'd brought Jo out, by the front door or down the fire escape. The front, probably, that's where the fire tenders would have been parked.

'Very stylish part of town,' he said, rubbing the palms of his hands together to remove the dirt. 'He knew what he was doing, our friend Jo. He could easily have set up shop in the middle of town, Covent Garden or Soho or someplace, got the interior designers in, smoked glass in the windows, audio-visual displays in the foyer, all that crap. The GLC would have picked up the tab, no questions asked. But out here looks better, down among the Real People, all very egalitarian.'

She gave him her Look. Miranda's Look could flatten a glass of beer at thirty paces.

'What's the matter, did I say something wrong?'

'It's so bloody easy, Harry,' she said pleasantly. 'Concentrate on the fuck-ups and you don't have to bother with the issues.'

They turned into Wood Lane and headed north towards the Kwikfit Exhaust depot and the railway bridge.

'What the hell, Latchkey's academic now. I'm off to Birmingham with Ben Webb in the morning.'

'You are, but I'm not. I'm working on Terry Pattichis.'

Harry looked at her.

'Says who?'

'Roger Carlisle.'

Roger told Joan to hold his calls, closed his office door behind him and perched himself on the corner of his desk. Miranda sat on the sofa, Harry standing behind her leaning against the bookcase.

'I thought you weren't interested in Terry any more,' said Harry.

Through the glass he could see Robert studying a map of Merseyside, *Good Food Guide* in hand. At least they'd eat well this week.

'I wasn't,' said Roger, 'not until the fifth floor called.' The fifth floor was where the mighty lived: director-general, managing director TV, the channel controllers, the secretary to the board of governors. 'They told me to drop it.'

They should have known better.

'Shit,' said Harry.

'Precisely.' Roger unwound a paperclip and started cleaning behind his nails. 'First, how did they know we were doing it; secondly why the hell were they interested, thirdly why do they want it stopped.'

'Who's this they?' asked Miranda.

'DG's office. I don't know where it came from before that. Who have you talked to about it?'

Harry shrugged.

'Inside the building or outside?'

'Either.'

He ran through the options.

'You, Miranda, the rest of the office. I mentioned it to Tony Mangan, I think, but I'm not even sure if I mentioned any names. I phoned Terry's solicitor, a woman called Catriona Clark. I had a drink with Archie Bain last night, but Archie's not the type to call in the heavy brigade. And I talked to Angela Webb on Saturday. I suppose it must have come from her.'

'Why did you go for Angela?' asked Roger. 'Why not Ben?'

'Because he fancies her,' Miranda explained.

'I didn't want to alarm him,' said Harry.

A word with Ben, a call to Broadcasting House, that sort of thing happened from time to time. Not often, but it happened, provided there was a good enough reason. Harry asked Roger if he'd been given any explanation.

'No, not really. I was asked to take it on trust.'

'And what did you say?'

'I said we weren't treating it as a priority, you were off on the election, I had someone else looking at it in their spare time, but only as a minor ingredient in a thing we were thinking of doing on the working of the Mental Health Act.' He allowed himself a little grin. 'Which is what we're going to do. Miranda handles Terry, you look after Ben.'

'Which Mental Health Act?' asked Miranda.

'Any Mental Health Act,' said Roger.

15

THE DEBATE WAS ORGANIZED by Birmingham's Central TV: Benn Webb for Labour, Chris Patten for the Tories, Alan Beith for the Liberal Democrats, the wryly authoritative figure of Phil Tibenham in the chair. Ten minutes per speaker, and then another half hour of questions from the public. Central TV being part of the BBC's opposition, Harry's role was strictly that of observer.

He sat with the studio audience, lined up three deep on narrow scaffolding rostra facing the set, maybe a hundred of them. Like Peter Sisson's audience on Friday night they belonged to that rarest of breeds, The Politically Active Citizenry – nice, reasonable, articulate people, well-versed in economics and sociology and world affairs, well-mannered enough to do what the floor manager told them, clap when he clapped, shut up when he wanted them to stop.

Harry loved the floor manager, who reminded him of Sidney Greenstreet, so fat that he carried a camping stool to balance himself on when his duties became too onerous. The upper reaches of his arms and legs had been absorbed into his mountainous torso, so that the limbs seemed absurdly short, like humpty-dumpty. Sweat poured down his face, and he kept wiping his forehead on the sleeve of his special-occasion suit.

Ben did well against what was a class opposition. He

was a strong speaker, less mannered than Michael Foot, less apocalyptic than Enoch Powell, but not shy of oratory; he could be funny without being frivolous, passionate without being excitable, sincere without sounding pompous. And Archie was right: he listened to what his opponents were saying, weighed their arguments, instead of just jumping in with a cheap point. The good looks he was born with, but the gravitas was something he'd learned.

Not that it stopped him going on the attack when the moment seemed right.

'It's screamingly obvious what the bulk of this country wants from its politicians,' he told Patten, brushing back a blond forelock. 'Alleviate poverty, create jobs, educate our children, look after the old and sick, improve public transport' – pause for emphasis – 'all the old, all the sick, all our children. Only, some politicians aren't interested in the obvious, what they're interested in is looking after their own. That's the Tory secret. In this country the votes of four out of ten electors gets you a working majority in the House of Commons. Four out of ten,' he repeated. 'So what you do if you're a Tory is find the easiest forty per cent to keep happy. The easiest people to keep happy are the ones who are happy already – the comfortably off, the middle aged, the healthy, the employed. The rest can go hang – it doesn't matter what happens to them. In fact the worse things are for them, the more the lucky forty per cent cling on to what they've got.'

'Is he part of the sixty or part of the forty?' hissed the retired civil servant on Harry's left.

'Ask him,' Harry suggested.

But there wasn't time: the final half-hour's questioning had been scrupulously divided up in advance across the political spectrum, with no space left for afterthoughts. At eleven o'clock it was over. Tibenham thanked them for coming, and everyone clapped and went home to watch themselves on their video recorders. Except Harry, who wandered out into the night air and walked across the windswept forecourt of Alpha Tower Plaza to the Holiday Inn. A perfect tableau of Birmingham architecture: a TV station, a Holiday Inn, an underground car park and an office high-rise, nothing between them but walkways and paving stones, motorway on all sides: an island of damp concrete in a sea of traffic.

Harry went upstairs and bought himself a drink in the first-floor bar. It had been a long day, up at six to catch the early train from Euston. Robert Kettle had travelled up the night before, and met him at New Street station. They'd had breakfast together at the hotel, and driven across the city to Ladywood where Ben was inspecting a new mosque, shoes off, hands clasped behind his back, nodding thoughtfully as he listened to the Muslim elders. Fifteen years ago the National Front used to stage anti-immigrant riots in Ladywood, but not any more.

There'd been no sign of Angela: an aide had told Harry she'd gone back to London for a couple of days to nurse Ben's constituency for him.

The Sikhs came next, a walkabout down Handsworth's Soho Road, then a communal lunch in a converted Methodist chapel, now a temple and social centre, Robert lining up shots and worrying about lighting levels while Harry poked around among the bystanders, talking to people, listening, looking for an angle. It was a bizarre but familiar scene, the tightly choreographed inner circle of party officials and plain clothes policemen steering the politician through the crowd, the herds of Press and television pressing in on them from all sides, trampling the long-suffering electors underfoot.

And so it went on all afternoon: a visit to a shopping centre, afternoon tea in a council flat, a Trade Union rally in the city centre. Every politician does these things, but Ben did them better than most – he seemed utterly at ease with ordinary people, knew who to flatter and who to tease, without ever seeming awkward or patronizing. Time and again he broke away from his schedule, turned left when his minders wanted him to turn right, accepted spontaneous invitations into people's shops and houses. He laughed a lot, and he made other people laugh, but underneath it all there was a seriousness of purpose, a sense of things to be done, as though he was recruiting volunteers for a better future.

Harry knew Ben was good, but he hadn't realized quite how good. Handling yourself on television is one thing – most politicians get there in the end, given enough coaching. But you can't teach people to be likeable in the flesh.

The unpredictability of the schedule caused Robert a lot of problems. He was a pictures director, used to setting up elaborate pans and zooms across the landscape, discovering his subject moodily reflected in the oily waters of a canal, or perfectly framed between lines of foreshortened tree-trunks. But by the time he'd finished a slow lyrical pan off the city skyline (for music, he liked to use plenty of music) Ben wasn't there any more: he'd have jumped on a passing bus, or ducked into a corner shop, or turned on his heels and gone back the way he'd come. The only way to catch Ben Webb was to stick close, or wait until he was up on the rostrum, trapped by his own audience.

Harry couldn't make his mind up about Ben. There was a lot that was refreshing about him, a feeling of optimism, a belief in the possibility of change. And even after you'd discounted the professional technique there was still a sincerity there, a love of life, an enjoyment of the company of other human beings. But once in a while the mask slipped for a moment, and there was a glimpse of something else – a man who had discovered a talent that was incidental to his real self, and was using it to bedazzle the punters while he got on with the main business, the pursuit of power. You needed both, of course, to get on in politics, the knife and the magic wand.

They'd finished shooting at seven, and Robert had gone off with the crew to eat. Harry wasn't hungry, and went back to the hotel to phone Miranda before going next door to Central to watch the debate. She'd been out. He tried her again now, from the hotel bar, but there was still no reply. He carried his drink back to a corner table and sat down with his notepad.

It was almost midnight by the time Ben arrived. Harry saw him come out of the lift, just him and a detective and Sam Dickinson, a head-office gopher with an armful of files. Sam was one of those twenty-three-year-olds who are born wearing suits, short hair; the world's full of them nowadays. Ben bought a Coke for the policeman and a short for Sam, but both of them looked too tired for serious drinking. Not Ben, though. Ben was still tanked up with adrenalin and looking for action.

Harry was the action.

'Kapowski, what the hell are you doing here?'

Big grin, head back, arms open and hands raised like a priest praising God. He had a way of making people feel special, be they old friends or total strangers.

'You're what I'm doing here, Ben. Been with you all day.'

'I thought I saw you – you were in with the Sikh's, weren't you?'

'And the Moslems. We're doing the bio-pic, didn't anyone tell you? Success hasn't changed Ben Webb, he's still an arrogant little shit, all that stuff.'

The politician gave Harry a bear hug, then separated and held him at arm's length, hands on Harry's shoulders, inspecting him.

'Probably. If so it didn't register. Sam handles all that stuff – I'm afraid I've rather given up paperwork at the moment, there isn't time to read all the bumph. It's a bit like roller-skating down the Eiger. Your crow's feet are coming on nicely, Kapowski. Women like crow's feet in a man, it suggests character. What are you drinking?'

He introduced Harry to the detective and Sam. Sam left shortly afterwards, and the policeman retired discreetly to a table by the door. Discreet, but not discreet enough for Ben. After two brandies he invited Harry upstairs.

'Bedrooms are off the record, by the way,' he reminded him as he unlocked the door.

He had two rooms joined by a party door to form an improvised suite. Both rooms contained two double beds, but one was clearly for sleeping in, the other an office: there was a lap-top computer and a portable fax machine on the desk, and heaps of newspapers and folders on the sofa. There was evidence of hotel sycophancy at work too, a large bowl of complimentary fruit and an ice-bucket of champagne with a ribbon tied round its neck on the coffee table. Neither of them fancied champagne: Ben disappeared into the bedroom and returned with glasses and an almost full bottle of Glenmorangie. Through the open door Harry could see a Samsonite suitcase open on the bed, a clean shirt in a polythene dry-cleaning wrapper beside it. He moved the papers off the sofa and sat down. Ben handed him a whisky and a cigar.

'Cheers. So what did you make of the show?'

'You really want to know? I thought you were very good.'

'Patten's a clever bugger, isn't he,' said Ben, lighting up. 'Doesn't bother with the party line too much – whatever you throw at him he still manages to seem reasonable, aware of the difficulties. He's none too specific as to what he'd do about them, but you feel he's sort of on the side of the angels.'

'Takes one to know one,' said Harry cheerfully.

Ben smiled back.

'You think it's all crap, don't you, Harry. You watch us poor monkeys out there on the job, and all you're doing is looking for the joins. The same way I bet you watch television programmes, clocking the professional tricks, checking edits, mentally unpicking the sound mix. Of course politicians use television, they'd be mad not to. If a man can't communicate, as Tom Lehrer used to say, the very least he can do is shut up. Before television a politician had to know how to write a good pamphlet, that's how he got his ideas across. The same goes for public speaking. Gladstone and Lloyd George were quite happy to manipulate an audience from the rostrum, people admired them for it. But for some reason TV and radio are different.'

Harry wasn't saying much, waiting for Ben to unwind. The politician was sitting back in the chair, tie undone, legs crossed, tapping the armrest with his finger for emphasis.

'But it's true, Harry. No one believes politicians. You get up and make a speech attacking unemployment and the papers say ah! Labour's worried about the working-class vote. No one ever credits you with an ounce of altruism.'

'And that's what you're in politics for, is it?' asked Harry. 'To change the world.'

'Yes. I don't have any great illusions about it, but I think things could be better than they are, and that it's worth trying to make them better. That's the easy bit. The hard bit is how you do it. You do it by hard work and compromise, and you use any tricks you've learned along the way. Which I bet is the way you work, too, isn't it?'

'I don't have your idealism, Ben.'

'I don't suppose you do, Harry. Idealism's a dirty word in the Press. You think we're all the same, closet despots who need to be kept in order. Half the time you're telling us what a terrible society we live in, the other half you're screaming murder at anyone who tries to change it.'

'We do our best,' said Harry.

'So do we, believe it or not. So what's this movie about?'

'You. It's a profile. The news boys are covering the day to day excitements of the campaign, the rest of us are meant to add a bit of depth, give the voters an insight into the people and issues. At least that's the official line. News covers the Press conferences; we film you eating breakfast, show what a real person you are.'

Ben grinned.

'Cynical bastard.'

He refilled Harry's glass for him.

It was hard not to like the man. Hard not to like him, and equally hard not to be cynical. Harry sort of believed in his idealism, but there were plenty of contradictions – the affluent lifestyle, the womanizing, the trade-craft. Even now – a private conversation in a hotel room at one o'clock in the morning – Ben still talked in sound-bites, short quotable sentences that news editors could cut in and out of, user-friendly modules of comment and opinion. And at the back of Harry's mind was the memory of the Honda mounting the pavement outside the Bombay Duck, the distant possibility that Ben might have had something to do with it. But why?

The fax sprang to life. Ben walked across, waited for it to finish, tore off the two sheets, read them and passed them across.

'The punters agree with you about the Central show.'

Harry ran his eyes down the print-out. Page one was

a telephone poll: two columns of figures, a paragraph of summary. Twenty-three per cent of two hundred viewers questioned after the programme said they were more likely to vote Labour as a result of Ben's performance, three per cent were less likely.

'You get these every night?' he asked Ben as he read on. Patten had done well too: viewers found him credible and open-minded – it was his party they had reservations about.

'No, just sometimes. They don't mean a lot. Someone did some research on it in the States. On most issues the punters don't know enough to make up their own minds – why would they? After a TV debate they wait for the commentators to tell them who's won. In the US a single comment by a TV anchorman changes the minds of four per cent of the electorate. It's you lot who matter.'

Page two carried a resumé of the main polls from the following morning's papers. Labour still had a slight edge, but the number of Don't Knows showed no signs of shrinking.

Ben sat down.

'People still don't trust us. They trust our intentions, but they don't trust us to be able to deliver on them. Not surprising, really, when you look back, the record isn't great. Other way round with the Tories; people don't like their intentions, but they think they're competent. The sad thing is that whether we win or not has very little to do with us – the voters will take a judgement on how they think the economy's doing, whether they're getting richer or poorer, and that'll be that. All we can do is try not to make too many mistakes along the way.'

'It's a wonder people vote at all,' said Harry. 'You look back at the last thirty years and it's like a succession of Biblical plagues. You wonder what horror's in store for us next.'

'So tell me who do you admire.'

'I don't,' said Harry. 'I know whose side I'm on, but I can't say there's anyone in politics I admire very much. Present company excluded, of course. And some backbenchers, you occasionally get the odd backbencher who's not afraid to ask awkward questions.'

'That's my Harry – Guardian of Civil liberties, Scourge of the Bureaucrat, People's Friend, Baker of Exceedingly Good Cakes – did I miss one out?'

'Salaried Hack,' said Harry.

Ben tossed him the whisky bottle.

'It's been a long time, Harry. It's good to see you again. I'm sorry if I've been pompous, the long days get to you after a while. How are you? Are you happy at the BBC?'

Harry took more whisky. Ben was right: it had been a long time – but since what? They'd never known each other particularly well: he remembered a Ry Cooder concert at Hammersmith, maybe 1984; the three of them, him and Ben and Angela, drinking beer out of plastic pints, a Greek meal afterwards. Two or three other times when they'd been guests at the same dinner parties. Long lost acquaintances, that was all.

'After a fashion, Ben. Still doing much the same.'

'It's funny, isn't it. Politicians come and go, but journalists last for ever. I don't think there's a candidate in this campaign who served in Ted Heath's Cabinet, but I bet half this year's TV anchormen covered the 1970 election.'

'I saw Angela on Saturday,' said Harry. He didn't want to talk about Terry yet, but he didn't want to seem to be hiding anything. 'She probably told you.'

'Yes, she said you were doing something on the GLC, you wanted to know about Latchkey and Jo O'Brien. Did you fuck her?'

'You're the second person who's asked me that, Ben. No.'

'I didn't think you did. I didn't kill Jo O'Brien either, in case that's what you were thinking.'

Harry smiled. He wondered how much Ben knew about him and Angela. Husbands and wives often tell each other these things, either in trust or in anger.

'You haven't married?' Ben asked.

'No.'

'You should, Harry. It's a ridiculous business, but it's worth it. You must have thought about it.'

'I have. To no great effect.'

'Jo O'Brien.' Ben shook his head thoughtfully, as though remembering. 'God, all that seems a long time ago. Jo couldn't stand Angela, he had that gay's thing about pretty young women, I suppose he found them sexually threatening. Older women he had no trouble with, particularly if their lives had gone wrong. Eartha Kitt, Shirley Bassey, Elizabeth Taylor, anyone with a sniff of tragedy about them. Why this sudden interest in the GLC?'

'Roger Carlisle,' Harry lied. He wondered whether to tackle Ben about the trial, about why he'd sanitized his CV so thoroughly, then thought better of it. Ben would have an answer to that: if there were going to be questions he'd need more substance to back them up. 'Roger has an infinite appetite for political archaeology. It's quite a relief to be back in the present again.'

But Ben wanted to keep talking about the past. It occurred to Harry that he might be lonely.

'The tragedy is that when people think about the GLC now, all they remember is the Jo O'Briens. There weren't even that many Jo O'Briens. There was a list of GLC-sponsored bodies the Tories used to wave around all the time – Babies Against The Bomb, the Gay Bereavement Trust, the Marx Memorial Centre, Southall Black Sisters, all that lot. You'd think payrolling the lunatic fringe was all the GLC did – in fact the sums involved were tiny. If I remember rightly the GLC gave money to something like two thousand organizations, and even the *Daily Mail* could only find eighty to object to. Granted that the GLC was socialist and the *Mail* was hard-line Thatcherite, eighty out of two thousand seemed pretty modest to me. The figure I do remember was that seventeen per cent of Londoners were black at the time. When Labour took over the GLC there were six and a half thousand people employed by the London Fire Brigade and only seven of them were black. A bit of positive discrimination isn't unreasonable in that sort of situation.'

'There don't seem to have been a lot of blacks on the Latchkey payroll.'

Ben smiled.

'Maybe not, but we had a reasonable ethnic mix. One Brit, one South African, one Turkish Cypriot. It wasn't such a dumb idea on paper. The rich and skilled were moving out of London in droves, the poor and unskilled coming in to take their places. A lot of them were refugees from provincial attitudes, gays and misfits and single parents looking for a bit of metropolitan toleration. Not just adults – kids. You'd be amazed how young some of them were, hardly into their teens. Most of them not very articulate, not very good at working the system. Latchkey was meant to be a mixture of political lobby, advice bureau and referral agency.'

'It was?' asked Harry drily.

'That was the theory. Easy to mock now, I know. Jo was a bloody good operator, you had to give him that.' Ben smiled at the memory. 'At least he had me fooled for a while.'

'How long?'

'Three or four months, I suppose. I'd never worked with anyone like Jo before, all that showbiz stuff can be very dazzling if you're not used to it. It didn't occur to me to question how he ran things, I was too eager to please. And to be honest it was fun, a lot of the time.

Hard work, but fun; Jo kept me busy. He reckoned that as long as there appeared to be enough activity going on no one would look too closely at what was actually happening. We were forever holding Press conferences and photo-calls and staging publicity stunts. Good ones, very professional, I learned a lot. And printing appeals in the papers. The GLC money paid for the office and the ads, but it was the public that put up the real cash.'

'And where did that go?'

Ben tossed a hand in the air.

'You tell me. Believe it or not I was very naïve in those days, Harry.' Naïve – the same word Angela had used. 'Shockingly so, when I come to think of it. In retrospect I should probably have done something about it, but I wasn't involved in the money end. I liked Jo and Terry. I thought Jo must have money of his own.'

'You didn't suspect anything?'

'Oh, in the end I did. I even wrote to Willie Walpole about it. But that was right at the end, not long before Jo died.'

The whisky bottle was half empty. Ben poured them each a last inch.

'So is Latchkey going to feature in this movie you're making at the moment?'

Harry shook his head.

'I wouldn't be allowed. Even if I wanted to.'

'Why not?'

He downed his whisky and stood up.

'A funny thing happened on Monday, Ben. Someone phoned the Director-General's office and advised the BBC not to go digging into Ben Webb's past.'

Ben looked at him blankly.

'What are you trying to say, Harry?'

'I don't know, Ben. I'm just telling you what happened.'

Ben kept staring, then put down his glass.

'You're sure about this?'

'That's what I was told.'

'Who by?'

'Roger Carlisle, via Tony Mangan. Deputy Head of News and Current Affairs. Those guys don't lie, they haven't the imagination.'

Ben was on his feet now, clearly agitated.

'You think it came from me?'

'I don't think anything, Ben. I just don't like men in grey suits pulling me off a story. Particularly when I haven't even had time to find out what the story is.'

'Tell me something, Harry. If someone tells you not to follow something up, what do you do?'

'Keep digging, of course.'

'Mangan would realize that, wouldn't he.'

They looked at each other for a long time.

'I suppose he would,' Harry said finally.

Ben walked over to the window. The curtains were open, the lights of the Rotunda glimmering in the darkness.

'I promise you one thing, Harry. It didn't come from me.'

16

THE PHONE WOKE HARRY. It was dark in the room.
He felt like death.

'Your morning call, sir,' the voice sang sweetly.
'Would you and your lady friend like breakfast?'

He felt across the bed. There was no one there.

'What lady friend?'

'The former Miss Walsall you met in the nightclub,
big tits and bad breath; you told her she had nice eyes.'

Harry pulled himself up on his elbows, turned on the
light and looked at the clock. It was ten to seven.

'Do you realize what time it is?'

'Don't be mad at me, Harry,' said Miranda. 'I'm only
doing my job. How did you sleep?'

'Like a log. My head hit the pillow at four, and first
thing I knew it was ten to seven.'

'Have a swim. They have pools in Holiday Inns, don't
they?'

'Possibly. Talking of nightclubs, I tried phoning you
last night.'

'I went out. I'm allowed to go out.'

'Depends who with. Do I know him?'

'Her. I went out on the town with Shirley Pattichis.'

'You did what?'

Miranda giggled.

'We went to see a male stripper, in a pub in Hackney.
A young brickie called Geoff, the D. H. Lawrence type,

twelve stone of muscle and a pair of mauve Y-fronts with lime-green trim until they got removed. Well hung, in case you're interested.'

'That's what they're saying about the next Parliament,' said Harry, trying to picture Miranda at a Hackney hen party. 'This was research, was it?'

'Of course. How about you?'

'I did in a bottle of Glenmorangie with Ben Webb. It's official: the world is an imperfect place but we shouldn't give up, there's still hope for the human race. Oh, and he denies he's been leaning on the Beeb. What the hell were you doing with Shirley?'

'I told you, research. Twenty Things You Always Wanted to Know About Her Brother-in-Law.'

'Give me three,' said Harry.

He was out of bed now, towel round his waist, phone tucked under his chin while he fiddled with the coffee-maker.

'For starters, he loved his mother,' said Miranda. 'He was raped by a Turkish policeman at the age of twelve, the year the Turks invaded Cyprus, nineteen seventy-six I think it was. As a teenager he spent all his spare money on clothes, he'd rather starve for a week than go without a shirt he fancied. Shall I keep going?'

'Please.' Harry was looking for coffee. Six tea bags, four plastic nipples of milk, no coffee.

'He kept a diary.'

'What kind of diary?'

'The usual kind. Thursday, woke up, had a shit, fucked a merchant banker. Or was fucked by, I'm never very clear about the mechanics of these things. Then how much he got for it, and his expenses — bus fares and stuff. Somewhere inside Terry Pattichis is a very tidy mind.'

'Did he name the bankers?'

'Initials.'

'And where is it now?'

'Shirley thinks the police took it. She and Pete collected the rest of Terry's stuff from Jo's flat after his arrest, it wasn't there then.'

Harry's kettle had boiled. He dropped a tea bag in the cup and bit open a sachet of sugar.

'What else did she tell you?'

'She talked about Jo's parties. He entertained a lot – dress informal, bring your own sex aids. And she wanted to know about you.'

'What did you tell her?'

'I didn't know a lot, so I sort of made it up. Your father was a rugby international and a Battle of Britain pilot. After the war he decided to devote his life to lepers in Africa. He died young, an elephant sat on his tent.'

'Is that a fact?' said Harry. 'I was under the impression he was alive and well and living in Somerset, dusting the lawn and pruning his hedges three times a day. What about my mother?'

'She never remarried. Didn't have any money, supported herself by working as a hotel receptionist; you were brought up in hotels, sharing a room with your mother. When the hotel was full you both had to move out and sleep in the coffee lounge. That's why you never learned to cook, you were weaned on hotel catering.'

'She's in Somerset too. Walking round after my father with a clothes brush and washing the curtains once a week.'

He made a mental note not to introduce her to his parents. He was fond of them, but they weren't the kind of parents you wheel out to impress Miranda Cunningham with, expatriate Poles with an inflated respect for British institutions in general and the Royal Family in particular.

'So what else did you do with your day?' he asked her.

'Not a lot, most of it was taken up with Shirley. I met

her at lunchtime. She showed me her family photographs, which took rather a long time. Then we went and picked up the kids from school, and took them round to Taki's for tea, and Taki gave me a lecture on the second-hand car business. He has Tory party posters in all his windows and some rather unusual views on the benefits of the enterprise culture. The kids stayed there while we went to Hackney to see the stripper. It was rather an entertaining day. Oh, and there were some messages for you in the office, hold on while I get my notes.'

There was a pause. Harry switched on the TV and turned the sound down. Breakfast television was doing its cookery slot, edible presents for Christmas. Buy a bar of chocolate, melt it down into dollops, put a glacé cherry on each dollop, and olé! Home-made chocolate dollops.

'You still there?' asked Miranda.

'Fire away.'

'First call was some dreary harridan called Angela Webb, wants you to ring her back. I said you'd gone to Ulan Bator.'

'Thanks. Who else?'

'Your friend Pigfoot Walker. He thought I had a sexy voice but I told him I was paralysed from the waist down. He said he knew the feeling. We have a date for Sunday night, he's taking me to a Richard Clayderman concert. Meanwhile he's at home if you need him. Oh, and Terry called.'

Harry stopped making notes.

'What do you mean, Terry called? Where from?'

'Broadmoor. They're allowed phone cards, apparently, so many units a week. They can phone you but you can't phone them. At least that's the theory. Joan talked to him. She didn't know when you were going to be where, so she told him to call back and she'd find out and give him a time and a number. It has to be before half past nine at night, that's Lights Out in Broadmoor apparently.'

'Give him the number of Robert Kettle's mobile.'

'Is that safe?'

'More or less. I can't think of any other way of working it. We're on the road all day. I miss you, by the way.'

'Why?'

Miranda always seemed surprised by other people's emotions.

'You keep my mind alert.'

'Do I? Good. I'm seeing Terry's solicitor this morning – Catriona Clark. What else do you want me to do?'

'Try and run down ex-Detective Superintendent Brian Natkeil, the guy who interrogated Terry.'

'Will do. Tell me something, Harry – do you have any idea where all this is leading?'

'No,' said Harry. 'I'm just sniffing.' He looked across at the TV: it was after seven. An all-in wrestler was reviewing the morning papers. 'I'd better go.'

'Have fun,' said Miranda. 'And remember me to Robert.'

Harry hesitated before hanging up.

'There's something else, isn't there,' he guessed. 'Something you've found out that you're not telling me.'

'No.'

'Would you tell me if there was?'

'No.'

She had a natural talent for lying, did Miranda, but she reserved it for unimportant occasions when the truth was too complicated to bother with.

Harry crossed the room and opened the curtains. Beyond the damp little balcony a pink-and-grey November dawn lit up the mucky glass of the Birmingham skyline. It had been raining in the night, and the underpasses and overpasses lay like shining eels at his feet. Bloody Birmingham, it wasn't even decrepit, just ugly. He knew and liked people who liked Birmingham, listened to them telling him about the Symphony Orchestra, and the leafy suburbs, and how hospitable the people were. They were, too, it was just the accent that made them sound thick. But the city itself was beyond redemption, an elephant's graveyard of the architectural disasters of the past thirty years. Worse still, the architects were at it again, superimposing a nightmare veneer of conference centres and shopping malls on the ruins of the last fiasco.

He showered and shaved and got dressed and started thinking about the film they were making. They had twenty minutes of air-time to play with, five days to get it all together. Today was Thursday: they'd finish filming on Sunday, transmit on Monday evening in the Campaign Report slot on BBC2 as part of a trio of films, each featuring one of the major parties – Liberal Democrats on Sunday, Labour on Monday, Tories on Tuesday, the order decided by picking names out of a hat. After the film, Harry would interview Ben live in the studio. The election itself was three days later, on Thursday.

The usual formula for a film like this was quite straightforward. A brief biography using library material and stills; four or five sequences featuring the candidate in action, and excerpts from a couple of his speeches. Mix in some of Robert's pretty visuals, an occasional piece to camera from Harry, pour on a bit of music, rough cut it to thirty minutes and then take out the dross. Always assuming everything went smoothly, no one got shot or resigned along the way.

There were other ways of going about it, but there wasn't much time. They were due to meet the crew downstairs at half past eight, bags packed and ready for the road. Today's itinerary took them north to Wolver-hampton, then Stoke-on-Trent, a diversion east to

Derby, and then a final cross-country rush to Manchester.

Harry talked it over with Robert at breakfast. Robert was in his element. He'd tried to get a helicopter to film the motorcade on its way through the Black Country, but the cloud level was too low. Instead he'd rented a Steadicam, an arrangement of counter-weighted braces which attached the camera to the operator's body and enabled him to run, jump and climb over furniture without jolting the picture. It was a wonderful toy: people like George Lucas and Alan Parker used one all the time. But not on current affairs documentaries: on current affairs documentaries you didn't have time for that sort of gear. The cameraman just put the camera on his shoulder and mucked in as best he could.

Harry downed his orange juice in one swallow and took a fork of damp scrambled egg.

'You're mad,' he told Robert.

Robert grinned, and arranged a tableau with the crockery.

'I've got an opening shot planned. The camera's inside the back of the car with Ben.' He drove the toast rack between the marmalade and the milk jug. 'The car stops, we don't know where we are, Ben gets out, the camera follows him.' He picked out two pieces of toast, one in each hand. 'The camera tracks back, gradually widening shot, Ben's on the pavement now, we can see the whole car, Ben's shaking hands with the welcoming committee, but we keep going.' His left hand stayed on the table, his left rising into the air. 'Up the steps of the Town Hall, the crowds pushing in around Ben, smaller and smaller as we keep widening, backing up the steps. There are fifty steps on that Town Hall, it's like climbing on top of a building. By the time we stop the crowd is way below us: the camera tilts up and we can see the whole town centre, the hills behind.'

Harry gave up on the egg and took a slug of coffee.

'Have you talked to Paul about this yet?'

Paul was the cameraman, a workaday Welshman in his early fifties with a low opinion of flashy young Londoners like Robert.

'He knows about the Steadicam.'

'Has he ever used it before?'

'Sure,' said Robert. 'He went on the course.'

Paul had indeed been on the course.

'Useless,' he told Harry as they loaded up the cars. 'Absolutely fucking useless. By the time you've rigged the bloody thing up it's time for lunch. What the hell does he think he's shooting, *Heaven's Gate?*'

They set off at nine, a ten-car convoy led by a police car, roof-light flashing; then the Labour party contingent, Ben and his entourage in a black Rover, a second Rover crammed with local party officials; then another police car, and the Press bringing up the rear. Robert and Harry were in a rented Ford Sierra, Paul the sound man in the Volvo with the engineer, the sparks following behind in a Fiat van. The rain was torrential, wipers battling to clear the windscreens as they negotiated the motorway system, through West Bromwich, heading for Wolverhampton.

Miranda sat very upright on the edge of the sofa, notebook on her knee, trying not to appear nervous. Two weeks into her new career she still found it ridiculous to think of herself as a representative of the BBC, someone with an office and colleagues and a brief that was largely outside her control. There were dozens of impertinent questions she wanted to ask Catriona – about the law, about what you did when you had to defend someone you knew to be guilty, all that shit. But she needed to get the day-job business out the way first.

Catriona Clark was pretty, slim and dark, with very short black hair and wine-red rims to her spectacles; a nervous, funny, hyper-energetic woman in her middle thirties. She wore a pale blue linen dress, expensively cut, and high heels. Her office was on the first floor of a Victorian terrace in Fulham with long sash windows looking out across Parsons Green. The room was spare and modern, white walls and a soft grey carpet, a scattering of minimalist furniture. Miranda sat on the sofa under a framed diploma, drinking fresh coffee out of a white French porcelain cup: Catriona perched on the cusp of a stainless steel chair.

'Terry Pattichis?' She had an eager voice with a slight lisp. 'What would you like to know?'

'Everything,' said Miranda, 'within the limits of professional discretion.'

She didn't get everything, but she got a lot.

Terry hadn't seen a lawyer when he signed his confession. Nor had he asked for one.

'Most people don't, it's odd, isn't it,' lisped Catriona. 'The one piece of law everyone thinks they know, "I demand to see a lawyer", and when it comes to it they don't bother. Not that they're automatically entitled, that's just TV movie talk. All the Home Office Instructions required at the time Terry was arrested was that someone be told where he was. If and when the police decided it wasn't going to obstruct the course of justice. The Instructions were magnificently vague on things like that.'

Not that Terry had minded. He signed his confession and went to bed in his cell. It was only the next day, when he got to West London County Court in North End Road, that he got a lawyer. Catriona was the duty solicitor at North End Road, hanging around for whoever happened to come in.

'Did he contest the confession?' Miranda asked.

'He did and he didn't. It was the same all the way through. He didn't deny it, but he didn't admit it. He didn't want bail either, I think he thought there wasn't any point. The only person he knew who had the money to stand bail was Jo O'Brien. He was very nervous, very fidgety. And very upset about Jo, he couldn't believe he was dead.'

The trial was a foregone conclusion.

'Tony Tree was Terry's defence brief. He's good, he did his best, but there wasn't much to go on. Terry had a motive, he had the opportunity, he'd signed a confession. There were no other suspects. We tried to catch the police out on technicalities, but it was all sewn up. They had witnesses who'd seen Terry and O'Brien arguing in the Balzac and the Beaumont Arms. O'Brien was accusing Terry of infidelity, threatening to chuck him out on the street. O'Brien's neighbours heard them rowing a lot the week before. Terry's fingerprints were on everything. Judges and juries don't like homosexuals at the best of times, and on top of that there was the whole Latchkey business, the papers had declared open season on the GLC for sponsoring Nicaraguan Lesbians and CND Paedophiles. The prosecution loved it. They had boxes of evidence on Jo and Terry's lifestyle, it was painful to watch. We pleaded manslaughter on the grounds of intoxication. You can claim intoxication for manslaughter but not for murder. But there was also the question of arson: he might have killed him by mistake, but setting fire to the office was clearly *mens rea*.'

'How about Ben Webb?' asked Miranda.

'Ben wasn't a witness as such, he'd left the office long before it happened,' said Catriona. 'We didn't want to put him in the witness box in case Brabazon started asking him about Terry's character. Ben was as helpful as he could be, but we decided it was too risky to put him in the box.'

She asked her about the forensic evidence.

'A mess. The police were naughty, especially Natkeil. They kept losing things, but that's par for the course.

And since Terry kept changing his mind about the confession there didn't seem a lot of point in hammering home on the technicalities. Everything was stacked against us: a client who didn't seem to care much what happened to him, a working-class jury with strong views on gays and drugs and GLC spongers. Everything pointed to Terry, no one suggesting an alternative explanation. Add in Mr Justice Wasson, seventy-three years old and proud of his reputation for plain speaking: it was a miracle Terry escaped the gallows.'

'Do you think he did it?'

Catriona sighed.

'I'm not meant to think in those terms.'

'I know,' said Miranda. 'But you must have a hunch.'

'I don't know, I really don't.'

'Do you have a copy of the transcript?'

'Sure.' She got up from her chair and stood with her finger poised over the intercom on her desk. 'Is there anything else you need?'

'Clues,' said Miranda, trying not to sound too desperate.

Catriona thought for a moment.

'Walpole,' she said finally. 'Try talking to Willie Walpole.'

Harry let Robert do the driving. It was a familiar routine, Robert at the wheel plotting ambitious visual sequences, Harry sitting beside him worrying about the editorial content. No two reporters and directors have the same working relationship: there are reporters who let their directors do everything, plot the story-line, script the interview questions and pieces to camera and block out – sometimes even write – the commentary; and there are reporters who do the same in reverse, leaving the director with nothing to do except supervise the technicalities. Harry's relationship with Robert tended towards the latter, but with a certain flexibility over who chose what sequences to shoot, and during the final edit. As a packager Robert had talent. Less than he gave himself credit for, but enough to give his films a certain style.

Wolverhampton was a washout, a grim battle of wind and umbrellas which even Ben had trouble finding funny. Conversations had to be shouted through the gale, streets and pavements were negotiated at a fast gallop, the public stayed away in droves. After twenty minutes the politicians retired to a Trade Union office for coffee. Harry and Robert stayed in the car and got out the newspapers.

'In 1932,' Robert read aloud from the *Daily Express*, 'scientists imported a hundred cane toads into Australia from Latin America to control beetle infestations on sugar crops.'

'Bufo marinus,' said Harry. 'They're called *bufo marinus*. Huge fuckers.'

Robert wasn't listening.

'The female,' he read on, 'can deliver forty thousand eggs at once, and also produces a hallucinogenic called bufotenine which can kill cats and dogs. The toads, lacking natural predators in Australia, have become a major environmental nuisance.'

'Big as melons, they are, Bobby. I've seen them.'

'Quote, Imbibing in toads, unquote can get you life imprisonment in Queensland. The State suggests getting rid of them by putting them in the freezer.'

'As opposed to playing golf with them, or hitting them with baseball bats, or drop-kicking them into the barbecue.'

'People really do that?'

'Sure,' said Harry. 'You never been to Australia? They do that sort of thing all the time.'

At eleven o'clock they set off again for Stoke. The rain eased a little as they drove north. Harry's hangover eased too, responding to a heavy dose of paracetamol.

They were on the M6 just south of Stafford when Robert's phone buzzed.

It was Terry.

'Is that you, Kapowski? Can you hear me?'

'Crystal clear. You should get yourself one of these machines, Terry. Keep it in your bedside locker. Payphones are a thing of the past. What can I do for you?'

'I've been thinking, Kapowski. Maybe we should write a book.'

'What about?'

'Me.'

'A brilliant idea,' said Harry. 'You tell me everything, I write it up, then we charge people to have their names removed from the manuscript.'

Terry laughed.

'But that's not why I was calling. I want Shirley left alone.'

'You do? Who's bothering her?'

'You are.'

'She told you that?' asked Harry.

'No, but I want you to back off.'

'You're asking the hedgehogs to lay off the traffic, Terry. I can't keep her off the phone. She even invited Miranda out for a piss-up on the town last night.'

'Who's Miranda?'

'She's the one who does the work around here, she's a researcher.'

'Then tell her – Jesus,' he interrupted himself, 'this call's costing a fucking fortune. I've only ten units left.'

'Then let me ask you one question. Who is it you're so scared of on the outside, Terry?'

'What do you mean?' asked Terry.

'I mean, who suggested you call me.'

There was a pause, Terry sucking on his cigarette.

'Does there have to be someone?'

'That's my guess.'

And then the line went dead.

'Was that the Cypriot?' asked Robert. 'I thought you'd given up on him.'

'That's what he wants me to do. I don't know why, but he's a very reluctant hero. Tell me something – how long does it take to stage a reconstruction?'

'What, a Scene of the Crime? Not long. Depends on what you want. How many actors?'

'Four or five,' said Harry. 'And a fire, a fire in an office. At night.'

'A couple of days. A day to set it up, a day to film it. Fires are difficult, though. Do you want it big?'

'Not that big. Plenty of smoke.'

'When do you want it for?'

'I don't know,' said Harry. 'I don't know.'

Harry had to admire Robert's driving. Other traffic kept breaking up the convoy, pulling out between them and the police car ahead. Robert was cool as a cucumber, one hand on the wheel, the other tapping the dash, casually swerving from lane to lane. Harry looked over his shoulder to make sure the crew were still behind him, then looked at his watch. It was five to twelve. He got out his address book, looked up Angela's number, and dialled. A Spanish woman told him Angela was out.

'Tell her it's Harry.'

'One moment please,' said the au pair.

A moment later Angela came on the line.

'This has to be quick, Harry, I'm meant to be down town knocking on doors in ten minutes' time.'

'I bet someone else does the knocking,' said Harry.

'Not at all,' said Angela. 'I do all my own stunts.'

'So I remember. Enough of this shit, what can I do for you?'

'When are you coming back to London?'

'Saturday or Sunday, I'm not sure which yet. It depends how things go. Ask Ben, where he goes I go.'

'I need to talk to you again.'

'Alone?'

'Alone.'

She dropped her voice. Harry guessed the au pair was still in the room.

'How about now?' he suggested.

'I told you, I haven't got time. And I'd rather it wasn't on the phone. Ben's in trouble, Harry.'

'I know, I've seen the polls.'

'Not that kind of trouble.'

Up ahead the convoy was indicating left for Stoke-on-Trent.

'Call me when you know your movements,' said Angela. 'I'd better go.'

17

IT WAS A GOOD CROWD, maybe five hundred people, arranged on rows of stacking chairs. Up on the rostrum, behind Ben, four local Labour candidates were lined up in a row, three men and one woman in red rosettes, arms folded across their chests, big grins on their faces.

'Tory leaders are quick enough to visit the scenes of natural disasters,' said Ben, hands in the pockets of his corduroy trousers, looking down at a point on the ground some eighteen inches in front of the microphone stand. Then he looked up at the audience, shaking his head. 'But they never show up to look at the human disasters of their own making.'

The audience broke into a round of applause, but Ben raised his hand to stop them.

'You can just see it, can't you. A steel mill closes: Central Office lifts the phone to the BBC, tells them to have a crew standing by, Kenneth Clarke's on his way by helicopter to commiserate with the work force.'

This time he let them clap, stepping back from the microphone, scratching the back of his neck. Harry's eyes were on Paul. The cameraman was stuck halfway down the aisle, looking up philosophically at the cast-iron tracery beams supporting the roof of the Victorian hall while the engineer tried to free the Steadicam's arm with a screwdriver. Robert was a yard behind, leaning forward, hands in the back pocket of his Chinos, offering whispered advice.

'There's no shortage of human disasters, if they're interested,' Ben went on. 'Central Office may not have noticed them, but the rest of us have. The eighties was an economic holocaust for much of this society. Not for bankers, not for interior designers, not for car importers, or for those people lucky enough to have gold credit cards in their pockets: not for spenders. What the Thatcher years did was to turn us from a nation of shopkeepers into a nation of shoppers.'

That's what bugs me about Ben, Harry realized. He crusades against materialism and marketing techniques, rants at the Designer Society, the triumph of presentation over substance. And yet he uses all the techniques he attacks.

He was standing at the back of the hall, leaning against a radiator, raincoat on, notebook in hand. His hair was wet from the monsoon outside, and a puddle had formed on the floor at his feet. He wondered what motivated all these people, the party members and envelope-stickers and Trade Union activists who spent the four or five years between elections squabbling with each other, and then came together for the three weeks of the campaign in a frantic display of Party Unity. Whether they won or lost they never seemed to get the government they wanted. The ones who couldn't face the prospect of Unity were outside, selling newspapers. The Communist party of Great Britain (Marxist/Leninist) on the left of the main door, the Communist party of Great Britain (Trotskyite) on the right.

'I wonder if you could explain,' Harry'd asked the Marxist/Leninist, a wiry Scot with long sideboards, 'the main ideological differences between you and the other comrade.'

The Scot pondered the question for some time.

'Basically,' he announced finally, 'they're out on a limb.'

The engineer had fixed the Steadicam, and Paul was lining up for a second attempt. Harry left him to it.

Outside the rain had stopped and the town was on the move again, pedestrians hurrying in and out of the shopping mall, queueing for buses among the municipal flower pots. He walked down the steps, found a pay-phone and dialled the number of Robert's mobile phone.

'Kettle,' Robert whispered.

'Kapowski,' said Harry. He could hear one of the candidates in full flow in the background. 'There are five men here with a Transatlantic crane for the top shot, they want to know where you'd like it.'

'A what?' asked Robert.

'Transatlantic crane. Big fucker, looks like one of those rigs they use to launch nuclear missiles, the kind the Russians used to parade through Red Square on May Day in the old days. It's on a double yellow line at the moment.'

'Shh,' said Robert.

'Are these phones really safe?' asked Harry. 'I mean, no one else can hear you? Tell me why I'm asking. There was a news crew sent to cover a speech Michael Foot was making once, they had a tight deadline, Foot was going to say something important, they'd film it, rush it back to base. Only Foot was waffling, taking ages to get to the point. Cameraman ducks outside and calls up the newsroom on the radio phone, tells them there's a problem, the old fart keeps droning on, still hasn't said what he's meant to. The PA in the hall picked it up, broadcast the whole conversation to fifteen hundred of the faithful sitting inside. A wonderful row afterwards. Are you still there, Bobby?'

'Roger.'

'Make sure you get plenty of cutaways of the audience, will you?'

'Roger and out,' said Robert.

Then Harry put through a transfer charge call to Miranda in the office.

'Terry says you're to lay off Shirley.'

'He says what?'

'I know, I told him. I've had another proposition from Angela Webb. Oh, and Robert wants to divorce me. How's your day going?'

'It's raining.'

'Here too, brings out the greys in the landscape. Did you find our ex-copper yet?'

'Who, Natkeil? Not yet, but I've got an address for him. He's not with the bookies any more, he's retired to Oxfordshire. The name Great Tew mean anything to you?'

'I went to a wedding there once, it's one of those unreal little Cotswold villages with mop-head thatches and leaded panes in the post office windows.'

She gave him Natkeil's address.

'You know what's odd about Ben,' he said. 'The money. Big house, two cars, good clothes, all on an MP's salary. Look him up in the Register of MP's Interests, will you? See if he had any other visible means of support. It's stupid, it never occurred to me before.'

'Maybe it's family money.'

'Could be. I'll ask Angela if I can think of a way of doing it politely. How did you get on with Catriona?'

'I'm not sure. She doesn't know much we didn't know already. She suggested I might talk to Willie Walpole.'

'Do that.'

'Yes, sir.'

'Sorry,' said Harry. 'You're not enjoying this much, are you.'

'It's fine. A bit confusing at times, but I'm getting three hundred quid a week, I shouldn't complain. Why are you doing it? You get paid anyway, don't you?'

'Because of the hypocrisy. I don't know if Ben had anything to do with Jo's death, or Pete's, but I hate a cover up. Politicians make the rules for the rest of us, then ignore them themselves, assume they're above the law. The real divide isn't between the Left and the Right, it's between insiders and outsiders. All politicians are insiders. Terry and Pete and Shirley are outsiders.'

'And which are you, Harry?'

'I'm a chameleon, I'm afraid. That's my problem.'

Across the square the doors had opened. Paul came out first, walking backwards. Steadicam strapped to his body, the sparks at his elbow holding up a sun gun. Behind came Ben and his party. Paul stepped sideways and panned round on to the square.

'I'll ring you later,' said Harry.

'If you feel like it.'

It was almost midnight by the time they checked in to the Midland Hotel in Manchester. There was a foolscap envelope waiting for Harry on the carpet inside the door. Inside was a sheaf of faxes from Miranda. The wonder of modern communications. He drew the curtains, undressed, got into bed and started to read:

STATEMENT

Shepherd's Bush Police Station   18 December 1983

I Terry Pattichis wish to make a statement. I want someone to write down what I say. I have been told that I need not say anything unless I wish to do so but whatever I say will be given in evidence.

                              sgd: T. Pattichis

My name is Terrence Pattichis, that's not my real name, my real name is Theo but I changed it to Terry when I came to live in England from Cyprus where I was born.

   On the evening of 17 December Mr O'Brien and I worked late at the office preparing for a charity function. I had a headache and had taken pills, I don't remember what they were, Mr O'Brien gave them to me from a bottle he kept in the drawer of his desk. Mr O'Brien also kept a bottle of vodka in the office and we had some drinks while we were working.

Where's Ben? Miranda had written at this point.

At around eight o'clock we went out to eat at the Balzac Bistro at the bottom of Wood Lane. I drank a Campari and Soda before the meal and shared a carafe of red wine with Mr O'Brien. After the meal we each had two brandies. At around half past nine we went next door to the Beaumont Arms public house.

We were still arguing but not all the time. At one point Mr O'Brien went off to make a telephone call and was gone about five minutes. When he came back we had more drinks until closing time. I would estimate that during the time we were in the public house I consumed three pints of beer and three measures of spirits.

We then returned to the office. Mr O'Brien continued to question me about other men I had been seeing. Mr O'Brien became upset and started to cry. I produced a packet of cocaine and we divided it up between us. As well as the cocaine we drank two or three vodkas mixed with Coca Cola from the fridge. I do not know how long we talked, but Mr O'Brien continued to question me about my liaisons with other men.

'*Who?*' Miranda wanted to know. '*Ask Natkeil about diary?*' she'd added.

Harry too wondered what the police had done with the diary, both at the time and later. Had they talked to any of Terry's lovers?

He became aggressive, and threatened to end our relationship. I was aware of certain improprieties in the way Mr O'Brien had been conducting the business of the charity. In particular I knew Mr O'Brien had been using monies intended for charitable work for his own purposes.

Not just Jo: Terry was in on the whole scam, must have been. You don't get through a quarter of a million quid without asking where it came from. If indeed they had got through it all: it crossed his mind that there might be more to the missing money than trips to Paris and crates of Bollinger. Enough to get a young proto-politician of limited means up and going.

The argument became heated. I was upset and frightened at what might happen to me if he terminated our relationship. I was also physically afraid of him. My mind was not working very clearly because of the alcohol and drugs I had taken. I struck him on the head with a chair, and he fell down, but he was still conscious. I then hit him again repeatedly until he stopped breathing.

I was feeling sick, and went out on to the fire escape to get some fresh air. At the bottom of the fire escape there was a shed where I knew the tenant of the shop downstairs kept his motor bicycle. I went down to the shed, which was open. I found a can of petrol inside, and brought it back upstairs and spread petrol over the body and around the office. I then took the remaining pills from the desk drawer, but there were fewer than I thought so I drank the rest of the vodka. That is all I remember.

I have had this statement read to me by Detective Inspector Peter Smithwick. I have been told I can add, alter or correct anything I wish. This statement is true. I have made it of my own free will.

sgd: T. Pattichis

Written by Detective Inspector Smithwick and read over by Detective Inspector Smithwick.

Also present: Detective Superintendent Natkeil and T/Detective Constable Denning.

Statement commenced at 2.45 a.m. and finished at 3.20 a.m., 18 December 1983 at Shepherd's Bush Police station.

Harry went through the confession again, singling two or three passages with a Hi-lighter, then put it to one side and picked up Miranda's second fax. This was an excerpt from the transcript of the trial itself.

Antony Tree (Defence Council): You were the officer in charge of interviewing the accused.

Detective Superintent Natkeil: Yes.

Q: You were present when the accused was cautioned?

A: I was.

Q: Did you inform the accused of his right to legal representation?

A: That would be the normal procedure, yes.

Q: And what you describe as 'the normal procedure' was followed on this occasion?

A: The accused was informed of his right to make contact with a lawyer or with his friends.

Q: And he chose not to?

A: He said he didn't want a lawyer.

Tree was doing his best, but he didn't have a lot to go on. He took Natkeil through the procedures, trying to catch him out, but Natkeil was a pro. The nearest he came to catching him was over the drink.

Q: In the statement we have heard read to us, the accused admits to consuming a considerable quantity of drink and drugs. It is reasonable to assume, is it not, that he must have been – to put it mildly – intoxicated?

A: I'm not in a position to comment on the accused's condition prior to his arrest.

Q: But it's fair to assume that he was drunk, to put it mildly.

A: That's not for me to say.

Q: Speaking in general terms, would it be your opinion that a man or woman who had consumed that much alcohol would be capable of giving such a coherent account of his or her actions?

A: In my experience people sober up pretty fast when they find they're in trouble.

Miranda had added on part of the evidence of Dr David McLennan the Divisional Police Surgeon who examined the body.

Tree: On the fifth of March last, in consequence of a message you received from the Police in the early hours of the morning, did you go to a premises on Shepherd's Bush Green?

Dr McLennan: I did.

Q: Arriving there, I think, at about four a.m.?

A: Yes, sir.

Q: Did you carry out an examination of the body of a man who was found there?

A: Yes, I did.

Q: There had been a fire on the premises. Was the body in any way harmed?

A: There was some scorching.

Q: From the signs you saw on the body, what did you conclude was the cause of death?

A: The deceased had received multiple blows to the head from a blunt metal instrument, causing severe haemorrhaging and multiple fractures to the head and neck.

Q: At what time do you believe death occurred?

A: I would estimate the time of death at between ten o'clock on the previous evening and two a.m.

Q: You can't be more precise?

A: In certain circumstances, where a body has been subjected to extremes of temperature, the onset of rigor mortis can be accelerated. I would not wish to be more specific as to the time of death.

Q: But you are satisfied that death had already occurred at the onset of the fire.

A: That would be my conclusion.

Miranda had written 'Time of Death???' *in the margin. She'd also appended the evidence of Peter Ceresole, the fireman who had discovered the body. His answers to the defence came first.*

Tree: What were conditions like in the office?

Ceresole: There was a great deal of heat and smoke. The flames by this stage had been extinguished.

Q: But the visibility was poor?

A: Yes. I was obliged to feel my way. I searched along the outside of the room and found nothing. Having established the layout of the office I proceeded to search the main floor area. I discovered what I took to be a foot. I moved my hand up over the body to the arm to search for a pulse, but there wasn't any. Then I tried to lift the body, using my back, but it was stiff and awkward, so I called for help.

Q: I imagine that in your work you have a certain amount of experience of discovering bodies.

A: Unfortunately, yes.

Q: Based on that experience, would you say that the body had been dead for some time?

A: That thought crossed my mind.

But the Prosecuting Counsel was having none of it.

Sir Patrick Brabazon: Mr Ceresole, you have told us that you have previous experience of discovering bodies at the scenes of fires.

Ceresole: That's right.

Q: Can you tell us how many? Approximately, that is. Ten? Twenty?

A: To the best of my recollection, four or five.

Q: And on the basis of that tragic but, it must be

said, numerically rather small number of incidents, you feel qualified to estimate the time of death?

A: No, I said the body felt to me as though it had been dead for some time.

Q: Speaking, as it were, as a layman, with no specialist knowledge of pathology?

A: Yes, that's right.

Q: And as a layman who is making that guesstimate under somewhat difficult circumstances – in the dark, with as you yourself have told us, a considerable amount of heat and smoke in the atmosphere?

A: That's right.

No one was trying, not even Brabazon. They all had their minds made up. Whenever a contradictory fact or an accidental revelation surfaced both prosecution and defence blinked, coughed into their cuffs and got on with the main business of sending Terry down with as little distraction as possible. It was that kind of trial. You couldn't even blame Tony Tree, who was young and overworked and knew he was on a hiding to nothing. In many ways defence lawyers prefer a client they secretly believe to be guilty, because losing the case leaves their consciences in the clear.

Harry looked at the clock: it was ten past two. He picked up the phone and rang Robert's room number.

'Did I wake you?'

'Yes,' said Robert.

'I'm sorry. Listen, I need the car,' said Harry.

'What, now?'

'Yup. I'll have it back by lunchtime. You don't need me in the morning, do you?'

'I suppose not. But I need the car.'

'You can travel with the sparks,' Harry suggested. 'I'll come over and pick the keys up now.'

Robert was too tired to object.

18

BRIAN NATKEIL WAS A fatty. Not flabby, but firmly fat, podgy hands with fat little fingers, like cocktail sausages stuck on to an orange, one hand grasping an invalid's walking stick, the other a half-smoked cigarette. He had a thick bull-neck, damp oyster-grey eyes, and a black hairpiece arranged too far forward on his head, so that at the front it reached almost to his eyebrows. He was clearly not a well man.

'You have a nerve, I'll give you that,' he told Harry. 'If I want to talk to you, which I probably don't, you write a letter, or telephone, that's the usual procedure.'

'I know. But you might have said no.'

The ex-policeman studied the tip of his cigarette, then dropped it. Ten feet away his pug lifted a leg and pissed against the wheel of Harry's Sierra, parked on a slight rise running up one side of the village green at Great Tew. The air was damp, and wisps of morning mist floated over the paddocks that led down to the stream in the valley below. It was ten past nine.

'What makes you think I'm going to say yes now?'

Harry didn't have an answer to that. He'd spent three hours on the drive down from Manchester trying to think of a pretext, an excuse for arriving on Natkeil's doorstep, and another hour sitting in the car waiting for Miranda. She'd been due to rendezvous with him at quarter to eight. He wondered if she was all right.

Great Tew was the sort of village that used to feature on railway company posters between the wars: two lines of thatched cottages and a village green set in a hollow in the Cotswolds, hemmed in by ancient woods. There was a half-timbered pub, the Falkland Arms, with an orchard and a duck pond and a dovecote; a post office-cum-village shop, also thatched, and a phone box, and up the hill in the forest a gloomy Edwardian manor house and a perpendicular parish church with a long yew avenue. An estate village, except that the estate was no more, and the yeomen's dwellings had become retirement homes and weekend cottages: there were Range Rovers and fun jeeps parked in the weedless gravel drives, the lawns were trimmed with mathematical precision, the roses pruned, the thatches almost bouffant in their manicured splendour. You could buy porcelain models of the Falkland Arms in the craft shops up the road in Banbury, and off-duty bank managers and town clerks came regularly to dress up in loose white suits and Worzel Gummage hats to Morris Dance on the green.

Natkeil lit another cigarette.

'Who are you working for?'

'The BBC,' said Harry.

Somewhere in the trees a peacock screeched. There were guinea fowl, too, scrubbing around in the undergrowth at the edge of the woods. You probably needed planning permission to own a guinea fowl in Great Tew.

'I guessed as much. You might as well come in.'

'What made you choose Great Tew?' asked Harry as Natkeil steered him through the timber gate and up the path to his cottage.

'The wife,' said Natkeil. 'And then she died. Bloody awful place, two parts Birmingham furniture magnate to one part London yuppie, queueing up in the pub to talk to an authentic farm labourer. Or discuss dry rot, they're very interested in dry rot round here.' He unlocked the door. 'Give me Tower Hamlets any day, villains and all. Except even Tower Hamlets isn't what it used to be.'

A narrow stone-flagged corridor led to an open-plan living room, low oak beams, Constable prints on the wall, two framed family photos on a mock-regency corner table, chintz armchairs arranged around an inglenook fireplace, all except one which had been turned round ninety degrees to face a large colour television. A *Radio Times* was open on the coffee table beside a full ashtray.

'If you're looking for breakfast you're out of luck, I don't eat it. You can have a cup of tea if you want.'

Harry had stopped on the motorway in the small hours and eaten a full fry – wet toast, rubber egg, lukewarm brittle bacon, grey bread-filled sausage, homogenized baked beans, long-dead tomato, the lot. Not because he was hungry, but to try and stay awake. He was past mere tiredness now, on into that floating state where the blood inched through his veins like yoghurt. Mentally his clutch had gone, and he was struggling to stay alert.

Natkeil disappeared into the kitchen and returned carrying a tray with a teapot, two cups, a bag of sugar and a carton of milk. He balanced it on top of the television, poured the tea, picked up the ashtray and emptied it into the fireplace.

'You a Londoner?'

Harry reached into his bag for a packet of cigarettes and switched the Walkman Professional to record. He didn't know if he was going to get anything, but if he did he might as well have it on tape.

'Sort of.'

'No such thing. That's half the problem, people like you, "sort of" Londoners. London's like,' – he searched for a cliché – 'a clock. A very delicate mechanism, all checks and balances. People like you come in and start fiddling with it, then you turn round and shit on us when it stops working. It's a mug's game being a city copper nowadays.'

He sat down heavily on the sofa. The pug wandered in from the kitchen and arranged itself at his feet. Harry helped himself to sugar.

'Is that why you resigned?'

Natkeil gave him a look.

'I didn't resign. I was told to.' He stubbed out his cigarette. 'What was it you wanted to talk to me about, anyway?'

Harry didn't want to ask him about Terry yet, he wanted to find out why Natkeil had been kicked out of the force.

'Negotiations with criminals. I'm interested in how ordinary policemen go about solving crimes.'

'They don't, not any more. What they do now is keep their whistles clean. You familiar with the Police and Criminal Evidence Act?'

Harry nodded.

'Villain's charter,' Natkeil continued. 'You nick someone, by the time you've cleared everything with the Duty Officer, got them a solicitor, read them their rights, rigged up tape recorders for the interview, taken fingerprints and statements, searched their house for stolen goods and labelled up your exhibits, that's your day gone. For one bleeding shoplifter.'

He broke off into a fit of coughing. Harry looked at the floor, studying the ugly pink roses woven into the orange carpet. Natkeil took out a handkerchief and wiped his mouth.

'And that's not the end of it, either – you been in court recently? Bloody chaos. They've got this thing called the Crown Prosecution Service now, meant to improve cost efficiency. The way they improve cost efficiency is to pay their lawyers so badly no one wants the job. The whole thing's so understaffed it backs up like a blocked sewer. You turn up in court, there's no one there for the prosecution. Or if there is it's some teenage barrister who's so overworked he hasn't had time to read his brief properly. Days on end you can spend down there, sitting in the office reading the papers, waiting for the brief to remember who he's meant to be prosecuting and what for. There's only two kinds of copper left in the force now, career bureaucrats and canteen cowboys, the rest have all left. Or been told to leave.'

'Why were you told to leave?'

Natkeil looked at him suspiciously.

'You really don't know?'

'No.'

'Clash of personalities.'

Harry kept going.

'Over what?'

'We had a suspect who got tongue-tied in the interview room, so we took him for a ride in a squad car instead. The Police and Criminal Evidence Act doesn't cover what happens in squad cars – no lawyers, no tape recorders, it's what you might call a more intimate atmosphere. Perfectly legal, I'll show you chapter and verse if you're interested. Only the authorities aren't interested in the letter of the law, they're more worried about left-wing MP's sounding off in the House of Commons. I took early retirement.' He smiled. 'A mate got me a job in the Leisure business. Dull work, but it paid for this lot.'

'Leisure as in bookmaking?'

'That would be the bulk of the business, yes. Supervising their security, going down the dog track once in a while to make sure no one's tying rubber bands round the animals' toe nails or filling them up with water or pinching their testicles in the trap to encourage them to run faster. People can get a bit carried away at the dogs.

I'm told that in Ireland they use day-release lunatics to put the dogs in the traps because they're the only punters who can be relied on not to be on the take. A bunch of blokes brought a hot greyhound across from England, swopped it for a local dog with no track record, laid bets up and down the country, a lot of money. When it came to the off the traps opened, all the other dogs raced away, but their's stayed inside. Eventually it backed out arse-first – the lunatic had put the poor bastard in the wrong way round.' He poured himself more tea. 'So tell me again what it is you wanted to talk about.'

'Terry Pattichis,' said Harry. 'The night of the seventeenth of December nineteen-eighty-three.'

Natkeil looked up.

'The Cypriot boy? What about him?'

'I wanted to know how much pressure there'd be on you for a quick conviction in a case like that.'

'Not a lot. Didn't need any pressure, the facts spoke for themselves. Might have been some if we hadn't picked up Pattichis, on account of O'Brien being a bit of a celebrity, but the situation didn't arise. And there was nothing funny about the way it happened, if that's what you're thinking – even the bloody judge commended us. You're not seriously suggesting Pattichis was innocent, are you?'

Harry said he wasn't suggesting anything, he was just curious. He was also beginning to worry about Miranda. She hadn't sounded at all surprised when he'd phoned her in the small hours and suggested they ambush Natkeil together. Maybe she'd got lost. Maybe her alarm hadn't gone off. Maybe she was strapped to a chair in a darkened cellar being punched around the face by hooded gunmen.

A milk truck stopped outside: there were footsteps on the path, and then a knock on the door. Natkeil heaved himself out of his chair, made his way slowly into the kitchen, came back with a wallet in his hand and went to the front door. While he was paying the bill Harry checked out the books on the shelf beside the fireplace. There were four: Philip Paul's *Murder Under the Microscope*, signed by the author; a Dick Francis thriller; a picture-book on the Cotswolds inscribed by Natkeil to his wife on their twenty-fifth wedding anniversary; and *Our Story* by the Kray twins.

Then his eye fell on the note pad beside the telephone. There were two names scrawled in thick pencil: Kapowski, and Terry Pattichis. A wonderful thing, the communications revolution. But if Natkeil had been forewarned – when? by whom? – then why was he playing the innocent? Harry wasn't being obstructed, he was being monitored. At least at the moment.

'Did you work on the Kray case?' he asked Natkeil when the policeman came back into the room.

'Who didn't? Now that was pressure for you. I'm not saying the twins weren't villains, they were. But the East End's a funny place, or used to be. The Press were on at us all the time to do something about the Krays, but the people they lived among weren't. You didn't get a lot of rape or drugs or child molesting or old people being mugged in their beds when the Krays ran their manor. The twins only mixed with their own kind, they mixed with other villains. Unlike the class of offender you get in London nowadays.'

'They did run drugs though, didn't they?'

'Not in Bethnel Green they didn't, that was just for the West End. I can't honestly see the harm in making a few bob out of the class of person who hangs around in West End clubs.'

'The Leisure industry,' said Harry, still worrying about Miranda.

'Precisely. What people do with their leisure is their own business.'

'And the same goes for Jo O'Brien?'

Natkeil put his teacup back on the tray.

'Up to a point. He gave parties, people knew what to expect. Not my kind of parties, but it's a relatively free country; if people want to dress up and enjoy themselves in private I can't see a lot of harm in it.'

'Did you find any evidence of blackmailing?'

'Not that I remember. What makes you think he did?'

'Terry kept a diary. Logged everything that happened.'

Natkeil shifted in his seat.

'A diary? What kind of diary?'

'Lovers, financial transactions, how he spent his day.'

'Who told you that?'

'His sister-in-law.'

The policeman shook his head.

'News to me. I'd have known about it if he had.'

The trouble with coppers, Harry reflected, is that they spend so much time playing out roles that they become like bad actors, the kind you get in Australian soaps: serving up a bit of sincere concern here, a knowing smile there, respectful when it seems appropriate, caustic when it doesn't, routinely lying to the Press unless there's a tactical reason not to. Which means that it's easy to overestimate the significance of a policeman's lie: it may be no more than a habit. And maybe he didn't know about the diary, maybe it was destroyed in the fire, maybe someone else got to it first.

He looked at his watch. It was after ten. Miranda's dead, he decided. And it's my fault.

'Did Ben Webb go to any of Jo's parties?'

'Oh, so that's it is it?' Natkeil took a long draw on his cigarette. 'You don't seriously expect me to answer that, do you?'

'No. But I thought you might tell me why his name never cropped up in Terry's confession. Or why no one called him as a witness.'

'He wasn't Ben Webb then, he was just an ordinary,

well-mannered young man who was in over his head.'

'No,' said Harry, glancing across at the photos on the corner table, one of a woman he took to be Natkeil's wife, the other of a wedding, Natkeil and the wife with a tall bearded youth in a morning suit and a girl in a lace dress, two lines of policemen forming an arch of truncheons in the background. Natkeil followed his gaze.

'Detective sergeant now, down in Southampton, two kids, his wife's in the force. What age was Webb at the time O'Brien got stiffed, twenty-four? Twenty-five? I didn't know he was going to end up running the country. He hadn't done anything, he hadn't seen anything, he hadn't heard anything, so I decided to leave him out of it. They teach you that on courses, don't involve bystanders if you can help it.'

'As a matter of interest,' asked Harry, 'did Ben Webb have an alibi?'

'He went off to play squash, had a meal with friends, went home to bed.'

'Any corroboration?'

'You don't need to corroborate alibis unless some-one's charged with something. Ben Webb was not a suspect. I've interviewed a lot of murderers, Mr Kapowski. Some I charged, some I couldn't prove, but I knew. Ben Webb wasn't one of them.'

Not if you're already convinced you know who did it.

'You said in court that Terry didn't want a lawyer when you pulled him in.'

'That's right.'

'But you didn't say who else he phoned.'

'Didn't I?'

Harry got the transcript out of his bag.

'The accused was informed of his right to make contact with a lawyer or with his friends. "And he chose not to?" Tree asked you. "He said he didn't want a lawyer." Full stop.'

'Tree wasn't having too good a time of it.'

'Nor was Terry Pattichis.' Harry put down the transcript. 'But he did phone someone, didn't he.'

'Are you asking me or telling me?'

Harry didn't answer.

'I haven't a clue. It's a long time ago.'

'But if he did you'd have known about it at the time.'

'Possibly.'

'Because you were there when he said he didn't want a lawyer,' Harry continued. He was watching the policeman's face. Natkeil was blinking.

'To the best of my recall he might have.'

'And if he did you'd have heard what he said, you'd have stayed in the room.'

'If he did make a call it can't have been important.'

He was back in control now, eyes steady.

'One last question,' said Harry. 'Did Jo O'Brien die where the fireman found him?'

'Of course he bloody did.' Natkeil had had enough. 'What's your name, by the way?'

'Kapowski, Harry Kapowski.'

'Russian?'

'British.'

'Well let me tell you something, Mr Kapowski. I don't mind you raking muck on Labour politicians, that's your job. But I do mind false pretences, I mind people barging up to me in the street at nine o'clock in the morning and telling me they want to talk to me about one thing then asking me about something entirely different.'

Which sounded to Harry like a remarkably accurate description of the way a lot of cops went about their business. Natkeil was on his feet now, advancing towards the front door. Harry picked up his bag and followed.

'If you want to know anything about the police handling of the Pattichis case you write to the Met Press office and ask for an interview. But if you've got it into your head that we sent the wrong man down for O'Brien you're barking mad. And if you think Webb had anything to do with it you'd better get yourself a good lawyer.'

'Thanks for the tea,' said Harry.

He had one key in the ignition when Natkeil came out of the house again.

Miranda was on the phone. She wasn't dead: her distributor had packed in on the Oxford ring-road.

19

HE MET UP WITH Miranda outside Boots in Banbury, fifteen miles to the north. He'd suggested Boots because he didn't know Banbury but he was sure it'd have a Boots The Chemist. Only Boots didn't call themselves Boots The Chemists any more, they called themselves Boots Health and Beauty, which seemed less than honest to Harry since the reason people went to shop there was because they were either ill or ugly.

The Boots in Banbury occupied about half an acre of a shopping mall concealed behind the Victorian brick frontage of what had once been a covered market.

'I think the plan is that W. H. Smith take over Menzies and The Body Shop,' he told Miranda as they skirted the Christmas tree in the central plaza. 'Then Dixons take over Smiths, Boots take over Dixons; the management of Menzies buys out Boots, sells off Smiths and The Body Shop to Marks and Spencers and uses the cash to buy a MacDonald's franchise. Or maybe it's vice versa. You're looking wonderful, by the way.'

He was right, she looked terrific. No guile, just the nearest clothes in the cupboard when she woke up: a pair of jeans, canvas sneakers and a faded floral blouse under an old blue sweater.

'Is the car OK now?' he asked her.

'Fine. I think it's probably in better shape than the garage man.'

'That I can believe,' said Harry. 'He make a pass at you?'

'No, he just had some entertaining thoughts about women and engines.'

They found themselves a table in a fast food joint that someone who'd never been to the States imagined looked like an American Pizza Parlour. The coffee was unmistakeably English. Harry ordered croissants and a Danish pastry. Miranda had waffles.

'What's happening in Manchester?' she asked.

'I'm learning to delegate,' said Harry. 'It hurts, but I'm learning. Robert's discovered a late vocation as an auteur director. Today we see the world through Ben Webb's eyeballs. Ben eats a bun, we see the bun the same moment he does. Ben takes a pee, we're there too, peering over his shoulder, when he looks up to the ceiling we pan up too, when he looks down again to shake off the drips we're following him all the way. At this very moment cinéma vérité is alive if not well somewhere in Manchester Mossidé. I love you, incidentally.'

'So you keep telling me. How did you get on with Natkeil?'

'He's a real charmer, you'd like him. He admits Terry phoned someone from the police station but he's not saying who. He says he kept Ben out of it because he has a soft spot for the young. He has a lot of soft spots, does Natkeil, but the rest are all physical.' He got the Walkman cassette out of his bag and passed it across the table. 'Take a listen, the quality isn't great, you might see if you can get anything done with it back at Television Centre.'

'Why are you worried about the quality? You're not planning to broadcast it, are you?'

'Maybe,' said Harry.

'Isn't that against the rules?'

'If we get round to broadcasting it we'll be breaking

a lot worse rules than that. Oh, and he was expecting me – you didn't phone him, did you?'

Miranda looked surprised.

'No.'

'He had my name and Terry's scribbled on a piece of paper by his phone.'

Harry was tired and speedy at the same time. He needed to sleep, but mostly he wanted a shower. Miranda looked so fresh. Fresh and prickly.

'You're really getting off on this, aren't you Harry.'

'What do you mean?'

'You're like a gun dog working against the clock, running here and there, quartering the field, sniffing a scent, chasing it into the brambles, losing it, finding another. You've decided Ben Webb's out there somewhere, and you've only got a week to find him, bring him back in your mouth to the cheers of the crowd. You're not really interested in Terry Pattichis, it's Ben you're after. What's he done to you? Is it Angela?' She broke into a grin. 'That's it, isn't it – Angela. You can't forgive him for carrying her off from under your nose.'

Harry was indignant.

'That's bullshit. There was never anything serious between me and Angela, it was entirely casual.'

'Then what have you got against Ben?'

'Nothing. Or not a lot. I'm suspicious of his Golden Boy politics and I'm curious to know how he's managed to be quite as successful as he has. That's the first of Kapowski's Golden Rules of Journalism – always start from the assumption that the villain's innocent and the hero's guilty, that way you ask all the unaskable questions. If, come the end of the day, the villain turns out to be a villain and the hero a hero, then so be it.'

'What's rule number two?'

'If someone evades a question, ask it again three times, nicely, then stop. At that point the audience know he's got something to hide. Number three is if a politician calls you by your Christian name keep calling them by their surname. There are more if you want.'

'That'll do to be going on with. What happens if the villain turns out to be half hero, and the hero half villain?'

'Then you say so. You don't get a great programme, but you say so. What you don't do is lay off someone just because they happen to be the Deputy Leader of the Labour party.'

'And where does Terry Pattichis come into all this?'

'I'm not convinced he does. But sure as hell something's going on. It may have nothing to do with Ben Webb, but if it has then we owe it to the punters to let them know before they go electing him to high office. Suppose Ben did get his hands dirty over Latchkey, and someone knows about it. Someone who'll keep quiet in return for favours.'

'Like who?'

'That's what we're trying to find out. And what I suspect someone is anxious to stop us finding out.'

'OK,' said Miranda. 'Just remember I'm watching you, Kapowski.'

She scratched her head. Harry loved watching her do little things like that, poking around in her bag, scribbling notes, ordinary mundane little gestures she didn't even think about.

'I checked the Member's Register, by the way,' she continued. 'Ben's incredibly conscientious. He's an unpaid director of three charities, and he has a small number of shares in one of those unit trusts that won't invest in armaments or tobacco companies. He's a parliamentary consultant to two trade unions, they pay him on an ad hoc basis but it's peanuts. They bought the house on an ordinary Building Society mortgage before Wandsworth got fashionable. The money's Angela's.'

Harry blinked.

'How do you know?'

'Friends in low places. She inherited a quarter of a million from an aunt, five years ago. Out of the blue, she had no idea it was coming to her.'

'She told you this?'

Miranda smiled.

'Of course not, I'm not that bold. Roger told me, he was at a dinner party on Thursday. Angela's name came up in the course of the conversation; someone had been at school with her. Apparently she was a right little madam, started wearing lipstick at thirteen.'

'What were you doing when you were thirteen?'

'Reading Jean Paul Sartre and hiding behind my glasses and trying to come to terms with the ridiculous, disgusting rumour that men stuck their thing into you.'

She lit two cigarettes and passed one to Harry.

'We need to talk to Terry again,' he announced.

'I know. How?'

'Have a word with Catriona. Lawyers are allowed access, we might be able to tag along with her.'

'What happens if he doesn't want to see her?'

'Something tells me he will.'

By the time they'd finished their coffees it was ten o'clock. They walked back through the mall to the car park.

Harry didn't know Miranda had a car. If she did he guessed it'd be one of those expensive little foreign cars career girls drive, a top-of-the-range Peugeot 205, or a Lancia Fire, or a Polo, new and pristine, with a sun roof and electric windows and a Residents' Parking Disk on the windscreen. Either that or something Green and ozone-friendly, a deux-chevaux or a Renault 4.

'Is that yours?' he asked, gazing at a rusting ten-year-old Datsun estate the size of a small truck, rusted through at the lintels, bent coat hanger for a car aerial, no rear bumper, seat six in comfort and room for a chest of drawers in the boot.

'Yup,' said Miranda.

'Why?'

'I move house a lot.'

He put his arms round her, her body relaxed and easy against his.

'Let me take you away from all this,' Harry whispered, 'and dump you somewhere else.'

'You need a bath, Kapowski.' She kissed him gently on the mouth. 'And a shave. Or maybe you should make a feature of looking like you've been living rough. Really successful presenters all look or sound odd, I've noticed that. Robin Day has a cold, Jeremy Paxman an arched eyebrow, William Woollard the Dorian Grey look, David Bellamy the stutter, Alastair Burnett the sand-blasted skin. Harry Kapowski sleeps in his clothes, it's worth a try.'

Harry kissed her again.

'I promise,' he whispered. 'When this is over I'll take you away for a dream weekend in Oldham.'

'Meanwhile you'll be back on Sunday?'

'At the latest. You still have a room free?'

She reached in her pocket for her car keys.

'For the moment. Did you phone Pigfoot?'

He hadn't. Pigfoot Walker and Nine Elms Lane had assumed a distant perspective in his mind.

He was in the outside lane of the M6 passing Newcastle-under-Lyme when the midday news came on. Ben made the lead story with a leaked Central Office memo listing policies the Tories had decided for political reasons to omit from their manifesto but would consider implementing if elected. These included privatization of the Universities, further cutbacks in Social Security payments, and the index-linking of old age pensions.

Harry had never met anyone other than a journalist or a politician who had ever read anyone's manifesto. People occasionally glanced at the idiot-speak pamphlets the parties rammed through their letter boxes, and if they were really conscientious they might read a précis in the papers, and that was that. Manifestos aren't meant to be read: they're there to give an aura of competence, to make it look as though a party knows what it's doing. In politics you don't need to do anything, you just need to appear to be doing it.

The Tories were on next, screaming foul and alleging dirty tricks. Could be, Harry reckoned, you never know these days.

He stopped at the Sandbach service station, partly to wash and shave and phone Robert to find out where he was meant to be going, partly to see who else pulled off the motorway. He parked by the phone booths and watched his mirror, noting the traffic coming up the slip road behind him. A red Toyota, a semi-artic container truck, a grey Citröen estate, two black-leathered bikers, a yellow Volvo with a back seat crammed with kids.

Robert was in Bolton.

'Is he on schedule?' asked Harry.

'More or less. We'll be here another hour or so, then lunch in Farnworth, we're due in Wigan around three.'

'Me too, I'll see you there.'

'You're sure you can spare the time?'

Harry grinned. Robert was obviously having a good time.

'Get to fuck will you, Kettle.'

Next he rang Pigfoot. Yvonne answered.

'Mr Walker's secretary?' asked Harry.

'Speaking,' said Yvonne.

'That's not speaking Yvonne, that's grunting. Am I interrupting something?'

'Not interrupting, joining in. My body's tied up, Kapowski, but you welcome to my brain.'

'It's your brain I'm after,' said Harry. 'You're sure it's not a bad time to talk?'

'Doesn't bother me, man. Anything to fill in the time

while he's doing the business. Sometimes I knit, sometimes I read a book, sometimes I just close my eyes and think of England.'

'You don't like England.'

'Precisely. So talking on the phone's no problem at all. Easy, honey,' she told Pigfoot, 'you in no condition to try that these days.'

Harry smiled.

'Let me ask you something. Suppose in the course of an evening Pigfoot grazed his way through the best part of a bottle of vodka, half a carafe of wine, two brandies, three pints of beer, and three whiskies, peppered it up with amphetamine sulphate, a couple of lines of coke, a fistful of non-scrit librium, maybe a red or two and the odd black bomber – what sort of shape would he be in?'

'You planning a party?' asked Yvonne.

'Maybe.'

'Depends. In training he'd be a little vague, a little confused who he was, what he had for his lunch. Out of training he'd be gone for two days, maybe find him asleep in the fridge or someplace. You really got some librium? That stuff's hard to come by these days.' She let out a gasp. 'You want me to move on to my back, sweetheart? You gonna do both of us an injury you keep doing that much longer.'

'In training he might still make sense?'

'Not a lot. He'd come and go. Full of life one minute, dead as a breeze block the next. But he's a big man, plenty of room for chemicals.'

'You weighed him recently?'

'Doing it now. Feels like around seventeen stone. That includes his socks, the man still has his socks on.'

Terry couldn't have been much over ten.

'Suppose he's in training, but a lot lighter. He'd still be able to hit someone over the head with a metal chair?'

'No problem. Tanked up like that he'd lift a bus. Small guys are even worse, don't know they can't do things. I've known an eight-stone weakling take a tap off a bath with his bare hands thinking it was the soap. What the hell kind of party is this you're planning?'

'My niece has a First Communion coming up, I thought I might arrange something a bit special.' Harry cupped the receiver under his chin and lit a cigarette. 'The guy with the bath tap, he knew what he'd done afterwards?'

She laughed. Harry wasn't sure who'd caused it, him or Pigfoot.

'Up to a point. Might have if he was in a calm moment. You planning to stop at the reds and the black bomber?'

'That makes a difference?'

'Makes a difference if you stop there or go on to something else. With that load on board you might manage all kinds of things if the mood was right. Much more and you'd be laid out on the floor for people to wipe their shoes on. Listen, I better go.'

There was a commotion on the line, then Pigfoot came on.

'That you, Kapowski? Where you been?'

'I miss you too,' said Harry. 'How's business?'

'Fucked up, man. You're causing me a lot of pain, Kapowski, you know that? I got cops following me round like I was the Queen touring Ireland. Any time I want to conduct a little business someplace I turn round and there's pigs watching me. I got pigs watching my door, I got pigs tailing me down the street, I got pigs two stools down in the bar drinking fruit juice and giving me winks – why you doing this to me?'

'Hold on while I get more Kleenex,' said Harry. 'Maybe it has something to do with a piece of meat I found on my pillow the other morning.'

Pigfoot was unambiguous. He hadn't done it,

wouldn't have done it that way if he was going to do it.

'You're talking to a Muslim, man, you know that? Muslims don't touch pork.'

'You're a Muslim, Pigfoot? Since when?'

'Long time.'

Harry put more money in the box.

'Muslims don't deal drugs, Pigfoot. They don't loan-shark, they don't sleep with women they're not married to and they don't drink alcohol. They're not allowed to reproduce the human body, let alone paper their walls with photographs of wet boobs and women in leather underwear. Muslims are good people.'

'I didn't know that, man, the brother I talked to didn't say nothing about posters, all he said was blacks and Arabs should stick together against the white man. Makes a lot of sense. And the pork,' he remembered, 'you are not allowed to touch pork.'

'No drink and no hard drugs, stay away from fast women,' Harry insisted. 'It's all there in the Koran.'

'Maybe there's more than one kind of Muslim.'

'I'm sure you're right.'

'And it wasn't me that trashed your flat. Not me, not anyone I know.'

'If not you, then who?' asked Harry out loud.

'You asking me? A woman, Kapowski: that's who'd do a thing like that. You been in any woman trouble lately?'

'No.'

'You sure? How about that no-tits tomboy you're messing with, looks young enough to be your daughter.'

For a moment a terrible thought crossed Harry's mind. But no, not Miranda, he couldn't think of any reason why she'd do a thing like that. He went back on the offensive.

'It's a funny coincidence, isn't it. There's a fellow called Pigfoot who's mad at me; one week he takes a run at me on a motorbike, the next someone entirely different wrecks my flat and leaves a pig's trotter on the pillow.'

'Don't ask me, man, ask the police. I got more alibis than the Pope at Christmas.'

'I'll tell you what I reckon, Pigfoot,' said Harry. 'I reckon you did the bike job. You didn't mean to get Pete, you didn't necessarily mean to get me either, you just meant to scare me.'

'Why would I want to do a thing like that?'

'Because someone paid you to. You were set up, someone phoned you up, knew you had a grudge against me, offered to do business. I don't reckon you're the killing kind, Pigfoot. The deal was simple, you take a run at me, snatch Pete Pattichis' notes, also scare the shit out of me for old times' sake. In return for which you get an envelope of bank notes. The same envelope of money you subsequently put in the mail to Shirley Pattichis after things started to go wrong. Is this making any sense?'

'I'm listening,' said Pigfoot.

'But that's not the end of it. Because the people who phoned you are still at it. Only anything they do now they can blame on you. When they smash up my flat all they have to do is leave a trotter on my pillow and bells start ringing all over the police force; your name's the first one in the suspects folder. You still listening?'

'Uh huh. I'm not saying I did the bike job, but I'm listening. You got any idea who these people might be?'

'I was hoping you might tell me.'

'People like that don't tell me who they are. They just call up, leave off packages.'

'You get any more packages, let me know.'

'I'll do that,' said Pigfoot.

Pigfoot was right about his alibi. When Harry phoned Chief Inspector Calloway, Calloway told him that Pigfoot had spent Saturday evening in police custody in

Luton after a fracas in a club. No charges, just six hours in the cells.

'Handy, that,' said Harry suspiciously.

'I suppose it is,' said Calloway. 'Very handy. You got any other suspects in mind?'

Harry could think of none.

He bought himself a can of coke from a machine, and checked the car park. The three cars and the bikes were still there: the container truck had just left and was moving slowly back down on to the motorway. He drank the Cola, picked up a set of morning papers from the newsagent, got back into the Sierra and headed north.

The hypotheses he'd been trying out on Miranda and Pigfoot sounded good, but they were no more than speculation: he still had nothing that would get past a libel lawyer, no hard facts, no Deep Throat. Hypotheses, just that. And he still couldn't make his mind up about Ben.

The traffic was heavy, and it was raining hard, lashing the windscreen. Three miles north of Sandbach, cruising at seventy in the outside lane, he checked his mirror. The Citroën estate was right behind him, headlights flashing, a sales rep in a hurry. Peering through the spray he could just make out the truck up ahead. As he began to pass the truck it veered to its right, edging him towards the centre reservation and the thin steel rail that was all that separated him from the oncoming traffic on the far side. The realization of what was happening and the need to do something about it happened simultaneously and just in time. He slammed the engine into third and hit the accelerator. The side of the truck hit the Sierra a glancing blow, bouncing off the centre rail, but Harry kept control enough to steer the car back into the outside lane, surged ahead until he was clear of the truck, kept going for another hundred yards, then pulled over on to the hard shoulder.

By then both vehicles had vanished ahead of him into the spray. No names, no numbers, just another throw of the dice in the daily roulette game of winter driving on Britain's motorways.

Harry got out of the car and threw up. He was in total shock, standing in the rain, buffeted by the traffic streaming past. No one stopped, no one seemed particularly interested. He examined the car. The bodywork was a mess on both sides, panels battered, wing mirrors gone. But mechanically it didn't seem to have suffered. He smoked a cigarette to calm his nerves, then drove on, slowly and carefully, as far as exit 18, where he turned off and doubled back to Crewe, dumped the car at the station and caught a train to Wigan.

20

Three whiskies in the buffet car had helped to steady Harry's nerves a little by the time the train reached Wigan. He phoned Roger from the station and told him what had happened.

'Pull out,' said Roger.

'What from? Webb or Pattichis?'

'Both.'

'Is that an order?'

'No, it's advice from a friend.'

'I'll think about it,' said Harry. 'Did Miranda call?'

'She checked in about half an hour ago, she's going straight to Willie Walpole.'

At least she was safe, at least they hadn't tried to give her the rollerball treatment too. Or not yet.

He found Robert and the crew in mid-walkabout in the town centre, Paul with the camera on his shoulder stalking Ben through the crowds, Robert dancing around behind him trying to keep out of shot. This wasn't the moment to break the news about the car.

'What happened to the Steadicam?' he asked the director.

Robert smiled. The Harrys of this world might laugh at him now, but he knew that come the viewing they'd be impressed. Of course they'd slag him off then, too, but only to stop his head getting too big.

'Wait till you see the breakfast,' he grinned.

'Good stuff?' asked Harry.

Robert kissed himself on the hand.

'Stunning.'

'Tonight on *Election Special*,' Harry mimicked, 'the deputy leader of the Labour party reveals the secrets of his muesli.'

'Kippers,' Robert corrected him. 'He had the kippers. Where did you park the Sierra?'

'Crewe station. I'll tell you about it later. What else is on today?'

Robert checked his schedule.

'Liverpool. Trades Council, local radio, candidates' meetings in Walton and Broadgreen. Broadgreen could be bumpy.'

'That's the Militant mob?'

'Yup.'

The walkabout was coming to an end, the minders looking at their watches. Harry found himself walking next to Ben as they made their way to the waiting cars.

'How's it going, mate?' asked Ben, arm on Harry's shoulder.

'To be honest, I haven't a clue,' said Harry. 'I missed this morning. Robert tells me the breakfast is a serious Oscar contender.'

'I hope so. He made me eat it three times, we nearly missed the Press conference. Are you coming to Liverpool tonight?'

'Of course.'

'I'll give you a lift.'

Harry hesitated.

'You're sure?'

'Absolutely. Sam can go with your people.'

Ben and Harry rode in the back of the big Rover. The detective sat up front with George the driver. The mood was relaxed – Harry could tell that Ben got on well with his entourage, neither aloof nor patronizing.

'You know something, Ben?' asked the copper. 'Seventeen years in the force and no one ever offered me so much as a bottle of vodka.'

'Disgusting,' Ben commiserated, 'I don't know what the country's coming to.'

He settled back into the upholstery, legs crossed, elbow on the back sill. Harry turned round to look out the back window. Robert was two cars behind, talking earnestly to Sam.

'So what are you going to say about me in this film, Harry?' asked Ben.

'The basic thesis is that you're a shy, sensitive and inhibited man masquerading as a Rabelaisian demagogue who'd sell his mother for a plate of profiteroles.'

Ben laughed.

'Sounds accurate enough to me. How about my unpublicized work for charity and the way I nursed my crippled baby sister through nine years of terminal cancer?'

'We only have twenty minutes.'

'How much have you shot so far?'

'About three hours, I'd guess. Six-to-one's a very respectable ration for a documentary. Anyway, tape's cheap, it used to be a different matter when we worked on film.'

'But you still want more?'

'Not a lot. We haven't time – we're on air in four days' time.'

Whatever was going to happen was going to have to happen fast.

'Your friend Kettle was asking about the possibility of doing something at the house. We're having a few people round for drinks on Sunday. I'll have a word with Angela, but I don't suppose it'll be a problem.'

Bloody Robert, you couldn't leave him alone for an hour without a banal idea bursting through the top of his skull.

Ben asked George to turn the radio on for the two o'clock news. The Tories were mounting a counter attack on the leaked memo, dismissing it as a mere discussion document, something drawn up for testing at Focus Groups, where selected members of the public were sat down and asked to respond at leisure to ideas and proposals.

'Where did you get the memo from?' Harry asked.

Ben was grinning.

'We have trained moles inside Central Office, recruited when they're still at Pony Club, told to lie low until they're called on.' He gave Harry a wink. 'There's a rule in this car, nothing said or heard here is repeated outside.'

'Fine by me,' said Harry.

'I made it up. A dull news day, I thought we might as well give you boys something to talk about.'

The detective was laughing. Harry was incredulous.

'Hold on. Isn't there a law against that sort of thing?'

'Not that I know of,' said the copper.

'Not even in the Bible,' Ben confirmed. 'I checked. You're not allowed to steal, or covet your neighbour's ass, or cast your seed upon the ground. But it doesn't tell you not to lie.'

'Have you been doing this long?' asked Harry.

'Off and on. All you do is think of something completely beyond the political pale, accuse the Tories of planning to do it, count to ten, and back comes a statement from Central Office saying that no definite decision has yet been taken.'

He handed Harry a cigar.

'The Press does it all the time. Ring up the Archbishop of Canterbury, ask him if it's true he's having an affair with Princess Anne, the Archbishop says no, the papers run it in ninety-two-point bold across the front page, Archbishop Denies Sex Tryst With Princess. After that it's up to the punters – they believe what it amuses them to believe. The same goes for politics. By and large the public don't like the Tories, they think they're smug and selfish and greedy. They think there are circumstances in which they may be the best people to run the country, but they don't like them. Which is why there's an almost infinite public appetite for Tory scandal, political or otherwise.'

'And what about scandals in the Labour party?'

'Oh, we have them. But they tend to be dull affairs. They're mostly to do with policy, not behaviour – reds under the beds, not in them. All the great scandals are Tory scandals – Profumo, Lampton, Parkinson, Selwyn Gummer . . .'

'Gummer?' Harry interrupted. 'What the hell's Selwyn Gummer done?'

'Nothing, as far as I know. But I'm working on it.'

Miranda dumped her car in Marylebone and took the Bakerloo Line down to Piccadilly to see Willie Walpole. She had no idea how you were meant to dress when calling on elderly homosexual peers, so she went as she was, the same sweater and jeans she'd worn for breakfast with Harry in Banbury.

Sometime in the late eighteenth century someone built a life-size replica of an Oxbridge College on a square of land between Piccadilly and Burlington Gardens – courtyards, grass, Old English flower beds, ornate covered walkways, porters' lodges, Georgian architraves and cold stone stairwells leading to self-contained gentlemen's chambers, with additional but considerably more spartan accommodation for servants in the attics.

Albany is still there today, invisible to the outside world, an oasis of dignified seclusion a decanter's throw from the noise and commerce of Regent Street and Piccadilly Circus. The rooms' tenants down the years have included Byron, Macaulay, Gladstone, J. B.

Priestley, Harold Nicolson, Graham Greene and Edward Heath. All men: until recently no women were allowed, not even wives, and children are still excluded.

Willie Walpole had kept a set of rooms there since the 1950s, long before his colourful behaviour attracted the kind of notoriety that the Albany committee are anxious to avoid. And once in a tenant, like a Church of England vicar, is very difficult to remove.

Miranda walked up the steps of the main entrance, watched with some aloofness by a uniformed porter, passed through a hallway and out into the courtyard. Walpole's chambers were on the ground floor behind a baize-lined double door.

'Come on in, my dear.'

Willie Walpole was a big man, running to fat, with a drinker's face that was blotched and beginning to sag with age, but still full of character. Such hair as he still had was long and white. He wore a double-breasted suit and carpet slippers, and a pair of half-moon gold-rimmed glasses slipped halfway down his nose. He led her through the small hall into a handsome book-lined living room – marble fireplace, old but tasteful carpet, three piece suite in wine velvet, watercolours on the walls where there weren't bookcases, a big chinese vase on a table beneath a gilt mirror. A half-read copy of that morning's *Daily Telegraph* lay open at the racing pages. Through an open door she could see his bedroom, carved oak bedstead, unmade.

Walpole's secret, according to Harry, was that he didn't mind what anyone thought about him, leaving him free to broker information on those who do. He was reliably reported to have run a one-man Dirty Tricks department for the Labour party during the sixties and early seventies, for which he was granted his peerage in Wilson's retirement honours – an appropriate reward, given the low level of probity among his fellow-recipients.

Harry also said there'd been a rumour over the years that he was on someone's payroll, though the paymaster varied according to who told you – the Czech secret service, the CIA, Aims of Industry, the Mafia, the Moonies. He certainly had plenty of friends in low places, particularly casinos and boxing halls. The role of Latchkey in these conspiracy theories was vague, the assumption being that he had helped Jo set it up knowing that Jo would abuse it, that it would collapse in tatters and thus help to further discredit the Loonie Left.

The general consensus was that Willie earned his money not from international espionage, but by hawking his services as a lobbyist and political consultant to companies and organizations who felt in need of a hired hand in the Palace of Westminster. Quite legally – everything was above board and on the record.

How such a colourful reprobate could ever have been accepted by the political establishment of any political party was a mystery until you met the man. In the flesh Willie was all charm. He also had a clever and astute brain, a dislike of cant, and a sharp and witty eye for the shortcomings of his fellow politicians. And a nickname: Bugger-Me-Gently. And the reason he still held a curious influence in the political establishment and was considered a Good Seat at dinner parties was that he didn't give a damn: people used him both as a source of gossip and as a testing board, someone whose opinions were untrammelled by ambition or ideological preconceptions.

He settled Miranda into a chair, and disappeared into the miniature underground kitchen, installed in what must once have been a coal cellar. Two minutes later he returned with a tray of coffee.

'So tell me about yourself, Miss Cunningham. No – let me guess? He pushed his glasses up his nose. 'You're twenty-four, unmarried, anti-establishment but drawn to it against your better judgement.'

Miranda blushed.

'Twenty-five.'

'You're also pretty, you may not like it but you are. Have you been in the job long?'

'Two weeks.'

'Long enough. You know, the reason why no one has ever written a decent book about the BBC is that no one with the right spirit has ever stayed in the Corporation long enough to do the research.' He tapped his cigarette lighter against his signet ring. 'So tell me about this programme.'

'It's a profile of Ben Webb. You've known Ben a long time, haven't you?'

'Have I?' said Walpole, sipping his coffee. 'I suppose I have. At least by your standards. A long time for me is rather different. How old did you say you were?'

'Twenty-five,' said Miranda.

'I'm seventy-four.' He wasn't, he was seventy-seven – Miranda had read the cuttings. 'I must have known Webb what – twelve years? Twelve years doesn't seem all that long at my age.'

'How did you meet him?'

'Wrote me a letter, they all do. "Dear Willie, I want to be a politician when I grow up, I wonder if you could tell me how to go about it." There are two kinds, the ones who want to make the world a better place, and the ones who want it to stay as it is but fancy the idea of being in charge. Both utterly impractical ambitions. I tell them to go away and become accountants or belly-dancers or whatever. There's no money in politics and almost no chance of office, the best you can hope for is the back benches, a more dreary, thankless and socially inconvenient life than which it's hard to imagine. Have you ever been into the Commons? Most of the time it's empty, three or four people making pompous speeches to the panelling. But the tough ones don't give up, they keep writing back, telephoning, even turning up on your doorstep. In the end, if they seem at all intelligent, I try to get them a job to shut them up. MPs like cheap labour around the place, keen young researchers to look up facts for them and so on.'

'Ben was keen?'

'Certifiably, dear girl, certifiably. Utterly dedicated.' He put down his cup. 'Where was I. Oh yes, the job – he kept pestering me so in the end I put him on to a fellow I knew in the charity business.'

'That would be Jo O'Brien?'

'The very man. South African, something of a maverick, ended up getting shot.'

'Bludgeoned,' Miranda corrected him. 'Someone hit him over the head with a chair and set light to his office.'

'Poor old Jo. Still, it was probably the way he'd have wanted to go if he'd had the choice. Full of delicious pills, he can't have known much about it.'

'Did you?'

'What, kill him?' Walpole laughed. 'Not as far as I remember. It's possible though, my memory's shocking these days. That's the wonderful thing about old age, you forget all the worst parts. No, it was that Cypriot boy, Terry something.'

'I didn't mean that,' said Miranda apologetically. But a bell had gone off in her head, an instinct that Walpole was playing deeper games than his cheerful banter suggested. 'There's some doubt about who killed him – I just wondered if Ben talked to you about it at all.'

The peer examined his cigarette.

'Doubt among whom?'

'Terry's family.'

Walpole chuckled.

'Well there would be, wouldn't there. It's possible someone else did it, I suppose. What have you come up with so far?'

'Bits and pieces, nothing very substantial,' said

Miranda. 'It's not really what I'm interested in, we just came across it by chance when we were looking into Ben's background.'

'Ah, but you're absolutely right, my dear. Ben did it. Jo refused to sleep with Angela, Ben treated it as a personal insult – every one else seems perfectly happy to go to bed with her. Greater gift hath no man than this, that he lay down his wife for his friends. Ben Webb on a murder charge – I love it. Tell me what you want me to say and I'll sign it on the spot.'

'What have you got against him?' Miranda asked curiously.

'Nothing, absolutely nothing. I think Ben's the best thing that's happened to the Labour party since Dick Crossman died. He's not as bright as Dick, but he's a heap more realistic. It's no good being holier-than-thou in politics, you have to play by the rules, keep your eye open for the main chance. No, don't get me wrong, I admire the man, it's just that a good scandal now would brighten up the campaign no end.'

'What do you mean by "play by the rules"?'

Walpole picked a hair off his sleeve.

'I mean be aware of other people's strengths and weaknesses. Don't get sentimental about your colleagues. Find a crowd and get in front of it. Be all things to all men. If you can't be wise at least be funny. Commit yourself to generalities but not to specifics. Remember that fear is the most potent emotion in politics – Ben's very good at all that stuff.'

'Who taught him?'

'Official Secrets Act job, that.' He laughed. 'No, I'm not a believer in conspiracy theories, my dear. I think he taught himself, but he's had help along the way. Nothing sinister, just good advice. Whitehall likes him. They've had a lot of autocrats at the tiller lately, and Ben's a pragmatist. If this was Jerusalem he'd be a Jew, as the saying goes.'

Miranda wondered if it was true. She liked Walpole, but she didn't trust him, suspected he often came up with a theory just to test the credulity of his audience.

'You were a trustee, weren't you?' she asked.

'Of Latchkey? Possibly.' He thought for a moment. 'Yes, I think I was.'

'Were you surprised to discover what had been going on?'

'About the money? A little. It didn't seem to me to be that important. What was it, a quarter of a million? Peanuts by charity standards. Prince Philip and the World Wildlife Fund handed over a million dollars to the Chinese to help save the panda not long ago, and the Chinks used it to build a dam that wiped out the poor animal's habitat. Jo may have had his fingers in the till, but at least he spent the loot on something constructive.'

'Did Jo have many enemies?'

'No. Or not that I knew about. People took him for what he was. You could disapprove of him, I suppose, but it was hard not to like the bugger.' He looked at his watch. 'Anyway, that's how I first got to know the young Webb.'

'Would you be happy to say it again on the record?'

'I don't see why not. When would you want to film it? I'm off to Spain next week.' He got a diary out of his breast pocket. 'Sunday's hopeless.'

'Then it would have to be Monday morning,' said Miranda. 'We transmit that evening.'

'Wouldn't that be leaving it too late?'

'Not at all,' said Miranda blithely, hoping it wouldn't.

21

HARRY WOKE A LITTLE after seven; got up, showered and dressed and went downstairs. Saturday morning, this must be Liverpool. The hotel was in the Grand Victorian style, recently refurbished, with a wide marble staircase running down into a pillared central hall. The theme of the reception was ice cream — moccha woodwork with blueberry cheesecake panels, a lime-sorbet carpet, frosted cornet wall lights, neapolitan cushions on strawberry-syrup sofas. He passed through the revolving doors out into the street.

He was a block from the waterfront, and could smell the sea air blowing in on a warm damp wind from the west. Friday-night Liverpool had only recently gone home to bed, and a small sad-looking Indian in an anorak was mopping at a line of vomit which stretched from the door of the Star of the Ganges to a nearby bus stop; further down the street a woman in her late forties, a shopping bag in each hand, was being kissed on the mouth by a man in a donkey jacket. Invitations to a Troops Out meeting, a Marxist rally and a born-again Argentine's evangelist convention were pasted beside the rock posters on the hoardings. He walked a hundred yards down the street, turned left into an alley, then stopped and waited to see if he was being followed. He wasn't. He bought an armful of newspapers from a Chinese newsagent and went back to the hotel in search of breakfast.

His head was full of Miranda again. It was a ridiculous affair, fragile and brittle, with no prospects. Everything about it reeked of danger – danger to his dignity, danger to his career, danger to his habits and self respect. He valued his habits not out of idleness but because they took care of the mechanics of his life and left him free to worry about other things. With Miranda, however, he worried about everything: how he dressed, what he ate, what he said, who his friends were; only when anger or frustration overcame him did he feel the strength and confidence to be his own man. He was forced to take her views and opinions seriously, not because he wanted to change his ways but because he wanted her affection, and if you wanted Miranda's affection you had to take the rest too.

The hotel dining room was a cross between a flower show and the booking hall at St Pancras Station: a high ceiling with deep plaster reliefs, pillars painted with custard-yellow marbling, dome lights and Raffles ceiling fans on brass chains, urns of palms and swiss-cheese plants, tame ivy hanging from baskets on the walls. There was a buffet of steam-trays lined up beside the door, overseen by a shirt-sleeved Lebanese maître. The waitresses came from further East, Malaysia and the Philippines, and circulated erratically among the tables with glass jugs of Kona coffee. Harry glanced around his fellow guests – a middle-aged couple on a wedding anniversary break, a table of young business executives studying a folder of display materials, a Frenchman in a double-breasted suit writing notes on an A4 pad: all very innocent. He collected his food from the buffet and sat down to read the papers.

Ben's Tory revelations had made almost all the front pages: 'LABOUR'S LAST-DITCH SLURS' in the *Sun*, 'SOAK THE OLD!' in the *Mirror*, 'TORIES DENY UNIVERSITY SELL-OFF' in the *Telegraph*. Ben had been right, a slow news day. Labour had moved up two points in the

Guardian's opinion poll, mostly at the expense of the Liberal Democrats.

'Morning,' said Robert, dumping his orange juice and scrambled eggs down on the table beside Harry. He was wearing his North Country rig, lumberjack shirt with rhinestone buttons, neatly ironed stone-washed Levis, dustless trucker boots. Harry folded up his paper and reached for his coffee.

'Sorry, that seat's taken.'

Robert smiled.

'We have company today. Roger's coming up.'

'Why?' asked Harry incredulously.

'Day out of the office, I suppose. Pleasant train ride, free lunch, show his face to the troops, back in time for the theatre.'

'It's Saturday, he wouldn't be in the office.'

A day out from Mrs Carlisle, he guessed.

'Whatever,' said Robert. 'He's arriving at noon. We ought to think about a stand-upper today.'

Stand-uppers being Robert's phrase for pieces to camera: he wanted Harry to perform.

'Sure. What would you like me to say?'

'Oh, the usual,' said Robert.

The table to their right had been taken over for a business meeting, two groomed women and two dull men, bleary-eyed, all with matching business accessories and portfolios and presentation materials.

'Which usual had you in mind, "there's-a-man-in-this-building-behind-me-who-won't-talk-to-me" or "on-the-one-hand/on-the-other-hand/only-time-will-tell"?'

Reporters always claim they hate doing pieces to camera, but they don't. They hate writing them, and they hate getting them wrong, re-doing them time and time again in front of crowds of jeering onlookers. But for most of them the stand-upper is the embodiment of their self-image, the ultimate Being There. Harry was no exception. He didn't like admitting it to himself, but

233

he liked seeing himself on the screen, a successful man on top of the job.

'Twenty seconds,' said Robert. 'Sixty words or so. With the Mersey in the background.'

'Finishing with a brief reference to the Beatles to cue some music?'

'Precisely.'

'If you'd thought of it earlier I could have done a piece about the Spencer Davis Group while we were in Birmingham.'

'Who?' asked Robert.

'Never mind,' said Harry.

The young were so ignorant these days.

Pigfoot had enough flowers in the back of the big Chevie to open a florist. Roses, irises, white lilies with phallic yellow stamens, all dew-fresh from the Clapham cemetery where they'd been lying unappreciated on the grave of some old widow who'd been buried the evening before. Yvonne thought it was wrong to take flowers from a cemetery, but Pigfoot couldn't see the harm in it, people have other things on their minds the day after a funeral than wondering what happened to the floral tributes. He hoped Shirley liked flowers.

It took him a while to find the house: Finsbury Park was unfamiliar territory to him. Or maybe he took time because he wanted to put off doing this. Also ten o'clock on a Saturday morning was early for him, normally you could hit him on the head with a pick-axe on Saturday mornings and he wouldn't feel a thing. But business was business.

Shirley was still in her tracksuit, making a pot of tea for Taki while the kids watched TV in the corner. Taki was reading a woman's magazine.

'Mrs Pattichis?'

'Those for me?' asked Shirley, eyeing the irises incredulously.

'Uh, huh,' said Pigfoot. 'More in the car if you need them. Can I come in?'

Shirley was dubious.

'You tell me who you are and what the garden festival's in aid of and I might think about it.'

'It's about your husband.'

'What about him?'

'That's why I need to come in. I want to talk.'

This was as far as Pigfoot had planned. He knew what he had to do, but he didn't know how to do it.

'You got a name?' asked Shirley.

'Walker, Bartholomew Walker.'

'Pigfoot,' she realized. 'You bring your motor bike with you this time?'

'That's what I want to talk about.'

'You got a lawyer with you?'

'No, ma'am.' A long time since Pigfoot called anyone ma'am.

Shirley sent the kids through to the kitchen. Taki got to his feet.

'No, you stay,' Shirley instructed him. 'I want a witness for this. Sit down, Mr Walker.'

Pigfoot cleared a space among the toys on the sofa, balanced the flowers on his knee, and started to cry.

Shirley lit a cigarette.

'This going to take long? Only we live busy lives, I have shopping to do.'

Pigfoot was wondering the same thing, how long he could keep the tears up before his sinuses started giving him trouble.

'Wasn't meant to happen,' he muttered.

'What wasn't meant to happen?'

Pigfoot didn't answer.

'You married?' Shirley asked him.

'Not exactly.'

'What does that mean? Either you married or you not married.'

'I got a woman I live with.'

'One born every day,' said Shirley, very matter of fact. 'You love her?'

'Shit, man.' Pigfoot wiped his face on his sleeve. 'I came to say sorry.'

'You did? For what? For killing Pete? You gonna tell me why?'

'It was an accident.'

'The accident was you didn't kill half the street. I know about the accident, what I want to know is the bit that wasn't no accident.'

'I only know about the phone call. Man calls me up, says I hear you got a grudge against Kapowski, maybe we can do some business.'

'What kind of man?'

Pigfoot wasn't too sure, except that he was English – real English, not Brixton or Finsbury Park.

'Like a policeman?' asked Shirley.

Pigfoot thought about it.

'Yeah, that sort of voice. Could have been a policeman. Only the police don't need to go hiring black men to do their dirty work, they skilled enough at that themselves.'

'Not any more,' said Shirley. 'The police got to be careful about these things nowadays.'

Pigfoot was thinking.

'Could be a policeman, yeah. Or someone's friends of the police. That was in the deal: anything went wrong, I didn't have to worry too much about the law. Might be some unpleasantness, maybe I have to answer some questions, come up with an alibi and stuff. But nothing serious, he said I got good insurance if I do the business.'

'What business, you still not telling me what the business is.'

'The business is snatch, the Greek – I mean your husband, he walks in the restaurant with something and

Kapowski walks out with it, then I make a snatch, and sometime or other I'll get another phone call and arrange to leave off the snatch someplace and pick up my fee. Only I never made the snatch. Kapowski reckons that's where I got the money I sent but he's wrong, that was my money. You need to be careful believing what TV people say.'

'And this man who hired you, he called back?'

'Just to say no snatch, no cash, but not to worry, maybe something else might come up.'

Shirley butted her cigarette.

'You got any way of getting back in touch with him?'

'That's what I'm trying to figure.'

'Well you better keep figuring if you want out of this shit you got yourself into.'

Roger's train was half an hour late getting into Lime Street, and it was almost two by the time his taxi managed to track the crew down in Walton. He carried no luggage, just a copy of *The Economist* tucked in the pocket of his black raincoat.

'Nostalgic for the old days?' asked Harry.

They stood in a strong cross-wind watching the crew set up the tripod on top of a block of flats.

Roger smiled.

'Nostalgic for filming, no. For Liverpool, yes. My first job was on the *Echo*, fresh out of college in a safari jacket and hipster flares. Sideburns too, as far as I can remember. It's a great city to be a cub reporter in, full of freaks and rebels and people who think it's the government's fault they haven't won the pools. And I fell in love for the first time, a girl called Brenda. A bit like Miranda, a woman of very strong convictions. How are you getting on with Miranda, by the way?'

'She's a very good researcher,' said Harry.

They took a late lunch in a Chef and Brewer in Widnes, Ben's last call before flying to Southampton for an evening meeting. Harry and Robert hadn't decided whether to go with him yet.

'He's in London from tomorrow – it's his turn to take the Walworth Road morning Press Conferences,' Harry explained. 'We're shooting a drinks party at home with him tomorrow lunchtime, that's about it, unless a big story breaks. In which case we can borrow the footage from news.'

Roger waited until Robert had gone off to talk to Paul before raising the real reason for his visit.

'What have we got?'

'Not a lot,' said Harry. 'Most of it's circumstantial. Ben was at Latchkey for part of the evening, then went off to play squash. There's nothing to suggest he went back to the office afterwards. Someone made sure his name stayed out of the newspapers. Terry Pattichis is being looked after, he still gets money from somewhere. I genuinely believe he doesn't know if he killed Jo or not. He made a phone call from the police station, we don't know who to. Jo made a call too, from the Beaumont Arms, about an hour before he was killed. No one bothered to check exactly where Jo died, or when, they simply took Terry's confession at face value. And someone somewhere is sufficiently jumpy about what we're doing to take the risk of leaning on the DG's office to call off the bloodhounds. Very little of which we can prove.'

'So what do we do next?'

'Angela wants to talk to me again. I also want to talk to Terry some more, we're trying to fix it with his solicitor.'

Roger was dismembering a beer mat. He looked up.

'You'll be careful, won't you Harry. We have to cover our arses in sheet iron on this.'

Harry nodded, saying nothing.

'What about Angela?' Roger continued. 'She's an old flame of yours, isn't she?'

'More of an ember than a flame. But I can hardly dupe her into grassing on her own husband.'

'Of course not,' said Roger. 'Even if Ben does have something to hide, there's no reason to assume she knows about it too.'

'She knows he's in trouble.'

'That could mean anything. When are you seeing her?'

'I haven't fixed anything yet. We're meant to be shooting her and Ben and the kids at home tomorrow. Tell me something, Rog – in your experience how easy would it be for someone to convince the powers that be that you were mad if you weren't?'

'Someone like me or you, very difficult. Psychiatrists would spot it a mile off. But someone like Terry, it's possible. Guys like that do their homework, they can be very convincing. They also have access to drugs, they can do a lot if they put their mind to it. You think Terry's faking it?'

'It's crossed my mind. I think there's someone he's scared of on the outside. Someone who looks after him as long he's where he is, but on condition he stays there. He's certainly got money from somewhere, enough to keep him in silk shirts and pay off the HP on his brother's car.'

Roger finished his drink.

'What other lines are you working on?'

'Miranda's doing some background on Ben. Catriona Clark is trying to get the Met Forensic Lab to do Electro Static Data Analysis checks on Terry's statement to see if it was altered, only she can't track down the original. That's about it at the moment. Oh, and in my spare time I'm making a documentary for *Election Special*.'

'Keep that as the day job, Harry. The other business doesn't have to happen now, we can keep it on the back burner until after the election. The worst thing that could happen is to rush it.'

'Mangan's been hassling you again, hasn't he.'

Roger smiled a sad smile.

'Not hassling, just reminding me. He likes to cover his arse too. But whatever you do, don't get Ben Webb's private life confused with the election, they're different animals. Get it wrong and the country has to live with the consequences for the next five years.'

'You think Labour's going to win?'

'That's what the private polls are saying. Both of them, Labour and Tory. It'll be close, but Labour should manage enough to get them a working majority.'

'Don't worry,' said Harry. 'They'll find a way to screw it up between now and Thursday.'

'Probably. But don't do it for them.'

Robert was making his way back across from the bar, looking at his watch.

'When are you coming south?' asked Roger.

'Tonight, I think,' said Harry, draining his lager. 'By train. I need to make some calls.'

'You still OK for a bed?'

'I think so.'

They spent the afternoon shooting vox-pops in the street, and then Harry's piece to camera. Robert positioned the camera a long way off, shooting down a long lens that foreshortened the perspective so that Harry appeared to be suspended between a motorway and the docks. Trucks piling by in the foreground, a container ship moving slowly past in back of shot, a big orange sun sinking into the mist over the Mersey. Very stylish, very pretty, and fuck-all to do with Ben Webb or the General Election.

Robert wanted Harry to appear to be walking towards the camera, but the evenness of the ground meant that he would disappear from shot halfway through his piece. Harry was so far from the camera that he and Robert could only communicate via the sparks, crouched behind an oil barrel holding a battery lamp and walkie-talkie. The walkie-talkie didn't work, so in the end Roger acted as a runner, thirty-five thousand pounds worth of BBC executive sprinting to and fro across the puddled waste ground.

The solution they arrived at was for Harry to walk on the spot: from where the camera was he'd look as though he was coming towards it. Harry started off word perfect for once, but a fault developed on the camera battery and they waited five minutes for a replacement. By now the container ship had gone, and they stood down again, waiting for a humble dredger to come up the river. The ground under Harry's feet had turned to mud.

'If Pigfoot was a hired gun,' said Roger, doubled up beside the sparks behind the oil drum, watching the skyline for Robert's cue, 'who paid him?'

'Not just who,' said Harry: 'Why?'

Whoever it was, they didn't have much time left to find out.

22

IT WAS NINE-THIRTY that evening by the time Harry got back to Marylebone. He found Miranda in the kitchen, sitting on one chair, her feet stretched out on another, rolling a joint, licking skins and arranging them on the table in front of her. She looked tired too, but cheerful. When Harry bent down to give her a tentative kiss she made him linger and slipped the tip of her tongue briefly between his lips.

'Good day at the office, darling?'

'Murder.'

Miranda giggled. She lit a match and singed the edge of a small block of black resin, blew out the flame, crumbled a pinch between her finger tips and spread it carefully on the skins.

'Are you really called Kapowski?'

'Afraid so,' said Harry, sitting down beside her. 'I was born Fitzgeorge-Parker but I changed it by deed poll when I decided to get famous. Kapowski sounds sort of interesting, breaks the ice at parties.'

She shook her head and moved her feet off the chair on to Harry's lap.

He helped himself to a joint. He had a lot of catching up to do.

'What's all this business really about?' Miranda asked.

'Social engineering,' said Harry. 'What happens in the

end is Ben Webb confesses to the killing of Jo O'Brien, gets three years' suspended because he went to school with the judge, and goes off to run a youth club in the East End. Roger Carlisle and Tony Mangan swop wives, Shirley Pattichis marries either Taki or Pigfoot Walker, she hasn't made her mind up yet. And you and me set up a *ménage à trois* with Angela. Angela stays home and looks after the babies while we research a series of documentaries on Unspoiled Beaches of the South Pacific for Channel Four.'

They moved through into the sitting room. Harry glanced across at the answering machine: the red light was on, the switch set to record. He wondered how long it had been that way. Miranda put on a tape, Robbie Robertson, 'Somewhere Down the Crazy River'.

Harry stretched out on the sofa, Miranda cross-legged on the floor beside him. It was a long time since Harry had anyone to come home to after a hard day. Most evenings he either went out or stayed in at Nine Elms Lane on his own doing his expenses or writing up notes or watching current affairs TV. He didn't know if it was impending middle age or bachelorhood, but he'd noticed that he found it increasingly difficult to do things that had no practical purpose. Lounging around getting stoned and listening to music was something other people did.

He dropped his hand over the edge of the sofa and found Miranda's neck, and she reciprocated, resting her arm on his leg, playing with the hem of his trousers.

'Are you hungry?' he asked her. It was quarter to ten.

'Mmm.'

She got up and put her shoes on, and they went downstairs and round the corner into Paddington Street.

This time Harry was sure they were being watched. A single male, sitting in the front of a Vauxhall Cavalier parked under the trees at the corner of Ashland Place, directly across from Miranda's Datsun.

'You got your car keys on you?' he asked Miranda.

'Sure.'

'Gimme,' said Harry.

He opened the passenger door for her, got into the driving seat and started the engine, then turned it off again.

'What's going on?' asked Miranda.

'We have company. Stay here for a moment, I want to make a phone call.'

He got out of the car, crossed the road and went into the phone booth in Nottingham Place.

Pigfoot answered first ring.

'Kapowski? I need your help, man.'

'Mutual. You busy, big man?' asked Harry.

'Head's busy, body ain't doing nothing.'

'Stockwell underground, half an hour. Miranda and I will be in a yellow Datsun estate, heading south down Clapham Road. Red eighty-seven Vauxhall Cavalier, EGB 414F, following us. Fellow at the wheel might be of interest to you. I'll turn left down Stockwell Road, then right into Landor Road. Thought you might be able to lay on a party.'

The Vauxhall kept its distance as they drove south across London, and was maybe forty yards behind as they forked left at the traffic lights into Stockwell Road. A small crowd was gathered on the pavement outside the underground, but there was no sign of Pigfoot.

Landor Road was an archetypal south London inner-city street, two lines of brick artisan terraces, some with small shops and fast food outlets on the ground floor, interrupted by the occasional piece of dull municipal architecture. For Sale notices littered the windows, and a number of the shops were boarded up. The traffic was light. He was three hundred yards down the road when three West Indians waved him down. He pulled over.

'You the Polak?'

'More or less,' said Harry.

'Second right, Edithna Street.'

Edithna was a long straight residential cul-de-sac leading to a patch of mud and grass, beyond which the lights of a high-rise receded upwards into the drizzle. The road was almost empty, just two lines of parked cars, a builder's skip, four youths playing football under the street lamps. Harry waited until the last minute before indicating right, turned the corner and kept going.

The Vauxhall's driver took the bend at speed, then hit the brakes hard when he saw the dead end, the Datsun parked by the kerb, but not hard enough to avoid the football or the teenager who ran out on to the road after it. The kid gave a shout of pain but took the fall well, rolled over the bonnet like a gymnast, gave an Oscar performance writhing on the wet tarmac. By the time the driver was halfway out of the car Pigfoot and his friends had him surrounded.

Harry and Miranda, innocent bystanders minding their own business, didn't wait to find out what happened next.

Neither of them spoke much as they drove north.

'You still hungry?' asked Harry as they crossed the river.

'Not really. I'd just like to know what the hell's going on.'

'Me too.'

Miranda hunted in her bag for cigarettes. A week ago she'd been giving up, now she was back on twenty a day.

'You're scared, aren't you.'

'A bit.'

'What of?'

'Truck drivers, motorcyclists, burglars.'

'Then why are you doing this? What are you trying to prove?'

'I'm not trying to prove anything, I'm trying to find out the truth about what happened to Jo O'Brien.'

'No you're not, you're looking for a good story, your very own Watergate. Except this isn't a Watergate, this is a meaningless little vendetta against Ben Webb. What the hell does the truth matter in a case like this?'

'The truth always matters.'

'Does it?'

Harry could hear a storm about to break in her voice.

'What's bugging you?' he asked.

'Ben Webb. You've got a thing about him, haven't you?'

'Not particularly.'

'Ben Webb believes in what he's doing,' Miranda continued. 'He's not a fool, he's not just a soap-box demagogue, he knows politics is a complicated business, that you have to play by the game to get things done. He makes no bones about it. But he's prepared to do the work. Which is a terrible reproach to the know-all classes, TV liberals and newspaper columnists.'

Harry had decided not to argue, or not yet: he wanted to hear it all.

'What's the other half?'

'Angela, of course. Ben won the girl. We're not talking about Starsky and Hutch any more, this is a Western. You lose Angela, shed a few tears, shrug your shoulders, get on with life. But you never forget. And ten years later you get your chance, you're on a job and you run into Ben again. And Angela. She's still beautiful, you arrange to see her on the pretext that you want to talk about Ben, you end up spending an evening together – am I getting this right?'

Harry had had enough.

'One: if Ben is such a guiltless hero, why has he resprayed his CV to remove all trace of Latchkey and Jo O'Brien? Two: who apart from Ben would know enough about what we're doing to try and stop us? Three: what is it he's afraid we'll find out? Four: why has no one checked his alibi? Five: I've spent the past fifteen years as a journalist and the worst thing that ever happened to me was I got hit by a half-brick in a riot in the Falls Road. Then I start looking into Latchkey and within a week I've been hit by a motorcycle, bulldozed off the motorway, had my flat broken into and been followed round town by hired hands in unmarked cars. We're not talking about political realpolitik, we're talking about a murder, and a frightened screwed-up kid who's spent the last eight years inside. Anyway, this isn't about me, or Ben Webb, or Pigfoot Walker, or Terry Pattichis. You're jealous.'

They'd reached Trafalgar Square, Harry negotiating his way across the traffic lanes heading for the Charing Cross Road.

'Should I be?' asked Miranda.

'Do you want an honest answer? No – I'm not about to have an affair with Angela Webb. The thought crossed my mind, and kept going.'

They'd stopped at traffic lights.

'Look me in the eyes and say that again.'

'I'm not about to have an affair with Angela Webb.'

'Then lay off her husband. What do we know about him? He left the office five hours before Jo was killed. He had no motive, there's not a shred of evidence to link him with what happened later. Or to what's been happening this week. But you're not interested in that, what you're interested in is Angela. An affair may be too complicated at the moment, but you still want to go to bed with her some day. You'd like to keep her on the long finger, if that's not too crude an expression. A spare fuck for a rainy day.'

'I suppose there may be something in that.'

Miranda smiled a distant smile. Distant, but at least she was in sight again.

'You bastard – are you turning honest on me? When all else fails disarm her with the truth?'

The traffic was moving again.

'The other way didn't seem to be getting me anywhere.'

'OK, let's keep going on the truth, then. How much of this are you going to put in the film?'

'That's simple,' said Harry. 'We're shooting two films.'

Miranda looked at him.

'Does Roger know about this?'

'Up to a point, Lord Copper.'

'And what's in the second film?'

'All sorts of stuff. They're shooting the reconstruction tonight.'

The top floor of Shirley's house wasn't a bad match for the Latchkey offices once Robert and the designer had reefed out the beds and cupboards, whitewashed the walls, stuck up posters and calendars, and installed desks and filing cabinets. Shirley, the only person present who had ever set foot in the original office, was supervising the decor.

'The light, it's wrong, they had one of those paper ones, like a globe, from China or someplace. And more postcards, there was a whole wall beside the window, nothing but postcards from people on holidays. Or from Terry and Jo, they used to send themselves cards to have them waiting when they got back from someplace, remind them what a good time they had.'

Downstairs in the kitchen Taki was serving coffee to the four actors. Close up none of them looked much like Jo or Terry or Ben, but they had the right builds. A costume lady was unloading clothing from a van, hanging the shirts and trousers and jackets on a makeshift rail beside the back door. Across the room a fake police sergeant was preening himself in front of a wall mirror, smoothing down his jacket, picking hairs off the shoulder. The uniform was his own: plenty of small-time actors own police uniforms and hire themselves out as a complete package, notebook and all. There were special effect boys there too, tinkering with a smoke machine in the back garden.

'Jesus,' Miranda said quietly. 'Where did you get all this shit?'

Harry handed her a coffee.

'That's the advantage of working for the BBC, it's all stacked up waiting for you. As long as you have a Project Number all you do is call up and order it.'

They went next door to the sitting room, where Robert was waiting with a VCR.

'These are the exteriors,' he announced, starting the machine.

The screen flickered and stabilized into a VT countdown clock. At zero the clock cut to a shot of Shepherd's Bush Green at night, street lamps and car headlights burning through the darkness, a silhouette of buildings beyond. Then a window lit up. There was a flash, followed by flames, then dense smoke.

'It's a combination of interactive digital video techniques,' Robert explained knowledgeably. 'Using ADO's and a machine called Harriet. We had to mess around on the master with Quantel paintbox to get rid of anachronisms.'

'I'm sure you did,' said Harry. 'It's brilliant, run it again. How much did it cost?'

'Not a lot, I used spare overnight downtime at the Framestore.'

'And what's it for?' asked Miranda.

Robert reset the machine.

'The night of the fire.'

They watched it through again.

'But how can you do a reconstruction? You don't

249

know what happened,' Miranda protested when it was over.

'Precisely,' said Harry. 'No one does. Or we know more or less what happened but we don't know who was involved. We're not supplying answers, we're asking questions.'

'Bullshit, you're showing how Ben Webb could have knocked off Terry.'

'No we're not. We're showing that the case against Terry Pattichis is shot full of holes. At this stage Ben is just a witness who may know things he hasn't yet chosen to put on the record.'

'Then why not just ask him?'

'I will.'

Miranda shrugged her shoulders.

'You have an odd way of going about things.'

Harry lit a cigarette.

'We're only doing it this way because we have no alternative. The BBC's so shit scared of the politicians it falls over backwards to do what it's told. Tony Mangan doesn't give a shit about Terry, he's only interested in his CBE.'

Shirley was at the door, holding a jar of instant coffee.

'You meant to have this in the office?'

Robert looked up.

'Sure.'

'It's Maxwell House, Terry never drank Maxwell House, only Gold Blend.'

'Does it matter?'

'You tell me, I don't know what you people think is right or wrong. I'm just telling you he drank Gold Blend.'

Paul was ready for a take. The office was arranged pre-fire, three of the lookalikes in position, Jo at his desk working the phones, Terry rummaging in a filing cabinet, Ben typing in a corner. Miranda and Harry crouched in a corner out of shot, trying not to get in the way of the sound recordist. Miranda was still in shock.

'Trust me,' Harry whispered.

'Give me one reason why.'

Robert called for Action. The camera started tight on a wall clock set at seven o'clock, panned down the wall to Jo, panned slowly to Terry, and then pulled focus to reveal the Ben-clone staring vacantly into space.

'Cut,' said Robert. 'Could we have a bit more animation from the actors this time please?'

They did it again three times before he was happy. Then Paul moved the tripod into the middle of the room to do close-ups.

And so it went on for another hour and a half. Each shot had to be individually re-lit; they had problems on sound, and with the video recorder. At one stage a light exploded, showering them with hot glass.

'How long is this going on for?' asked Miranda, looking at her watch. It was quarter to two in the morning.

'Don't even ask,' said Harry wearily.

Next they did Ben getting up from his desk, collecting a squash racket from the stationery cupboard, saying his farewells; then Ben pouring drinks; then Terry complaining of a headache, Ben fixing him up with pills. On and on. Harry and Miranda left at three.

'You're really going to transmit all this?' she asked as they got into the car.

'Probably,' said Harry.

'But what if it turns out Terry did it all along?'

'Do you think he did?'

'I've no idea, Harry. I'm just doing what I'm told.'

'But you must have a hunch.'

'Not really. The only hunch I have is that Ben Webb had nothing to do with it.'

'Any particular reason?'

'What's happened this week just doesn't feel like his

style. He may have his flaws as a politician, but he doesn't strike me as the kind of man to put out contracts on BBC journalists.'

'Do you fancy him?' asked Harry.

Miranda smiled.

'Not really.'

The phone rang. Shirley answered it, spoke briefly, then put her hand over the receiver.

'Your friend Walker,' she told Harry, passing him the phone.

Pigfoot sounded nervous.

'You know what you just done to me, Kapowski?'

'No, but you're about to tell me. Let me guess, you just assaulted a police officer.'

'Ain't no ordinary police officer, man says he's working for the government but he ain't no policeman. And no one laid a finger on him yet, he's just worried he hurt someone driving too fast round a corner.'

'Does he have a name?'

'Knight,' said Pigfoot. 'Stephen Knight. Least that's what it says on his driving licence.'

Harry reached into his pocket for his notebook and wrote down the name and licence number.

'Does he have any other ID?'

'Nope. What do you want me to do with him?'

'You got any plans of your own?'

'I given up having plans, Kapowski. As far as business is concerned, I retired.'

'Then let him go,' said Harry, and put the notebook back in his pocket. 'Unless Shirley has other ideas.'

Shirley's idea was for someone to find out who Mr Knight was and who he worked for.

'That something you can do?' she asked Harry.

Which was exactly what Harry was trying to figure out. Time was not on his side. There were less than two days until transmission, under five to the election itself.

23

THE SUNDAY PAPERS ALL had their final opinion polls, which showed little movement in the position of the parties. The parties themselves had lined up a cornucopia of photo-opportunities – humourless economic spokesmen were to be seen sharing jokes with showbiz comedians, designer-dressed women candidates in high heels climbing on to tractors, their male counterparts bouncing round children's hospital wards on pogo-sticks or disappearing down sewers in hard hats and white wellies. The fun of it all.

Harry scanned the headlines briefly, and then hit the phone, but Sunday morning was a bad time to try looking up neglected contacts. He left plenty of messages, but by half past ten had made little progress. What he really needed was a bent copper or a civil servant with access to the DVLC computer in Swansea, where the ownership details of Stephen Knight's Vauxhall Cavalier would be stored, but none of his contacts were home. He rang Television Centre and checked in with Robert, entombed in the basement briefing his tape editor before setting off for Wandsworth, where they were due to film Ben and Angela at noon. Miranda was off to Broadmoor with Catriona Clark to see Terry. If he let her.

She dropped Harry off at Nine Elms Lane on her way west. Mrs Perrymede had done a comprehensive job:

the flat had been cleaned, scrubbed, dusted, the surviving contents arranged not as they had been but as she thought they should be. The air stank of bleach and polish, the walls had been washed down, most of the stains were gone from the carpets. Harry pawed his way from room to room, putting things back in their correct places, made himself coffee, and changed into a suit. Half an hour later he was back on the road, heading for Wandsworth.

There were cars parked on the pavement for thirty yards on either side of the house in Baskerville Road: Volvo estates, Mercedes, big Saabs, top-dollar Peugeots, sporty little Lancias – the weekend chariots of leisured London. The house itself was one of a row of detached Edwardian villas with fake-Tudor appendages. There were mountain bikes in the clematis-encrusted porch, and the heavy half-glass door was open, the sounds of voices pouring out into the street.

There must have been fifty people inside, drifting in and out of the rooms, sitting on the stairs. Paul and his crew were rigging lights and laying cables in the hall, Robert sitting on an oak seaman's chest making notes.

'You sure he wants us to film all this?' he asked Harry. 'It's not exactly an East End street party.'

'Sure. There aren't a lot of votes in being cockney these days, what people want is success. He's made it, but he still cares, the perfect combination. If he didn't have a house and family like this the Walworth Road image-sculptors would hire him one. This is how we're all going to live when the People's Party have had a chance to run the country for a couple of years.'

Two already substantial ground-floor rooms had been knocked together to form an open area that ran the full width of the house and on out into a wrought-iron conservatory, from where steps led down into a pleasantly chaotic urban orchard. The room had a high moulded ceiling, oriental rugs on a timber floor, a lot of good Victorian furniture, mirrors and hangings and careful but interesting oil paintings on the walls – semi-abstract landscapes, boldly executed portraits and over-age nudes. Downstairs Harry glimpsed a big live-in kitchen, quarry-tiles and scrubbed pine. There were two more storeys above, and sounds of a TV coming from what he assumed to be the kids' quarters.

He steered his way through the guests to the conservatory, past chattering groups of men and women in their thirties and early forties, barristers, merchant bankers, journalists, fashionable academics, maybe the odd writer – well-fed, confident people who had country cottages in Suffolk, spent their Christmases in the Alps and alternated their other holidays between the Scottish highlands, Tuscany and exotic beaches in the Indian Ocean. A hired-in barman in shirtsleeves and a black tie was uncorking a bottle of Chablis behind a long and well-stocked table covered with a Moroccan blanket. There was music playing from the hi-fi, a medley of sixties hits, loud enough to disturb the conversation, not loud enough to dance to.

He looked around to see who he knew, but the faces all looked the same, middle-aged public schoolboys with wives who were trying to look glamorous in cheeky short skirts or colourful ethnic silks. Ben and Angela's friends were drawn from the Interesting Rich of their generation, not a career failure or hair-shirt to be seen.

'Harry!'

Ben bore down on him. Loose brown cotton trousers, open necked denim shirt.

'I thought there was an election on, Ben. Shouldn't you be off rallying the troops?'

'Later, later. Who don't you know?'

'Everyone,' said Harry.

Ben laughed.

'Wise man. I probably shouldn't have you here at all. It's Angela's party, really. You're not going to take the piss, are you?'

Harry grinned.

'Just promise me you won't turn into a Kinnock if you get the leadership.'

'In what way?'

'Friend to all the world until you get to be King, then slam the door and appoint some harridan woman to filter all your calls and blame it on her when no one gets to talk to you any more.'

'Promise,' said Ben. 'If and when. Have you said hallo to Angela yet? She's here somewhere, though God knows where. I haven't seen her properly for about a month.'

A tall Nigerian in tribal dress had just appeared in the doorway.

'Excuse me a moment,' said Ben, and vanished.

Harry was left admiring a five-foot wooden carving of a whale alongside a woman with gobstopper eyes and a long skirt. She introduced herself as Celia. Celia had a husband called Vance, built like a water tower, with stilt legs and a barrel chest and half-moon glasses. Vance was convinced he knew Harry. Harry didn't know Vance from Adam.

'Didn't I meet you in Groucho's with Johnny Lloyd and Ed Victor?'

'Possibly,' Harry smiled.

The real answer was No: you've seen me on TV. Once a week it happened to him, a stranger in the street, someone at a dinner party, confused by a familiar but not instantly famous face. The trouble with appearing on the box was that you never saw the audience but they saw you all the time.

'Have you known Ben long?' asked Celia.

'Two or three minutes,' said Harry.

'Ha ha,' Vance snorted.

Robert backed into the conservatory, arse in the air as he laid a curved length of plastic rail on the floor, the last link in a circle of tracks that ran like a toy railway around the entire edge of the room. Behind him Paul and the engineer were unpacking a long flat aluminium suitcase containing a lightweight camera dolly.

'You know Goddard's shot of the Rolling Stones in the recording studio in *Sympathy With the Devil*?' he explained to Harry. 'The camera circles endlessly round them — I don't think there's a single cut in twenty minutes.'

'How long are you looking for from this sequence, Bob? To the nearest hour?'

'We'll mix in and out of the track, lay voice over and commentary. It doesn't need to be that long.'

A teenage child, borrowed from a neighbour, was handing round snacks on a tray.

'You don't have any pre-Chernobyl cheese, do you?' asked Celia.

Harry had caught sight of Angela over by the door. She saw Harry too, and gave him a quick wink. She wore a short black dress, unadorned except for a Bedouin necklace. Say eight hundred quid for the dress, another three for the necklace. Harry left Celia and Vance discussing the wooden whale and joined her.

'You do this every weekend?'

She looked him straight in the eye.

'More often than you'd think.'

'Business or pleasure?'

'Mostly business. You have to, in politics. It's called making contacts.'

'What kind of contacts?'

'All kinds.' She glanced around the room. 'That's Jules from Faber and Faber, for example. He's publishing a book of Ben's speeches.'

Someone had turned up the stereo. The man from Fabers was dancing with a big-arsed corn-fed American woman with bad skin, shifting his weight from one foot to the other, nervously swivelling his bottom, clapping his hands above his head and looking at the ceiling. His partner danced with her eyes closed, hips swaying out of time to Chuck Berry.

Angela pointed out half a dozen other guests – a city analyst, a fashionable academic, a moneyed computer-software mogul, a visiting *Newsweek* columnist.

'Ben's on a roll at the moment. They need us, we need them, it's a symbiotic relationship. Do you disapprove?'

'Of course,' said Harry.

Paul had the camera on the dolly and was rehearsing the track round the room, Robert tiptoeing beside him to clear the way.

'The trouble with this lot,' Angela was saying, 'is that all they're interested in is the sound of their own voices.' She smiled. 'I was like that when I was twenty; I wanted to sit up all night talking about Proust and existential-ism: all the men wanted to do was fondle my tits. It's the other way round now: I want them to fondle my tits, all they want to do is talk.'

Harry grabbed another glass of Pimms off a passing tray.

'What's it like being married to a pathological liar?'

Angela looked at him blankly.

'The Tory memo,' he explained.

'Oh, did he make that up?' She smiled. 'I can't really see the harm in it. You're not going to blow the whistle on him, are you?'

'I promise not to.'

She looked across the room. Ben was standing by the fireplace with his back to them, deep in conversation with the woman from *Newsweek*.

'Have you seen the garden?'

'Should I?'

'I think so.'

She took him downstairs through the kitchen and out

across a patio piled with bicycles and potted shrubs on to a lawn planted with old apple trees and fringed by flowerbeds. The sounds of a Sunday morning football game floated across the bottom wall from Wandsworth Common. The air was fresh but not cold.

'What are those,' asked Harry, pointing at random at a clump of greenery.

'Dead nettle, I think.' She took a sip from her glass. 'To old times, Harry.'

'To old times,' said Harry. They walked on down the lawn, pretending a mutual interest in the herbaceous border. Angela bent down and snapped off a leaf.

'Maybe we should have got married. Do you ever think about that?'

'Sometimes.' A lie, but he thought about it now.

'I do. I was carrying your baby when Ben got back from the States.'

Harry froze.

'You were what?'

'Pregnant. I didn't tell you at the time because I didn't want to blackmail you. You used to be very upright in those days.'

'Good God!' said Harry.

'I wish he was.'

'What happened?'

'I miscarried. A girl, flushed down the sluice at the Middlesex Hospital. Ben thought it was his, he was terribly upset.'

They'd reached a small fibreglass pond sunk into the earth beneath a leafless lilac bush. Harry sank down on his haunches and dipped a finger into the water.

'Because of the kid?'

'That came into it. And there were other things — family pressure, people's expectations, a desire not to hurt him.'

'But you also loved him, didn't you?'

'I think I must have. It's perfectly possible to love

more than one person. I meant what I said the other night: he's been good to me, in his own way, he's just not the monogamous type. The whole success thing hasn't helped, either. It's had its advantages, but it's changed both of us. And not for the better.'

Harry got up again.

'Have you ever known anyone whose character has been improved by money or fame?'

Angela looked him in the eye and smiled.

'It looks to me as though you didn't turn out too badly yourself, Harry.'

Her hand was fiddling with the bedouin necklace. He hadn't noticed before quite how drunk she was.

'I'm not at all sure about that. And anyway, I'm not that rich or successful.' He lit a cigarette. 'Does Ben have money?'

'No, the money's mine.' Her hand had moved to her ear lobe, fingering it absent-mindedly. 'I had a great aunt who died — we knew she was well off, but it honestly never occurred to me she was as rich as she was. We thought we might get enough for a new car. It turned out to be a little over three hundred thousand pounds.'

Harry put a mental verification tick beside Roger's dinner-party gossip.

'Does it bug Ben to have you bankrolling him?'

'Not as far as I know. I think it probably rather suits him — he can live comfortably without compromising his socialist principles.'

'If he has any.'

'Oh yes, he's serious about all that. Don't be put off by the tradecraft, he only plays those games because he thinks they're necessary. He can't see the point in feeling virtuous on the periphery: if you're going to play the game at all, you play hard.'

'You said he was in trouble,' said Harry.

They turned and walked back towards the house.

Harry glanced up at the first-floor windows, but there was still no one watching them.

'Are you still working on Latchkey?'

'Not exactly.'

'What the hell does that mean?'

'It means someone told me not to. I'm also up to my neck in the election.'

'How much do you know?'

'Not a lot. I know what you told me, that Ben was there earlier in the evening. I know Jo O'Brien resorted to blackmail once in a while, but only with strangers, he wouldn't touch anyone he was fond of. I know Terry made a phone call from the police station, but I don't know who to. And I know someone has been paying Terry off, sending cheques to his mother in Cyprus.'

They'd stopped. Angela was nodding, fingering her hair.

'I don't know who Terry phoned. But I can tell you about the money. I sent it.'

Harry took a drag of his cigarette.

'Why?'

'If I tell you, will you use it?'

'It depends on the reason.'

'I swear this has nothing to do with Jo's death. You have to believe me, Harry.'

'I'll try.'

Her eyes were on him, watching for his reaction.

'Ben had an affair with Willie Walpole,' she said softly. 'Nothing serious, it was over long before Jo was killed. I'm not even sure Ben's properly bisexual – there's never been a hint of anything since.'

Ben and Willie: it sort of made sense. Not good sense, but plausible sense. He could even see them together, Willie's mischievous nihilism, Ben escaping from the dead tedium of the overcrowded committee rooms of the Chartists and Tribunites, plotting revolutions and internal coups and blaming the late arrival of the

Socialist Millennium on the ideological deviations of their fellow party members. Compared to all that, Willie Walpole and Jo O'Brien would have been a lot of fun; and if the price the embryonic young politician had to pay at the end of the evening was going to bed with Willie then that wouldn't exactly harm his career – Willie could still open plenty of doors in those days.

'Terry wasn't averse to a spot of blackmail, either,' Angela continued. 'He was very reasonable about it – what was it, a hundred quid a month? He knew we could afford it even in those days, before the real money came along. His mother was crippled with arthritis, she was living in cramped conditions, a hundred quid a month made a lot of difference. Pete didn't have any money, he had Shirley and the kids to look after. A bit of redistribution of wealth didn't seem unreasonable to Terry. He was fond of his mother. The funny thing is, if we'd said no, I don't think he would have done anything about it, I don't think he would have crucified Ben, it wasn't his style.'

'How did Terry know?'

'About Ben and Willie? He bugged them. He was at a party at Willie's flat, left a transmitter in the bedroom. Jo bought back a suitcase full of gadgets from Hong Kong one time, they played endless games with them.'

'You heard the tape?'

'Some of it.'

'And a hundred quid a month – that was it?'

She looked down at her hands.

'Not entirely. Terry wanted a bit of pocket money as well.'

'Enough to pay for Pete's car?'

'That and a few other bits and pieces.'

'Are you still paying?'

'Not for his mum. But the rest, yes, he still gets his allowance.'

'Does Ben know?'

Angela didn't answer.

'Why did you say Ben was still in trouble?'

'If any of this got out it could be misconstrued. Not by you, I'd trust you. But the tabloids would have a field day.'

She bent down and scratched at a speck of mud on her sixty-guinea soft-leather shoes. Harry said nothing. The old Desmond Wilcox interview technique: act sympathetic to your subjects, but don't help them, leave them with the echo of their own words, and sooner or later they'll say something else, if only to get rid of the silence. Always works.

'There's something else as well,' Angela said, straightening up and taking a sip of whisky. 'Ben's alibi on the night.'

'You were his alibi.'

'I know. After he left the office he went to play squash round the corner. You don't have to check, I already did. He had a court booked for seven. A foursome: him and three mates, they played for an hour.'

'Do you know who the mates were?'

'Friends from Oxford. I knew two of them, Andrew Kavanagh and Roderick Murphy, the third was a friend of Roderick's called Damien Harrington. They all went off to eat afterwards, but Ben left at half past ten, said he had work to do. I was meant to be out of town, I had a ticket for a Vivaldi concert in Croydon but I had a headache and decided not to go. Ben didn't get back to the flat until midnight.'

'Did he seem upset?'

'More surprised than upset, he didn't expect me to be there. We had a row, I accused him of being off with another woman. He'd thought I was out of town, the perfect opportunity.'

'What did he say?'

'He admitted it. He was full of remorse. I forgave him and we had a screw. I've always believed that cuckolds should behave incredibly well, make their partner feel like a real shit. I thought that was the end of it until we heard the news on the radio the next morning. To start off with we were just freaked by Jo's death, then it dawned on me. And him: he went to pieces. Partly because of Jo and Terry, but also because he realized he had no alibi, or not one that he was about to admit to.'

'Who was the other woman?'

'I don't know, he's never told me. A married woman, he admitted that much.'

'Does Ben do drugs?'

'No. He does food and alcohol and sex, but as far as I know he's never touched drugs.'

'Why are you telling me this?'

'Because I'm scared, Harry.'

'Of what?'

'I don't know. Of what would happen if people started asking questions again, I suppose.'

'All this is about sex, isn't it. Death, politics, blackmail, fame, money, but in the end it all comes down to sex.'

'I suppose it does.'

'What I really want to know,' said Harry, 'is what you meant by the note you left on my pillow the night before you and Ben got hitched.'

'I meant I wanted that night to be a disaster, I wanted it to be a fumbling mess, I wanted you not to be able to get it up, I wanted to feel disgusted with myself for being there, I wanted to get you out of my system before I tied the knot with Ben. That was to be the final fuck. And it was. How long is it now, eight years?'

Harry did the sum in his head.

'About that.'

They'd reached the patio.

'We still could,' she said.

'Could what?'

'Get married.'

She was right, they could; and it would probably work, at least for the first few years, which is about as much as you can say about most marriages. In fact marrying Angela would probably be a safer option than life with Miranda. Less exhausting, certainly.

'I'd have to get divorced first, of course,' she went on. 'I'm sure it could be tastefully done once the election's out of the way. Then there's the children – how would you feel about becoming a stepfather?'

'Terrified, frankly.'

'I'm joking, of course.' Her hand was on the door. 'But I do still love you.'

Upstairs the party was still in full flow. No one seemed to have missed them. Celia was dancing rather awkwardly with the Nigerian. Ben was talking to a crew-cut young man in a double-breasted suit. Robert and Paul had the camera set up looking back into the room, whale in the foreground, guests behind. Harry went across to join them.

'I need a shot of you with Ben, Harry,' said Robert.

'Doing anything in particular?'

'Looking relaxed.'

The two of them went over to Ben.

'Do you just want me and Harry together?' asked Ben.

'Whatever seems most natural,' said Robert, and cued Paul to turn over.

'Then let's have the three of us together. Harry, I'd like you to meet Fritz Buber. Danny, this is Harry Kapowski.'

Harry extended his hand.

'What do you do?' he asked.

'I'm a lawyer,' said Fritz.

'What kind?'

'Libel.'

'Best in the country,' said Ben, smiling through his strong white teeth.

24

Terry Pattichis wanted the Tories in by a majority of eleven, or Labour by thirty-three. He'd got twenty to one on the former and seventeen to one on the latter, via a male nurse with a line to a bookie's in Newbury. He also had to-the-nearest-ten laying off bets on both of them, an accumulator of startling complexity on the positions of the minor parties, and a quid each way on Billericay to declare first, second or third on the night.

Catriona and Miranda both laughed. Half the laughter was spontaneous, the other relief that he'd agreed to see them in the first place. They'd been there a little over half an hour now, and the mood was getting more relaxed. He'd volunteered little new, but he'd answered their questions civilly enough.

'This is still to do with Ben Webb, I assume.'

Terry crossed his legs and pinched the seams of his immaculate grey worsted trousers to make sure they hung straight. The shirt was creaseless too, white linen, open at the collar.

'Not entirely, Terry,' said Catriona. 'It's also about you and Pete.'

Terry put down his teacup.

'Poor bloody Pete. Do they know who killed him yet? Shirley was on about some West Indian dopehead with a daft name – Trotter? Footless?'

'Pigfoot, Pigfoot Walker,' Miranda corrected him.

She was hypnotized by Terry. Despite what Harry and Catriona had led her to expect, she'd still been anticipating a rough diamond, not this immaculately dressed, quiet spoken young man with the Cliff Richard manners, who stood up to shake their hands, pulled out their chairs for them, fussed over refreshments and took credit for the flower arrangements on the tables in the visitors' lounge.

'Have they charged him yet?'

'Not with murder,' Catriona explained. 'Reckless driving.'

'Is that what it was?'

'He was aiming for Harry,' said Miranda.

'Any particular reason?'

'He was paid to.'

Miranda thought she saw a worrying thought cross Terry's face.

'Who by?'

'That's what we're trying to find out.'

'Any ideas?' asked Terry. 'Apart from Ben Webb,' he added, smiling through well-polished teeth. But the cheerful mask was beginning to slip, his brow contracting into a frown. He glanced round the room to see who might be listening.

'If Ben's involved he's not in it on his own,' said Miranda.

'And Pigfoot claims not to know who hired him?'

She shook her head.

'They've had another try at Harry since. They also ransacked his flat.'

'So what's his theory?'

'Very straightforward. Whoever stitched you up is worried that the stitching is about to come undone.'

'Assuming I was stitched up.'

'Assuming you were stitched up.'

'And if I wasn't?'

'Then we're back to square one.'

'And I get left in peace.'

'Unless you want to know who killed Pete.'

Terry offered them more biscuits.

'Yeah, I'd like to know who killed Pete,' he said quietly. 'But I'm not sure how much I can help you. The police know all this?'

'Not all,' said Catriona.

'Why not?'

'Harry doesn't trust them.'

'Wise man. Trust no one and always carry a condom, that's what Jo used to say. Have you talked to Willie Walpole yet?'

Catriona looked at Miranda.

'Briefly,' said Miranda. 'We're seeing him again tomorrow.'

Terry scratched the back of his neck.

'Yeah, Willie might be able to sort all this out. Tell him Terry thinks he may be in danger of getting his memory back.'

Harry and Robert went straight from Wandsworth to Television Centre to check on the editing. They edit underground at the BBC, somewhere beneath the statue of Hermes, in charm-proof bunkers divided by glass windows and linked by an incomprehensible labyrinth of identical corridors. A whole race of engineers lives in this gloomy tomb, pink-eyed and pale-skinned after years of subterranean incarceration.

Steve Curtis was an engineer's engineer: spectacles, Terylene shirt, BBC Club tie, slept-in tweed jacket, C & A jeans and socks inside his sandals. He was known to his colleagues as Caravan Curtis: there were caravan magazines and catalogues beside his Tupperware lunch-box on the shelf, torn-out photographs of caravan sites and rallies Sellotaped to the walls, a half-repaired ball-hitch on a shelf beside the door.

Harry had brought three polystyrene cartons of Vendomat coffee, and handed them round. It was half past two.

They'd been sending tapes and cutting orders back to London all week, and an off-line rough-cut was already in the can. Harry pulled up a chair and sat down while Steve ran back to the beginning.

The tape opened with Ben in the streets of Birmingham, a quick montage of handshakes and smiles intercut with vox-pops; then a long pan across the city skyline, ending in a leisurely zoom to the Sikh temple, Ben's speech laid over, then a cut inside to Ben in close-up at the microphone; a sound and vision mix to a second exterior zoom to the Islamic centre, more speech, a cut to the rostrum, Ben addressing the Pakistanis; then the same again in Stoke, this time with an English audience. A longer chunk of speech this time, with plenty of cutaways of the audience. On top of all this Robert had superimposed newspaper headlines. The sequence ended with a slow dissolve to a still of Ben as a baby, on a beach with his parents, at school, at University, getting married, at his first Labour party conference.

'First commentary comes here,' Robert explained. He checked his clipboard. 'Sixteen seconds, say forty-five words.'

Harry made a note. Next came archive footage of Ben campaigning for his parliamentary seat.

'Hold it there,' said Harry. 'We need a shot of Latchkey.'

Steve stopped the tape.

'But I thought . . .' Robert started to say.

'Just a shot. There's nothing to prevent us saying he worked there, it's part of his CV. We're not suggesting anything, we're just stating a fact.'

'Mangan won't like it.'

'Of course he won't. But put it in anyway on the Townson Principle.'

Under the Townson Principle – named after a producer of the same name – you put in something you knew your boss would take out to distract his or her attention from other more subtly controversial ingredients.

There wasn't a lot else Tony Mangan or anyone else could object to. Steve had left gaps for Willie Walpole's interview and the footage from the drinks party, but otherwise the sequences cut together well and logically. A bit rough still, but Harry knew it would come out fine in the end. The whole thing ran twenty-seven minutes, which would cut down to twenty without too much pain. It ended with a rousing plea by Ben on behalf of the Common Man, a perfect cue for Harry to pick up in the studio interview afterwards. Mr Webb – do you really see yourself in the role of the Common Man?

Harry ran through his notes, checking the commentary durations, what he had to pick up from and where he needed to take the narrative before the following sequence.

'Version two,' said Steve, changing tapes.

Harry checked the corridor to make sure they weren't about to be disturbed.

'It's only a very crude assembly at the moment,' Robert apologized. 'We're still short of pictures in places.'

The second film began the same as the first, but moved much more rapidly through Ben's life and career, with no reference at all to Latchkey. After five minutes it faded down to black, held there for three seconds, then mixed to a picture of Jo O'Brien. Robert talked Harry through it.

'Part one is the popular conception of his career, very upbeat and eulogistic. Then we stop dead and tell the Latchkey story.'

'Whatever that may be,' said Harry.

'Precisely.'

Steve ran on. After Jo there was a wide shot of Shepherd's Bush Green, then three Latchkey posters in quick succession, the ones with the ethnic kids in street doorways; then archive of Jo surrounded by celebrities at a charity rock concert in Richmond Park. The picture froze, and a graphic circle picked out Ben in back of shot, talking to Willie Walpole, indistinct but unmistakeable, and a youth in a white shirt. Two more circles appeared around them.

Harry peered at the screen.

'That's Terry?'

'I reckon,' said Robert.

He produced a newspaper photo of Terry Pattichis taken at the time of the trial and held it up beside the monitor.

Harry asked Steve what he thought.

'Who's going to say it isn't?'

'An awful lot of people,' said a voice behind them.

Roger Carlisle was leaning against the door jamb, hands in his trouser pockets.

No one spoke. Roger came into the room and sat down.

'Before you do anything else, take that bloody machine off the circuit, it's on ring-main – it's being piped all round the building.'

Steve reached forward across the desk and punched a button.

'Next,' said Roger, 'you can explain what the hell this is about.' He picked up a plastic coffee-stirrer and began bending it in his fingers. 'And no bullshit, I want the truth.'

Harry was thinking fast.

'It's a standby, Roger.'

'A standby for what?'

'In case the story happens in a hurry. We've more or less finished the election movie, so we've used the spare

271

time to cut together a sequence about Latchkey which can drop in at the last minute if we need it. If the story doesn't happen this week then *Not Proven* can have it, if or when we do something on Pattichis.'

'Show me,' said Roger.

'It's not finished yet. Give us an hour.'

'If I give you an hour you three will slash together thirty seconds of anodyne garbage to shut me up. I want to see what's here now. Run it, Steve.'

Steve looked at Harry. Harry swivelled round in his chair to face the editor, so that he had his back to Roger. He made two small hand gestures, turning down an imaginary sound control with one, shortening the duration with the other.

'Run it,' he agreed. 'It's still mute, I'm afraid.'

Steve started late and came out early, so that what Roger saw was the news coverage of Terry's trial, night exteriors of the Balzac bistro and the Beaumont Arms and the West London Squash club, a few newspaper headlines and still pictures of Jo and Willie and Ben and the reconstruction. No voice-over from the illegally recorded interview with Chief Superintendent Natkeil, no artist's impression of the motorbike piling into Harry and Pete outside the Bombay Duck. Total duration maybe six minutes.

'That's it?' asked Roger, finally snapping the stirrer between his fingers.

'That's as far as we've got,' said Robert.

'Or as much as you want to show me. You're mad, Harry, you know that? Have you even talked to a lawyer about any of this?'

'Yes,' said Harry, which was technically true: Catriona was a lawyer. Not a libel lawyer, but a lawyer.

'And what did they tell you?'

'The usual. Probability isn't enough, all that shit.'

'And you're seriously considering transmitting some of this tomorrow night?'

272

'Either we do it now or we do it when he's deputy prime minister. Or party leader. You know what the odds are on getting it past the thought police then. We're talking about murder, Rog: we're talking about a man in Ben's position against a kid like Terry Pattichis. Better to have him exposed now than blackmailed in office.'

'Who the hell's about to blackmail him, Harry – you? And I thought Terry was happy where he is.'

'That's because he thinks he did it.'

Roger was on his feet again.

'I don't know what the hell you think you're up to, but I'll tell you this. Sometime tomorrow afternoon you and Robert and Tony Mangan and God knows who else from the politbureau are going to sit down in a viewing theatre and watch a twenty-minute programme about Ben Webb's career in the context of the current General Election. Knowing what Tony thinks of you there'll almost certainly be a BBC lawyer present as well. You're going to watch it, and then you're all going to talk about it, and before you leave the theatre you're going to decide between you if it needs any changes, and if it does you and Robert and Steve are going to make those changes, and that is the film that goes out tomorrow night. If, at some stage, we want to make a programme about Terry Pattichis, we'll make a programme about Terry Pattichis. And we'll do it in the usual way, in our own time. That's the good news.'

Harry was looking at his feet.

'Get on with it, Roger.'

'The bad news, at least as far as you're concerned, is that the live interview which follows will be conducted by your erstwhile *Panorama* colleague Tim Green.'

'Says who?' demanded Harry.

'Tony Mangan. And if he hadn't made that decision, I would.'

*

Harry needed to get out of the building. He had a script to write, phone calls to make. He also wanted a drink. He grabbed a cab off the rank in Wood Lane and went home.

Inside the flat he poured himself a whisky, turned on the TV, slumped down on the sofa and picked up the phone.

The first person he rang was Miranda. There was no reply. He left a message on her answering machine and hoped that for once in her life she'd remember to check it. Then he rang Robert in the edit suite.

'Are you OK, Harry?' asked the director.

'Not really. The whisky's helping.'

'You haven't forgotten about the dub this evening, have you?'

Harry was due to record his commentary at nine. Mercifully there wasn't a lot of it to write. The commentary for the other, Who-Killed-Jo-O'Brien, film was already recorded, wild with no pictures on to quarter inch sound tape: even now Steve was laying it to the master.

'I'll be there. Is Roger still around?'

'He's upstairs in the office. Do you want to talk to him?'

'Why not.'

Robert transferred the call. Harry could picture the Northerner in his glass-sided hutch, feet on the desk, black Lakeland clouds clinging to his upper slopes. Roger lifted the phone.

'Thanks a lot, Rog,' Harry said sarcastically. 'You're a real mate.'

'Any time. Where the hell are you?'

'Hammersmith Bridge, ready to jump. This is by way of a farewell call. What the hell's going on?'

'I might ask you the same question. You can't go mounting major drama shoots in the middle of the night without anyone knowing. We're in the communications business, people in this building talk to each other sometimes.'

'Who knows?'

'The fifth floor. Costume department phoned up Tony Mangan this morning to complain that you and Robert had been keeping their people up all night without a meal break on a shoot in Finsbury Park. Mangan said what shoot. They told him it was something to do with reconstructing a murder. He went through the roof, tried finding you but you were out on location. So he called me. You can count yourself lucky I was around to break his fall.'

'Sorry about that,' said Harry.

'So am I. In the event it doesn't matter much, we can put Latchkey on hold until the election's over. If you really feel strongly about it you can always hand the story over to the papers, I'm sure the *Sunday Times* would love a good anti-Labour smear at this point in the campaign.'

Harry said nothing, just looked at the TV. They were showing a Japanese game show in which the contestants were given a chain saw and two locked wooden boxes, one containing a beloved household pet, the other a pile of gold coins. The pet was a loveable little chow, visible to the audience in a little bubble at the top of the screen. Harry wondered why Japanese game shows had so many hosts – this one had four, all glitzed up in lamé jump-suits, novelty stetsons and grins that met round the backs of their necks.

'Are you still there, Harry?'

'More or less. And I do feel strongly, since you ask.'

'If it's any consolation Steve showed me the other film. You and Robert did a good job.'

'Thanks,' said Harry sourly, and rang off.

The Japanese had given way to an ad break, a blonde in a business suit loading a brass bedstead into the back of an estate car outside Harrods. Not a traffic warden in sight. Harry switched off the set, moved over to his desk, turned on his computer and started working his commentary notes up into a script.

It was after five when Miranda arrived. She was hungry. Harry poked forlornly round the kitchen, but between them Mrs Perrymede and the burglars had stripped the fridge clean.

'So how was our friend Terry?' he asked, triumphantly producing an overlooked packet of digestives from the store cupboard.

'First the good news: he didn't chuck us out. Then the better news: he was happy to answer questions. The bad news is I'm not convinced he was telling the truth all the time.' She got out her notes. 'He jumped around a lot, so this may not all make sense. First the phone calls: he says he phoned his mother.'

She settled into the sofa while Harry made tea.

'From a police station?'

'Why not? She was his next of kin. He says he doesn't know for sure who Jo phoned from the pub, but he thinks it was either Ben or Willie Walpole. He says Walpole goes to bed with people as a way of getting to know them, screw first and ask questions afterwards. Under all that louche urbanity Willie's a big fat jelly, apparently, only he doesn't like to let it show in public. Jo was promiscuous, but he was also very jealous, that's what the argument in the Balzac was all about. He said it was a stupid row, they kept accusing each other of going with other men.'

'Did you ask him for names?'

'Of course. He just smiled.'

'And what did he have to say about Ben?'

'"Nice young man," he kept saying. "Took a while to settle in, but a nice young man. He did well, didn't he?" Period.'

'Why would Jo have phoned him from the bar?'

'Work, he presumes. They were worried about the

Press do they were lining up. Jo was very obsessive about his work, believe it or not. If he decided to do something he went for it, no shirkers. Worked hard, played hard. I suppose that's why he got away with everything for so long – people who'd seen him in action were impressed.'

'Did he have anything else to say about what happened later?'

'Not a lot. The last thing he remembers they were screwing, they made up and dropped ecstasy.'

'You know a way of hitting someone over the head with a metal chair while you're making love?' asked Harry.

'I'm sure it can be done.'

'What else?'

Miranda thumbed on through her notes.

'I asked him about Angela and the money. He didn't say anything at first, he just smiled. And then he quoted Marx: From each according to his abilities, to each according to his needs. The Open University has a lot to answer for.'

And then she told him what Terry had said about Willie Walpole.

'So which bits didn't you believe?' asked Harry.

'I'm not sure. The phone call to his mother sounds a little far-fetched. And terribly convenient, since the woman's dead.'

'Do you think he is mental?'

'You can't tell. The madder some people get, the saner they act. And he takes a lot of pills, you can't really tell what's the pills and what isn't.'

'And how's your hunch doing?'

'Do you mean do I think Ben did it? Why? What's his motive?'

'He'd written to Walpole complaining about the way Latchkey was being run. Willie warned Jo. Jo knew all about Ben and Willie's affair, and threatened to spread the news around. Knowing the way Jo worked he also made sure that Ben's name was all over the Latchkey paperwork. If Latchkey fell apart Ben was going to go down with it. His career would be ruined. Angela was meant to be away for the evening. He went out and played squash, had a meal, then went back to his office, saw the lights were off, assumed they'd gone home, got in via the fire escape and started going through the papers.

'He was halfway through when Jo and Terry got back from the Balzac. Ben hid, waited until the other two were otherwise engaged, then tried to sneak out. Jo spotted him, they had a row. Terry was out of his head by now, he may well have just wandered off. Jo told Ben to wise up, Ben went berserk and hit him with the chair. He then torched the place to destroy the evidence, and Jo with it. Terry got picked up by the police, who put two and two together, took him down the station and gave him a statement to sign. Terry phoned Willie, the only person he knew who could be any help to him. He hadn't a clue what had happened, he just knew he was up shit creek. Willie assumed Terry had done it, but said he'd do what he could. He didn't want to get involved himself, he wanted to distance himself as far as he possibly could from the whole Latchkey fiasco. So he waited a couple of days and then rang Angela – or got someone else to – and told her Terry was threatening to make trouble for Ben. Angela agreed to pick up Terry's bills. And that's the way it stayed until Pete decided to get involved.'

'And that's what you're going to broadcast to the nation?'

'Of course not. All I'm going to do is list the known facts and ask the relevant questions.'

'But suppose it was Willie? Suppose all that happened, only it was Willie not Ben. Willie was up to his arse in Latchkey. It's possible he set the whole thing up to discredit the Left – he already had one foot in the Tory party by then. If Jo had found out about it he'd have gone ape. Not because of the politics, but because the whole scam depended on Willie not exposing Latchkey. Ben had already started to smell a rat, that's why he wrote to Willie. Willie got the letter and realized he had to act fast. He went round to Latchkey to pick up the documents he needed to get his own name off the files. Jo and Terry interrupted him.'

Harry gave up on the tea and collected a bottle of Bushmills from the kitchen.

'The trouble is it's all guesswork, there's not a shred of evidence to support any of it.'

Miranda reached into her bag.

'Try this.'

'What is it?' asked Harry.

'A diary,' said Miranda. 'Terry's diary.'

25

'WHERE THE HELL DID you get it?' asked Harry.

'Shirley gave it to me. We called in on the way back – Terry had knitted some place-mats for her, we were dropping them off.'

'How touching.'

'Shirley thought so. She found the diary when she was clearing Pete's papers out of the attic for the filming. He'd never mentioned it to her; she thinks he was worried there was stuff in it that might reflect badly on Terry's lifestyle.'

Terry Pattichis had small, precise handwriting, surprisingly neat for a youth who had enjoyed such a brief affair with the education system. It was a business diary, intermittent and economical, often no more than a line a day, made up largely of abbreviations and initials. It covered a period of two and a half years, starting in the summer of 1981 and ending abruptly on 16 December 1983, the day before Jo was killed. With few exceptions the entries referred to sex, money or shopping.

Harry opened it at random at July 1983.

15.7 Trsers £18.70, shrt £14.99. T* PK, Monmouth Place/£25, Tx £3.20.

18.7 Brghtn, J bt antqs, row then J*T.

19.7 Pty @ MMs, AR* RJ and TQ, HJ*B, W left w KA T* RN/nc, T*HG, £20.

And so on: expenditure, lovers, social events. Tx stood for taxis, antqs antiques; an asterisk he presumed meant sex, nc no charge. T for Terry, J for Jo, MM Jo's flat in Monmouth Mansions; the other initials were less clear.

'How did Pete come to have it?' he asked Miranda.

'He picked up Terry's gear from the flat after the trial, it must have been in there somewhere.'

Harry took a sheet of A4 out of his bag and began taking notes.

'J for Jo, B for Ben, W for Willie Walpole, I presume. Jo was killed on the Thursday.' He thumbed through to the end of the diary. 'There was a party on the Tuesday: GK screwed SD, TY and GR and AS had a threesome, Jo screwed Willie, or vice versa. Must have been like a battery farm in there. B for Ben left alone. The following day Ben, Jo, Terry and Willie met up at the House of Lords. No asterisks, they were probably too knackered to walk straight by then. Or they were at lunchtime. But things picked up in the evening, asterisks all round, except W; W seems to have had enough.'

'Whatever happened to AIDS?' Miranda wondered out loud.

'Nothing had happened to AIDS, or not yet, this was 1983. At least it was happening but they didn't know about it yet. AR on the seventeenth might have been Alan Richtbladt, the actor. He died a couple of months ago, there was a big memorial service at All Souls, Langham Place. And I think DM might be David Martin, that awful Scots filmmaker; he snuffed it last year sometime.'

'You're sure B is Ben?'

'Has to be. He's around at all the office functions.' Harry opened the diary at random. 'Latchkey reception, B J T W etc. Housing Conference, Scarborough, B, J, T. There's loads of it.'

'You mean he's gay?'

'Bisexual. At least he has been.'

'Can you prove it?'

'Angela says so.'

Harry told her what Angela had said.

'Which also means Ben doesn't have an alibi,' said Harry. 'What about the diary? Ben's all over it, living it up with druggies and blackmailers and embezzlers. And then someone got killed. The high-living hedonist doesn't exactly fit with an earnest young whistle-blower. This thing may be bigger than just Ben, but he's involved.'

Miranda put her notes back in her bag.

'You're the boss, Harry. I only work here.'

She got up. Harry realized she was leaving.

'Where are you going?'

'Home.'

'To do what?'

'I haven't decided yet.'

'For fuck's sake. Did I say something wrong?'

'Not particularly. I just feel like being somewhere else.'

Some day soon Miranda was going to give him a coronary. One minute she was a lover, the next she didn't seem to give a damn.

'Please yourself.'

'Don't worry, I will.'

She was at the door now.

'Will I see you later?'

'Maybe.'

And that was that. Harry looked at his watch: it was six o'clock. He had three hours to finish his script. He got himself another drink and sat down at the computer.

The way you write a film like this is to start with the sequences, arrange them so that they flow naturally into each other, either chronologically or to illustrate a theme. Then you decided on which bits of sync sound to use from the actuality, speeches and conversations and so on. While you're doing that a sort of structure begins to emerge. Then you think about what you want to say, and try matching it up with the sync and the sequences. They'd already reached that stage: what Harry had to do now was to write the words which linked the story together: a sentence of commentary here, a paragraph there.

He opened his desk drawers to get out the disc on which he'd made his original notes on Pete and Terry. Miranda was right: he had a tidy mind. Everything was neatly arranged: envelopes in the top right − just envelopes, in neat stacks arranged by size, no spilled paper clips or elastic bands or biro-caps or bottles of dried-up Tippex. Next drawer down was a virgin block of foolscap, the one below that postcards and stamps and a box of new pentels.

He opened the bottom left-hand drawer, which was where he kept the floppies for the Apple Mac. Three plastic trays, like miniature album racks, subdivided by plastic markers, each with a label in a bright primary colour. Blue for scripts, green for research, yellow for correspondence, red for personal documents and so on. Each disc was labelled according to specific content.

He flicked through the discs, doubled back, ran through them again. There was no sign of Latchkey. Maybe it had got thrown out by mistake when Mrs Perrymede was tidying up. Except that all the others were there, all fifty of them. One in fifty missing was too much of a coincidence. Harry checked again, then slammed the drawer closed.

It was the bloody disc they were after, that's what the break-in had been for. Someone wanted to know how much he knew. Someone who understood computers, and had access to another Mac to run the disc on. Most people used IBMs or compatibles, but Apple Mac discs only ran on other Macs.

Walworth Road had Macs for the Labour party's

desk top publishing operation. Central Office probably did too. And if you didn't have one of your own there were loads of bureaux that would do the job for you.

There'd been nothing of any great importance on the disc. He switched his concentration back to the script, working up the handwritten notes he'd made during the week. Twice during the subsequent three hours he tried ringing Miranda at Marylebone, but there was no reply. He finished the script at half past eight and was reading it over when Archie Bain rang.

The Scots MP was one of the people he'd tried to contact that morning looking for a way to trace Stephen Knight and his car. Members of Parliament sometimes had informal ways of penetrating government computers. Archie was returning his call.

'You still on about bloody Webb?' asked Archie.

'A favour,' Harry told him. 'I need to trace a car, a Vauxhall Cavalier, registration EGB 414F. Driven by a punter called Stephen Knight, who may or may not be working for HMG.'

'Hold on, hold on,' said Archie. 'What the hell is this about? I'm in the middle of an election campaign, pal. I haven't got time to go gumshoeing for Harry Kapowski. You're grubbing round Ben Webb looking for tabloid tittletattle and you have the balls to ask one of his colleagues to lend a hand. You have neck, I'll give you that, Harry.'

'It's important, Archie. I promise.'

'Important to who?'

'All of us.'

'Oh yeah? All of us in general, and you in particular? Who is this Stephen wotsisname?'

'He or his mates tried to kill me on the motorway the other day.'

'Wise man. And what has this got to do with Ben Webb?'

Harry wasn't at all sure how much to tell him. He

284

could trust Archie to a point, but he was still a Labour party man four days off polling day.

'That's what I'm trying to find out. One way of finding out is Mr Knight.'

'And if he leads to Ben?'

'Then you've got a rotten apple in the barrel, Archie.'

'In which case I'm not sure I want to know.'

'That's up to you. But if it's nothing to do with Ben, you're in the clear.'

'So that's the deal, is it? I do your leg work, you get the applause.'

'Not a lot of leg work.'

Archie said he'd think about it. No promises, no guarantees, and above all no using his name as a source.

'Not now, not ever. And if I don't like what I find I may not call you at all.'

That was fine by Harry. Next he rang Angela Webb.

They talked for twenty minutes. It was ten to nine by the time Harry finally left the flat, twenty past when he got to Television Centre.

Steve and Robert were waiting in the dubbing theatre, Steve head down in the *Caravan Times*' small ads, Robert giving the sound supervisor a lecture on how his equipment worked. Harry walked in the door like a train going into a tunnel and slammed his papers down on the mixer desk.

'Bad day at the office, darling?' asked the soundman, grabbing his coffee mug for safety.

'Sorry. Yes, fucking awful since you ask.'

And then he noticed Miranda, sitting quietly in a corner thumbing through the Sunday papers. He ignored her and handed Robert a copy of his script. Robert read it through to the end, then doubled back to the second page.

'His election to the National Executive – are you sure that was eighty-six?'

Harry hesitated. He wasn't sure, and he didn't have

the cuttings with him. Miranda had put down the papers and come over to join them.

Harry handed her the script.

'Make some calls, will you sweetheart?'

'Who?' she asked.

'I don't know. News Information, Walworth Road – '

'Are you talking to me?'

'Of course I'm bloody talking to you.'

'Then don't call me sweetheart. Ever. Don't call anyone sweetheart, come to that. It's an arsehole name, it's what rednecks call their wives when they come home drunk. My name's Miranda.'

He felt even worse now. He wanted to grovel, but a crowded dubbing theatre is not a suitable place to try and salvage a personal relationship.

'I'm sorry, you're right, it's an arsehole name.'

Somehow he'd ended up with his face to the control room wall, talking to a sculptured foam acoustic panel.

Miranda was on her feet, heading for the door.

'I'll see what I can find out. And I need to talk to you sometime.'

Harry made his way through into the glass booth and sat down at the microphone. There was a colour monitor on the desk in front of him and a set of headphones. He put on the cans and spread the script carefully on the cloth surface, got out a pen and started to read out loud to himself, underlining words for emphasis, inserting hyphens for pauses. The monitor flickered and came to life, and Robert's voice appeared in the headphones.

'You taking the cues off time code, or do you want us to flash you, Harry?'

'Flash me, Bob, I need all the help I can get.'

'We'll run it once for rehearsal.'

Harry didn't watch the run through. His eyes registered

the green cue light going on and off, his mouth voiced the words, but his mind was elsewhere. Worrying about Ben Webb, worrying about Miranda, worrying about what was going to happen to his career over the next twenty-four hours. All this for an alcoholic drug-abusing Greek-Cypriot rentboy who didn't want to get free in the first place.

Maybe it was time he got out too, found a way to earn a living that didn't entail spending your life suspended between suspected murderers and the crass inertia of the BBC and the judicial system.

Robert wanted some word-trimming at points where the commentary overlapped synchronous speech. Two words here, a second there. Harry brought his mind back into focus and scribbled in the changes. Miranda was back. He watched her through the glass talking to Robert. Robert nodded, made a note. She crossed the control room and pushed through the door into the recording booth.

'You were right, it was nineteen-eighty-six.'

'Thanks,' said Harry.

'For nothing. I've told you, I can handle crises.'

'What's the crisis?'

'Walpole's dead.'

'Dead how?'

'Murdered, someone put a bullet through his head. In his chambers.'

Harry froze. Pete's death might have been an accident, the truck on the motorway a coincidence, the rest of the business – the burglary, Stephen Knight – shadow boxing, attempts to bounce him off the story. But killing Walpole meant that someone out there was running scared, the most dangerous state of all.

'When?'

'They don't know yet. The last time anyone saw him was last night. A porter found his body an hour ago. Are you thinking what I'm thinking, Harry?'

Harry nodded, then looked through the window at Robert.

'You heard the news?'

Robert pressed the talk-back button.

'Yes. Do you want to get this out of the way first and talk about it afterwards?'

'Why not,' said Harry.

Miranda went back next door and they went for their first take. Harry was on autopilot: the light flashed, he started talking, the paragraph ended, he stopped. Not very long paragraphs, most of them: 'There was a time when the Labour party could take Birmingham's well-organized Muslim vote for granted. Not any more,' and then sync sound of Ben doing the hard sell to the Pakistanis. 'It's half past two, and the Ben Webb roadshow has hit Stoke on Trent,' followed by a damp looking brass band welcoming Ben to the civic centre. Harry read it clearly and mechanically and tried not to think about Willie Walpole.

They finished just in time to catch the ten o'clock news on ITN. Walpole's death made the second lead, straight after a prime ministerial outburst against Opposition attempts to turn the election into a personality contest. The Albany authorities had banned the cameras from their precincts, but there was a long-lens shot through the entrance into the courtyard, and extensive footage of police vehicles coming and going. A senior Scotland Yard officer told reporters what had happened. The body had been found at seven o'clock, but first indications were that the shooting had taken place much earlier. There were no signs of forced entry, suggesting that the peer had known his killer, who could have reached the chambers either through the main entrance or by a side door which led into the Albany from Burlington Gardens. As far as they were aware nothing had been taken from the flat, and robbery was not thought to be a likely motive. They were pursuing a number of lines of enquiry, and appealed for witnesses.

Next they ran a short obituary, heavily slanted towards Walpole's social contacts with known members of the criminal fraternity. There were also a number of brief tributes from his fellow politicians, including Ben, who was interviewed on the pavement outside the house in Wandsworth.

'Whatever his politics, he had a great gift for friendship,' he'd told ITN. And a sense of humour, and a hatred of hypocrisy: all that had prevented him from achieving high office was his refusal to compromise his independent principles for the sake of his career.

ITN failed to ask Ben what Willie was like in bed.

The news moved on to the day's rioting on the West Bank. Harry turned off the set.

'Well Bugger Me Gently,' he said quietly.

Things were beginning to make sense at last.

26

HARRY AND MIRANDA WENT home separately, Miranda to Marylebone, Harry to Nine Elms Lane. They were both exhausted, but Harry took a sleeper anyway, just to be on the safe side.

He woke at nine, and spent the morning making phone calls and reading Walpole's obituaries in the morning papers. Obituaries aren't what they used to be: there was no need to read between the lines. 'Gay Peer Murdered', the *Daily Mirror* screamed across half its front page, though there were affectionate tributes to be found tucked away among the catalogue of drink-driving convictions and libel cases, and the general impression that emerged from the Press was that of a well-liked rogue.

It was twelve o'clock when Archie Bain phoned back.

'You still alive, pal?'

'More or less. You got any news for me?'

'The news is get off the story, Harry. Unless you fancy a head-on collision with the entire Security Services. Which I do not recommend.'

'Is this the former Reporting Scotland bloodhound I'm talking to, or the Labour party's Damage Limitation spokesperson?'

'Both. It's also a family man with a wife and five wains who is putting his career prospects on the line phoning you in the first place. Is this a secure line, by the way?'

'Not particularly,' said Harry. 'So tell me more.'

'There isn't any more, hen. Except that you never called me and I never told you anything. You want my advice, you get down to Television Centre and polish up a nice friendly little piece about The Coming Man in British Politics, have a few drinks and forget the rest. Utterly.'

Harry did just that. At two o'clock he was back at Television Centre, just in time for the management viewing of the Webb profile. Robert and Tony Mangan and the lawyer were already there, sitting on grey upholstered armless chairs, eating canteen sandwiches and drinking Vendomat coffee.

They watched the film in silence. Mangan and the lawyer both took notes. Roger arrived halfway through and stood at the back, leaning against the wall, reading the note Harry had left on his desk. When it was over Mangan helped himself to another sandwich and stood up.

'What do you reckon, Roger?'

You shit, thought Harry: never waste your own opinion when you can borrow someone else's.

Roger thought it was fine. Better than fine: stylish and informative.

'How about the Latchkey line?'

'I can't see the harm in that, Tony. It's a matter of historical fact that he worked there. We're not saying anything more about that.'

'We're not saying anything, but the innuendo's there.'

'It's only an innuendo if you know the other half of it,' Harry argued. 'Otherwise it's perfectly innocent. If you do know the other half of the story you're not about to draw attention to it by going to court.'

Mangan looked at the lawyer.

'What do you reckon, Peter?'

'I think it's probably all right.'

Harry noted the 'probably'.

'As a matter of curiosity, what is the other half?' the lawyer asked.

'We're not sure,' said Roger. 'It appears that Ben wasn't where he said he was on the evening Jo O'Brien was killed.'

'That's all?'

'Tell him what you know, Harry.'

Harry gave Roger a look.

'All of it?'

'All of it?'

Harry settled back in his seat.

'It looks as though Terry Pattichis was stitched up. He was too stoned to know what happened himself, so someone told him. The confession reads like a police pantomime, they write better scripts on *Home and Away*. Ben had an affair with Willie Walpole before he got married. Terry and Jo both knew about it. After the killing Angela Webb undertook to pay Terry's mother's old age pension for the best part of eight years. Shortly after we started looking into all this, someone broke into my flat and stole a floppy disc containing all my notes. On Sunday Ben went out of his way to introduce me to his libel lawyer.'

'Can you prove all that?' asked the lawyer.

'I can prove the libel lawyer bit.'

Mangan looked as though someone had just switched off his blood supply.

'I thought you'd stopped work on this.'

'I know you did,' said Harry. 'Can I ask why you told us to?'

The deputy Head of News and Current Affairs put down his sandwich.

'Because Ben Webb is a senior member of the Labour party. We're in the last three days of a General Election.

I'm not trying to protect the man, but I don't want him crucified on TV on the basis of a load of hearsay evidence in order to release some juvenile child molester back on to the streets of London.'

'Terry Pattichis is not a child molester,' Harry said quietly. 'Anyway, most child molesters are heterosexual – I can show you the figures if you want. And he's been sitting in Broadmoor for the past eight years for a crime he may not have committed.'

'Don't tell me, Harry, tell the Home Office.'

'I already did. They sent me one of those nice little printed notes, "The Minister thanks you for your recent communication, which is receiving his attention." Don't call us, we'll call you, sometime in the twenty-first century. And you still haven't told me who leaned on you, Tony. Ben Webb? Willie Walpole?'

'What the hell has Walpole got to do with this?'

Harry grinned.

'That's why he's dead.'

Mangan had had enough.

'Call your dog off, Roger, I've got better things to do with my time than listen to this rubbish. And lose the Latchkey shot,' he added on his way to the door. The lawyer nodded politely and followed him out into the corridor.

Roger closed the door after them and sat down. He was smiling.

'So do I get to see the other movie now?'

'Sure,' said Steve, and put a new cassette in the machine.

'Where's Miranda, by the way?' asked Roger.

'I've no idea,' said Harry.

They watched the tape through twice. Roger made notes, asked a few questions, then got to his feet.

'What do you reckon?' asked Harry.

'I'm happy if you are,' said Roger.

'I'm happy,' said Harry. He walked over to the

recorder, took out the cassette, and slipped it into his shoulder bag.

The lounge bar at the Beaumont Arms was almost empty. He bought himself a pint of Guinness and a double whisky and installed himself at a table under a dayglo poster advertising a disco. It was the same table Terry and Jo must have sat at. He drank the whisky down in one, followed it with a chaser of stout, went over to the juke box and programmed it to play Elvis's version of 'My Way' five times. Then he crossed the bar to the payphone and dialled Angela's number. No one was going to hear him over the sound of the boy from Tupelo.

'Where was Ben yesterday morning,' he asked her the moment she lifted the receiver. 'Before the party.'

'We went up to town first thing, he had to drop in to the office, I had to pick the kids up, they'd been staying over with friends up in Hampstead.'

'Ben came home on his own?'

'Yes, he took a cab.'

'Does he own a gun?'

'He has an old Beretta pistol, his father brought it back from the war.'

'Where does he keep it?'

'In his study.'

'Is it there now?'

'No.'

'Did he kill Willie?'

'I don't know. How are you getting on?'

'Not bad, all things considered. I feel a bit as though my brakes have failed. Tony Mangan just viewed Ben's film.'

'Who's Tony Mangan?'

'God. A talking suit. Come the revolution they're going to make him Minister for Euthanasia. Meanwhile he's marking time running the Beeb's election coverage.

I'm beginning to think he may have another job as well.'

'What did he make of your film?'

'He thought it was bland, predictable, cautious, and seven seconds over length. He loved it. But he made us take out the seven seconds.'

This was madness. He took another mouthful of Guinness.

'I've booked your flight. Check-in's at half nine, Turkish airlines, you'll be out of the country by the time the news breaks. I've booked you into The Dome in Kyrenia for a week, you'll like it. The Dome's on the harbour, a bit decayed in the Bournemouth style, bar full of Ancient Brits who migrated for the cheap brandy when India went native. Plus the odd Essex bank robber. Turkish Cyprus is still a pariah state. You can lie low until the initial row has died down a bit. What did you fix about the kids?'

'Maria will be here, she'll look after them until I sort something out.'

'Are you OK, Angela?'

'Just about. I'm trying not to think too much. And you?'

'Ditto. How are you getting to Heathrow, by the way?'

'Taxi, I suppose.'

'I'll organize a car to pick you up. I'll see you at the check-in. It's going to be rough. You realize that, don't you, Angela?'

'I know.'

The barman had had enough of Elvis. He reached across and unplugged the juke box.

'Good luck, kid,' said Harry.

'Good luck, Harry.'

TV studio control rooms are a fine mix of sophisticated engineering and medieval pageantry. The engineering side is a work of art, but engineering miracles have a low status in television. By now everyone knows that everything is possible: dream up an impossible machine and before you can say Alan Sugar they'll be selling one in Dixons for ninety-nine quid, with a box of C-90 cassettes and a last year's model food processor thrown in for free.

The pageant is much more complex, a thing of pure drama. A pool of harsh light illuminates a long High Table – the mixer desk – at which the Director/Monarch sits in his high-backed throne, his loyal henchmen and women lined up on either side waiting for their orders. The rest of the room in near-darkness. Runners and floor assistants and supplicants hover in the shadows awaiting their instructions; below them on the studio floor another thirty or forty vassals stand poised over their booms and cameras and set furniture, ready to do their master's bidding. The fetish through which the Director/Monarch transmits his orders is a ten-inch stainless-steel cock/microphone which rises from the desk in front of him. Whatever he commands the fetish to do gets done: cameras move over the studio floor, sets are built and dismantled, lighting adjusted, guests or actors summoned from the green room.

Tonight's God was called Sandy, a faintly louche man of around fifty in a Hawaiian shirt, Levis ironed to a seam that could cut cold butter, and white leather slip-ons with gold buckles. Sandy prided himself on his informality and technical mastery, which he displayed by arranging after-hours social life over the talkback and calling machines by their initials. The fact that he was in practice no more than a Constitutional Monarch, that the studio could run itself perfectly smoothly if his place was taken by a flying squirrel, never crossed his nicotine-encrusted mind: the image was the thing. No one kicks sand in the face of a studio director when he's on the job.

296

Why would they bother, Miranda wondered. She looked out through the darkened glass window of the gallery at the studio floor. The presenter's desk, which on screen would appear as a sophisticated piece of modern furniture, was in fact no more than a semicircular block of chipboard on a scaffolding base, clad in textured beige panels and indented to take a row of sleek monitors and computer terminals. Behind the desk a pyramid of stage-weighted flats rose to a giant neon *Election Special* sign. Four scene-shifters were sheltering behind the flats playing cards. It was half past eight, and camera rehearsal was about to start.

'Sequence one's opening titles,' Sandy told The Cock. 'Tim link to camera three, then the movie, then a one-plus-one in area B. Any sign of Tim yet, Maureen?'

'He's on his way,' a voice came back.

Tim Green's lugubrious features appeared on the monitors.

'Tell him not that jacket, Maureen. The check'll strobe. Has he got anything else?'

'Topless,' said the voice. 'He says he'll do it topless.'

A phone rang on the desk. Sandy picked it up, spoke briefly, covered the mouthpiece with his hand, and looked back over his shoulder.

'Is there anyone around from production?'

Miranda realized he meant her.

'Trot down to VT and see how the Webb tape's coming on will you love?'

Angela put the note in an envelope, wrote the boys' names on it and left it on the hall table where they'd be sure to see it when they got back from the Pig'n'Vid. Pig'n'Vids being the way Wandsworth kids spent their evenings nowadays, round at a neighbour's watching over-fourteen videos and filling their faces with burgers and coke. Then she opened the front door.

The black man facing her was six and a half feet tall

and built like a tank. He had on purple trousers held up by a wide rhinestone-studded belt, a loose lime-green shirt in some shimmer fabric, and a chauffeur's hat.

'Mrs Webb? Car service.'

She looked beyond him to the big white Chevie convertible with the white hood and white-walled tyres. Music was coming from it, loud enough to bring the neighbours to their windows.

'That's the car?'

'Yes, ma'am,' said Pigfoot, 'that's the car, I'm the service. You got any luggage?'

She let him pick up the two suitcases from the porch and walked with him to the car. He opened the back door and ushered her in.

The back seat was already half occupied by Yvonne; Yvonne in a black leotard, black stockings and high heels, purple lipstick and purple nails.

'This is Yvonne, she's your hostess Mrs Webb.' He had to shout to make himself heard over the music. 'Any way she can make your journey more comfortable, just say the word.'

Angela smiled. Bloody Kapowski.

'Heathrow,' she told Pigfoot as he moved off down Baskerville road. She looked back once at the house, then settled back into her seat.

'That's an airport?'

'Yes.'

'I always wanted to visit an airport,' said Pigfoot. 'You got a map there somewhere, Yvonne?'

Miranda sat in the editing suite watching Steve line up the Latchkey tape on the machine.

'Drop-out on the Beta-to-one-inch transfer,' he announced.

'Is that a problem?'

'Of sorts.'

He had his glasses off, eyes glued to a luminous panel that reminded her of an electro-cardiac machine. She wondered what 'of sorts' meant, but didn't like to ask, fearful of the lengthy technical explanation that might follow.

'What's all this business about, anyway?' asked Steve, switching the monitor to colour bars.

'Two versions of the same story. We won't know which we're running until the last moment.' Two weeks in the Beeb and she was already using the 'we' that separates production from engineering. An uncrossable, unspoken barrier as invisible and impermeable as the class system.

Steve wasn't really interested, what concerned him was the picture drop-out. Fifteen years of editing other people's programmes, shift after shift, every producer convinced that theirs is the only important programme ever made, assuming the editor thinks likewise. They don't want your opinion, they want to be told how brilliant they are. For the first couple of years you try offering an honest opinion, but after that you give up and concentrate on the job in hand.

The phone on the wall rang. Steve reached out to get it, his eyes still on the monitor.

'It's for you,' he said, swivelling round in his seat to hand her the receiver. It was Harry.

'Is the tape ready?'

'Almost. We have drop-in problems.'

'Drop-out,' said Steve philosophically.

'But you'll be ready in time?'

'How long?' Miranda asked Steve.

'Five minutes.'

Miranda passed on the news.

'Good luck,' said Harry.

Angela wished he'd turn down the bloody music. Doggerel rap and a backing that sounded like a slow motion

299

traffic accident. Yvonne had balanced two plastic cups on the seat and was trying to open a bottle of champagne. They were across the river now and heading north through Earl's Court. At this point they should have turned west onto Hammersmith Road, but Pigfoot kept driving north up Holland Road. She leaned forward and tapped him on the shoulder.

'You missed the turn,' she yelled.

'Story of my life,' said Pigfoot, and kept driving.

Yvonne aimed the bottle out of the window and pushed the cork with her thumbs until it shot out, spraying foam on the upholstery.

'Don't worry, Mrs Webb. We have one stop to make, a friend wants to see you before you leave.'

Angela tried not to look worried.

'Am I allowed to know who?'

'Sure. Harry Kapowski. Friend of yours, isn't he?'

They'd reached Shepherd's Bush. Pigfoot drove along the south side of the Green, then turned right up Wood Lane. TV Centre was half a mile ahead on the left hand side, but before they reached it the car slowed and turned right up a slip road into an industrial estate of modern flat-roof factory units. Pigfoot switched the lights to main beam, off and on, then accelerated hard towards the metal louvred doors of the loading bay. Angela just had time to glimpse the To Let notice before she closed her eyes.

There was no crash. At the last minute the louvred door swung upwards. The car bumped over a concrete ramp and then went into a skid, making a near-perfect circle of the empty warehouse before coming to a halt with its hose pointing back the way it had come. Yvonne leaned over and opened Angela's door for her.

'We figured you might want a little privacy. Five minutes, we'll be back.'

Angela got out on to the bare concrete floor. Pigfoot revved the engine, slammed it into first, and vanished back into the night. The garage door slid closed behind them.

It was dark in the warehouse, just a single bare bulb hanging in one corner. And then the lights came on. She turned around. Harry was standing by the door of a small glass-windowed office, his hand on the switches.

'Hallo, Angela.'

Two plastic chairs were arranged on either side of a packing case, on top of which sat a portable TV, a VCR, a bottle of Bushmills and two glasses. Angela relaxed.

'Don't ever do that to me again, Harry. You're crazy.'

Harry grinned.

Angela sat down. He poured an inch of whisky into each of the glasses, slipped a cassette into the machine and pushed the start. The monitor flickered to life, a VT clock counting down from thirty, then up came Latchkey.

Angela lit a cigarette and sat back in her seat, watching the reconstruction. The piece was complete now, commentary and visuals in place, the story told firmly and economically, first the known facts, then the questions they raised. If there wasn't enough there to convict Ben, there was more than enough to wreck his career.

When it had finished Angela said nothing for a while, just stared at the screen, biting at her lower lip, taking it in.

'They're going to transmit that tonight?' she said eventually.

'They are, but they don't know it yet. Miranda switches the tapes at the last minute. For rehearsal they have the other film, come transmission they get this. The first anyone else will know about it is when it hits the screen.'

'You're sure it's going to be OK, Harry?'

'Of course I'm not sure. It's bloody madness, but

what can they prove? Jo's dead, Walpole's dead, Terry's happy with the way things are. The only person who can substantiate Ben's alibi is you.' He took a handkerchief out of his pocket and blew his nose. 'That's my version. You still haven't told me what really happened.'

She looked down at her hands for some time before answering.

'How much do you know?'

'I know Ben's affair was with Jo not Willie. B for Bugger-me-gently, W for Webb – at first I thought it was B for Ben, W for Willie.'

Angela lit another cigarette and put the lighter back in her bag.

'That's what the row in the Beaumont Arms was about. It wasn't Jo who phoned, it was Terry. Jo said it was long over, Terry didn't believe him, Jo said ring the man and ask him. I was meant to be away for the evening, he thought he'd get Ben. When he got me instead he asked him anyway. I went berserk, got in the car, drove straight to Shepherd's Bush.'

'What time was this?'

'About eleven, I suppose. Ben still hadn't got back. I didn't mean to kill Jo. It was almost dark in there, all I could see was Jo screwing someone. I knew he'd screwed Ben before, so I assumed that was who it was. I was screaming at him, he started taunting me back. That's when I hit him with the chair. He went down and I just kept hitting him. Then I looked around for Ben, but he wasn't there, Terry was. Out of his head, but he still wanted more pills, he kept asking for pills. I asked him if he's seen what happened and he said "yeah, isn't sex wonderful?" Then he wandered off, he said he was going to the pub to find Jo. I panicked and phoned Willie. He said what's done is done, you'd better get rid of the evidence, make it look as though someone was after the paperwork. And get yourself an alibi.'

'You didn't set the fire straight away?'

'No, I wanted to make sure I was somewhere else by the time it went up. I found a box of candles on top of the electricity meter, cut an inch off the top of one and used it as a fuse, stacks of papers and a pint of petrol in a coffee jar to help the blaze along once it got started.' She took a slug of whisky. 'It was an accident.'

'Not for Terry it wasn't.'

She shrugged her shoulders.

'He likes it in there.' She put her cigarettes in her handbag. 'You're taking a hell of a chance, Harry.'

Harry got up and retrieved the tape from the recorder.

'Not as big a chance as you took shooting Willie.'

'I had to, he was the only one who knew.'

'He wouldn't have talked.'

'He might have.'

'But you didn't have to frame Ben for it.'

She smiled a half-smile.

'That's the least of his troubles. I'm scared, Harry.'

'Stop worrying.'

Outside, Pigfoot gave a blast on his horn. He looked at his watch.

'We'd better go.'

As they headed for the door Angela slipped her arm around him. The horn sounded again.

'Who the hell books your taxis for you?'

'Friend of mine called Pigfoot Walker. He's the one who killed Pete Pattichis. He didn't mean to, it was me he was trying to scare.'

'I know all about Pigfoot, I left his signature on your pillow, remember?'

'You needn't have bothered, I didn't know anything at that stage. What did you do with the disc, by the way?'

'I had it printed out by a place in Mortimer Street. Dull stuff, I was disappointed in you. How come Pigfoot's still on the loose?'

'Shirley forgave him. It's an old Islamic custom, the relatives can choose their own retribution. She decided to go for the money. Very practical.'

They'd reached the door.

'Is this for real, Harry?'

He reached into his jacket pocket and took out an airline ticket.

'Would I tell a lie?'

She kissed him gently on the cheek.

'Probably.'

Harry switched off the lights, put his hand on the door lever and pulled it open.

The headlights were dazzling. Angela shielded her eyes. There wasn't one set of lights: there were half a dozen. Behind them, in the darkened warehouse, Paul emerged from the glass-windowed foreman's office, Betacam on his shoulder, red indicator light flashing on and off to show he was still turning over.

Angela looked at Harry, then at the cars. Two silhouetted figures were walking towards them: Roger Carlisle on the left, Chief Inspector Norman Calloway on the right.

'You bastard!' Angela screamed.

27

'MANGAN,' SAID HARRY. 'Where's Mangan?'

'Across the road in hospitality,' said Roger. 'Waiting for Ben.'

'How long before he gets here?'

Roger checked his watch.

'Twenty-five minutes.'

The deputy Director of News and Current Affairs was sharing a drink with Robert Kettle and Tim Green in room B29, a plush dungeon along the corridor from the video-tape suite whose wall of heavy curtains concealed not a window but a blank concrete wall. He looked up and smiled as Roger and Harry came through the door.

'You hanging around for the kill, Harry?' he asked.

'We all are.' Harry went across to the drinks trolley and poured himself a whisky. 'The thing that interests me, Tony, is how much they pay you.'

Mangan smiled.

'What, the BBC?'

'No, the government.'

The smile was gone.

'What are you talking about?'

'The security services, Tony old chap. Those nice boys with the OBEs who take people like you out to lunch and invite you to do a little something for Queen and country. The State within the State.'

'He's drunk,' Mangan told Tim and Robert.

'Not yet,' said Harry.

'Is this true, Tony?' asked Roger.

'Is what true?'

'That you work for the security services.'

'Of course not.'

Harry looked at the clock. Ben was due in fifteen minutes.

'Don't be daft, Rog – he works on the need to know principle. He hasn't told his brain yet.'

'Need to know what?' asked Mangan.

'That Ben Webb killed Jo O'Brien,' said Harry. 'Any fool could have figured that Terry's trial was a farce if they'd bothered to think about it. Only the police didn't bother to think, it's not what they're good at. They had a corpse and a prime suspect and pressure for a fast conviction. But your friends in Whitehall aren't fools. They had their eyes on Latchkey already – a left-wing charity with political connections, staffed by promiscuous homosexuals – why wouldn't they? Three for the price of one. Jo may even have been on their payroll all along. And they had their eye on young Ben, too: bright young lad with political ambitions, you never know, may get somewhere some day. They knew Ben had been making noises to Willie Walpole about the state of Latchkey's accounts. So when Jo's found dead after a fight, they have another suspect, just as promising as Terry and twice as interesting. What's more Ben didn't have an alibi: he played a game of squash, had supper with friends and then went home to an empty bed, because Angela was off at a concert in Croydon. Or so he thought.'

'You're mad,' said Tony. Tim and Robert were watching him, gob-smacked.

'For most of this week I've wondered if I am. I didn't use to believe all this State-within-a-State stuff either. But the heavy brigade convinced me.'

'Keep talking,' said Tim.

'There isn't a lot more to say. Except that for the past eight years Tony's friends have been under the impression that Ben Webb was a murderer. And rather than do the decent thing they've sat on their little secret, waiting until the day when Ben became a power in the land. Which he now is, I suspect with a little unnoticed help along the way. He might well have made it anyway, if a little less smoothly – he's a bright boy, with a sharp eye for the main chance. Personally, I don't happen to think much of him as a politician, I think he's a slick opportunist: optimism and honesty happen to be marketable commodities at the moment, so that's what Ben sets himself up as. In a different climate he'd be just as likely to sell himself as Mr Shrewd or Mr Technocrat or Mr Call-A-Spade-A-Spade. But that's something the punters have to suss out for themselves. Big stakes. And then poor old Pete Pattichis gets it into his head to start digging around, and muggins here sets all the fire alarms off ringing people up asking them about the Latchkey business. That's when the Heavy Mob came on board. All they wanted to know initially was what was in the bag Pete was handing me, whether he had the missing diary. But when that screwed up, things started to get more drastic. Up to and including driving a truck at me on the M6. Failing to rub out Kapowski was a minor detail. The big fuck-up was that Ben Webb didn't kill O'Brien in the first place. His wife did.'

He checked his watch again. Less than ten minutes to go.

'Did Ben know?' asked Tim.

'I suspect not. The first he was meant to know about it was after the election, when the men in grey suits would present themselves and reveal they knew his little secret. A spook's dream: a senior politician with a guilty past shared only by the forces of Law and Order, which is how I imagine those dinosaurs see themselves.'

Mangan got up. His face had gone white, whether through fear or anger Harry still had no idea.

'Your play, Tony,' said Roger.

But he was already halfway to the door. The others were still watching him when the phone in the corner rang. Ben Webb was in reception.

'You going to tell him?' asked Tim.

'Not yet,' said Roger. 'Let him do the show first.'

Harry and Miranda watched the programme upstairs in the *Not Proven* office. Harry perched on the edge of the conference table, Miranda slumped in the chair behind Phyllis' desk. They were both too tired and tense to talk much. After the opening titles, Tim Green came on the screen, and started into his introduction. Harry leaned forward, waiting for the camera to cut to Ben, waiting to see his expression.

'In a moment,' said Tim, 'I'll be talking to the deputy Leader of the Labour party . . .'

And there was Ben, looking authoritative but unstuffy in a grey wool suit. Harry relaxed and lit a cigarette.

'Who's going to tell him?' asked Miranda.

'I am,' said Harry. 'Has to be me.'

He stood up and walked across the office and pulled up a chair beside her.

'Thanks.'

'For what?' asked Miranda.

'For trusting me.'

'Trusting you? What on earth makes you think I trust you, Harry?'

Harry sighed.

'OK, for staying on the story.'

'I told you, Harry, I'm doing it for the money. What do you do it for?'

'Habit, I suspect.'

She gave him a tired smile.

'Are you going to keep doing it?'

'I thought we weren't going to try and change each other's habits.'

'I'm not, I'm just curious.'

'Then the answer is, probably. And you?'

'I haven't decided yet.'

'About us, or about the job?'

'You. I don't give a fig about the job.'

'I don't suppose you'd be tempted by a few days away from it all?'

'Like where?'

'North Cyprus. I still have the tickets.'

Miranda looked up at the screen. Ben Webb was in Handsworth, glad-handing Sikhs.

'How about Birmingham?'

'You serious?'

'Absolutely. I've never been to Birmingham.'

Ben handled the interview with Tim Green like a pro: confident, witty, unflappable. Harry and Miranda waited until it was almost over, then took the lift down to reception.

'Do you want to be in on this?' asked Harry.

Miranda shook her head.

'I'm going home, Harry. I'll see you later.'

Across the foyer Ben's driver was sitting reading the evening paper.

'How you doing, Harry.'

'Not great, to be honest.'

As soon as the interview was over Roger Carlisle collected Ben from the studio floor.

'Have you time for a drink, Ben?'

Ben looked at Sam Dickinson, who had joined them.

'Up to you, Ben.'

'Not tonight, thanks Roger.'

Ben's detective was there now too, and Roger led the entourage out into the circular corridor that rings the inside of the building, through the double doors and out into reception.

'Hallo, Ben,' said Harry.

'Harry!' A double-fisted handshake: looking down Harry could see how raw and blistered Ben's hands were after two weeks pumping flesh. 'I didn't know you were in tonight. Were you happy with your film?'

'Ben, I need to talk to you in private.'

'What, now? Just the two of us?'

Harry looked at Roger. Roger gave him a nod.

'Three.'

'Is this really important?'

'Yes,' said Roger.

Ben shrugged his shoulders.

'OK. Where?'

Harry didn't want to go back down to the hospitality room, which would by now be full of production staff finishing off the left-over claret while they waited for their taxis home.

'Do you mind fresh air?'

'How long are we going to be?'

'Not long,' said Harry.

It was a soft night, a warm damp breeze blowing from the south-west. They walked out down the ramp into the car park, away from the floodlights that illuminated the front of the building. 'This place used to be a Chinese Garden, do you know that?' asked Ben. 'Some Victorian eccentric built it for his own amusement. I've met people who grew up here in the fifties, the great game for kids was to break in at night and go swimming in the lake. They must have demolished it to make way for the BBC.'

Half way down a line of parked cars Ben stopped and leaned back against the side of a Range Rover, hands in pockets.

'So what's the great secret, boys?'

Harry looked around to make sure they were alone.

'The police arrested Angela two hours ago for the murder of Jo O'Brien.'

Ben looked straight at Harry.

'For what?'

'For Jo's murder. It also looks as though she shot Willie Walpole.'

Ben was shaking his head.

'This is a joke, isn't it?'

A hundrd yards to their left the audience from a game show was pouring out into the night, making its way towards a line of parked coaches, ready for the long trip home to Coventry or Southampton.

'I'm afraid not,' said Roger.

And then Harry told Ben the whole story, as simply and directly as he could. The politician stood in silence, running his fingers through his hair. In the distance the detective stood at the top of the ramp, watching them.

'Where is she now?' asked Ben when Harry had finished.

'Shepherd's Bush Police Station,' said Roger.

'I'm sorry, Ben,' Harry said quietly.

Ben reached across and put his hand on Harry's shoulder. Harry didn't much like the man, but he felt for him now. He also suspected that Angela had been right, Ben did love her in his own way.

'I'm sorry too, Harry.'

Above and behind them a commissionaire came out through the reception doors, eyes straining in the darkness.

'Mr Carlisle or Mr Kapowski out there anywhere?'

'Over here,' Roger shouted back.

'Chairman's on the phone for you.'

'Tell him we're in a meeting,' Harry joined in.

'Don't worry, I'll take it,' said Roger, and started off up the ramp towards the building.

Ben was staring at the wall behind Harry's head.

'What are you going to do?' Harry asked him.

Ben's eyes came back into focus.

'When are they likely to charge her?'

'They can hold her seventy-two hours first, if they need to.'

'Without the papers knowing?'

Harry nodded. Seventy-two hours took them through until Thursday evening, ten o'clock, an hour after the polls closed.

'Then in the meantime,' said Ben, 'I'd better get back to the job. You too.'